Praise for Lost Angels: As Above, So Below #1

"There is a truth which neither heaven nor hell can ignore: souls that are meant to be joined will be, regardless of the cost. Any angel can be tempted, any devil as well. But when that temptation offers something beyond understanding, anything is possible...if they are able to believe in each other."

— Succubus.net

"*Lost Angels* is an erotic paranormal romance that is story-driven, but has enough erotic, romance, and paranormal elements to satisfy the reader."

— Looking for a Good Book

"If you enjoy theology and the idea of angels and demons at war among us, you need to check this book out. You won't be disappointed."

— HorrorAddicts.net

"Aside from the framing of the war between Heaven and Hell through well-developed characters and a familiarity with theology, Rhoads and Thomas's depiction of temptation make this book. Any fan of erotic horror fiction, male or female, is going to have fun reading this one. Lost Angels has a creative plot, vivid descriptive imagery, relentless temptation, graphic horror, and fiery, fun sex."

— Up All Night Horror Fiction Review

"Beautiful, intoxicating and strange as only a relationship that spans heaven and hell can be, *Lost Angels* is the most evocative and entertaining novel you're likely to read this year. Just keep a strong hold on your soul as you do so; you don't want to become a victim in the eternal war."

— John Everson, author of *The House by the Cemetery* and *Sirens*

"Fans of paranormal romance, urban fantasies, kick-ass fights, and some damn hot sex, check out *Lost Angels*!"

— Dana Fredsti, author of the Spawn of Lilith trilogy

"Lorelei is mesmerizing and oozes sex. You'll be as addicted to her as I was."

— Dreadful Tales

Angelus Rose: As Above, So Below #2

Published by Automatism Press, San Francisco

Copyright © 2020 by Loren Rhoads and Brian Thomas.

All rights reserved.

Cover art by Carmen Masloski.

Cover design by Mason Jones.

Interior design by Automatism Press.

First edition.

Paperback ISBN: 978-0-9636794-8-2

e-Book ISBN: 978-0-9636794-9-9 .

DEDICATIONS

ANGELUS ROSE

AS ABOVE, SO BELOW: BOOK 2

LOREN RHOADS
&
BRIAN THOMAS

AUTOMATISM PRESS

SAN FRANCISCO

CHAPTER 1: MORNING IN THE CITY OF ANGELS

Morning dawned brown in Los Angeles, just the way Lorelei liked it. The air smelled of car exhaust and dust, with a hint of charred human flesh. The succubus breathed deeply, savoring.

Although she felt a flicker of loss for the human soul who had possessed her for the past week, she had to admit that it felt really good to be alone in her infernal flesh once more. She stretched, letting the borrowed suit jacket fall open to reveal that she wore nothing beneath it but thigh-high stockings and a towering pair of black Ferragamo pumps.

Lorelei sensed a current of desire eddying on the breeze. She looked down from her position on the bodega's roof to find her angel gazing up at her.

"What do you see?" Azaziel asked.

"I think the nightclub has stopped burning." She hopped lightly down from her perch, assuming her mortal guise as she did so. The angel's regard warmed her as he caught her and set her feet on the sidewalk.

After he sank back down to the bodega's stoop, Aza asked, "Where did you get the jacket?"

"It's your sister's." Lorelei posed for him. "Like it?"

"I'm not sure it suits you." In mortal seeming, Azaziel looked ashen in the morning light. Angelic blood smeared his white button-down shirt. Dried ichor flaked off his blue jeans. Lorelei snuggled against him on the stoop. She petted his blond hair back into place, but there was little she could do here on the street to ease the exhaustion in his gray-green eyes.

"Look," she purred, "we could both use some shut-eye. If you've changed your mind about taking me back to your church, fine. I know a place where we could crash."

"We're not going back to your sister's den," Aza countered wearily. "I met her last night, before the exorcism. She didn't like me much."

"Don't take it personally, Lover. Floria doesn't like anyone very much." Lorelei stood once more, twisting around to make sure the seams on her stockings were straight. She grinned at the angel. "Don't you worry, though. I'm in no hurry to catch up with Floria again, after the last couple of days. Aspersions were cast... She and I are going to need some distance, if we're going to repair our friendship."

"I'm sure that's true of my family as well."

"I don't doubt it." The succubus held her hands down to him. "Come on, Lover. The longer you sit, the harder it will be to get moving again."

Azaziel rubbed his thumb over her long thin fingers to sneak in a caress as she pulled him to his feet. His tone was less affectionate. "We are not putting one of your projects out of his bed, either."

She smiled, letting the dawn sparkle in her lavender eyes. "Nice idea, Aza. Jealousy always works in my favor. But I'm not in a mood to invite complications. Work can wait."

"I thought you were always on the clock when you were with me."

"I don't see anyone checking my timecard just now," she teased. "C'mon, Lover. All I want is a bath and clean sheets and a little more of your company. We can debate philosophy later, if we're still awake."

He engulfed her in a hug. "Simply holding you makes me feel better."

She laughed. "How you talk, Angel. Let's get a room."

When he turned her loose, Lorelei stepped back to open her Louis Vuitton clutch. She drew out a slip of shadow which slid up under her borrowed suit coat. The shadow molded itself into a form-fitting dress that sheathed her from knees to wrists. Then she pulled an antique silver compact from her purse. A few quick strokes with her fingers touched up her makeup and smoothed her hair.

Azaziel watched the transformation with a bemused smile. He surprised her with a rare flash of humor. "Now that you've got your armor on, what's your plan?"

"Watch." Lorelei stepped to the curb and thrust up her right hand, hip cocked.

Aza stared at her. From the crimp of his sandy eyebrows, she guessed that confusion wasn't an emotion he was comfortable with. He watched mortals and knew what they were doing, why they were doing it, and how they justified their actions to themselves. Now that Ashleigh's soul had been removed from Lorelei's flesh, the succubus was once again infernal enough to be confounding. She found that a relief.

Luckily, Aza didn't have to wait long to decipher Lorelei's pose. An Uber pulled up at the curb. Lorelei opened the car's back door and slipped inside. The driver was a dried-up ex-soldier, old before his years, counting the days until he could jump this chickenshit world. Definitely something she could work with, if she didn't already have a date.

"I don't know what I'm doing in this neighborhood," the driver grumbled. "I never come out here."

"I'm glad you did," Lorelei answered. She watched Aza climb painfully in beside her and close the door behind himself. "We're going to the Chateau Marmont. Take us in the back way, all right?"

"Sure," he said, not at all sure.

"It's on Sunset Boulevard."

"I know where it is," the veteran snapped. "I just don't know where the back entrance is."

"I'll direct you."

Aza leaned over toward her and whispered, "Chateau Marmont?"

"The staff is very discreet." Lorelei grinned. "You'll like it."

Riding down Sunset Boulevard as the city came awake was a pleasure Lorelei hadn't indulged in for a while. The neon had been turned off. The crowds of drunks had all staggered back to their cars to negotiate the freeways. No one wandered the street save those who lived on it, most of whom were destined to become some devil's breakfast.

At the thought of breakfast, Lorelei's mouth watered. She hadn't eaten a soul since the quick snack at Lost Angels the night she met Azaziel.

She licked her lips and cuddled up against her angel. He put his arm around her shoulders and held her close. Lorelei breathed deep, savoring his scent: devils' ichor, angelic blood, and beneath that, myrrh, solitude, loneliness. Still not fallen, but hers.

The last time they'd spent the night together, he'd jammed a mortal soul inside her and fucked the poor girl silly. Lorelei wondered where Ashleigh's soul was now. Unwilling to ask Aza and bring the girl between them again, the succubus forced the thought away.

She leaned forward to point out the inconspicuous turn up into Crescent Heights, then the nondescript drive which would bring the cab around above the crenellated castle walls of the old hotel.

Chateau Marmont, emblem of 1920s-era Hollywood, was modeled after the Loire Valley's Chateau Amboise: all fluted pillars and pointed turrets, somebody's fantasy of a magic castle. Greta Garbo came to Chateau Marmont when she'd had enough of being alone. The ghost of John Barrymore, forever drunken, still frequented the baronial living room. Jim Morrison used up the eighth of his nine lives hanging from a drainpipe as he tried to swing from the roof into his seventh-floor window. Members of Led Zeppelin rode their motorcycles through the lobby with Lorelei, clad in lingerie, riding pillion. She'd partied with John Belushi—who of her sisters had not?—before the final speedball brought him screeching to a halt in one of the bungalows around the swimming pool. Good times, she thought. Damn, it felt good to get back on her own turf.

As the taxi glided to a halt in the empty parking lot, Lorelei turned to the angel. "Pay the driver, would you, Love?"

Before she saw her direction followed, an ex-college linebacker—now a uniformed doorman—opened the car door for her. "Nice to see you again, Miss," he said softly enough that she could ignore him if it suited her.

Instead, Lorelei turned a radiant smile on him. "Thank you, Roger. It's heaven to be back."

Aza snorted as he followed her through the Gothic archway into the antique-packed lobby. The high-ceilinged room was sleepy at this hour, recuperating from the post-bar pandemonium. Lorelei strode across the scattered carpets, loving the echoes that her heels struck on the bits of bare marble in between. She hoped the sound would wake the ghosts.

A woman she didn't recognize looked up from her computer screen as Lorelei approached the desk. "May I help you?"

A man hustled out of the back office with a keycard outstretched. "You room is ready, Miss."

"Thank you, Suresh. Any messages?"

"I hesitate to tell you that the roses eventually stopped coming."

She laughed. "I finally got that resolved. How did your girlfriend enjoy them while they lasted?"

"She's my wife now." He puffed with pride. Lorelei smiled. *Boy, that tasted good.* Suresh continued, "I took her back to Mumbai to meet my family in February."

"May you have many sons," Lorelei said. Then she collected Aza, leading him toward the silent bank of elevators.

"You keep a room here?"

"A girl needs a closet," Lorelei said. "I can only carry so much of my wardrobe in my purse."

The succubus Floria let herself into Tuan Nguyen's penthouse. The apartment was quiet inside, a nice change from having Lorelei stay over the previous week. Stupid slut left nothing but chaos in her wake.

Floria and Lorelei had been littermates, hatched together in the first years of the French Revolution. They'd come up the ranks together, clambering over each other over the years. Their competition had always been friendly, until last week when Lorelei started chasing that damn angel.

Floria's infernal flesh crawled at the thought. She had enough work to do to get herself promoted to temptress. Luckily, Lorelei seemed to be providing Floria a good steppingstone. Asmodeus said he was pleased with the job Floria had done with the invitations to the exorcism. Her star was rising.

As the succubus strode down the hall toward the kitchen to fix herself a

Corpse Reviver, she discovered her contracted host, Tuan Nguyen, hunched over the latest Halo game in the living room. Even though the boy had been home alone, he had his headphones on. She had him well trained.

Floria smelled smoke from the nightclub fire in the boy's clothing. Too bad Tuan made it home safe. She'd looked forward to finding herself a better class of prey. She smirked. It was time to help the pretty young man find his death. Then Floria could send his soul to its just reward and move on.

Tuan caught a flicker of the succubus's reflection in the TV screen and jumped. "When did you come in?"

Floria arched one eyebrow at his tone. "Just now. Don't you have work today?"

Tuan pulled off the headphones and set the game aside with a sigh. "Hai's truck was inside the police tape, so it took us a while to get home," he explained. "I told Sammy to sleep. Hai hung out here until dawn. He's gone to see if he can get the truck now, or if it's been towed. I'm waiting for him to check in."

Not placated, Floria asked, "And the others?"

"It's barely Saturday morning," Tuan protested. "They're still asleep."

Floria rolled her golden-brown eyes and reached back to unzip her gold lamé dress. "If you've got nothing better to do, come to bed."

The boy shut off his game console and obeyed, but not with the enthusiasm he once might have shown. Yep, Floria thought, time to be trading up.

Lorelei's "closet" was nothing more than a hotel room, full of overstuffed furniture upholstered in shades of blood and sand. She rounded the room, closing the drapes. Although they could both see well enough in the darkness, Aza switched on the gold-tone table lamp.

Lorelei realized that she didn't have a plan beyond getting him alone here. Her heart thudded hard in her chest. "Should I run us a bath?"

"I'll shower, if that's okay with you." The angel was already withdrawing toward the bathroom.

Lorelei let him go. Why did this feel so strange? Last week, when she'd accompanied him back to his lair in the warehouse district, she hadn't second-guessed herself. Following people home was what she did. Or she brought them somewhere like the Chateau that played into their fantasies of wealth or fame, then flattered them into damnation.

She still didn't know how to play Aza. She knew he'd taken a wife in the years before the Flood, a girl named Anah, who'd been meant to die when the waters rose. Rather than consign her to that fate, Aza had tucked Anah up under his wings and carried her off to another plane. There they stayed as the years passed, until Anah aged and died. Lorelei understood that Aza had disobeyed the Enemy and fled the Earth in pursuit of love. Because of that, she knew that artifice wouldn't entrap him now. He'd selected Lorelei for reasons that were entirely his own. She hoped to understand them before long. Measuring up to them would be another story. Odds were that he'd kick her to the curb as soon as he discovered the creature he craved didn't match the reality in front of him. Lorelei wasn't sure what—if anything—she could do to prevent that.

She heard the shower turn on and imagined the angel undressing. Should she follow? He hadn't invited her. If she gave him time to think, he might regret having come home with her. Maybe he'd use her powder room, then skip out and get down to work with a new attitude.

Speculation got her nowhere, she decided. Raiding the in-room bar, she cracked open a bottle of Absolut and some Ocean Spray and mixed herself some breakfast.

She thought about the various mortals she'd had on the agenda before Aza's interruption: Tino, the transitioning wannabe model. Tom Chin, the computer geek who couldn't believe his luck when a real girl dragged him into bed. Petey, the dyke mechanic with the strong right arm. Jenna—no, Jenna was dead now, suffering in Tantalus's Hell. There were others whose names Lorelei couldn't remember without checking her black book. It didn't really matter. At the moment, she wanted a damn vacation. Of course, Hell recognized no days off for good behavior.

"Lorelei?" the angel called softly.

The succubus tossed down the rest of her liquid courage, then came to stand outside the bathroom, face turned away to allow for his modesty. "Yes, Lover?"

"Come look at this, will you?"

She laughed, twisting the double entendre, and pushed into the bathroom. He'd stripped down to his 501s, allowing her a clear view of him partially undressed for the first time. Long muscles striped his shoulders and chest, vestiges of the wings he didn't manifest inside the washroom. He'd gone a little soft around the middle, she noted with amusement. Her diagnosis was too much five-spice lamb gobbled from a takeout box.

He stood in front of the mirror, head twisted awkwardly to look over his shoulder at the wounds he'd suffered at Lost Angels. His injuries concentrated on his back, which surprised her not at all. Few in Hell would attack an angel face to face. She saw the bruise where Nebiros's serpent had pierced Aza's shoulder blade with its fangs. No wonder it hurt the angel to fly.

Aza guided Lorelei's hand to a jagged puncture left by an infernal slingshot. Without hesitation, the succubus nuzzled the dark laceration, feeling the throb of the projectile embedded there. She probed the ragged tear with her tongue, felt Aza squirm in response. She wondered if he would like a belt to bite down on. She grinned into the wound, then drew the shard of obsidian from it into her mouth. The angel's sigh of relief was followed by a pulse of the fiery stuff that served him as blood.

Swallowing the blood with a grin, Lorelei crunched the obsidian noisily in her teeth, as if it were an ice cube. "Yum. Tastes like home." She found herself abruptly nauseous at the mix of holy and profane in her stomach. She swallowed bile.

"Guess you lost your taste for home," Aza observed.

She shrugged. She'd swallowed far nastier things over the centuries. "Can you say the same?"

"We both know the answer to that, Lorelei."

"That's a shame," she hissed, hanging back. She felt his blood slicking her face and wiped it away with the sleeve of his sister's suit jacket.

The angel shrugged noncommittally. "I am what I am."

"So am I, Lover. So don't rub my face in the fact that I've chosen to be with you just now. I could go anywhere with anyone. I *should* go back to work, or at least to my boss, and beg him to forgive the last week I've wasted mooning over you."

"Stop." Aza reached out to tuck a strand of dark hair behind her ear. "I know. I'm sorry. Let's clean up now and rest. I'm amazed either of us survived last night. Let's not ruin that by thinking of our responsibilities right now. We should be counting our blessings."

Lorelei gave him a smile that would have lit up half the city. "Go ahead and shower. I'm going to run a bath. I need to soak the toxins out of my skin."

True to her word, Lorelei turned her back and bent over the tub. She was aware that the position strained the Lycra of her dress just so, but also aware that the angel didn't spare her much more than an appreciative glance as he stripped off his jeans and stepped into the shower stall. She wondered if he liked to sing in the shower. Maybe a little Morrison for old times' sake? She hummed to herself as she swirled one languid hand in the quickly filling tub. *Come on, baby, light my fire…*

Aza closed his eyes against the shower's spray. He ached in a way he hadn't in millennia. The battle had been hard: all Hell's forces focused on him alone, until Shebniel and his sisters had joined the fray. In the end, Shebniel lost his mortal form and went home to glory.

As much as he missed his friend, Aza couldn't begrudge him the escape from this world. Shebniel had been steadfast and loyal, watching over the children of this sprawling city. He deserved to enjoy a Heavenly respite until the Word sent him forth again.

For the first time in centuries, Aza found that he'd lost the craving to return home. When he interrogated the feeling, he discovered that all he truly wanted was to stay here in this evil place, to lie down beside Lorelei once more, and rest.

Across Sunset Boulevard from the Chateau, an angel sheathed in a dove gray tracksuit sat atop the Victoria's Secret billboard. Muriel kicked the heels of her blazingly white Reeboks against the billboard's face, denting it a little deeper with each kick.

At the end of last night's battle, the archangel Rafael had cautioned Muriel against judgment. He listened to her pour out her frustration and fury as she begged to assist her friend Samael, one of the angels of death. To soften his refusal, Rafael reached out to embrace her. The contact with the archangel still resonated through Muriel—and brought tears to her eyes. She'd been stunned to realize that Rafael believed everything could be resolved through physical contact.

Look where physical contact had gotten Azaziel, Muriel growled. Azaziel, instigator of the battle last night, was now holed up with his harlot.

And yet, even as Muriel watched them, Azaziel did not fall. He slipped into a healing meditation, trying to mend the wounds he'd taken fighting Hell's general on earth. The succubus poured herself a tub of scalding water. If they hadn't both been naked, it might seem almost innocent. The lion lying down with the lamb, as it were.

Then again, Muriel was hard-pressed to see anything lamblike about Lorelei.

Every fiber in Muriel's body quivered with the desire to tear the succubus apart. Muriel was desperate to spare Azaziel any more temptation. She pulled her sword from its scabbard and began to hone its mirrored blade.

Rafael appeared suddenly as if summoned. Resplendent in a brilliant white suit, he smelled like sweet breezes and honey, like the sun-drenched meadows of Heaven. "Put the blade away, Little Sister. It isn't needed this morning."

"You can see what is about to transpire," Muriel argued. It pained her to watch Azaziel skating toward Perdition with no one to reach out to prevent his fall.

"Azaziel has a choice in his destiny," Rafael argued.

Why, she wondered, did Azaziel have something she could not? "I've never recognized a choice in mine."

Rafael raised a single ivory brow. "Be that as it may, you are forbidden to harm the succubus. What is in motion must continue to its end."

Rafael reached a hand down to Muriel's shoulder, as if to comfort her. Instead, Muriel wrenched herself away and fled across LA.

As Lorelei sank into the tub, the bathwater felt like lava. She rubbed down the goosebumps that shivered up her arms. She loathed the sensation, a souvenir of being trapped in mortal form. She lay back so the scalding water closed over her face, then breathed out a sigh.

It *had* been a long time since she'd been home. She didn't often miss it. There was no privacy there, never a chance to do exactly what you wanted. Someone was always lurking, ready to report you if it would give them a leg up the infernal ladder. Some devils preferred life in Hell to working in the world, more turned on by torturing the damned than chasing after new ways to sin. Lorelei had always been the opposite. She was born to prey on mortals. In her centuries in the world, she'd fallen in love with it. She tried, unsuccessfully, to imagine leaving it. There were too many things she wanted to taste, too many places she wanted to see, too many risks she wanted to take. How could she pursue a relationship with the angel—and make her boss, the Prince of LA, see that she was still valuable to his organization?

All the same, the angel's advice had been good: stop wasting time worrying about her responsibilities. She pushed herself into sitting up, glorying in the sensation as the water sheeted over her shoulders. She poured the hotel's complimentary white ginger shampoo into her hands and lathered her hair.

After she rinsed and repeated until she was sure she'd gotten the infernal muck out of her hair, she realized that Aza had finished his shower and left the bathroom. She could hear him moving around in the bedroom beyond. She wondered if he was touching her stuff. She smiled, hoping he'd select some lingerie to his liking.

She scrubbed every inch of her body, washing away the indignities she'd been subjected to before the exorcism. She chose to ignore the sludge settling on the floor of the tub. It didn't merit close examination.

Reaching for one of the luxurious towels, she rubbed herself dry, raising the blood to her skin. It felt so good to be alive. As a concession to the angel, she wrapped herself in the hotel's robe, turbaned her hair in an extra towel, and left the disaster in the bathroom for the help.

To her amazement, Azaziel had already crawled between the sheets. He lay there with eyes closed, his breathing steady and even.

Lorelei eased herself down beside him and watched him sleep.

Still damp from his shower, his gossamer hair was darker now. Instead of sun-brightened gold, it looked almost the color of caramel. His nose seemed sharper since his face had relaxed, the shadows under his eyes duskier, but his sweet soft lips looked all the more kissable.

Let him sleep, Lorelei commanded herself. He'd earned it, fighting hand-to-hand with the General of Hell's Armies. She hadn't been able to stay and watch the battle herself, since Aza's sister Barbelo spirited her away. Lorelei had stayed long enough to see fiends swatted down like flies and succubi slashed in half like paper. Devils could not stand against angels. She wondered if Hell's General survived. Probably. Spite had a way of surviving almost everything.

She released her hair from the towel and rubbed it drier, before getting up to retrieve her brush from her purse. Untangling her mane gave her hands something to do while she pondered the enemies she'd made in the last week.

At least Yasmina had been stripped of the boss's favor. The elder temptress had slithered out of the exorcism in disgrace, her pathetic attempts to bend the rules in order to bring Aza down revealed for all to see. Yasmina was still out there—undoubtedly still gunning for Azaziel—but she'd be less of a threat without Asmodeus's organization backing her.

Floria was another concern. Lorelei and Floria had hatched together, trained together, and leapfrogged each other up Hell's ranks. Floria wouldn't forgive the past week, when Lorelei struggled with genuine love for another creature for the first time in their existence. Lorelei would have to figure out how to make peace. Floria wasn't the sharpest tool in the box, but she held a grudge for a long, long time. In fact, Floria's grudges had often been a source of amusement for Lorelei. Now, though, Lorelei knew Floria well enough not to leave her back turned. If she couldn't mend the fence, she'd have to broker a truce. Until one of them got reassigned, they had to work in the same city.

There were more problem relationships she should think about, plans she should make, but Lorelei found herself yawning. *Sufficient to the day is the mischief thereof*, she told herself. If you counted a day as one period of wakefulness, then this 'day' had been more than sufficient.

She unwrapped the robe and draped it over the club chair across from the bed. Her hand was on the lamp before curiosity got the better of her. What did her angel sleep in?

She eased the duvet back and laughed out loud. Aza wore cerulean blue boxer shorts, adorned with hearts, clouds, and cherubs. She knew they were a joke for her amusement. That charmed her all the more.

She switched off the light, then snuggled under the covers against the angel's back. Aza rolled over to nuzzle her hair.

Lorelei met his lips. A shock passed through her, followed by his compassion flowing into her. This time she met it with her own. "I know you're wounded," she whispered. "Let me make it better."

He gazed at her in the dark, lambent eyes reading her. She closed her eyes to kiss him again. She focused as much sincerity as she possessed into the kiss. It had been a horrible week. She'd endured much because of what he'd done to her, but there had been moments, back in the beginning, that had been magical. She wanted to recapture that magic for them both now.

Something changed and she felt his assent. She moved back far enough that he could slip off his boxers. When he rolled back to face her, he dropped his mortal glamor. Light surrounded and infused him, bright as the sun behind clouds. His eyes changed color, sliding from gray to sea-green to almost blue.

"Thank you," Lorelei whispered.

Aza answered, "Be yourself, Lorelei."

She let her own mortal glamor fall away. Sometimes she let the transformation take her gradually, but this time she simply was: nubs of horn, crimson skin, barbed tail.

Aza's hand hovered above her collarbone, as if feeling her heat on the air.

He was clearly as into this as she was, so she hooked her leg up over his hip and pulled herself closer. She knew he had control issues and expected him to push her over onto her back, but he didn't. Lorelei smiled into his kiss. What was he waiting for? Permission?

Maybe so. She'd told him that the first time he'd fucked her had been problematic. After he'd inflicted Ashleigh's soul on her, the possession locked Lorelei into mortal flesh. Aza seemed to consider the possession some kind of kinky devil-girl bondage, apparently not realizing that without negotiation, a safe word, or any way to escape, the restraint had been terrifying for Lorelei. It had been erotic only for him.

This, in a way, would be make-up sex. And yet Azaziel made no move toward her.

Lorelei faked a pout. "Don't you want me?"

"I shouldn't."

"I didn't ask that." She leaned away from him, but he guided her back for another kiss. Keeping in mind his injuries, she nudged him onto his back. Then she crawled atop him, glowing red in the darkness. He'd made love to her parasite slowly, drawing out the moment of connection. Lorelei didn't bother with that. She thrust down to the root of him and rode him in a slow grind. They were already connected. She wanted to enjoy it to the fullest.

As she'd expected, the sex was amazing. She felt herself light up inside, each nerve aglow with sensation. Aza held her hips, not guiding her, but letting her work. His smile was a work of art.

"I love you," Lorelei whispered. The words felt strange in her mouth.

17

She'd said them before, when a mark required her to, but never truly meant them. She felt the substance of them now, the contract.

Aza didn't echo her. Instead, he reached up to touch her face, to draw her back down for another kiss. "I know," he said.

Fucking angels, Lorelei thought, loud enough for him to hear.

He laughed, then kissed her like he meant it.

CHAPTER 2: GOODBYE TO THE PAST

At the sound of a footfall beside the hotel bed, Aza jolted out of his meditation. Even as he summoned his sword to his hand, he moved to shield Lorelei. Instead of Muriel, as he expected, he found his sister Barbelo standing inside the room. She remained far enough from the bed to appear unthreatening. Barbelo's warm hazel eyes twinkled as she offered folded clothing in her outstretched arms.

"Rise and shine, Big Brother," she encouraged quietly.

Aza lifted the blankets and stepped to the floor, but Lorelei didn't stir. He reached out, gentle as a breeze, and lifted a lock of her shadowy dark hair away from her throat. Her luscious, slightly parted lips invited him to leave a kiss, but he knew one kiss would lead to others. His sister waited.

He tore his gaze away and turned toward Barbelo to accept the clean—if not new—clothing. Relieved not to have to put his bloodied battle gear back on, Aza stepped into a comfortably worn pair of jeans. As he buttoned on a clean chambray shirt, Barbelo collected the torn clothing he'd worn to the nightclub, along with the blazer Lorelei had borrowed, and put everything into the bathtub. Barbelo burned the lot with a brief, bright flame.

Standing at the bedside to gaze down at the sleeping succubus, Aza knew—as clearly as he'd ever known anything—that he had to leave Lorelei. There were mortals in need, souls in torment. Aza knew at his core that he had been created to serve them. Still, he hated to leave Lorelei like this, without a goodbye.

As she'd anticipated his need of fresh clothing, his sister had also foreseen his difficulty in bidding the succubus adieu. Barbelo appeared at Aza's elbow to offer him a single long-stemmed red rose.

Aza lifted the bud to his lips. Its petals were as warm and soft as Lorelei's skin, without the electric musk of her perfume. He left a kiss on the rose for Lorelei to find later. The flower shimmered from crimson to a deeper, more passionate hue. He laid it on his pillow.

Then, without looking back, he followed Barbelo from the room. If he gave in to second thoughts, the succubus's gravity would trap him. He set his shoulders and fought it.

Once the door closed behind him, Barbelo reported, "Shebniel sent word from the Realms of Glory."

Aza said nothing, unwilling to voice what felt almost like envy in his heart. Shebniel, his friend for many years, had returned home after the fight in the nightclub.

"There is a place for Ashleigh, if you release her spirit," Barbelo continued. "Shebniel will shepherd her now that her work on Earth is done."

Crushed by the impending loss of yet another soul he had loved, Aza nodded. He had set this ascension up for Ashleigh, hoped and dreamed it for her. He would participate in her liberation willingly, because it meant she was free from torment at last. Still, he had to voice one protest: "Lorelei would wish to bid Ashleigh farewell."

"No, Brother. Your succubus has come a long way, but our rituals are not for her." Barbelo smiled, as sympathetic as ever. "Not yet, anyway."

Lorelei rolled over inside the blankets, seeking warmth. She wormed her way across the entire king-size bed before finally registering that she was alone in the hotel room. Aza had gone.

She swam out of the bedding to find a single long-stemmed rose lying on the pillow beside hers. The angel's goodbye kiss lingered on its petals.

Not coming back. Anger flared through her. A flower was no substitute for a real goodbye kiss. She snatched the flower up and pitched it across the room.

The succubus flopped over onto her back to stare at the featureless ceiling overhead. It felt like mid-afternoon, a strange time of day: stranded between the pitcher of mojitos at lunchtime and Happy Hour, a time for lazing in bed with a sated conquest. Not a time to wake up alone.

It registered that she was hungry. Her last meal had been the night at Lost Angels when she first saw Azaziel. That had been…Tobias, who played bass in a psychobilly band and taught reading at the Boys & Girls Club, but who couldn't tell the difference between a live wire and a ground. He had been tasty.

To be honest, Lorelei felt all rumbly and hollow inside. Somewhere in the massive Chateau, there must be some gray soul ready to lay down his or her burdens, to walk away from pain and disappointment, someone not good enough to be saved or evil enough to be truly damned. Someone ready to be devoured. Dinner.

Lorelei stretched and let the covers fall away.

As if to delay her, Azaziel's rose perfumed the hotel room, as rich and luxurious as romance. Its petals glowed the color of blood smeared across obsidian. Was that how the angel envisioned his feelings for her? If so, why had he left her?

It didn't matter. She was hungry. She pulled the hotel's plush robe back on, slipped the keycard into its pocket, and laid her ear against the inside of her door. The hallway was vacant at this hour. She sensed that the whole building was somnolent, awaiting evening and the beautiful people to bring it to life again. Fucking afternoon, Lorelei thought.

She let herself out of her room and drifted down the silent corridor, touching each door in turn. Most rooms were empty. She'd gone down the length of the hall and started back around when she hit the jackpot. Snoring leaked through the door to her. He sounded like a 747 revving for takeoff. No doubt that the occupant was alone, making a racket like that. No partner could sleep through it.

Lorelei slipped her keycard into the reader on the door, waited for the lights to cycle, and shoved. When the door whooshed open, the occupant's breathing caught, a slight cough as his tongue slipped backward down his throat, momentarily choking him.

Lorelei eased the door shut and engaged the bar lock. When she turned back around, the businessman stared blearily at her. "Am I dreaming?"

Sloughing off the robe as she crossed the room, Lorelei slipped under the covers and snuggled up beside him. "If you were awake, would this feel so good?"

He shifted his hips to take better advantage of her touch. "What are you doing here?"

"You called me," Lorelei said. It was true in its way. She rubbed her cheek against his stubbled one. He smelled faintly of L'Air du Temps and unfinished sex. He'd come in for a nooner, but had been unable to climax with his call girl.

No special craving motivated him. Her flesh appealed to him, but he didn't lust after it. He had money enough, as indicated by this hotel room. No addictions called him. He ate intentionally, gambled moderately, and exercised not at all.

"Family?" Lorelei wondered.

"Divorced," he sighed. He forgave the ex for leaving, felt his snoring had driven her away. The anger had long gone cold. "This is a weird dream."

Lorelei swept her hair across his bare chest. He shivered with the sensation of it. "What do you want most in the whole world, Hamid?"

"To sleep a night through."

She smiled at him, hiding her sharp teeth. A gray man with a gray life: no sins or chance for salvation. Just what she needed.

Lorelei shifted closer and used the rhythm of her breathing to lull him. Hamid surrendered to her, drifting back to sleep. One twitch roused him, but she guided him back down. His snoring began softly enough, but soon crescendoed: LAX revving up again.

Lorelei slithered over him. She watched him closely in the darkened hotel room, waiting for the catch in his breathing. All the while, she continued to gentle him, calming him with the warmth of her body.

His tongue relaxed back into his throat, stifling his breathing again. Starving for air, his heart pounded wildly beneath her. Lorelei whispered, "Hush. Rest."

The sense of what she said penetrated his oxygen-starved brain. This was what he wanted, after all: the unbroken sleep of death.

Lorelei held him until his last tremors subsided. Then she sealed her mouth over his and sucked out his soul. It flowed into her eagerly, then settled in her stomach like a stone.

Before she'd been possessed by Ashleigh, Lorelei used to feel a sweet rush of energy as she absorbed a soul. Now she felt too full, almost nauseous. Lorelei forced a burp. That helped a little.

Hamid's untenanted flesh was now hers to do with as she would. Lorelei thrust her hips against the corpse a few times, experimentally. There were times when she'd humped the dead, but now she gave it up as a bad job. What was wrong with her? Lust was the element that defined her existence. If she couldn't work up some lust toward her prey, she was headed for a world of hurt. Too bad the only creature she desired had forsaken her.

Snarling at herself, she retrieved her robe from its puddle on the floor. As she shouldered back into it, she fought down a yawn.

The heavy meal was making her sleepy. Until Asmodeus summoned her, it wasn't like she had anywhere to go or anyone else to do. Might as well go back to bed and wait for night.

Azaziel pulled himself heavily up to the platform below the lighted cross that made Forest Lawn Memorial Park such a landmark. The small assembly waiting on the platform remained invisible to the stalled rush-hour traffic below. Rafael smiled at him gently. Muriel watched with calculating blue eyes. Joseph, the exorcist who had pulled Ashleigh's mortal soul from Lorelei's flesh, looked more at peace than he had in years.

The sun sank inexorably toward the west.

Beyond the emerald green acres of the dead, the City of Angels washed from the feet of the San Gabriel Mountains to the sea. Aza turned slowly, looking it all over. He could feel Lorelei still lazing in bed. He wished he was still with her.

Then, with a shudder, Aza opened himself to the web of life in the metropolis, trying to feel himself woven into its fabric. He had to know he belonged here, that he was needed.

As ever, cold logic intruded: it wasn't as though he could go anywhere else. He had been sentenced here after Anah's death. That was long before the valley filled with people, long before the metropolis sprang from the dirt. He was stationed here, whether LA needed him or not.

Gazing at Azaziel standing on the parapet, Joseph was lost in reverie. The old man remembered the day his friend Barakiel had escorted him to the apartment not far from here, to meet Lorelei and the mortal soul possessing her. Though it had only been days ago, it truly felt like a lifetime.

Joseph had recognized Hell's forces before. He saw them at work all over LA. He'd seen mortals possessed by them before. He'd seen succubi—how could you miss them in LA?—but they'd never particularly tempted him. Lorelei, trapped in mortal appearance by the teenaged ghost inside her, had been a creature undreamed of. Joseph hadn't lusted after her at all, but he'd ached with wanting to help her, wanting to rescue Ashleigh.

As if that was what he had been waiting to hear, Azaziel finally spoke. "It's time, Father. Would you be so kind?" He extended his open hand down toward the old man. "Never thought you'd be partaking in a sacrament again, did you?"

Joseph shook his balding head as he raised the chromed martini shaker as if it were a chalice. Then, hesitantly, he drew it back to his chest, as if he could hug the girl within. After all he'd been through with the teenager, he needed to say something. "Farewell, Ashleigh Johnson. Go with God." Heartfelt, if not original.

Joseph gave a gentle kiss—the kind he used to render unto the Bible at Mass—to the martini shaker's mirrored top. He felt the girl's vitality buzz like an electric current through the metal, as if she returned the kiss. It left a pleasant, almost forbidden, tingle on his lips.

Hollow with dismay, Joseph reproached himself. Such unpriestly thoughts—and in the presence of angels, too. Then again, he'd lost the right to think of himself as a priest years before.

Clad in an immaculate white suit, the archangel Rafael placed a comforting arm around the old man's shoulders. "Of course you're a still a priest, Joseph. How could you ignore faith, having seen all?" The angel waggled a cautionary finger. "Not that it isn't possible, I realize. I just wouldn't recommend it."

Rafael steered Joseph away from the platform.

"Can't I stay?" Joseph asked.

"You've seen enough of the unknowable for one lifetime, Father. But have you ever seen the stained glass mural of the Last Supper they have here at Forest Lawn?"

Joseph shook his head.

"It's spectacular at sunset." Rafael turned back. "Muriel, you might want to see it, too."

The hotel room's phone rang, buzzing like an insect inside Lorelei's head. She reached out of the cave she'd made in the blankets and swatted at it. The sound didn't relent.

Furious, she boiled up out of the bedding like wasps erupting from their nest. She snatched up the receiver. Before she could say anything, a fiend growled, "Car's here."

Fiends were Hell's enforcers, the ones who stuck the pitchforks in. Lorelei didn't have to obey their commands; technically they were lower in Hell's hierarchy than succubi. All the same, it didn't do to disregard them, unless you had more firepower within your grasp than Lorelei could access.

"Give me a minute," she purred. "I'm not dressed."

That garnered a predictable snicker before the connection broke.

Lorelei stretched. She wished Azaziel had left her a love mark or two she could show off as needed. Next time she'd have to make sure of it.

She called down to the kitchen for an extra-hot triple capp with lots of cinnamon and copious foam. Then she opened the closet to consider her options. It was hard to know how to dress, since she wasn't sure who she needed to impress. Not that the fiend would have told her, if she'd asked. Fiends only dispensed as much information as they were ordered to. Whoever sent him, they weren't in a tearing hurry for her company. They'd sent a car, rather than coming themselves. That meant she had time to fix herself up. That she was expected to.

She poked through the spectrum of black dresses in the closet. How long had it been since she'd stayed at the Marmont? Two years, maybe five? Long enough that her wardrobe had dated. She pulled out a Betsey Johnson sundress with spaghetti straps that gave the impression that it would come off with one good yank. The dress was far enough out of style that it could pass for vintage. It implied a sense of humor about fashion, but was fancy enough to take her from a meeting with someone higher up the ladder, then out for drinks with prey afterward. She might as well plan to get back on the horse, as one might say.

She tucked the black Ferragamo pumps she'd been wearing for the last couple of days into the closet and pulled out some strappy gladiator sandals, wrapping the laces around her calves Roman-style.

She closed the closet door to check her appearance in the mirror. Any lesser creature might have had to contend with bedhead, but Lorelei always figured that looking like she'd just rolled out of bed worked in her favor— like maybe she'd be just as happy to crawl right back in. At the moment, that wasn't far from the truth.

From the vanity table she took replacements for the cigarette case and lighter that had been in her purse. She found an antique gold money clip, still holding a couple of twenties and the company credit card, which she pitched into her purse. Finally, she added an obsidian dagger from the vanity's bottom drawer. It wouldn't provide much in the way of protection, but it was better than nothing.

She painted her lips, then looked around the room. Azaziel's rose had fetched up against the wall. Lorelei stormed over to snatch it up. The angel's kiss still burned there. With an exasperated sigh, she bent her face to the rose to retrieve it, savoring his apology.

As much as she might have liked to carry the talisman with her, she would have to fight to keep it if anyone guessed that it meant something to her. The rose was too fragile to withstand that. She opened the closet and tucked it onto the shelf. It should be nicely mummified the next time she discovered it.

Unable to look away from the martini shaker clasped to his breast, Aza listened to the others leave the platform at Forest Lawn. Barbelo went, too. That allowed him a moment alone with the girl who had helped him woo Lorelei.

With a gesture as careful as any caress, Aza unscrewed the martini shaker's lid and summoned Ashleigh into the honeyed light of the setting sun. As mist whirled around him, the girl's image and flavor filled his mind. He understood her longing, her uncertainty, and breathed her in.

They shared a crystalline instant of memory. A month ago, he had seen her on the statuary-filled balcony below this spot. Ashleigh had just been thrown out on the street after her boyfriend Deion discovered she was dying of hepatitis. Afraid to catch it himself, Deion hadn't wanted to nurse her as she died.

Aza recalled the girl's terror at her imminent mortality. She'd pressed her cheek against the marble feet of the Aphrodite statue. With the desperate sincerity of one who had so little left to lose that she possessed no limits, the girl begged the goddess—or any kindly spirit—to let her taste true love before she died.

Invisible to her eyes, Aza trailed Ashleigh to the streets below, whispering encouragement and hope, sounding her out. In the process, he confirmed what he had suspected at a glance: Ashleigh Johnson could be saved. He'd bided, visiting her dreams, never truly real to her until the instant of her passing. Then he gave her a choice. She was free to join the other souls cached at his church until the angels could make sure they stood in favor at Judgment. Instead, Ashleigh was willing to risk everything for him. For love. Her plea to Aphrodite may have been her undoing in Heaven, but it was without equal for Azaziel's needs.

The last rays of light sparked across the distant hills, spilling across the enormous City of Angels. This was a moment, brief and eternal, when the gates opened for those with cause. In that silver-gold instant, the way stood clear to Heaven's very source.

Azaziel gazed upon the home he might never visit again. He studied the countenance of the Almighty he hoped might still have uses for him. Speaking the tongue of the eternal host, Aza bade the Thrones of the Sun greeting and implored them to grant Ashleigh safe conduct.

The girl left with his sigh. Her soul lingered before him, glistening, begging him to follow, to take the path with her, to escort her home.

Tears blurred Aza's sight. More than almost anything, he wanted to accompany her, but he feared the heartbreak of being denied entrance. And there was Lorelei to consider. He couldn't leave her without saying farewell.

The only instruction that came to his heart was to let the girl go and prepare the way for those still in peril. Lowering his gaze, the angel told Ashleigh, "I have been set here. I must remain until I am summoned."

Ashleigh understood. She turned to follow the trails of light to her well-earned reward. With a peal of gratitude to Lorelei meant for every angel who could hear it, the teenager sped along until she was lost in the growing brilliance that sealed the gates behind her.

Azaziel knew there was justice in this. He also felt the loss of another love he could never touch again.

Then he heard the sound of his name in another's prayers and raised his head.

After Rafael escorted them to the Great Mausoleum and unlocked all the intervening doors, the archangel left Joseph alone with the blond warrior angel.

"Welcome back, Father. I'm glad you finally saw the light and found your way back to us." Muriel's voice was remarkably musical, in contrast to the harshness of her words.

Joseph examined the angel in front of him. She was trim and sporty, like one of those aggressively fit women always rushing from yoga to spinning, whatever that was, to bootcamp. Her sunny blond hair was styled in a pageboy, not a single hair out of place. If he was honest about it, Muriel looked exactly how he had expected angels to look, whenever he'd thought about it back in the day.

Gazing at her now, he could see anger simmering below her surface. Disappointment in the world gave a subtle crimp to her flawlessly shaped eyebrows.

He wasn't going to allow her bitterness to mar his mood. "It's good to be back," he assured. Then he couldn't help but add, "I have Lorelei to thank for it."

The angel's laugh was sharp as broken steel.

"Honestly," Joseph argued. "I wanted to see an angel in all its glory. I wanted to see evidence of the divine on Earth."

"And she dragged you into Hell's embassy to perform a Black Mass, followed by a Satanic exorcism," the angel scoffed.

"But I saw you there," Joseph realized, "with your sword drawn, attacking the fiends…" This creature hadn't seemed angelic then. Instead, she'd been righteous and terrifying.

He hadn't meant to flatter her, but Muriel puffed up, taking his words as praise. "There are so many more devils to destroy," she mused wistfully. Then she brightened again. "Perhaps the time is coming for all of us to take up arms."

Joseph could think of little more frightening than that, so he switched the subject. "Did you ever know Ashleigh?"

"No," the angel answered. "She was Azaziel's charge. It's a blessing to know he can do something right, after all." Muriel stared at the massive stained glass window with complete disinterest. "If it's all right with you, Father, I would like to get back to work. I feel I've been distracted from it for too long."

Joseph nodded. "Don't let me keep you. I'd like to pray."

She beamed at him and discorporated as he watched.

Inside the Grand Mausoleum, Father Joseph stood alone in front of the massive stained glass window. He bowed his head in prayer. With day fading from the sky outside, the pastiche of da Vinci's The Last Supper grew shadowy. Only the corpse-ivory faces still glowed with light.

Aza waited nearby, glad in his heart that the priest had rediscovered his faith. Praise Heaven that this unexpectedly positive thing had bloomed from Aza's experiment with Lorelei.

As he closed his prayer, Joseph blessed Lorelei for showing him his heart's desire. He apologized again for ever having doubted the action of the divine. Then he crossed himself in the correct order for the first time in years.

Joseph turned away from the darkening window. He startled when he saw Aza. "I didn't know you were there."

"I didn't want to interrupt."

"Did you hear it all?"

"Only the end. You know, of course, that Lorelei only invited me to the exorcism. The other angels came at our Master's direction."

Joseph nodded. "It's all the same. You are evidence of the divine at work—and the others came to your rescue."

Aza inclined his head, shamed and honored simultaneously. "The others were charged to retrieve you and Ashleigh."

"Which makes Lorelei the agent of my salvation."

Aza smiled, unwilling to carry the argument any further.

Joseph shook his head wonderingly. "I don't presume to understand your motives, but I think you should know what you've done. Lorelei admitted before Hell to loving you."

Beneath the weight of that revelation, Aza sank to one knee. Demons loved, for better or worse. Devils, created by Hellish science, did not. Although Lorelei had told Aza that she loved him, he had not fully believed her. If she'd confessed it before Hell, that was another matter entirely.

Joseph raised his hands as if to comfort the angel, but came no closer. "She loves you as fiercely as ever a woman loved a man. If she's lucky, she'll die for it. She will undoubtedly be made to suffer for it."

"Hell won't kill her," Aza assured the priest. "She has a soul now."

"That didn't protect Deion Gutierrez."

Aza had to concede that point. Ashleigh's boyfriend Deion had been killed as a way to tempt the girl into betraying Lorelei. "Still," Aza argued, "Hell won't kill Lorelei. Asmodeus would have done it at the exorcism, in front of an audience—in front of me—if it had been in his power to do so."

Joseph allowed the subject to be changed. "It seems as if Hell must have been empty last night."

"Unfortunately, there are more where they came from."

Sinking into one of the benches facing the window, Joseph said, "You would think that I could stop questioning. I just don't understand how the city of Our Lady, Queen of the Angels, was allowed to become like this."

"God's will," Aza answered. His own faith felt more solid than it had in a while. "Everything is God's will."

"Even what happened with Lorelei and Ashleigh?"

Aza joined the priest in the pew. "Only the Almighty could have created Lorelei's soul. It's outside my power." He clasped his hands and gazed at the old man, cheered by the changes the priest had undergone overnight. "Thank you for telling me about Lorelei. I hope she believes that I love her, too."

"Ashleigh believed it." Joseph smiled at the memory of the girl. "They grew to be very close, toward the end. But Lorelei had doubts."

"I'll have to prove it to her, then." After the words left Aza's lips, they echoed, taking on a weight that sounded like a vow.

Before either of them could comment, Barbelo appeared in the doorway. She had an army surplus duffel bag slung over her shoulder. "Here are the things you asked for, Father. The rest will be given to charity, as you suggested."

"And my friend Barakiel?"

"He wasn't at home when I knocked. One of us will try again to contact him."

Joseph shifted uncomfortably. "Have any of the fallen angels ever come back to the fold?"

Barbelo and Aza exchanged glances, then Barbelo smiled at the priest. "Our door is always open."

When the elevator arrived, the room service waiter stood inside the car. Lorelei stepped in and grabbed her cappuccino with a smile. She gulped the scalding liquid as they rode back down together. When the elevator doors opened on the lobby, Lorelei licked foam from her upper lip and handed the cup back empty. The whole transaction was accomplished without a word. Damn, she liked Chateau Marmont.

A limo waited in the flagstone breezeway. Lorelei had expected a town car. A shiver spilled down her back as she read the vanity plate: CD<3DSNK. Cold-hearted snake. Yasmina, that bitch. Last time Lorelei had seen the elder temptress, she'd been slinking out of Lost Angels in disgrace. Lorelei wondered if she could fling her wings out fast enough to flee.

The fiend leaning against the fender tossed down his cigarette. He stamped it out with a steel-toed boot that somehow managed to complement his slick black Hugo Boss suit. His presence forestalled Lorelei's flight. If Yasmina had come, her driver would have been poor, mutilated Jezebel, not this unfamiliar fiend.

"I was about to come drag your ass outta there," the fiend growled. He didn't stand as tall as yesterday's mortal linebacker, but this guy was as rectangular as a refrigerator. His face seemed all clashing planes and angles, as if he'd been hastily constructed.

Lorelei pirouetted so that the fiend could appreciate the lack of underwear under her skirt. "Perfection takes time, tough guy."

His squint measured the yankability of her dress. Then he deigned to open the back door of the limo for her and stood out of her way.

Lorelei bent down to make sure the car was empty before she committed herself to climbing in. The fiend didn't manhandle her into the car, which was a nice change from recent days.

Not a crumb marred the black leather upholstery. It didn't have that new car smell, but neither did it smell like despair and torment. It didn't even smell like the Reptile House at the zoo.

Lorelei wished she knew what she was getting into, but short of imminent disfiguration, it couldn't be any worse than the past week had been.

After the car pulled away from the curb, Lorelei ransacked the compartments built into the limo's seats and floor. Yasmina had all manner of things stashed away, some of which Lorelei tossed out the window. First to go were the temptress's changes of clothing. Lorelei loved the sight of a snakeskin dress fluttering from the branches of an oleander in the median. The bottles of Cristal she hurled against the pavement. After her last adventure in the back of Yasmina's limo, Lorelei would never drink that shit again.

In fact, last time Lorelei had been in this limo, Yasmina had threatened her with a curse. Lorelei's wrists itched with the memory of the nightmare vision: Yasmina had tattooed feathered cuffs around Lorelei's wrists, ankles, and throat, binding her to Azaziel. Lorelei searched desperately for the temptress's tattoo needles, but didn't find them anywhere in the car.

That meant that bitch still had them. Lorelei's blood turned to ice at the thought.

CHAPTER 3: THE ANGEL'S HOARD

Yasmina was in a fine mood by the time she slithered back into her Beverly Hills condo. She'd spent the day hiding underground, waiting to hear that she'd been forgiven for her little faux pas before the exorcism. No one had bothered to contact her, to let her know if additional penance was required. It felt as if she hadn't been spared another thought. To add insult to injury, someone had stolen her limousine. Yasmina had been forced to take an Uber home.

The temptress flung herself down onto the Le Corbusier chaise in front of the picture window. Greasy black smoke hung over the ruins of Lost Angels. Asmodeus's nightclub looked to be a total disaster. The club had been the public face of the demon's organization in LA, the centerpiece where everyone came to do business. Its loss was a huge PR fiasco, to say the least.

Maybe that was the hold-up in Asmodeus getting back to her: he must be setting up his new base of operations in town. Yasmina hoped he would call soon to let her know where it was.

She conjured herself a cigarette, but felt too agitated to enjoy more than a couple of puffs before grinding it out in the Hermès ashtray.

She fished her cell phone out of her little black Vivier handbag and stared at the blank-faced screen in disbelief. No command from Asmodeus. No commiseration from Jequon. No messages from the harpies to tell her that Azaziel had been destroyed. She'd never dreamed that Hell would carry this pretense of punishing her so far. She threw the phone back into her purse and roared, "Jezebel!"

The former succubus scurried into the room. Her large brown eyes remained downcast above the scar tissue that sealed her mouth shut. Whatever she'd been doing since they came home, Jezebel hadn't yet removed her long black velvet driving coat. It hung open to emphasize the purple-red scar tissue that swirled flame-like across her scrawny white torso. The scars disappeared into the featureless junction between Jezebel's grooved thighs. The sight of her mutilated minion raised Yasmina's spirits.

"Mix me an eye-opener and go find me someone to eat."

Jezebel bobbed her head and went to comply.

The breeze shifted the nightclub's smoke in the direction of Yasmina's building, obscuring the view. She needed to know for certain that Azaziel had been slain. She pulled out her phone again, but Jequon's number went straight to voice mail. "Hello, darling," she breathed. "Did you stay for the end of the exorcism? I'm dying to know who had the pleasure of devouring Lorelei's shiny new soul. Call me soonest."

With a growl, she tossed the phone into her bag again. Then she accepted the Dirty Bloody Mary from Jezebel and sent the ruined succubus on her way with the flick of an overlong fingernail.

The angel Muriel walked past the hospital doors like anyone else, drifting through the waiting room to see who might need her. A massively pregnant woman grimaced in the corner, while two of her four kids squabbled over a broken green crayon. Between contractions, the woman called everyone she knew on her cell phone, trying to find anyone who could watch her children while she gave birth to another. A middle-aged daughter paged through an out-of-date magazine, one eye on her mother hovering near the door to the examining rooms. They were waiting for a man with "chronic indigestion." He was drawing his final breath. A young man held his head in his hands, wincing at the pain shooting from behind his right eye. An elderly man coughed despairingly into a threadbare handkerchief.

None of these people recognized the crises in which they were enmeshed. Most had already made up their minds about their predicaments, denying the evidence or blaming others. Muriel could have stopped to offer comfort, but she didn't see the point. She hadn't come down from Heaven to comfort humans. She'd volunteered to teach them to sing the Everlasting Hymn, praising their maker until they were called to meet Him. She was only interested in humans who could fully invest in singing. Unfortunately, early in her time in Los Angeles, she discovered that most humans were too wrapped up in their brief, ugly lives to praise anything higher than money or lust.

Muriel chose to spend her energy on those who had an immediate stake in learning to sing, those at the precipice where their choices might affect how they spent eternity. Beyond the gangland battlefields, where she did a fair amount of her proselytizing, the surgical suites of the big warehouse hospitals offered an opportunity to do some real good for people.

The angel rode up in the elevator with a crop of sinners whose transgressions ranged from the banal to tedious. She hummed softly to herself, raising blood pressures throughout the car. She didn't look up from her gleaming white leather tennis shoes.

As the elevator reached the first surgical floor, things felt promising. Muriel pressed the button to stop the car, deaf to the alarm it set off. She opened the door to a "locked" ward, where only people armed with the appropriate badge were permitted. When she left the car, she released the stop and allowed the doomed contingent to proceed on their merry ways.

She peered into each surgical suite until one called to her. The woman on the table was practically invisible beneath blue drapes. Her heart tolled with alarming slowness, shoving congealing blood through her narrowed veins. The surgeon shook her head.

As Muriel neared the table, the patient's eyes popped open in shock. She moaned low in her throat. The anesthesiologist misinterpreted her fear as pain. He made an adjustment that nudged the woman farther down her slippery slope. She would have protested, if her voice hadn't been stifled by the breathing apparatus in her throat.

Muriel bent down to be eye to eye with the woman. "Hi, Theresa," she chirped. "I'm here to retrieve your soul when you expire, then pass it on to the guardian of the appropriate direction."

The word expire tapped a deep well of terror. The woman's heart rate skyrocketed and she tried to twitch her heavy limbs to protect herself. Regrets, things left undone, words unsaid crowded her mind.

"She's seizing," one of the masked figures misdiagnosed. Phenytoin was added to the cocktail in her IV.

Muriel stroked the woman's forehead. Theresa's brown eyes pleaded, but they might as well as beseeched a boulder.

"It doesn't matter if you were Christian," Muriel explained. "Those distinctions matter less than you expect." The angel smiled, exuding fierce joy. "Let me teach you a little song that will praise the Creator. I'll sing with you until you know the melody."

The succubus Floria sashayed through the doors of the Hollywood Park Turf Club, kicking some extra flirt out of her crimson lambskin mini skirt. Behind her stomped a matched pair of Asmodeus's fiends.

Floria enjoyed the way the track's patrons pulled their dazed attention up from their racing forms when they sensed her near. She watched them clock her in sequence: heels, hemline, rack, face, goons. Then their startled gazes dropped back to the seventh race.

She was surprised that the fallen angel Barakiel let her stride right into his place of business. Every moment she lured someone's attention away from the ponies was a drop in revenue. Maybe Barakiel already bailed, jumping ship as soon as he glimpsed her escort. If she'd been in his loafers, she wouldn't want to take the blame for losing the exorcist either. Then again, she might have been sympathetic if he hadn't demanded Floria pay him a couple of her Vietnamese boys to borrow the priest for Lorelei's exorcism.

One of the fiends stepped up alongside her and jerked his misshapen head at the freight elevator. Floria realized the fiends were probably too big to fit in a regular elevator.

No one moved to question where they thought they were going. Floria wondered if the fallen angel had simply given himself the day off. She supposed these fallen assholes felt themselves equal to the demons who ran the cities—as if, once they'd stepped off the straight and narrow, that accorded them all the rank and privileges of those who'd actually taken up arms against the Enemy. Floria had seen Asmodeus do shit that would make a fallen angel molt.

She bared her teeth. She had hoped that her boss would do something permanently disfiguring to Barakiel, but Asmodeus made it clear that the feud between Floria and Barakiel didn't particularly trouble him. The only point that their boss was interested in underlining was the loss of the priest.

Floria wondered if she would have stood half a chance to get satisfaction from the fallen angel without the borrowed muscle at her back.

The elevator took them down a couple of levels to a vacant cinderblock hallway painted industrial green. Floria followed the fiends to a featureless black metal door. One of the fiends took hold of its chromed knob, laid his other oversized paw on the wall, and tugged. The door's locking mechanism sheared off with a snap.

Beyond the door lay a cramped office crowded with video monitors. Barakiel sat there alone.

He was handsome, Floria had to give him that. His tall body was tucked nicely into a pinstriped navy suit. His straight, severe features had a Chinese cast. In the flickering light, Floria glimpsed a hint of his black-feathered wings and shuddered.

Preempting her speech, Barakiel said, "You've come for your boys."

Floria nodded.

He flipped a pair of polished slot machine tokens at her. Floria fumbled and caught one. As soon as her hand closed over it, she felt TN's soul squirm across its surface.

A fiend stomped down on the other token. He scooped it up and handed it to Floria.

"Is that all?" Barakiel asked wearily.

"I'm satisfied," Floria said. "I have a message for you from the boss. He wants you to burn down the exorcist's church. Asmodeus says the next time he asks about it, there had better be nothing left but ashes."

The fallen angel nodded unhappily.

Floria turned on her Louboutin heel. She didn't look to see what the fiends were up to as she pulled the office door shut behind her. Of course, it no longer latched. She heard the first blow land and smiled.

She wondered if Barakiel would take his beating like a good little lapdog.

She would've liked to stay and watch the show, but the room was so small, she might have gotten snarled up in the beating by accident. Better safe than spying.

Floria tucked the tokens holding her boys' damned souls into her bra, pulled out her phone, and called the boss for her next assignment.

The limo stopped across town at a strip mall that would have been nondescript if not for the line of people outside. A valet opened the limo door for Lorelei before the fiend got out from behind the steering wheel. As the succubus stepped out of the car, paparazzi descended. Should've put on her sunglasses, she realized. This might make the video shows: pretty young thing arrives alone in a big black car. Generally Lorelei liked to play farther under the radar. Limelight brought official inquiry when things ran their inevitable course and the LA County Coroner got called in. A decade or more ago, her sister Floria had been run out of LA after one of her stunts. Then again, Floria never could resist a flashbulb.

Inside the restaurant's velvet-curtained doorway lurked a mouthwateringly lovely Syrian coat check girl. Lorelei wondered how many coats were getting checked this sultry evening. What else did the girl sell?

The maître d' swept up to the podium. He was a tempter Lorelei recognized: Barbatus, something like that? He wore Asmodeus's glyph burning in the ruby of his lapel pin.

That Asmodeus had summoned her somewhere public, rather than disciplining her on a nameless dirt road in the Angeles Forest, meant Lorelei was in no immediate danger. Still, the last time she'd seen her boss, he was trying to use her as a bribe to cause Azaziel's fall.

Lorelei suddenly craved a cigarette. Damn California and their anti-smoking laws, anyway.

"Wait in the bar," the maître d' told the fiend. To Lorelei, he simply said, "Follow."

Barnabas—or whatever his name was—led her through the crowded bar and into the restaurant beyond. The dining room was lit like a stage set. Warm yellow lights reflected up from the pristine white tablecloths to gently gild the diners' faces. Although the evening was young, it seemed as if every chair was full. A dining room this small had to be exclusive.

Behind massive architectural arrangements of flowers in black blown-glass vases, mirrors lined the walls. It would be possible to spy on diners everywhere in the room while you enjoyed your amuse-bouche. Lorelei liked the place already. She turned slowly, admiring the reflections that ghosted after her.

"Don't dawdle," the tempter said.

Lorelei followed Barbas to a table in the corner. He pulled the table out so she could slip behind it. "Absolut and cranberry," she told him, even though it wasn't his job to bring her a drink.

"Don't press your luck, Hot Stuff," he sniped. "The ashes are still smoldering over at Lost Angels."

"Since when are we afraid of a little fire?" Lorelei returned. Still, she took his point. Lost Angels had been the crown jewel of Asmodeus's operations in the city, both in terms of cashflow and in souls brought to damnation. It wasn't Lorelei's fault that the club burned down, but the boss could blame her for it, if he liked.

Asmodeus limped from behind a floral masterpiece built around a taxidermy peacock. Leaning on his silver-headed cane, the demon adjusted the length of one black silk cuff beneath his brocaded jacket sleeve and surveyed the room. One curl of his tightly wound black hair drooped above one eye. Lorelei's heart missed a beat when his black gaze turned to her, but then he smiled.

He came to the table and stood over her until it was pulled out again. He settled onto the banquette beside her. Taking both her hands in one of his, he pulled her close for a deep kiss. When he released her, his smile was smug. Clearly, he'd tasted the angel's kiss on her lips. "How is my friend Azaziel this fine evening?"

"Satisfied," Lorelei hedged.

"Not entirely, I hope."

"He's got the taste now."

"So you consummated your relationship? One to one, with no pesky mortal girl to chaperone?"

"Yes," Lorelei admitted. She wondered where Asmodeus's spy had been. She thought they'd been reasonably discreet.

"Good." Asmodeus stroked his goatee, considering.

A heartbreakingly pretty mortal girl arrived at the table with both Lorelei's cocktail and an ice bucket with a bottle of champagne. She set the martini glass on the table in front of Lorelei, where it burned crimson in the theatrical lights. Then she uncorked the bottle with a flourish and poured the bubbly before vanishing again.

The demon handed Lorelei some champagne and rang his flute against hers.

"What are we drinking to?" Lorelei asked cautiously.

"The ascension of the angel Shebniel to the Realms of Glory."

She sipped the dry wine, trying to decode the words. Finally, she shook her head. "Shebniel is...?"

"Boon companion to your boyfriend. Shebniel was originally one of the Seventy Childbed Angels, named on amulets to protect innocent infants from us." He rubbed his hands together like a silent movie villain.

"Eventually the Sacrament of Baptism replaced the amulets and our boy Shebniel got banished to this corner of Paradise. Last night, immediately after the exorcism, Nebiros's warriors stripped him of his flesh and sent him home."

Lorelei felt more shocked than victorious. Had Aza witnessed his friend's escape from this mortal coil and chosen not to tell her? Asmodeus watched her, waiting for a reaction. Lorelei sipped some more champagne and said, "One less angel to oppose you here."

"And one more angel sent down to replace him, embodied and primed to fall. That would be Shebethiel, another babysitter." Asmodeus closed his eyes to savor his champagne, but his smile was ironic. Then his depthless black eyes opened again to entrap Lorelei with their gaze. "The angelic hosts are limited," he reminded. "There are only as many of them as were created before the birth of the world. One by one, we'll put them to the test and drag the losers to Perdition. I'm pleased that you've stepped up to bigger game than your average lecher or junkie."

Another mortal girl, even prettier than the last, opened a folding stand one-handed and rested a huge brass tray atop it. She off-loaded a series of dishes: cucumbers floating in yogurt, feta cheese and fat round olives, crunchy rice laced with saffron, sliced tongue. Asmodeus filled his plate and began to tuck in.

Lorelei tried to pace herself. Her appetite was still dulled by the soul she'd swallowed earlier. She laid a smooth slice of tongue on her plate, then copied her boss by sprinkling a purplish red powder over some rice. Its flavor was sour, fruity, slightly astringent. In contrast, the tongue was succulent and very fresh. She wondered if the sinner to whom it belonged was still draining in the kitchen. She took Asmodeus's warning and promised herself to be truthful.

Of course, the demon set the rules of the game. "In case I haven't made myself fully clear, I am keeping a tally," he told her. "You may have the credit for Shebniel's ascension and Shebethiel's sojourn here on earth, but I haven't forgotten that you cost us a perfectly serviceable priest and failed to damn your little parasite's soul."

Lorelei flinched.

"At the moment, you're in the black, my girl. But I expect to see Azaziel firmly in our corner before very much longer. Clear your schedule. His fall is your only priority."

Gulping down a bite of tongue, she promised, "I live to serve you, my prince."

"The better you serve, the longer you'll live." He sliced off another bite of tongue. "With your shiny new soul, you will be privy to many...shall we say, enticements? I'm particularly interested in all you can find out about

Azaziel's other companions. Maybe we can weed out a few more of them."
He stared at her, eyes half-lidded. "I got to where I am by never taking my
eye off the ball. Unlike Yasmina. Reject her example and you'll have people
working for you before long."

Temptress? Could it be that the promotion was finally within her grasp?
With shaking hands, Lorelei picked up her vodka and cranberry and sipped
it. "So Yasmina's off the case?"

"That bitch?" Asmodeus teased, echoing the sentiment shared by most
of his staff. "She wants your angel fallen, but can't get the job done. I
expect you to have more luck with it."

"Why did you give me her car?" Lorelei begged. She rubbed her wrist,
remembering the nightmare tattoos.

"Because you deserve it more than she does," the demon said. "She will
understand that it represents my aegis. Even so, I doubt you can stay out of
her way. That fiend of yours might make her think twice about taking you
face on—but you needn't rely on him alone. "

Asmodeus placed a matte black cell phone, slimmer than the company
credit card, on the snowy tablecloth. "Keep in close touch, Lorelei. You're
moving up quickly and there's bound to be back-stabbing, so if you need
help, ask."

The phone had a button marked with the demon's glyph. She could find
that in the dark or even in more dire situations, if need be. She thumbed the
phone off and gazed up at him, biting her lips to plump them up.

Asmodeus gathered her closer with a firm arm around her waist. His
other hand traced her hemline. Lorelei's thighs parted automatically. His
manicured nails masked sharp black claws that explored her, claiming
ownership.

Conscious of the mirrors all around her, Lorelei kept her expression
composed, her breathing measured. She was a young woman fascinated by
an older man, not a succubus being pleasured by her demonic master.
Asmodeus nuzzled his face in her hair and held Lorelei on the verge of
climax, toying with her.

She wondered if he wanted her to beg for orgasm. When she realized
that she didn't need his permission—that, with the slightest hitch of her
hips, release could be hers—something within her slipped beyond the
demon's grasp. Lorelei felt the change. Surely Asmodeus did, too. Taking
responsibility for herself opened a door to freedom. That went to her head
faster than the champagne—or the orgasm—had.

Asmodeus removed his hand and wiped it on the napkin in her lap.
Then he brushed the heavy mass of Lorelei's dark hair from her shoulder.
He clamped his teeth on the nape of her neck, the way a tiger would
discipline a cub. The pain was so sharp it took her breath away. She took

his point: she wouldn't enjoy being devoured.

The demon sat back, licking her blood from his teeth. "On your way," he directed with a nod. "Have fun tonight. I look forward to catching up with you soon."

Lorelei scuttled across the banquette, out from behind the table. As she stood, she wiggled enough to switch her hemline back down into place. The gesture echoed in the mirrors all around her. It was the sort of movement that would raise a smile, if the viewer understood what he spied.

Asmodeus watched her with measuring eyes.

After he locked up at Forest Lawn, Aza flew out to Venice Beach to enjoy a moment alone. He stood on the darkened sand, staring at the waves rolling in one after another in the moonlight. He wanted his thoughts to still, not to draw parallels between the years he'd spent, the mortals he'd served, the creatures he'd loved—and the endless waves breaking on the beach. He wanted to see only the infinite.

But that was impossible. He'd been sentenced to this world for so long that even as he struggled, it was hard to see the Maker's perfect will behind the slow dissolution of everything.

Instead, he saw the sparkle of Lorelei's eyes, the luster of her hair, the grace of her walk, the blackness of her figure-hugging dress. His arms ached to hold her again.

An ugly cough caught his attention. Half a mile away, two harpies perched on the lifeguard chair, staring at him. Damia and Keisha, self-proclaimed friends to his Ashleigh. They'd waited to devour the girl's soul, but Aza had snatched it up first.

He turned his back on them now, unwilling to let them infect his thoughts.

Ashleigh Johnson had been the antithesis of Lorelei: stick-thin, eaten up by methamphetamine abuse and hepatitis. More than anything in her life, Ashleigh had hungered for love. And Lorelei, however unwillingly, taught her what love felt like.

Aza wished the girls could have had a chance to say goodbye. He wished he'd thanked them both for what they'd meant to him, what they'd both given him. He wished he'd been able to prove his love to Lorelei and make Ashleigh proud.

Now Lorelei was in terrible danger. He sent up a prayer that Heaven would extend its protection over her or allow Aza to guard her himself.

The waves continued their inexorable march. He received no acknowledgment.

Aza remembered the last time he'd opened his heart to beseech the Almighty. Mastema, Director of the Fallen on Earth, had appeared with an offer. Of course, Barbelo had rescued Aza from that. Azaziel offered up a quick blessing for his younger sister, who must be neglecting her work to watch over him.

His own work had certainly suffered in the past week. He turned resolutely away from the tumbling waves to see what good he could do.

Another angel was working in the shadows of the palm grove. This angel's hair stood up in a royal purple mohawk. He wore a black T-shirt emblazoned with a white-inked skull above two syringes like crossbones. The angel was handing out clean needles, bleach, and providing directions to the methadone clinic.

Aza recognized the new angel at once: Shebethiel, brother to the lost Shebniel.

Aza wondered at the feelings that rose inside him. To feel that clean again, to look so bright... Aza had been posted to this corner of Creation for so many centuries that sometimes, like this moment, he could feel the weight of each individual year.

Aza watched Shebethiel handle the addicts gently, easing their aches and lifting their spirits, making it seem possible that life could be worth living beyond the addiction that shackled them. Aza forced himself to straighten, sent a prayer winging skyward, and went to help Shebethiel with the needle exchange.

Lorelei's fiend waited at the bar, drinking what looked like mud and smelled like sulfur. Though plenty of pretty young things of every gender jammed the area—eager to be discovered—they left a vacant margin around the fiend. He seemed pleased by that.

As Lorelei drew nearer, he rumbled, "Are we out of here?"

"Time to hit the road, Sugar." Lorelei put her hand on his arm to test his allegiance. He didn't shrink away. She'd never had a fiend of her own before. The prospect was heady.

The fiend cleared a path for her just by walking to the door. People scrambled over each other to get out of his way.

By the time Lorelei and the fiend left the restaurant, the valet had the limo waiting. If anything, the number of paparazzi outside had doubled. Lorelei dodged behind the fiend, feigning shyness. The fiend was with the program enough to move to shield the door as she slipped inside, blocking the flash of her crotch so he alone could enjoy the view.

His tongue slipped out to lick his practically nonexistent lips. Lorelei grinned at him, not helping his situation in the least.

He closed the limo door and came around to climb behind the wheel. The car sank under his weight.

"What's the name of this place?" Lorelei asked.

"Isfahan."

Lorelei repeated that to herself. She wondered if the boss was feeling homesick.

The fiend interrupted her thoughts. "Where to?"

Lorelei gave him directions back toward downtown. When they neared it, Lorelei said, "Drop me off and stay in the car. Give me fifteen minutes. If I don't come right back, I'll be working."

He nodded once.

This was easier than she'd expected.

"What's your name?"

"Tibor," he said grudgingly.

"When we stop, I want you to program your call into my cell. I want you on speed dial, Sugar. In case I need some...muscle."

He chuckled, as she intended. More importantly, he didn't argue.

The sketchy neighborhood near the 405 was deserted, although it was still relatively early for a Saturday night. Not a sound broke the stillness as Lorelei stepped out of the limo. She expected to hear the rustling of small scavengers, but even the rats seemed to be asleep. The silence, in the midst of LA, set the hairs on the back of her neck creeping. Lorelei rubbed at them, disgusted. She had hoped the physical sensations of fear would vanish with her possession. No such luck.

Azaziel's mostly-abandoned church threw a towering black shadow against the smoggy purple night sky. Since she'd been here last, fresh plywood had been bolted over the church doors. Just to make a point, a padlock hung chained over them, too. The rest of the building looked as she remembered it: sooty tendrils ghosting above the boarded-up windows, staining the adobe-yellow paint.

She saw no indication that anyone was home. Dammit. She'd hoped to swing by, find Aza in his room in the back, and drag him out to celebrate in her new car. It seemed only fair that he enjoy some of the trickle-down effect, since she was coasting on his ascended buddy's good name.

But if Aza wasn't haunting his usual places, how was she supposed to contact him? She didn't imagine he carried a phone or any other convenience of the modern era. Last time she'd needed to reach him in a hurry, she'd hung herself, guessing that he would appear to retrieve the soul of her parasite. Now, without Ashleigh to provide insurance, a suicide attempt was much less appealing. Lorelei was fairly sure the angel would come if he could, but he had less incentive to drop everything. The succubus didn't like her odds.

Maybe she could just leave a message, like he'd left her the rose. As soon as she'd decided on that, she wondered how long it might be before he swung by the church again. What if one of his other angelic buddies found it first?

Nothing struck her as a better idea. Careful not to snag her dress, she climbed through a hole in the chain-link fence surrounding the church. Last time she'd visited, she'd been locked in mortal form and Aza made her climb up the fire escape. This time, she merely opened her wings and hopped up to the window ledge. The newly replaced window hung open a crack to catch the evening breeze.

A man lay asleep in Aza's bed. Although he lay face down, with little visible beyond his balding head, Lorelei still recognized Father Joseph. From the window ledge, she could see the glow that indicated he had been saved.

Lorelei eased the window sash up all the way and stepped inside. The scents of myrrh and loneliness lingered inside the room. Aza had been here recently. She inhaled deeply.

The priest threw himself over onto his back, squinting at her silhouette in the twilight. He sketched the sign of the cross over himself. "Who's there?"

"Sorry to wake you, Joey," Lorelei purred. "I'm looking for Aza."

"Lorelei," he guessed.

"Right in one." She eased into her familiar human shape before he had a heart attack. "Staying here awhile?"

Joseph fumbled around in the darkness to light a candle beside the bed. "This used to be my church, before the fire. I told you that, didn't I?"

He'd told her, but she'd forgotten. Lorelei settled on the foot of the bed. "This is the mattress where Aza banged me and Ashleigh, quite the little ménage à trois. Did he tell you that?" She was glad the priest had wanted the light, because it meant she could savor every nuance of the dismay that crossed his face.

She changed the subject for him. "Do you have a way to get in touch with Aza?"

"Other than prayer?"

"You're not suggesting I try that, are you?"

"Not really." Joseph scrubbed his hands across his face. "You can leave a message with me."

She drew the lipstick out of her purse. When she crossed the room, the priest shrank away from her. Kneeling at his bedside, the succubus wrote her new phone number on the burning candle. "Ask him to call, would you? Tell him I want some advice on how to dodge Yasmina."

"She seems like bad news," the priest commiserated.

"Since I'm her second least favorite person, I ought to get some tips from Number One." Lorelei blew the old man a kiss and turned to leave.

Outside the church, the night lit up with the sound of singing. A lone male sang a quiet lullaby. Lorelei froze, riveted by the maddeningly familiar voice. Then a slow smile crept across her face. Azaziel. Right on cue. Lorelei wondered what little honey her angel was crooning to now.

Desperate to distract her, the priest asked quickly, "Call you about Yasmina? That's your whole message?"

Lorelei stalked toward the window. Joseph wrestled out of the bedclothes behind her, but hesitated before his hand closed on her arm. Lorelei could feel his heat at her back, his breath on her hair, but ignored him. What didn't Joseph want her to see?

She peered cautiously around the window frame. Outside, a winged angel stood in the center of the fenced playground: without a doubt, her Azaziel, clad in a pair of 501s and a button-down blue chambray shirt. Above and around him like traces of a molecule's orbit, swirled the souls of children. A multitude of souls, she saw, hundreds. Lorelei cataloged them instantly: none of them saved, many of them swinging toward the light, a few of them still shadowy with unshed mortal grievances.

Aza offered his lullaby to the souls of unsaved children.

Lorelei struggled to wrap her mind around what she saw. Her angel hoarded souls, children's souls: to what purpose? Demons collected the damned and sent them on their way; angels scooped up the saved. Devils consumed the remainder, removing them from the wheel of life. Very few mortal souls—those who had withdrawn from the eternal battle—had the determination to stick around as ghosts. What were these children doing here?

Behind her, Joseph dropped his bible on the floor. The noise resounded in the little room, magnified far louder than the action justified. Outside, the angel immediately stopped singing and manifested his sword and armor.

"You'd better go," Joseph warned.

Lorelei worked up a vicious grin. "I'm here to see Aza," she reminded.

"He might not be alone."

"I've been ordered to work my way around to his friends."

Before the priest could answer, she stepped up onto the window ledge and sprang out.

Aza's face lit up, thrilled once again to see her. His armor evaporated.

But Lorelei was too angry to fully appreciate his welcome. No wonder the angel had come to her exorcism with a Childbed Angel. Lorelei wondered how many of the other sixty-nine guardian angels had come to LA to protect Aza's ill-gotten flock.

Like a cat scattering pigeons, Lorelei's appearance shattered the precise geometry of the children's adoration of the angel. Their souls shrieked and fled the devil. She noted that they seemed trapped within the confines of the chain-link fence.

Lorelei reached out for a young man—Erik, all gothic doom and gloom—and trailed her talons through his soul. She found lust there, drooling admiration for the devilish charms straining her yankable black dress. That one she caught in the reflection of the buckle of her purse.

Aza put his sword away. He jumped upward, opening his wings as he leapt toward her. "Come away from here," he ordered.

"We'd better go somewhere we can talk," Lorelei answered. "You have some explaining to do."

CHAPTER 4: TRUTH AND CONSEQUENCES

Lorelei beat her batlike wings hard, gaining sky. Aza's huge gray-feathered wings overtook her effortlessly. As he banked his wings to reach for her forearm, the angel ordered, "Stop."

Flicking one wingtip, Lorelei darted out of his grasp. She was relieved to know that her membranous wings had better maneuverability than his. While she might not be able to match him for speed and power, she might win an aerobatic contest.

"We need a place to talk," she protested. "Anywhere down there, we're going to have to worry about being overheard. What you need to explain to me you don't want any of my kind to report. So follow me and think about how you plan to justify what I just stumbled across."

As soon as the words left her lips, they made her want to laugh. They echoed any number of lovers' quarrels she had inspired over the years. The laughter drained from her when she remembered what Asmodeus had said about being privy to things either side would hide from a creature without a soul. Had Aza revealed his cache of children to her on purpose?

She glanced over at him. The angel's face was a mask of unhappiness. No, she realized, he hadn't known she was there. Just as she hadn't known Joseph was in the bedroom before she broke in. Although Azaziel probably didn't think of it in those terms, his bedroom must have a glamour over it that shielded its contents—which was probably why he'd thought he could bring home a certain succubus and bang her without consequence.

Azaziel trailed Lorelei across the city. Though his wings were pearly gray rather than snowy white, the stained-glass shimmer of his halo hurt her eyes. She retrieved her sunglasses from her purse and concentrated on the mountains looming in front of her.

She had another realization: for a supposedly omniscient creature, Aza didn't appear to consider the repercussions of his actions. Everything seemed an experiment to him. She wondered if he was proving something to himself. Was he simply acting out to get his Father's attention?

That thought sent a shiver zinging down her back. She did not want any of that kind of attention.

Azaziel reached tentatively down to take her hand. Lorelei allowed him to weave his fingers between hers, enjoying once again the smoothness of his palm, the comforting strength of his grip. However, once he had hold of her, he began pulling her forward. He wouldn't—or couldn't—match his speed to hers. It felt like being hauled off to be disciplined.

He was really strong, she realized again. She reminded herself not to struggle. She would only tear her wings if she opposed him.

Azaziel eventually noticed he was dragging her forward and relented. "Did you have a destination in mind?"

Lorelei thrust one taloned finger toward the Art Deco confection perched on the edge of Mount Hollywood. Griffith Observatory commanded a view of nearly all of LA. Better than that, it stood above most of the listening posts that she knew about.

Aza angled them into a column of warm air and then rode it practically all the way to the observatory.

Yasmina loitered in the shadows outside the bar on Santa Monica. Midnight came and went, but Jequon still held court inside. She smoked one cigar after another, flicking the butts at the rats who dared poke their noses out of the gutter.

Finally the party broke up. This year's starlet left in the company of a man old enough to be her grandfather. Her potential co-star rode off on the back of an incubus's Ducati Diavel. The investors followed in a knot, queuing to climb into their town cars.

As soon as Jequon sauntered through the bar's door, the temptress peeled herself out of the shadows and stepped into his path. Jequon stared at her, his beautiful aquiline face closed off and unreadable. Three very large young men drew closer to him, waiting for a word from their boss.

"I need to talk to you," Yasmina told the fallen angel. "Please, Jequon. Please."

At the note of desperation in her voice, Jequon smiled. "Know of a good after-party?"

"I do," the temptress promised. "How depraved are you feeling tonight?"

"Abysmal."

"I know just the place."

Jequon turned to one of his entourage and sent him jogging after the car.

Soon as they landed on the observatory dome, Lorelei used the angel's grip on her hand to pull him around to face her. "What was that?" she demanded. "In the churchyard?"

Azaziel sighed. "Those children were like Ashleigh, neither saved nor damned. They never got a chance before death took them."

"That's what it means to be mortal," Lorelei argued. "They have the span they're given and they make the best or worst of it. Why would you gather them after they're dead?"

As the words crossed her lips, a realization blinded her: Aza might be auditioning new succubi shortly—and now the exorcist was on his team. Aza read the thought in her face before she could spit the words at him.

"No." He gave her a little shake. "Please don't even think that. I do not plan to put these children into your sisters. You are special to me, Lorelei. One of a kind. Those children are separate from what I was doing with you..."

"To me, you mean."

Aza moved to gather her into his arms, but she dodged backward and held one hand up, palm out. "Before the exorcism," she said coldly, "Ashleigh revealed you'd been watching me. How long had you been stalking me, Aza? How many souls did you audition to poison me with?"

"It's not like that." He held out his hands, trying to placate her. "I've been collecting the souls for a while—"

"Ten years?" she pushed. "Twenty?"

"Not as long as that," he shot back, too quickly. She knew he hadn't bothered to count. "I've been very particular about those I gather. I only collect the ones who would have been ours if they'd survived a little longer. The ones for whom death came as a shock."

The casual way he explained bending the rules horrified her. This was so wrong that it made her physically ill. Over the bile burning the back of her throat, she forced herself to ask, "Have any ghosts graduated from your little program?"

He didn't respond, so she knew the answer was yes.

Shaken, Lorelei took another step back. She struggled to wrap her mind around her new understanding: Azaziel had saved souls after their bodies died? "Oh, Aza, this is so wrong."

He stared at her, caught off-guard by the depth of her revulsion. "It's not forbidden," he protested.

That was so entirely in character. What he'd already done—stuffing a mortal soul into Lorelei and then fucking the poor girl trapped in the succubus's infernal flesh—had not been forbidden either. It hadn't needed to be spelled out, because no one in their right mind would believe they could get away with it.

Once again, Lorelei plummeted from her certainty that Azaziel felt something specific for her back to the sick realization that this was all an experiment to him. She was the only one in love. Clearly, she was a fool. The thought made her tremble. She threatened, "Hell could make such war..."

He cut her off. "You won't betray me."

She stared at the angel. His certainty burned around him, shimmering in his halo. Wow, did she loathe being dictated to. She asked, "Why not, Azazi-El?"

Nonplussed, he said the first thing that occurred to him: "Because you love me."

"Because I love you, I know you're not going to kill me to ensure my silence. You can't even kill the bitch who was your wife's sister millennia ago—and you loathe Yasmina."

"I won't kill you," he agreed. "But if you love me, don't do this. Don't turn me in as a career move. Sure, bringing all those souls within Hell's grasp will catapult you up the infernal ladder, but it will kill me, Lorelei. Asmodeus will kill me. I will die to protect those children."

Goosebumps shivered over her. She knew he would do exactly as he promised. Perhaps that was what Azaziel had been looking for all along: not a lifetime companion, not a one-time sex toy, but oblivion. Maybe he sought the one transgression that would push Heaven and Hell so far that they'd destroy him rather than condone his behavior.

It made her want to protect him from himself—and that made her angrier yet. "Go away. Go away and let me think."

"Please. Forget what you saw. It doesn't change anything between us."

"It changes everything," she said flatly. "I wondered why you hadn't seduced Ashleigh while the obviously willing girl was still in her flesh. You could have reversed her blood poisoning—or gotten her to a hospital, if you didn't want responsibility for a miracle. Instead you let her die. I thought that was because you recognized the immutability of the laws that govern the collection of souls. I thought that springing her on me had been a flash of inspiration, something that came to you when you couldn't figure out how else to fuck me guilt-free. Now I see that you'd been appraising souls and Ashleigh served your purpose best. You wanted me, but you wanted me tainted. You wanted me changed. You used me, Angel. Worst of all, you used my friend Ashleigh to get me."

Lorelei knew the flavor of truth when she spoke it. Azaziel didn't deny her words.

She continued, "So we'll see, Angel. You've taught me a lot of things in the last week. We'll see if turning a blind eye was one of the lessons."

"Please, Lorelei." He reached for her again, but she skipped backward, wings out and ready to flee. "You have to know that you're special to me."

"You said that before, Angel. But just because you don't currently intend to plop a soul into another of my sisters doesn't mean that one of your brothers won't decide that it sounds like fun. And since you've already got a stockpile of souls eager for improvement... What you're doing is dangerous. It's dangerous to me, now that I know it. So I need time to decide what I'm going to do with the knowledge."

He abruptly manifested closer to her, pulling her into his arms to kiss her hard and long. Lorelei struggled not to surrender to the kiss, not to be bought by it. Oh, he would take to Hell's ranks just fine. She sank her talons into his waist and pushed herself away.

"You're asking me to die for you," she said icily. "You know Asmodeus will kill me for keeping a secret like this. Even if he hadn't already vowed to devour me himself before you can have me—"

Aza interrupted her. "Is that true?"

"I came directly from meeting with him to see you." She pulled the heavy mass of hair over her shoulder to reveal the bite mark scabbed on the back of her neck. "Even if you could somehow win my soul back from him, how many centuries will it take before I am pure enough to ascend with your others?"

To her immense surprise, the angel had no more justifications. Azaziel tossed open his wings and leaned off the observatory's roof, letting the night winds pull him up into the sky.

Fuck. Lorelei sank down onto the dome. She pulled the new cell phone out of her purse, savoring its heat in the palm of her hand.

What was she going to say to Asmodeus? If she reported the stash of souls, the demon would order an attack on the playground. How many fiends would it take to bring an angel down? Maybe Nebiros was still in town, ready to take another crack at Azaziel. Her wannabe boyfriend could be dead before morning, all for the glory of hell.

The succubus stared off in the direction of Aza's church, blind to the constellation of streetlights burning below her. If the angel was serious about dying to protect his wards, could she live with his sacrifice on her new-grown conscience? Worse than that, what would it be like to live without Aza? As long as he survived, she could hope they might someday find a way to be together.

Now, furious that he had put her in this position, she was hard pressed to remember why their relationship was a thing she should want. Asmodeus told her to bring Aza down. This would certainly do it.

As Lorelei switched the cell phone on, the empty silence around her was broken by the sound of wings. Lorelei stared up into the night sky. The thought came unbidden to her: if Aza asked her to come back to his bed in the church, she would go with him. There had to be a way to resolve his hoarding without anyone needing to die.

Instead, another angel fell toward her like a lightning bolt. Lorelei had no time to open her wings—no time to gain the sky—before Barakiel slammed into her. They rolled across the domed roof, grappling. His fist connected, knocking her head against the copper plating. She saw shimmering lights. Then they were dropping over the edge.

"The priest was mine," Barakiel snarled. He looked like hell, bloody and bruised, eyes swelling and lip torn.

Lorelei brought her taloned feet up and kicked hard. Unexpectedly, the fallen angel released her. She found herself plummeting. She somersaulted, hurled open her wings, and banked right, seeking a thermal. The post-midnight air currents were weak.

Barakiel struck her again. This time Lorelei clung to him, pressing her body against his. She wound her tail around his thigh. She grasped his wings, feeling the softness of his tattered black feathers. "Wait," she insisted.

The fallen angel tried to pluck her off. Lorelei felt his flesh warming to hers, despite himself. She ground her sex more firmly against his leg.

"Look at you," she continued. "All Joseph wanted was to see an angel. You could've done that. You could've revealed yourself and persuaded him that his god was truly dead, that the only angels left were fallen. You could've given him exactly what he wanted and guaranteed his damnation, but you were afraid."

Barakiel stopped struggling. His wings beat powerfully, gaining height. Lorelei refused to look down.

"You were afraid of blaspheming your Father, weren't you?" she demanded. "Well, don't let me be the first to tell you, but you're fallen, Angel. You're damned never to see your home or your creator again. Sentenced to eternally walk the earth, right? But you hoped you could find salvation. You hoped the priest would save you, so you didn't do the one job our master set for you."

The fallen angel tore her away from him, throwing her downward. Lorelei shook shreds of his suit from her talons. She turned, alert for his next attack.

Rather than dive at her again, Barakiel winged away in retreat.

Lorelei screamed after him, "Wanting salvation isn't enough!"

He hurled a curse over his shoulder, but kept going.

Lorelei glided into a turn and returned to the observatory. No, she realized, wanting wasn't enough. It hadn't made Azaziel hers.

She retrieved the cell phone from where she'd dropped it. Before she could think twice, Lorelei pressed her master's glyph.

Floria surprised her by answering. "Help you?"

Lorelei looked at the phone, but yes, she'd pressed the right button. "Hello, Sister. I've got a message for the boss."

"Uh-huh?"

"I just saw your favorite fallen angel."

"Jequon?"

"No, the other one."

Floria's laugh was jagged. "Barakiel? You're dealing with losers tonight, aren't you?"

"Seems like. He sounds less fallen than I thought."

"He's just bitching because the boss disciplined him for losing the priest," Floria said. "I guess shit rolls downhill." She sounded smug about it.

"Yeah, well," Lorelei said, "pass the message on to the boss, would you?"

"Sure," Floria chirped.

Lorelei decided not to say anything about Aza's petting zoo until she could tell Asmodeus directly. She saw no reason for Floria to get any credit for all those souls.

Yasmina waited until she and Jequon were settled at a booth at the back of Pandemonium. There was a man tied to a Saint Andrew's cross up on the stage, being lashed with bouquets of long-stemmed roses by two of the younger succubi. Crimson petals scattered across the stage and stuck to his bloodied back.

Once Jequon had a martini in hand, its olive replaced by an eyeball, Yasmina rushed to get her apology out. "I should have told you about the mishap with the boy's soul. Those damn harpies got out of hand and killed him before I could prevent them. It wouldn't have mattered…"

Over the rim of his glass, Jequon's brown eyes shifted a shade darker.

Yasmina amended quickly, "I didn't think it would matter, if I could successfully tempt Ashleigh to our side or persuade her to betray Lorelei—or if Lorelei had agreed to help me topple Azaziel. The ends justifying the means and all that."

The fallen angel favored her with a sharp smile. "You forget your station, temptress. Those means aren't yours to use. Which is why you find yourself shunned now."

"I know I screwed up. But please, Jequon, I need your help."

He gazed at her, judging. "I want to see Azaziel brought down almost as much as you do," he agreed. "But you're going about this the wrong way. Lorelei is stubborn. You need to come at her sideways, so she thinks the idea is hers. How can you manipulate her into working for you?"

Yasmina's mouth closed with an audible snap. She frowned into her own glass, unsure how much to admit. Then again, this was Jequon: he would know soon, if he didn't already. "I can't go anywhere near her. Did you know that Asmodeus repossessed my limo and gave it to that stupid cunt?"

Jequon swirled the eyeball around in his drink. "As a matter of fact, I did know that."

One of the succubi on stage had backed the other against their victim and was grinding into her, using him as a backstop. Their submissive moaned into his lavalier.

Yasmina ignored them. "I can't believe Asmodeus would throw his aegis over Lorelei, after she cost him the dance club."

"You're too short-sighted," Jequon corrected. "He's tempting her."

"What do you mean?"

Jequon took his time to answer. He sucked the eyeball into his mouth, popped it between his teeth. "Lorelei has a soul of her own now. You've seen it."

Yasmina remembered the moment at the exorcism when the two souls had flown free of the succubus's flesh. "So?"

"So Lorelei invited Azaziel to the exorcism in order to retrieve her possessing ghost. She led Father Joseph back to the light. Before, in her unsullied days, she was a spirit in service to Hell, but nothing she's done since she sprouted a soul of her own has been in Hell's service."

"That's what I'm saying," Yasmina argued.

"No, it's not," Jequon corrected. "Lorelei is a succubus on her way to Heaven. Asmodeus can't allow that, so he's trying to tempt her back into being an asset. His asset."

"Oh." Yasmina grasped exactly how her mistake had played into Asmodeus's hands.

The fallen angel laughed at her expression, then polished off his drink. "If you want your place back at Asmodeus's right hand, then you'd better tempt that succubus back into being comfortably damned."

It was Yasmina's turn to laugh. "She hates me."

"Everyone hates you, my beauty. That's no secret. You've always made that work to your advantage before."

Yasmina waved at the succubus on table service to bring Jequon another martini.

"If you can't get to Azaziel directly," Jequon advised, "then use Lorelei. And if you can't get to her directly, then…"

"Use Floria. Perfect."

"There's plenty of jealousy to exploit," Jequon agreed.

Aza eased the playground gate shut behind him. As he crossed the crumbling asphalt, he savored the draw of the children's souls. They swirled around him in greeting. He had collected many of these souls himself, gathering each from the brink of some uncertain eternity. He'd intended for Ashleigh to join them when she left Lorelei's flesh, but her innate goodness—and Lorelei's friendship—had saved her instead.

He paused at the center of the yard, glorying in the unconstrained energies flowing around and through him. Each had a distinct pulse, tint, and voice just as in life, only now unencumbered by form and worries about the mortal world.

He recognized each soul in passing: Antonio, Dalisay, Jeff and Lyle, Shu, Eleni, Jorge, so many more. He heard voices full of vitality and joy. Angel and mortal were so close this way. Aza had long believed that mortals should be this pure but whole, with bodies and lives that measured in spans more fitting to the growth and change that Heaven required.

It might take decades, but here—or anywhere safe—these souls could be taught by his kind. Free from distractions and temptations, they could restore the broken mirror this world had become. Every time he walked among these spirits, it seemed to him that things could be made right at last.

Shebethiel drifted to the ground a few paces away. The children moved to greet him, then orbited both angels in a steady kaleidoscopic flow. "I don't understand how the succubus fit into your plan." Shebethiel's words echoed exactly what his brother Shebniel had said—before the exorcism that cost him his mortal form.

Aza chuckled bitterly. Even his moment of peace was infected by what he'd done with Lorelei. "She didn't fit into this plan," he answered. "That's all too obvious now."

Shebethiel considered that long enough that Aza turned to go. Finally, the other angel said, "She will betray you to Asmodeus. She must."

Aza countered, "It remains to be seen what Lorelei will do. She can be surprisingly stubborn."

Muriel arrived in a burst of righteous light. The dance of the spirits fell into chaos as they withdrew from her. "The devil's master set her as bait for you," Muriel said, her musical voice discordant. "She will do no more than she is commanded."

It didn't surprise Aza that Muriel had come to join the argument. It would have been bewildering if she'd missed a chance to scold him. To be truthful, her interruption didn't particularly irk him, except that she frightened the children.

"Love will guide Lorelei," Aza told the others. "She will do her best to protect me."

Shebethiel shook his head. "You're a romantic."

"Worse, he's a dreamer." Drawing her hands through the brilliant traces of a soul, Muriel pursed her lips. "Here's an observation, Azaziel: maybe you've spent so much time among mortals that you've begun to dream like them."

He made no effort to debate her. "That's a consequence of having dreamt for them long enough."

Barbelo appeared, wearing a fond smile as always. Aza thought again how blessed he was to have her as his friend.

Rafael manifested in the midst of the playground, bobbing gently in the night air. He burned with a light that cast the host of other LA angels suddenly gathered on the playground into stark relief. As one, the children moved toward the archangel, the nucleus of light at the heart of a living molecule.

"Muriel, Barbelo, and Azaziel, you are released from your supervision of this assemblage. Whether Lorelei tells what she knows or not, our estranged brothers will be sniffing around you after last night's cataclysm. They will soon be seeking a way into this place like foxes into a henhouse. It's best if you go separate ways and draw their attention away while we find new hideaways for your students."

Muriel glared at Aza, then stormed away in a huff. The children's souls drew as far away from her as possible.

Aza turned on his heel and followed Barbelo out through the gap in the chain-link fence. "Could you aid me with something more, my friend?"

"You have only to ask."

"Muriel and I visited a mother in crisis the other day, brought her the news of her son's untimely passing. I don't doubt the mother's faith, but Muriel..."

Barbelo didn't require him to finish the thought. "I'd be glad to check on Dolores for you."

His friend's unwavering kindness buoyed his steps as he walked away from her.

Muriel kicked through the wet ashes of Lost Angels, finding a polished Italian loafer, a delicately feminine Philippe Patel wristwatch, a cell phone with a cracked screen, a charred skull.

The Los Angeles County Fire Department had battled the blaze through most of Friday night, but once the flames reached the back storeroom, something exploded, shooting fire upward in a towering pillar. From that point on, the fire crew evacuated. Their game plan shifted from saving the club to containing the conflagration. Asmodeus's lucrative money factory was allowed to collapse inward and burn itself out.

Unfortunately, Muriel had not been allowed to join her friend Samael in reaping the mortals trapped inside. The disappointment felt like a physical weight in her chest.

The skirmish at the nightclub, facing off against fiends and tempters under the command of the General of Hell's Army on Earth: that woke something in Muriel that had long been dormant. Now she ached to join the battle again, to shake blood and ichor from her sword. She felt tempted to go on a rampage across Los Angeles, killing devils as she found them. One never had to travel far in the metropolitan area to find some scheming representative of Asmodeus's organization.

As she pondered where to begin, an archangel appeared amidst the wet ashes and the mouth-watering scent of barbecue. Muriel sank to one knee, blue eyes downcast. Michael was the commander of Heaven's host. He'd vanquished Lucifer and cast him down to Hell, where he bound the former Morning Star in chains. She was blessed that the holy archangel had come to deliver her orders in person.

Muriel had only met Michael once before, when she dwelt in the Celestial City and sang in the Choir Eternal. Then she'd simpered like a fangirl. Although her heart was singing, she tried to play it cool now. "Hail, Mika'il."

Michael had taken the form of a shaven-headed warrior with tidy black whiskers outlining his jaw. His skin was a shade paler than his warm brown eyes. Today he chose to appear dressed as an LAPD officer, complete with spit-shined boots and a baton in his belt. Oh, he was comely in appearance.

"Well met, Sister," Michael boomed. He reached down to raise her to her feet. "Well fought last night."

"I was surprised you didn't join us."

"And spoil the fun? Hell's cowards usually turn tail when I appear. It takes the pleasure out of scuffling with them."

She hadn't considered that. "But Hell's general—and Asmodeus himself—were able to escape."

"Nebiros often does," Michael mused. "And Asmodeus serves a purpose in the Almighty's plan."

Muriel swallowed and struggled to maintain her joy. "Still, there are so many devils…"

"More grown every day," Michael agreed cheerfully.

"If Nebiros were destroyed, others would vie for his position. They might thin the herd a bit."

"Assuredly." Michael grinned at her. "But one of those might be a better tactician than Nebiros. When it comes down to it, Hell's general has always relied on brute force to bull his way out of any situation. As long as that's the case, we needn't fear any action he might take against us."

Muriel found little satisfaction in that thought.

With surprising gentleness, Michael asked, "You didn't join us in repelling the apostates from the Plains of Heaven, did you?"

Certain that he knew the answer, Muriel shook her head, swinging blond hair into her face. Less than a third of Heaven's contingent had been directed into battle that day. The rest stood on the battlements, cheering. Muriel had joined her voice to the battle hymn. Even now the words reverberated inside her. Unfortunately, that glorious day had been the first moment that singing—formerly the delight of her existence—had no longer been enough to sustain her. Watching the pennants fly and weapons flash, hearing the exultation of Heaven's force and the enemies' curses as they were vanquished: something in Muriel's chest took flight. From that day forward, she lived to fight evil—preferably hand-to-hand.

"You will receive another opportunity before long," Michael promised. "This situation with the ensouled succubus will lead to a confrontation with the infernal prince of this city. Whether it troubles him personally or not, Asmodeus cannot allow the slight to go unanswered. Hell must protest what Azaziel has wrought or fret that we plan to dump mortal souls into all their devils."

Muriel shuddered. "We don't plan to do that, do we?"

Michael laughed. "It's actually not a bad strategy, but I doubt we'll have a crush of volunteers looking to become entangled with succubi in order to save some of them. Lorelei had a very rare soul possessing her. The rest can't possibly be so lucky."

The mere prospect made Muriel nauseous.

Michael relented and changed the subject. "You needn't search the ashes here. Samael did a thorough job of rescuing those who were redeemed and destroying or damning the others. There's nothing for us here any longer."

"It's not that," Muriel protested. "It's just...I feel at loose ends. While we were here, while I was fighting...I felt a sense of purpose. I felt needed, engaged. Perfected. Now I'm simply Muriel once more. I feel as useful as these ashes."

"All of us have our uses," he reminded softly.

But some of their uses were so much more glamorous, Muriel thought. Some were doomed to labor, unknown and unappreciated—unrecognized—while others were honored in legends. Michael had been the first angel to bow down before Adam. Michael had spoken to Moses and Joan of Arc. He was the most beloved angel, the one for whom more houses of worship had been named than any other. Muriel wanted to be like him so badly that it hurt.

"Find strength in your work," Michael counseled. "There are tasks enough for all of us."

Muriel nodded, taking encouragement from the archangel's assurance. Even Azaziel had a poem written about him: written by one of the greatest sinners in history, of course, but still Azaziel's existence was recorded and celebrated and set in verse. Muriel longed to inspire a mortal to lionize her. First, however, she had to do deeds worthy of remembrance. Perhaps her moment was at hand.

CHAPTER 5: WHEELS WITHIN WHEELS

Sighing, Lorelei leaned back against the observatory's dome to gaze up at the stars. Her shift in position revealed the angel sitting beside her as if she had been there all along. Lorelei flinched. "Holy crap, Barb. You startled me."

"Sorry." Barbelo offered a smile as if she really meant it. Today she was wearing a turquoise lace-neck T-shirt with blue jeans and beaded sandals.

Lorelei shook her head over the angel's sense of fashion. Rather than debate it, she asked, "Come to defend Aza's poor choices?"

Barbelo laughed, lovely and warm. Real amusement shone in her hazel eyes. "Unfortunately," she said, "I bring you joyous news that will make you sad."

"Wow, Angel. You really know how to sell a revelation. I can't wait to hear it." Lorelei rolled her eyes for effect.

"Last evening at sunset, Ashleigh Johnson ascended to her just reward."

The words stabbed through Lorelei. A Heavenly reward was what Lorelei had wanted for the girl, what she'd hardly dared to expect, but the loss of her first real friend still cut. Lorelei curled up around the pain and sobbed.

Lorelei had honestly loved Ashleigh, as goofy, awkward, and naïve as the girl had been. Ashleigh had protected Lorelei from Yasmina and saved Lorelei from being dissolved into madness before the exorcism began at Lost Angels. Ashleigh had been the first true confidant Lorelei had ever had. In the end, the mortal girl had only ever wished happiness on her rival for the angel's love. No one, in Lorelei's entire existence, had ever treated her so gently or so well.

And now her friend was gone forever.

Barbelo gathered the succubus close in her arms and merely held her, letting her grieve.

Seated on the crossbar of the H in the Hollywood sign, Muriel turned toward Samael. This was ostensibly some infernal's turf, but Samael often perched here, at least since that actress committed suicide.

The Angel of Death had drawn the hood of his cloak up, shielding the bones of his face from the predawn light. It was hard to see where her friend was looking, except that his head was turned away from the succubus and Barbelo.

"I don't understand," Muriel repeated. "Why are they lavishing so much attention on that devil?"

Samael didn't turn from whatever held his attention. "Lorelei has a soul of her own now," he reminded.

"Surely they don't imagine it can be saved?" Muriel snarled. "How many souls has she damned? You must be able to see that number."

"Yes," Samael agreed. "She has done well for her master, but that was before she was granted a soul. Since then, she perfected the girl-child's soul and led the priest back to the light."

"And swallowed the soul of one who might have been damned."

"She showed mercy," Samael pointed out. "She has tempted no one new."

At a loss for words, Muriel stared at her friend, puzzling over his tone. She knew without doubt that Samael had no mercy for Hell's minions. She knew that he performed his duties impartially, harvesting souls as he was directed, immune to bargaining and bribery. She knew that Samael had no affection for Azaziel and little patience for the Watcher's transgressions in the name of love. Despite her certainty of Samael's allegiance, Muriel didn't hear the hatred for the succubus that she had hoped.

"It's a shame someone can't annihilate her before she leads another of us into temptation," Muriel said, with a nod toward Barbelo. "Especially since our sister's methods are so questionable to begin with. How little it might take to lure her into doing Hell's work with the best of intentions."

Now Samael did turn toward Muriel. The stars that were his eyes glittered inside the darkness of his hood. When Muriel met his gaze, a wave of vertigo washed over her. To cover her shudder, she resettled her wings across her back.

"I have not seen Barbelo do anything questionable, beyond her affection for Azaziel. If she has been directed to minister to the succubus, then that is her burden. I have not received any orders regarding the succubus myself."

Muriel laughed unhappily. "I have." Then again, she had Michael's assurance that she would have another chance to fight evil soon. As far as Muriel was concerned, it couldn't come soon enough. She had one particular evil in mind.

Lorelei felt the change as the sun crawled over the horizon. She looked up to find the sky hung with shimmering sheets of gold. She grimaced and bent to pull her sunglasses from her purse. As she slipped the Persols on, Lorelei demanded, "Why didn't Aza tell me about Ashleigh? He should have invited me to her liberation—"

Barbelo shook her brown curls gently. "My brother is on probation.

You can imagine the dispute over his relationship with you. He didn't have permission to bring you along, although he wanted to."

Lorelei shrugged that off. "He could have told me about it afterward. Or gotten a message to me somehow, if he wanted to dodge telling me in person." Instead, Aza had forgotten all about her. He went back to messing around with his children's souls, taking comfort from them, rather than from her. Apparently, he hadn't spared another thought for his would-be girlfriend, until she sprang out of his bedroom window at him.

The sense of abandonment was just as crushing as any human girl might feel. Lorelei thought about the cell phone in her purse and realized she really should have reported the stockpile of souls long before now. She frowned at the Venice Beach angel at her side. "Where are you off to today?" she asked pointedly.

Barbelo laughed, dismissing the brush-off. "I'm attending a funeral. In fact, you met the boy, I believe: Deion Gutierrez."

A shiver trickled down Lorelei's back. "You're kidding, right? Deion, who used to be Ashleigh's boyfriend?"

"The same."

"You know I was there when he died, right? Well, not in an active, able-to-do-anything-about-it sense. That bitch Yasmina had shoved me down deep into my own flesh and left Ashleigh in charge. Yasmina and her harpies captured Deion as a way to tempt Ashleigh to become a succubus. To take over my life. And when my girl stood up for me and said no, Yasmina's pet harpies tore her ex-boyfriend apart and swallowed his soul. He should've been good and damned, but Yasmina had him erased to keep him from talking. It's one of the reasons she lost her status as Queen Bitch of Asmodeus's court."

Barbelo took in the whole sad story with a sage nod. "You know Deion was a good customer of your friend Tuan?"

Lorelei hadn't known that. She realized belatedly that meant that Tuan probably sold the speed to which Ashleigh had been addicted. Obviously the girl hadn't known herself, or she wouldn't have sympathized with Tuan and his enslavement to Floria.

Lorelei felt like she had to say something to keep the conversation going. "Will Tuan and the boys be at the funeral today?"

"Seems likely."

Thinking it through, Lorelei argued, "Not if Floria can help it. It's not good business to let dealers face the consequences of their deals." Then again, Floria sounded like she had her hands full with the boss's business. Maybe her grip on the boys wasn't as tight as she wanted to think.

Barbelo's smile held no hint of malice. "You're welcome to come along with me and keep an eye on Floria's gang."

There was a catch, Lorelei was sure, but in all likelihood, Floria wouldn't be at the funeral, so that made it as good a place to be as any.

Although Lorelei preferred wakes to funerals, she really didn't have anything else going on today. Besides, consolation sex could be really hot. Maybe Deion had a brother.

"Let's get some breakfast first," Barbelo suggested. "Fancy a burrito?"

Lorelei put a hand over her stomach and felt it grumble. "Lead the way."

Aza decided he was hungry. There were fewer restaurants open at dawn in LA than there used to be, but Canter's was still twenty-four hours. He would stop in, pick up a picnic, and go join Lorelei at the observatory. He would try to explain why it was important to make the children safe. Surely, he could make her understand somehow. Then, if neither of them got called away, they could watch the city come awake.

There was a line at the deli, even at this hour, but he knew the menu and passed the time people-watching. He catalogued those already fallen to gluttony and lust, as well as those saved by temperance, patience, and charity.

The cashier taking orders wore her hair backcombed into a perfect flip. It was an unnatural orange sherbet color. She cracked her gum at him. "What'll you have, Doll?"

"Egg and bacon sandwich on challah, two potato knishes, and a pair of chocolate egg creams." He handed over all the money wadded into the pocket of his coat. She patiently smoothed each bill before handing back his change.

Aza stepped back to wait for his order and bumped into an immovable object. The creature's sulfurous smell was familiar even before the angel turned to find Mastema lurking behind him.

"How did you know I adore egg creams?" the demon teased. This morning he wore a green sharkskin jacket buttoned over a too-wide tie adorned with a busty hula girl who could have been Lorelei's twin.

Aza wondered if Mastema intentionally dressed like a clown. "The egg creams are not for you," the angel said, "but I can spare you a five if you'd like to order your own."

"That's right kindly of you." Mastema held out a paw and accepted the bill, but made no move toward the counter. "Quickly, though, before you get your order and drift away, I have a proposition for you."

"I'm finished listening to your propositions," Aza said coldly.

"This one's about your honey."

The number before Aza's was called to come pick up their order. The crowd milled around to let the lucky couple pass.

Without losing the thread of the conversation, Aza answered, "She's not yours to offer."

"No, it's an offer for her," Mastema clarified. "I'd like you to present it to her for me."

Aza didn't turn toward the demon. He didn't want to admit, even to himself, that he'd felt the briefest flash of temptation. "Lorelei can make her own choices," he said with a pang.

"Thought you might like to sway her to make the choice you'd prefer."

Aza's number was called. He stepped forward to flash it at the man behind the counter. He exchanged the paper slip for a plastic shopping bag of parcels wrapped in white deli paper and two cups to go.

As much as Aza wished for it, the demon had not vanished.

"The deal is this," Mastema said, trailing Aza to the door but making no move to open it for him. "What if your girl could be persuaded to fall in your direction?" When Aza didn't ask for clarification, the demon spelled it out anyway. "What if you made her an angel second-class? A junior angel? She could tag along with you, doing the Lord's work, spreading her special kind of loving to the needy. Think of all the joy she could bring, with the right instruction."

There it was, all too enticing: Lorelei working at his side. Lorelei as his helpmeet—and there would be no reason for them ever to be parted. Aza forced himself to shake his head. "It's impossible."

"Why do you say that?"

"No one can be made an angel."

"She wouldn't be one of the eternal host," the demon conceded. "Hence the designation 'second class.'"

"No one can make an angel," Aza repeated.

"Wrong, boy-o. Two people can make an angel. One hasn't chosen to make any more...and me."

"You don't have that power."

"Trying to convince yourself or me?" Mastema asked. "The powers I have would surprise you."

While they were arguing, breakfast was cooling off. "No," Aza said more forcefully. "I will not tempt Lorelei to fall, even if it means falling upward. Anything more that happens to her must be her choice. I'm not going to be the agent of her destruction."

"So be it then." Mastema grinned at him. "Say, didn't you use to squat at that burned-out church near the freeway? I heard Asmodeus suggest that there better not be anything but ashes there next time he asked about it."

Aza's heart sank. Had Lorelei betrayed him so quickly? He rushed through the door and simply wished himself back to Santa Rosa's, the church that served as his home.

Lorelei decided her black Betsey Johnson sundress was a little flirty for a Sunday morning budget funeral. Disappointed that no one had tried to yank the dress off of her yet, Lorelei fetched a scrap of shadow out of her purse and formed it into a shrug that covered her shoulders and décolletage. Even so, she looked positively gussied up compared to Barbelo, who had added yet another men's blazer—albeit a sober, charcoal-colored one—to her T-shirt and blue jeans.

Lorelei wondered what had happened to the blazer Barbelo lent her after the exorcism. Last she'd seen it, it was wadded on the floor of the bathroom at Chateau Marmont. Lorelei hated to think that Barbelo had gone into her rooms to retrieve it.

For now, Lorelei trailed the angel into the rundown funeral home. Its scuffed cream-colored walls needed a coat of paint. The faded green carpeting looked brownish, stained and worn from the shuffling of hundreds of mourners. Beneath the overpowering perfume of chemically-produced lily burned a tang of disinfectant. Lorelei took a deep breath and found herself lightheaded from the aroma of despair.

Barbelo paused to scan the guest book, so Lorelei continued on into the viewing room alone. Of course, there was nothing to view. Deion's corpse had been partially eaten by the harpies. Putting him back together well enough to go on display was a job for a special effects team, not a cut-rate undertaker. The metal casket at the front of the room remained chastely closed.

Atop the casket, a yearbook photograph showed a young man in an ill-fitting suit and a cheap tie. With his wounded eyes and natural hair, he wasn't a bad looking kid. Lorelei thought she could glimpse what Ashleigh had seen in him. Speed, unfortunately, hadn't done his teeth any favors.

A middle-aged woman made a beeline toward her. Dolores Gutierrez wore a black polyester dress that had seen its share of funerals. She wore her short hair layered and frosted around her face, trying to look younger than her forty-five years. "How did you know my son?"

Lorelei offered the woman her hand. "I only met him once. I was a close friend of Ashleigh's."

"God rest her soul," Dolores breathed. Lorelei held herself tightly, so she didn't shudder.

Deion's mom was clearly saved, surprisingly at peace with the loss of her son and his ex-girlfriend. Lorelei extracted her hand. Just as she was going to excuse herself, Father Joseph insinuated himself into the conversation. "I'm surprised to see you here, Lorelei." His voice wasn't welcoming.

Lorelei flashed a quick smile to the mother before turning to find the old man back in his clerical collar. His face was still ruddy from years of drinking cheap whiskey, but his eyes were surprisingly clear.

"Morning, Father. I came with Barb." Lorelei waved toward the angel, saw him recognize Barbelo for what she was. The priest straightened in surprise. Lorelei grinned.

"Is Azazi—"

Lorelei cut across him with a hiss.

"Is Aza here, too?"

"He's avoiding me," Lorelei confessed, "since the big reveal last night."

Joseph steered her to a quieter corner. "Were you responsible for Deion?"

"No—he was someone else's account—but I was there when he was killed as a temptation to Ashleigh."

The priest formulated his indignation, but Lorelei cut him off. "I didn't have a hand in it. And you know she didn't fall for it."

Lorelei watched some part of him slide over into relief. Then he spoiled it by adding, "Just don't stir up any trouble in here today."

She winked at him. "Trouble is not my plan."

Even as the words left her lips, Lorelei heard her name roundly cursed at the back of the room. Her smile dissipated. She should have guessed that the harpies would show up here.

"No trouble, Lorelei," the priest reminded.

"Don't start none, won't be none."

She pivoted to find the pair of harpies, camouflaged in ratty human forms, glaring daggers her way. Damia, the blonde, wore her mangy rabbit fur coat over a cheap mauve leather mini skirt, torn fishnets, and black Chuck Taylors. Keisha was all baby dyke tough in Doc Martens and ripped jeans that had once been black. A ragged black hoodie molded itself around her muscular arms and covered the tattoos on her shaven skull. These two, working at the behest of that bitch Yasmina, had killed poor Deion while failing spectacularly to tempt Ashleigh.

Normally Lorelei wasn't one to start violence, but these two deserved to be slapped into a paste. They smelled terrible, their manners were abysmal, and Lorelei could take them easily. She opened her purse but, just as her fingers closed around the hilt of her obsidian knife, Tuan Nguyen stepped into the chapel, trailed by his boys.

Floria was nowhere to be seen.

Tuan nodded at Lorelei, then led Sammy, Lam, Kim, and Hai to pay their respects to Deion's mother. Hai Ng, Tuan's righthand man, goggled at Lorelei, giving her flirty little dress the appreciation it deserved. Maybe he would provide the consolation sex she was looking for.

When Lorelei glanced back into the corner of the room, the harpies had vanished. Unfortunately, the stink of them still hung in the air. Lorelei would have spat on the floor and cursed their names, but the dead boy's aunty watched her too closely.

When Aza arrived at Santa Rosa's, the church's playground was vacant. Even the echoes of the children's voices had dissipated. Nothing remained to indicate they had ever been there. He sent up a quick prayer that they could all be safely hidden.

When he opened his eyes, he saw a lone angel standing guard on the church's roof. Michael raised a hand in greeting. "Well met, Brother."

Aza tossed open his wings and hopped upward to join the archangel. "Thank you for standing watch." He paused, unwilling to admit he had just been talking with the demon in charge of the fallen.

"You've heard the rumors, too?" Michael asked. "That Asmodeus insists your home be razed?"

"Yes," Aza admitted unhappily.

Michael didn't pursue it. "It's good you've provisioned yourself," he said, gesturing toward the bag of takeout. "Other duties await me."

Aza nodded and sat down to unwrap his sandwich.

Before Joe could launch into today's homily, Lorelei slipped out the back door for a cigarette. Now that she'd ditched Azaziel's sister, the day stretched ahead. She ought to call Tibor and get herself a ride up to Asmodeus's mansion to report Aza's hoard of souls.

As she keyed the fiend's call into her cell phone, she wished her boyfriend had given her any reason not to turn him in.

Tuan followed Lorelei out into the sunshine. "You have anything to do with Deion's death?" he demanded.

Lorelei turned toward him. Tuan was a remarkably pretty young man, with delicate features and the sweetest bow of a mouth. Floria had been open before him pretty much since Day One. He'd seen more than most mortals survived. Lorelei could see that Tuan's soul was still damned, although altruism and a paternal sense of protection for his boys threaded through him. Floria had better watch that or she'd be sorry.

"No, I didn't have anything to do with Deion's death," Lorelei answered. "Deion didn't survive being one of Yasmina's pawns."

Tuan stared at her. Lorelei caught the echo of "that bitch" in his thoughts. He'd undoubtedly heard it regarding Yasmina more than once from Floria.

"Was it quick?" Tuan asked.

That wasn't the question Lorelei expected. "Not quick enough." She drew hard on her cigarette, then added, "I thought you'd ask if he was damned."

Tuan stared down at the cracked sidewalk. "Of course he was damned."

"Actually, not," Lorelei corrected. "He deserved it, no doubt. Especially after the way he treated my girl Ashleigh. But Yasmina's minions devoured him instead. At the last minute, Deion skated out of Hell. It wasn't quick and he was terrified, but he didn't end up in the fire where he belonged."

Tuan stared at Lorelei speculatively. "I didn't know that was possible."

Lorelei wondered why she was telling him this. Floria would be pissed if she found out that Lorelei had gotten the boy's hopes up. She added some damage control: "Escaping hell is not supposed to be possible, but demons can play fast and loose with the boundaries. Angels certainly do it. But now Yasmina's in trouble for breaking rules that weren't hers to bend."

Lorelei offered her cigarette case to the young man. Tuan accepted a cigarette, lit it off the butt of Lorelei's, and exhaled a long plume of smoke. "Have you talked to Floria since the exorcism?" he asked.

"Last night. She was answering the boss's phone."

"He's got her running all over town," Tuan explained.

Lorelei had another drag off her cigarette and didn't say anything until she was sure of her temper. "She probably thinks she'll make temptress after the invitation list to the exorcism," Lorelei said lightly, like it didn't matter to her.

Tuan knew her too well to be fooled. "You might want to make peace."

Lorelei laughed. "Floria can hold a grudge for a long time."

"That's for damn sure," Tuan agreed.

Sammy popped his head out of the funeral home's back door. He was the enforcer on Tuan's crew, the one who made sure the debts got paid. He thought of himself as vicious and scary, but Lorelei—having seen some truly scary shit in the last couple of days—turned away to light another cigarette. The position allowed her to roll her eyes in peace.

"They're gonna start the service," Sammy said.

"Thanks." Tuan crushed his cigarette out on the concrete. "You coming in?" he asked Lorelei.

She saw a limo weaving aggressively through traffic, completely out of place in this neighborhood. Something about it made her guess it was coming for her. "No rest for the wicked, Baby. I've got to get back to work."

Tuan started to say something, then thought the better of it. He followed Sammy into the mortuary.

As Muriel stepped into the shoddy mortuary chapel, an archangel turned from comforting the bereaved mother. His maroon suit was sharply tailored, setting off the dusky bronze of his skin. He'd pulled his dreads back from his face with a length of gold cord that shimmered like a crown.

Muriel crossed the room to him, but he made her wait until he'd finished whispering words of condolence to Dolores Gutierrez.

The woman turned away from Muriel, not snubbing her as much as completely unaware of the angels surrounding her. Muriel frowned at the woman's back. Muriel had been the one to find Deion's body, abandoned on a hillside, his motorcycle leathers shredded by a harpy's claws. In fact, she had accompanied Azaziel when he brought the news of the death to the woman and her sister. Muriel was about to remind Dolores that they'd met when Zadkiel released the woman and drew Muriel aside.

"Good day, Muriel," he said calmly. She loved to listen to his voice. Zadkiel, master of the Choir Eternal, made even the simplest words ring like music.

"It's been a long time," Muriel said. As a matter of fact, it had been too long. Seeing her former choirmaster made Muriel homesick. Zadkiel smelled of Heavenly breezes, flowers and sunlight and the burnished glow of voices raised in eternal praise. Zadkiel must have come directly from the Presence. Her eyes hurt from looking at him.

"How go things?" Zadkiel asked. He was walking her toward the front of the funeral parlor, toward the bright LA daylight that paled in comparison to the beautiful luminescence of home.

Muriel swallowed against a sudden lump in her throat. "It's more difficult than I expected. They have so many distractions, so many cares when really there is only one thing they should ever think about... I try to bring them the song in my heart..."

"With love?" Zadkiel asked.

Muriel gazed at him, unable to answer. She didn't love her charges, any of them. None of them appreciated what it cost her to move amongst them. They were all flawed, if not outright broken: clouded mirrors of the beauty of Creation.

Zadkiel led her into an empty, dust-smudged chapel. "Let's pray together, Sister. Hopefully it will bring you some clarity."

Time to get at least one creature cemented into her corner, Lorelei told herself. They had a moment for one detour before she headed up to report in.

She gave Tibor directions down into the heart of Hollywood and settled into the back seat of her limo. She snapped out of her reverie as Tibor drove past the Scientology building. "Turn right," she directed, "then park. We're here."

"Where's here?" the fiend asked.

Ooh, speaking out of turn. Lorelei liked that. She didn't bother to respond, savoring the tiny bit of power.

She waited for the fiend to come around to the passenger door to give her a hand out of the car. Then she stalked across the empty street, working the sway of her hips and unfurling her tail for emphasis. She looked over her shoulder, favored the fiend with a sharp-fanged smile, and asked, "Coming?"

She halted in front of the metal gate padlocked across the entrance of the former museum. "Would you open this for me, Sugar?"

Tibor wrenched the metal apart, crumpling the steel like yesterday's LA Times. A fist through the solid oak door took care of its lock. As Lorelei expected, the building's owners hadn't been keeping up payments with the alarm company. The site had been vacant too long. No one wanted the place after its last tenants. More than that, no one wanted to stand in the shadow of L. Ron Hubbard. Thick dust carpeted the floor.

The fiend turned slowly around in the lobby, trying to make sense of the warren of little rooms that filled the big space.

Lorelei asked, "Can you feel it? I used to love this place when it was open."

"Where are we?" he grated out, unaccustomed to curiosity.

"This was once the Murder Museum." Lorelei strolled into the unlit maze of rooms. "They displayed a working guillotine in the lobby. One of the rooms in the back had Charlie's bed from Spahn Ranch."

All the ephemera was gone now, leaving behind only memories and vibrations. Lorelei found the cold spot she was looking for and planted herself in it. She looked over her shoulder at the fiend again, appraising him from polished steel-toed boots to brush cut. He didn't take the bait.

She watched the fiend until his stone black gaze finally traveled up to meet her eyes. He looked uncertain what he was being offered. Lorelei started to dance, swaying like a flame. She hiked up her skirt with the barbed tip of her tail. "What's a girl got to do to get some service here?"

As she shimmied her skirt back down, Lorelei laughed. The fiend had been as rough as she'd expected, but that hadn't kept her from coming repeatedly and at full volume. She noted that his thin lips looked a little chewed up as he was tucking his equipment back into his black Hugo Boss trousers.

He didn't speak until they were on their way back to the limo. In the middle of the street, the fiend rumbled, "I could get used to having my own piece of tail."

"Pleasure to have been of service," Lorelei teased. Then she caught sight of the limo's license plate again. "Hey, Sugar, do you think you could steal me a different license plate? I hate that the car still looks like it belongs to that bitch."

"Sure," he said. "I'll take care of it."

He unlocked the car and opened the door for her. He waited until she tucked her legs inside, then closed her in with a smile playing around his lips. When he climbed behind the wheel, Lorelei had the definite sense that, if he'd had any musicality at all, he would have been humming. He clearly didn't get off the leash much.

One happy customer on her side.

CHAPTER 6: SAMPLING THE HONEY

Pleased with herself, Lorelei leaned back into the limo's black leather upholstery. She closed her eyes, wondering how Ashleigh was now. Was she happy in Heaven, walking the golden streets, shopping in the celestial mall for a toga and sandals, signing up for harp lessons? Lorelei's vague notion of what Heaven might be like convinced her that it was probably too clean and bright, too regulated and quiet to be particularly interesting. Paradise, in Lorelei's mind, had always consisted of a warm, dark cavern with wall-to-wall upholstery and a steady stream of lovers to cater to her every whim. She wasn't sure how Ashleigh would enjoy Heaven. Would she know anyone there?

Mud and sand, but Lorelei felt lonely. She wondered if there was anyone in the world she could talk to this afternoon, someone not bound up in the Eternal War, who could tell her what to do about Aza's pets.

Her thoughts drifted. Lorelei wondered if Ashleigh would look in on her from time to time. Could spirits in Heaven look down on mortal affairs—or was that a myth? If Lorelei spoke to her—sent prayers?—would Ashleigh hear? It seemed to Lorelei that she might need an advocate in Heaven. If not for her own sake, then for Aza's.

Then again, Azaziel chose to let the girl die, hoping to save her soul postmortem. That should provide a lesson on how the angel used others when it suited him.

Still angry, she dozed off, lulled by the purr of the limousine's engine.

When Lorelei woke, the sun was going down. Tonight's project, she realized, had better be straightening out her sister.

Floria lived out in the Valley with Tuan Nguyen. They'd plucked the Vietnamese boy off the street one night. One spectacular weekend later, Tuan had signed Floria's contract—which bought him a penthouse apartment, a BMW, and a gang of boys who sold coke, did speed, and ran around too fast on little Japanese motorcycles. There'd been moments when Lorelei envied her sister's domestic arrangements. Now, after fucking around with an angel and riding around in an angel-fucker's car, Lorelei wondered if she could ever be satisfied by sex with mere mortals.

Time to find out. Tuan's right-hand man was enamored of Lorelei. She'd never had any special use for Hai Ng—damned for lust and greed without her help—but if his presence could help her iron out the trouble with Floria, then his participation was welcome. Lorelei didn't think it would be difficult to get Hai on-board.

She dialed her sister's number.

"Floria," her sister said, by way of hello. Even Floria's voice shone bright golden, the epitome of a sun-soaked blonde. Too bad she was such a bitch.

"Hello, Sister," Lorelei purred.

"You're the last person I expected to hear from," Floria drawled. "Where are you?"

"The 134. I owe you a favor for arranging that beautiful exorcism. Wanna get together and let me start paying you back?"

"What did you have in mind?" Floria asked skeptically.

"Gather Hai and Tuan and work a few fantasies? We haven't done that in a long time."

Floria's good mood turned brittle. "I told you before that if you wanted to get off, get your own boys."

"Sister, I don't need to get off," Lorelei corrected. The fiend chuckled. Floria surely overheard him. "Oh?"

Lorelei chose not to elaborate. "It's your call. Either you want to get together and have some fun like we used to, or you're busy. I'll take my new limo and its driver and find some other trouble to get into. He seems amenable."

In the front seat, the fiend gave the slightest nod. Lorelei smiled.

"The boss gave you a car?"

"Yeah. You'll never guess whose car. Please come help me fuck it up."

"All right, Sister," Floria agreed. "Where shall we meet you?"

"We're on our way to you now. I'll call you when we get there." After she hung up, Lorelei asked, "You know where Floria lives?"

"I can find it."

"Good." Lorelei leaned back but didn't close her eyes, afraid to drift off again.

The afternoon had passed in a haze of boredom. Aza listened to conversations in the derelict neighborhood around him, but since he couldn't leave his post to aid anyone, he merely amplified their prayers and passed them along. This also was a worthy duty, but it was so far away from what he wanted to be doing that it made time drag.

There was a surprising dearth of devils in his neighborhood today. It was as if they'd all withdrawn to more populous parts of town. That seemed to contradict the notion that Lorelei had reported Santa Rosa's—or else it meant that the devils had spied the movement of the children's souls and were mounting their attacks elsewhere, wherever the children had been hidden. Not that Aza could do anything about it, either way.

Eventually, the sun sank behind the high-rises. Aza watched the glorious apricot light fade from the sky, his thoughts full of Ashleigh and Lorelei: both together and after they had parted. Melancholy seemed part of the air he breathed.

Once the night had taken hold, Aza gave up his vigil and went down to his room to collect the battered cigar box that held the few belongings he kept there. Asmodeus's command to burn the place down might not be carried out for days. Aza no longer had the patience to wait for it. He would take his mementoes somewhere safe.

As the fiend parked the limo in front of Floria's apartment building, Lorelei called her sister again. Before very long, Floria and the young men came out of the security door. Tibor heaved himself out from behind the wheel—without being told—and opened the back door for them.

Floria bent over uncertainly to peer inward. Lorelei watched relief wash over her sister's face, followed almost immediately by irritation. Still, Floria accepted air kisses from Lorelei while the boys admired the car's glossy finish. When everyone climbed into the back, Tibor closed the door behind them.

Floria asked, "Have you got a destination in mind?"

"Not really," Lorelei answered. "Anywhere you need to go?"

"Why don't we run by Lost Angels and see what we can pick out of the ashes?" Floria suggested. "Think of all that jewelry flashing around Friday night!"

Tuan and Hai exchanged glances, uncertain if she was serious.

"Ease up a moment," Lorelei scolded. "We can always garbage-pick later. For now, let's put on some music, check out the bar, and just enjoy life. I've got nowhere I'd rather be." She let her hand linger high up on Floria's thigh and added, "And no one I'd rather be with. Let's just party."

As if he expected Floria to start a fight, Tuan preempted her response. "Where did you boost the car?"

Lorelei mimicked Hai petting the upholstery. "Like it?"

Hai grinned. He stroked the leather even more sensually. "It feels almost like it's alive."

"Probably was, at one point," Floria groused. "Who knows what she used to upholster her car? That bitch always creeped me out."

Lorelei was amazed that Floria figured out the car's provenance so quickly. Although she wasn't normally quick-thinking, Floria grasped right away that Yasmina disgraced equaled an extra limo in Asmodeus's fleet. Lorelei wondered if Floria had expected the car to come down to her instead. What'd she do to rate it, other than throw an invite-only exorcism?

Lorelei composed her face before Floria could catch her expression. This little get-together was all about cheering Floria up. Which would be easier, if her sister wasn't determined to be a bitch.

"You got the car from your boss?" Tuan guessed.

"Mm-hm."

Hai whistled. "What'd you do to win this?"

Lorelei was stumped how to answer. The boys didn't know about angels. She offered, "Unmasked that bitch you've heard so much about."

"And burned down the boss's dance club in the process," Floria corrected.

Last Lorelei had seen her sister, Floria had taken Yasmina's place in the boss's entourage and was hightailing it away from the angels. The boys must have escaped the flames on their own. Lorelei wondered if Floria had meant for them to die there. Awkward.

Hai changed the subject. "Until we saw you at the funeral, we wondered if you made it out at all. I was scared when we didn't hear from you. I watched the news to see if your name was on the list of victims."

Lorelei realized she'd hardly spared the boys a thought until it came time to placate Floria. Floria derailed Lorelei's apology. "You were at the funeral, too?"

"Busy day," Lorelei pointed out. She opened the bottle of Patrón Añejo she'd sent the fiend to buy, pouring generous glassfuls without splashing a drop on the carpet. Damn, this car rode smooth.

Despite the tension in the air, everyone raised their glasses—even Floria—and looked to Lorelei to propose the toast. Luckily, she had one ready: "Great sex, great cars, great friends, great booze, great drugs, great sex."

Their glasses chimed together. As Hai drank, Lorelei nudged his elbow enough to spill a trickle out of the corner of his mouth.

"Oops! Sorry." She leaned over to mop it up with her tongue.

He laughed and hugged her. "I'm glad you got out of there okay. I was really worried."

"Me, too," Lorelei admitted. "Wanna get me high?"

Hai pulled an Altoids box out of his leather jacket and withdrew a joint.

As he entered his room, Aza found a touch of Lorelei's perfume lingered in the air. He turned his head, trying to track the scent.

He had no mementoes from Lorelei. The stocking he'd kept from their first night together, the rag with which he'd tied back her hair on their second night, and the few odd items she'd left behind in his warehouse room across town: all those things had been consigned to the flames by

Barbelo. Aza didn't begrudge his friend's attempts to spare him temptation, but he wished he could locate the object that vexed him now.

As he was about to give up, his gaze caught on the taper standing on the bedside table. The candle had a series of numbers written on it in lipstick in an exaggerated feminine script.

Aza lifted the candle to his face and inhaled. Yes, Lorelei had touched this, probably before she'd seen the children's spirits outside. She'd left him a way to contact her. Aza chuckled. If only he had a phone…

He placed the candle with the other things he wanted to rescue: his cigar box, some incense, a couple of books. None of the rest felt as irreplaceable.

Two hits into Hai's joint, the Viagra hit Tuan in a rush that took his breath away. He shifted, jeans suddenly too tight in all the wrong places. He noticed that the succubi didn't miss the motion. Lorelei's smile was conspiratorial. Floria's was predatory.

Before Floria could pounce, Lorelei leaned across Tuan to plant a sloppy kiss on her sister's mouth. Floria stiffened for a fraction of a second—Tuan wondered what that meant—then buried her hands in Lorelei's thick brown hair. The two devil girls exchanged kisses that were fiercely competitive and hotter than fucking hell. Lorelei's boobs were rubbing against Tuan's chest when Floria finally reached for his fly.

Tuan leaned back into the buttery leather seat, eyes rolled closed, to enjoy the attention Floria lavished on him. It had been a while since she'd spared the time to play with him like this. Damn, if he hadn't missed it.

He heard Hai moan, followed by Lorelei's wonderful throaty laugh. That might have made Tuan cum, but Floria knew him too well. She wrapped her fingers around his balls and tugged hard enough for the pain to cool him off.

Tuan opened his eyes to find Lorelei on her knees in the carpet, her belly against the seat. Hai knelt behind her, giving it to her as hard as he could.

Lorelei must have sensed Tuan's gaze on her. She opened those unnaturally violet-blue eyes. Without a word, she twined her fingers between Tuan's. She pulled his hand toward her, slipping his middle finger into her hot wet mouth. Floria swung her leg over his and ground her sex against his. She was dripping, actually wanting him for a change. Or maybe just wanting to be the one who got him off, instead of Lorelei.

Tuan told himself not to care. It had been a long time since the sisters played well together. Everyone would be happier if they were getting along again. Tuan closed his eyes once more and let them work their magic on him. As long as he could switch his brain off and go along for the ride, he could think of nothing in the world better than being at their mercy.

Aza waited until it was getting late to give up on guarding the church. It was too much of a temptation to chant Lorelei's name and summon her to join him.

Instead, he flew over Tujunga to stash his box of mementos and books at a storefront church where he sometimes stayed. Then he winged off to Chinatown. Dropping down into an alley, he put away his wings and walked over to Noc's restaurant, held the door open as a quartet of Latina girls came out. The young women continued to laugh amongst themselves, mostly ignoring the angel, but the last of the group cast a glance back at him. Some flirtatious quirk of her lips reminded him briefly of Lorelei. Aza gave the girl a genuine smile. The force of it wiped her expression blank.

Aza closed his eyes and let her go. Then he ducked into the Golden Door before the other girls noticed him.

From the kitchen, Noc called, "I'm closing soon, but I can give you fried rice to go..." Then he came into the dining room and recognized Aza's mortal guise. A smile revealed the cook's square, yellowed teeth. "What would you like, old friend? Are you very hungry?"

"Fried rice would be perfect," Aza said. "And a Tsing Tao, if you will join me."

"Of course." The Cambodian man crossed the restaurant to turn the sign in the window to closed. He locked the door's deadbolt and turned out the neon. Then he returned to the kitchen to make the angel some dinner.

The boys could barely stand when Lorelei returned them to Tuan's building. Even Floria seemed in a better mood, although she couldn't find one of her earrings. Lorelei promised to return it, if it showed up. It wasn't as if they'd left the car.

Lorelei watched the trio troop back into the building, pulling the security gate shut behind them. Then she sank back into her seat, lonelier than she'd expected to be.

It felt like forever since she'd seen Azaziel.

"Where to?" Tibor asked.

"I really don't know," Lorelei said. "Normally, I'd have you drop me at Lost Angels and see what kind of trouble I could stir up there..."

The fiend made a noise that wasn't a laugh.

"Just drive," Lorelei suggested. "I'll figure something out."

Noc settled across the linoleum-topped table and opened two bottles of beer. Aza lifted his bottle in a salute, then drank deeply.

"I will make some takeout for your lady friend," Noc offered.

Aza smiled, remembering the scent of Lorelei's perfume. How he must have reeked of it, last time he'd visited with Noc. "She's not staying with me any longer."

Noc clinked his beer bottle against Aza's, but said nothing.

The angel nodded, accepting the sympathy. He ate a few bites of the barbecue fried rice, remembering the days when Noc had first come to this country, desperate to escape the impoverished life he'd left behind in Cambodia. Aza had befriended him then, finding him a place in a Chinese family's kitchen. Noc learned to cook as he worked. Now he was a masterful chef, but in his own restaurant he kept his prices affordable to the surrounding neighborhood. He even cooked up extra "leftovers" at the end of the day to take to Lafayette Park, where he fed the homeless several times a week.

Aza found himself eager to unburden himself to someone who would judge the relationship purely on what the angel said about it, without looking for otherworldly themes. "We had an argument," Aza began. "She walked in on me at work and saw something I hadn't intended her to. She let me explain, but now she's angry at me."

When Aza found himself stymied by how to continue the story, Noc asked, "Are you ashamed of her?"

Surprised, Aza met the man's eyes. That had been a truly perceptive question. "No." When Aza said the word, its truth resonated through him.

"Does she know you aren't ashamed of her?"

This time the angel smiled. "No. I've tried to hold her apart from my life and my friends." He had another sip of beer. "I wanted to keep her all to myself."

The confession startled him. He realized that he had forgotten that he himself could not be divorced from his work. As individual as he often felt, he was simply part of a larger plan. There was no way to keep Lorelei separate from his work because she also was a part of it.

Noc sipped his beer as if nerving himself to ask the next question. "Does she know what she means to you?"

Aza turned the question over in his mind.

"I see you when you think of her," the restaurateur said. "She means more to you than perhaps you know. She gives your life light. This argument you had... It wasn't her fault, was it? She came to you, but you tried to hold her separate from your life, your work, your friends. Maybe you asked her to leave her friends, set aside her work, to wait for your attention to turn her way? No wonder she feels wounded and angry. She knows how she feels...but she does not know how you feel."

The man's insight comforted Aza. "Thank you, my friend. You always know what to say."

Once Hai settled into the hot tub up on the roof outside Tuan's penthouse, he lit a joint. He puffed on it meditatively a couple of times before passing it to Tuan. Tuan hit it once and leaned back into the hot tub, staring up at the stars as he blew out a long plume of smoke.

Hai watched him, but the older boy had gone off into his own world again. That was happening more and more lately. Whatever Tuan was thinking about never made him happy. Hai shook his head and scooted closer on the bench—not too close, of course, because he didn't want Tuan to think he was coming on to him—and plucked the joint from Tuan's fingers.

"Oh, sorry," Tuan said.

Hai waved the apology away as he exhaled a cloud of smoke. "I've been thinkin'," he drawled.

"That's never good," Tuan teased. He took the joint back and hit it again.

Hai raised a playful fist, but dropped it back into the water without swinging it. "About asking Lorelei to be my girlfriend."

Tuan coughed up a lungful of smoke. "Why?"

Hai snatched the joint before it could be doused in the hot tub. "What kind of dumbass question is that? She fucks like a porn star. You get it all the time," he said, meaning Floria, "but I have to wait for my number to come up." Hai looked at the tail-end of the joint but decided he'd had enough and stubbed it out in an ashtray somebody had stolen from a casino in Las Vegas. "It would be so sweet to have Lorelei bringing that home to me every night."

Tuan reached for the Modelo he'd set on the edge of the tub and had a long swallow. Finally he pointed out, "You know she works for Mr. Prince."

"Yeah. I'm not talking about making her stop being a call girl. I know she's not going to give that up for me. Well, not 'til I can buy her a limo."

Tuan sucked down more of his beer, but didn't argue.

"She's got to be lonely," Hai pointed out. "Bet she'd love to have someone to take her dancing and make her breakfast."

Tuan shook his head, but he had on his big brother smile.

"What?" Hai demanded.

"She's a free spirit," Tuan said. "I'm not sure she eats breakfast."

"Maybe she'd eat me for breakfast," Hai said, settling into the hot water so the jet could knead his back.

"Without a doubt," Tuan agreed.

Muriel walked unseen past the boys lounging in the hot tub, then passed through the glass door without opening it first. A minor bit of magic, not enough to impress on its own, but she wanted to make a point about how nothing a succubus could do would keep her out.

From the kitchenette the succubus she'd come to see slammed the refrigerator door and screeched unholy curses. Azaziel's name was roundly execrated—no love there, Muriel was pleased to note. Apparently, Floria saw Muriel's angelic radiance and misidentified it.

Now that they faced each other, Muriel got her first real look at Lorelei's sister. Where Azaziel's harlot was curvy and generously endowed, this one was willowy. The peignoir she wore was scarcely as long as a bath towel. She wore her platinum blond hair in a complicated layered cut. Her golden-brown eyes stared pure murder at Muriel.

"What do you want?" the succubus snarled, although the fury didn't conceal the terror that pulsed through her. "Lorelei's not here."

"I know," Muriel told her. "She's off to meet Azaziel."

"Why are you here, then?"

"I want to put an end to your sister's pursuit of my deluded brother."

"I'd like nothing more," the succubus agreed.

Muriel held out her hand to display a trio of bullets. "There's been some debate about whether your sister's shiny new soul bears the weight of her former exploits in the service of Hell or if she has only done good works since her possession—and now she's bound for the Realm of Glory."

The blond devil hissed angrily.

Muriel nodded in agreement. "If she's struck by one of these, neither option will matter. She will be removed entirely from Creation. Canceled out."

The succubus sidled closer, extremely tempted. "What are they?"

"They are repurposed from a very old and terrible weapon." Muriel closed her fist and turned it over, holding the ammunition out. "Will you do it?"

Floria swept a beaten copper bowl up from the coffee table and held it toward the angel. Muriel dropped the bullets in. They fell with the sound of a discordant gong.

Floria promised, "I can find someone who will do it. No questions asked."

Muriel let a slow grin creep over her face. Then she removed herself from this den of vice, straight to the nave of the Russian Orthodox Cathedral of the Holy Transfiguration. She hoped the frankincense burning there would wash the devil's stink from her nostrils.

While Lorelei debated where she might go to find some company, Tibor wheeled the limo into a parking lot.

"Where are we?" Lorelei asked.

"Hold up," the fiend answered. He parked in front of a dusty old liquor store and climbed out of the car. Frowning, Lorelei watched him circle the car and open the back door.

A demon clambered into the limo. Even for a demon he was strange-looking: red-hair shooting out in tufts all over his head, lemon-striped green vest mis-buttoned over a blue plaid shirt. She would have catalogued him as a used car salesman if she didn't already recognize him.

"Nice car," Mastema said as he settled in.

"I like it," Lorelei answered cautiously.

"Fight with your boyfriend?"

Lorelei sighed.

"No worries, Honey. He can't resist you for long." The demon twisted the cap from a bottle of Asti Spumante and poured two Solo cups full. He handed one to Lorelei. By way of a toast, he added, "I like to see a girl working her way up."

Lorelei drank the cheap wine, but the plastic cup didn't improve its flavor. "So you'll be the one in charge of Aza when he falls?"

Mastema smacked his lips over the wine. "Yes, ma'am."

"Can you protect him before that?"

"Our boy Aza can protect himself," Mastema said. "Did you see him fight at Lost Angels?" When she twitched her head no, Mastema said, "You missed out on something. Went toe to toe with Nebiros. If the demon's cadre hadn't lost their nerve and hauled Old Crickleback off through a portal, there might be a new general taking the reins of Hell's Army."

Mastema seemed pleased by the possibilities.

They sipped their nasty wine as Tibor pulled the car back onto the road. When the demon didn't seem to be in any hurry to get to the point, Lorelei prompted, "You're too busy to come just to chat. Chief cat-herder on Earth, right?"

"That's right: Administrator of the Fallen on Earth, although I like your spin better. I ought to get business cards made." Mastema grinned, showing yellowed teeth. "I wanted to quiz you about Aza's friends. Any of them I ought to corner in a dark alley?"

Lorelei thought about it. There weren't many of them she'd met—and to be honest, no matter what Asmodeus thought she should do, she really wasn't looking to change that. "Barbelo doesn't seem holier than thou."

"She's a special case." Mastema topped off Lorelei's Solo cup. "Her mother was Sophia. You know that story?"

Lorelei shook her head. She'd never heard of an angel with a mother.

"Sophia is the angel of female wisdom. She was gangbanged by a whole legion of her brother angels eager to sample some of that special honey. In consequence, Barbelo is the one angel who doesn't count the Holy Father as Daddy."

Lorelei struggled to come up with a suitable response. "That is messed up."

"Little Girl, there are an eternity of messed-up stories on the other side of the family."

"What's the story with the blonde bitch?"

Mastema laughed. "Narrow it down for me."

"Flaming sword? Hot temper? White tennis shoes?"

"Ah." Mastema toasted Lorelei and chugged his Asti, following it with a massive burp. "Muriel. Created to sing in the Heavenly Choir, but posted here because she wasn't allowed to fight off the invaders during the Siege of Heaven. She envies the other angels, especially your boy Azaziel. That could be useful."

"Glad to help," Lorelei said, toasting him with her Solo cup.

"Anyone else?"

"The only other two I've spoken to were Michael and Rafael. They both seemed pretty secure in who they are."

"The War will be over, if either of them switches sides," Mastema promised. "Don't know if there's much you can do about that, Baby Girl."

"I'll set my sights lower." Lorelei leaned close to breathe, "Anything you can do to keep that blond bitch off my back will be much appreciated."

"How much appreciated?"

"You wanna take it out in trade?"

"You good at your trade?"

Lorelei dropped her gaze demurely to puzzle open the demon's trousers. He leaned back, content to watch her work.

Lorelei straddled him. She let her hips work as her hands roamed the rest of her body. Her dress pooled in shadow beside them as she lifted her breasts, teasing her nipples with her sharp thumbnails. Performing for him was actually getting her heated up.

Mastema licked his chapped lips and grinned.

CHAPTER 7: THINGS FALL APART

Eventually, Mastema leaned forward in the limo to command Tibor, "Circle this block."

"Where are we?" Lorelei wondered as she reassembled her dress. She congratulated herself for keeping anxiety out of her tone.

The demon's answer didn't give any clues. "Wiltshire."

Lorelei puzzled over that as the fiend turned into a residential neighborhood off the main drag. He continued to the next corner and turned right again. The succubus was still confused when, after the third right turn, the demon ordered, "Pull over here."

Mastema opened the back door himself and stepped out. Lorelei watched him go, relieved that whatever test he had been giving her, it was over. Then he surprised her by holding a hand into the car. "You're coming, too, Missy."

She knew better than to argue. She scooted across the bench seat and let him assist her out of the car.

The street was quiet, empty of pedestrians save one. The demon inserted two fingers into his mouth and gave a surprisingly loud whistle. Only after the figure turned did Lorelei recognize Azaziel.

"Go make up," Mastema encouraged, nudging her in the angel's direction. "Give him a kiss for me." Whistling a bawdy sailing shanty, Mastema sauntered past Azaziel without a greeting and turned left at the corner of Wiltshire Boulevard.

"Hey," Lorelei said as Aza drew closer.

"Hey," the angel answered. "Have a nice meeting with the Prince of the Fallen?" His tone was less judgmental than she might have expected.

"It was pleasant enough. We didn't really talk about you, if you're curious."

"I'm surprised." The angel didn't continue on to ask what they did talk about. Instead, he said, "I missed you."

Lorelei smiled, but her heart hurt too much to make the expression stick. "It's been, what? Since last night?"

"Whatever. It's been too long." The angel tried a smile on her. "I found the message you left me at the church. I was going to call you, but it's not easy to find a payphone in LA anymore."

Lorelei shook her head at that, but didn't argue.

The succubus looked tired to Aza's eyes, as if she hadn't slept since he'd seen her last. Had worry kept her awake—or work? Aza noted she was still wearing the gladiator sandals she'd had on yesterday, so she hadn't been back to her room.

As if aware of his assessment, Lorelei pulled her lipstick from her purse. "What did you want to tell me?" she asked.

Aza swallowed. It was harder to find the words than he'd expected. "I've been a bad boyfriend."

"Oh?" Lorelei arched one eyebrow over the mirrored lipstick case at him. "Having sex doesn't make you my boyfriend."

Before she could work herself up into real anger, Aza cut her off. "I would really like to be."

"Huh." The indignation in her tone wasn't backed up by her expression.

"Let me take you to dinner," Aza offered. "I was thinking that we've never had a real date, just the two of us out on the town. Let me make it up to you."

"There are fewer places open all night these days," she pointed out.

"We can find something."

"I should be working," she argued. "I'm behind."

"It'll wait," Aza answered. "The one thing I know for sure: the work will always be there."

She smiled suddenly: beautifully, unguardedly herself behind her mortal façade. "Careful there, Angel. That sounded ever so slightly like ingratitude."

He nodded, conceding her point. "I didn't really mean it to. It's more like exhaustion." Aza pulled a flask from the inside pocket of his flight jacket. "Until you appeared, I was planning to drink somewhere quiet and contemplate my sins."

"I'm always glad to contemplate someone else's sins," Lorelei encouraged. "And I'll have a hit off that, if you don't mind." She let him hand her the flask, screwed the top off, then remembered to ask, "It's not holy water or something foul like that?"

"Just whiskey."

She had a slug and passed the flask back. "I like the idea of a date," she said thoughtfully, "but not in public. I'm worn out from dealing with people today."

"All right. I have another idea." He turned down an alley that led between the skyscrapers. An unmanned security booth stood there. They skirted the barrier across the drive and walked back into the darkened center of the block to find a little graveyard. A mausoleum wall took up the eastern side. In the northeast corner stood a little round chapel. On the north, a solid wall of office towers rose beyond the cemetery wall.

"Nobody here but the dead," Lorelei noted. Her voice held the approval he had been hoping for. "Marilyn's buried over in the corner." She pointed toward the mausoleum. "I should go say hello."

Floria waited until Tuan walked Hai downstairs to say goodbye for the night. Then she took the copper bowl and her phone and retreated to the bedroom. Tuan knew not to disturb her when the bedroom door was closed. She needed to think.

Why had the blond angel come to her? Did it understand that Lorelei was under Asmodeus's protection? If Lorelei's destruction could be traced back to Floria in any way, it would mean punishment...or worse.

Still, the opportunity was just too tempting to pass up. Floria and Lorelei had been rivals pretty much since their first breaths. Success came easily to Lorelei. People liked her, trusted her, worked to please her. Floria, on the other hand, had to scratch and scrabble for every step forward. There was no telling what she could accomplish once her sister was out of the game.

Floria put the copper bowl down on the fur-upholstered bench at the foot of the bed. Then she dialed Jequon's private number. As much as she hated the smug fallen angel, he had contacts every-fucking-where. He'd be able to hook her up with someone who could shoot Lorelei.

Whatever it cost, Floria was willing to pay it.

After they'd made a circuit of the darkened graveyard, Lorelei followed the angel to a bench under one of the massive trees. He sat down and gazed at her, eyes shining. "Thank you for not turning me in."

"You've been lucky so far," Lorelei observed. "Just because I haven't doesn't mean I won't."

"Understood."

She sat down, too, but didn't slide over close to him. If he wanted her, he was going to have to make the gesture. While she waited, she looked out across the cemetery. Red vigil candles burned on several graves, but the rest of the flat bronze markers were lost in the blackness. What a wonderful, peaceful place for their first date.

The angel ruined it by saying, "Barbelo told me you cried over Ashleigh."

The dead girl was still coming between them, Lorelei thought.

Aza must have seen irritation flare in her eyes. He continued quickly, "I'm sorry I didn't tell you the news myself. You caught me off-guard on the playground. I was grieving her and sought comfort from the others like her and...now I wish I'd come to you instead. I know you were friends..."

"We were friends," Lorelei agreed. "And I'm glad that she's safe, but I would've liked to say goodbye. Barbelo said that wasn't allowed."

"That's what she told me, too, when I asked."

"Do you trust her to be honest with you?"

"Of course," Aza said, legitimately bewildered that there would be any question.

Lorelei smiled. What would it be like to actually trust that your friends told you the truth?

Aza handed over the flask, waited until Lorelei had swallowed a sip before he said, "That's one of the things I wanted to talk to you about."

Lorelei bristled again. "What do you want now, Aza?"

"Please don't tell anyone about Ashleigh's destination."

Lorelei's laughter burst out of her, sudden and loud, shattering the silence of the graveyard. She said, "I can't believe you're asking me for another favor, Angel." She knocked back a hefty swallow of whiskey. Let him wait. Finally she added, "At least you're not dictating to me this time. Good job supporting the illusion of free will."

Hai got himself home and found a parking spot on the street not far from his mom's place. From the sidewalk, he could see that the nail shop was dark, but she'd left the light on upstairs in the kitchenette for him. It was her way of gauging whether he came home on any given night. He crept up the stairs, dreading to wake her. Luckily, nothing creaked this time.

He flicked off the kitchen light, shed his clothes in a pile, and stretched out on the sofa. Sleep took him instantly, chased immediately by a dream.

Hai knew that if anyone saw him, he would be dead. Still, it was impossible to tear his eye away from the keyhole. He was spying on the private room in the back of Lost Angels.

Floria and the woman she always referred to as "that bitch" shimmered into beautiful, half-naked sex monsters. Floria was still platinum blond, but her skin had turned bright red. Leathery black bat wings hung around her shoulders like a cape. The other woman turned into a snake from the waist down. She reared up on her tail, swaying above everyone else.

Lying naked on the table in the center of the nightclub, Lorelei had transformed into a devil girl, too. Her skin burned a rich, bloody red. She still had the same big round boobs—but now horns poked through her hair.

Hai was thrilled to discover the girls weren't just witches. The magic they were doing was more powerful than he had ever imagined. It made him sick to think that Tuan already knew the girls were devils. The most he had done to make use of their power was to become a petty drug dealer.

Hai wanted so much more for himself. Somehow, he'd have to figure out how to make himself indispensable to them.

The skylight above Lorelei burst and angels rained down. Hai's heart rose like a helium balloon. Then he heard curses screamed that he couldn't understand, in words that ran over his skin like rats and left tracks of electricity behind.

Lorelei slipped off the table she'd been lying on. She huddled on the floor, miserable and scared, trying to hide from the angels. Hai saw his opportunity. He reached up to turn the deadbolt and opened the storeroom door just enough to jolt Lorelei with a new wave of terror. Putting his mouth to the crack, Hai called her name.

A smile split Lorelei's face. Her bright white teeth were as sharp as a cat's. She folded her bat wings against her back and crawled the short distance to him on all fours. She had a long thin tail tipped with what looked like the ace of spades. The sight of her coming closer, breasts swaying and barbed tail lashing, hardened Hai instantly. It took his breath away, like a sucker punch. He wanted her so badly it was difficult not to fling the door open and pounce on her.

He punched his left fist into the doorframe. As he'd hoped, the pain cleared his head. He had to be smart now. He had to rescue her. It was the only way to make her truly his.

Lorelei slipped into the storeroom and pressed the door closed. In the darkness, he felt the heat of her flesh. The scent he had always assumed was her perfume—hash on the breeze in Griffith Park at night—was stronger. Lorelei pulled him against her bare breasts. She kissed him hard, filling his mouth with her burning tongue. His hips spasmed, thrusting against her belly. He nearly came in his jeans from the passion of her kiss. Just a kiss. This was better than winning the lottery.

The devil girl set him back on his feet. Taking his hand, she pulled him across the room, away from the door. "Is there a way out the back?" she asked.

"Can you see in the dark?" As he said the words, Hai realized it was a stupid question. Of course she could see in the dark. "Behind the liquor boxes. There's a freight elevator. That's how I got in here."

She led him onto the lift platform. Hai fumbled the Zippo out of his pocket and flicked it, giving himself enough light to figure out the controls.

As the machinery clanked to life, Lorelei asked, "Are you parked nearby?"

"Couple blocks away. Can't you fly?"

"I want to get away from the angels before I do." She reached overhead and shoved open the steel doors to the street. Hai saw the bolts shear off. Lorelei leapt out, reached down, and pulled him out before the lift came to a halt.

She ran, dragging Hai along behind her. Her hair waved behind her so thick and full that Hai wanted to wrap his hands in it and yank her to a stop and shove her against the alley wall. As if she could read his mind, she flashed a smile over her shoulder. It made him stumble.

"Soon, Tiger. We've got to get away first."

"The truck's over on Temple Street."

Lorelei nodded. She halted at the cross street, waiting for traffic to clear before she abandoned the shadows. Hai stared at her back, fascinated by the way the tail grew out of the perfect cleft of her ass. Its tip lashed with agitation. If he didn't remember seeing her huddled so miserably on the floor of the nightclub, it would be hard to believe this was the same creature.

Lorelei raised his hand to her mouth. She slipped his forefinger into the hot darkness between her lips. A shudder rocked Hai and he nearly fell. "What are you doin' to me?" he begged.

"Nothing like I'm going to do," Lorelei promised.

Hai was sure that if she turned back to look at him, he was going to cum instantly.

Instead, Lorelei navigated the maze of alleys, edging closer to where he'd parked the truck. Hai's agony was constant. The ache seeped into his lungs, made it hard to draw breath. He took each step because Lorelei forced him onward. He wanted nothing more than to stop and get some relief, even if he had to jack himself off. Scared as she was, determined to escape as she was, she was sex. He felt like it was killing him.

"Okay." Lorelei shoved him against the rough cinderblock wall and dropped to her knees in whatever ugly garbage was strewn on the alley floor. She peeled open his jeans and swallowed his sex in a gulp. Everything happened so fast that Hai had little time to appreciate any subtleties. His jeans were around his knees and he was banging the back of her throat for all he was worth. She did something with her tongue. White light exploded in Hai's mind, the most powerful orgasm he'd ever had pouring over him in waves. It went on and on, exploding in his brain like a twelve-inch line, amplifying itself like some bad DMT trip, whiting him out like a heroin OD.

The muscles in his legs melted. The cinderblocks scraped his ass as he sagged, but the pain did nothing to reduce the buzz

Outside the graveyard where Azaziel wooed his harlot lounged one of the ugliest creatures Muriel had ever seen. The fiend seemed cobbled together out of broken pieces that scarcely passed for human. Leaning against the limousine, it stood maybe half again Muriel's height and three or four times as broad.

This was the creature who had been squiring Azaziel's trollop all over town. Muriel grinned as she manifested her sword.

The fiend made no sound as he smashed his left hand down hard against the air. With a thunder crack, a pitchfork unfolded from his fist. It stank of sulfur.

Muriel feinted at him with her sword. He spun the haft of the fork to knock her blade aside.

She grinned wider. Fiends were Hell's enforcers, meant to terrorize sinners around the lakes of fire. This one must have been assigned to guard the succubus. Whether to keep her on the path to Hell or to protect her from Heaven's wrath, it hardly mattered to Muriel. Even if she couldn't exterminate the succubus herself, she could still thin Hell's ranks.

Muriel cut back at the fiend. He blocked her blade with the pitchfork's ironclad haft. Her sword blade sparked against an infernal curse soldered into the metal.

As Muriel sang a line from the Eternal Hymn, the blessing engraved along her blade flared into flame. The sword cut inexorably through the pitchfork. While she was focusing, the fiend punched her hard in the skull. Muriel twitched blond hair from her face, shaking off the pain. She'd allowed herself to become distracted by the beauty of the song, the purity of the blessing on her sword. She kicked the amputated part of the pitchfork away as she disengaged.

The fiend followed her, uneven teeth bared in a ragged snarl.

Muriel swung at him again. She let him tangle her blade in the tines of the pitchfork. Then she wrenched her sword sideways, breaking the tines as if they belonged to a disposable plastic fork.

The monster looked comically uncertain. Muriel let him pull his broken weapon free. Before he could raise it defensively, she launched herself toward him, manifesting her wings in mid-leap to add speed to her attack.

Her blade cleaved his skull like a stick slicing through mud. The fiend's flesh smoked and stank as it shriveled away from her holy sword.

Muriel turned her attention to the limousine behind the fiend's corpse. She snapped her fingers, causing a spark inside the gas tank to tear the vehicle apart. Then she settled down to watch the flames and polish her blade clean.

A massive fireball exploded on the street outside the cemetery, setting off car alarms all around them. Flickering orange light illuminated the graves, as bright as dawn. Lorelei leapt to her feet, aware that something had gone terribly wrong. She knew she was in trouble, without having any clue why.

A glance at Azaziel did nothing to reassure her. He had manifested his sword and donned his heavenly armor. Lorelei's throat went tight at the sight, choking off her breath.

Azaziel's gaze focused on the fire. "Fly," he told her. "I'll cover your escape."

She didn't hesitate. Dropping her mortal guise, she leapt for the clouds.

Hai opened his eyes from the wet dream, only to wade into a nightmare. On the molded plastic lawn chair in front of the X-Box sat the snake woman from the exorcism. She looked human now, a lot like one of the chicks in the Victoria Secret ads. Despite that, something about the pattern of the dress she wore still made him think of a snake.

"Now that you know what Lorelei really is," the stranger said, hissing slightly on the final s, "can you guess what her boyfriend is?"

Hai frowned, trying to wake up completely. He struggled to sit up, wadding the sheet into his lap to camouflage the wetness soaking his boxers. "Lorelei doesn't have a boyfriend."

"Of course she does, Hai. She just hasn't told you about him. Everyone else knows, even Tuan." The snake woman's laugh was mean. "In fact, she'll be with him again soon, if you want to go and spy on them."

Anger flushed through Hai, like corrosive in his blood. "Where?"

"I'll tell you," the woman promised. "But there's something I'd like you to do when you get there."

Dawn was brightening the sky when Azaziel joined Lorelei on the observatory dome. "Not the most defensible place in the city," he chided.

"Is there any truly defensible place for me?" Lorelei asked. "It's not like I can run to Asmodeus for safety, with your damn secret hanging over my head."

Aza didn't dispute that. "Come with me," he suggested, holding out his hand. "I'll find you somewhere safe."

She had thought she would run away with him, if ever he asked. But now she found herself so afraid that even breathing was hard to manage. "I can't. You know I can't."

"Won't," he corrected. "You can do anything you want to."

Did he believe that? She remembered the moment of freedom she'd tasted with her orgasm in Isfahan and shuddered. "Where would we go?"

The angel seemed caught off-guard that she'd considered it. He clearly hadn't thought this through. "I can't leave Los Angeles," he began, already hedging his bets.

Lorelei interrupted him. "Didn't Ashleigh give you my message? You have to leave. The boss vows that you'll fall or be destroyed—and you know he's not your only enemy here."

The angel combed his fingers through her wind-tousled hair, gazing at her through a new kind of pain. "My duties are here," he said at last.

"And you won't give up your duties for me?"

"I can't, unless I fall."

"That damned hope of Heaven." Lorelei grinned, despite the ache in her chest. "Let's say, for the sake of debate, that I do come with you. Do you think your 'friends' are going to accept me? Aza, that blond bitch will kill me as soon as she gets an opportunity."

"I can protect you from Muriel."

"I doubt that's one of your God-given duties," Lorelei argued. "And they wouldn't trust me to accompany you as you work. They're moving the souls, aren't they? Off the playground?" She touched her fingertip to his lips to make it clear she wasn't tempting him to reveal anything.

He slipped his arm around her waist and hugged her close. Lorelei lifted her head. Their lips met. Electricity thrilled through her. She clutched him to stop the sensation of vertigo.

With a sigh, Aza leaned back. "This cannot be wrong."

"Is your conscience finally troubling you?" Lorelei asked.

He stroked a lock of hair back from her face. "Come with me. Then you won't have to tell anyone what you saw."

Quaking, Lorelei stared at him. Every instinct told her to flee. In a choked voice, she wondered, "What are you asking me to do, Aza?"

"Stop working for Asmodeus. Join me."

She stepped back from his embrace, wrapped her arms around her shoulders, and dug her talons in to feel the pain. "Are you asking me to work for the Enemy, Aza?"

"Are we enemies, Lorelei?"

"Aza..." Tears prickled her eyes. "I only want to be beneath Heaven's notice."

He touched her face, wondering at her tears. "I don't ask this lightly. You may be allowed to sit this out, but I cannot."

"I thought...I'd hoped...this moment was between us."

"If you keep working for him, you will be forced to tell him," Aza argued. "I am responsible for those defenseless souls. I must stand between them and all the hordes of Hell."

Lorelei's head felt too heavy for her to hold up any longer. She couldn't bear the sight of Azaziel, burning with angelic conviction.

Dammit. She loved him, yes, and she'd hate to see him die, but he'd done wrong both in creating her soul and in corralling those mortal spirits. If he died for that, the order of the universe was served. She really could not leave her master and expect to survive.

Aza raised her hand to kiss it. "Ever have a moral dilemma before?"

"You are insufferable," she snapped. "All this amuses you, doesn't it?"

He looked stung. "I was trying to be sympathetic."

"You're not very good at it." She found herself too angry to give him the tongue-lashing he deserved. Gradually, she became aware of her hand still in his, of the heavenly coolness of his flesh against hers.

"I wanted you from the moment I saw you," Lorelei admitted, "hunched over that bar, the curve of your wings obvious beneath your coat."

Aza gazed at her, eyes shining, and let her speak.

"When I saw you in your cell in the candlelight, blazing with anger and glory, I knew you hadn't drawn your weapon because if you had to kill me, you wanted to derive all the torment from it you could, hurting yourself as much as me. I knew I couldn't let you go."

She marveled at the glow that surrounded him, the halo that never dimmed. It was amazing that his kind could ever pass unnoticed among mortals.

Humans, she corrected herself. She was mortal now, thanks to him: her soul waiting to be harvested by the right tempter.

"I've known about you for years," Aza confessed, "since you first came to LA. I've watched you work. The other succubi might as well be mantises snatching up their prey. You took a genuine interest in your charges. You seemed to make an emotional connection that the others didn't bother with." He met her eyes, watching for her anger to flare again. He seemed willing to brave it, to be honest with her. "I chose you, Lorelei. Of all of your sisters, I fell in love with you."

Trying to absorb that, she asked quietly, "When were you certain?"

"In the alley downtown. When you broke your attack. When you took on your human aspect in midair and fell into my arms—I realized I would love you forever."

Lorelei heard the sound of the gunshot even as the impact jarred Aza. His rich golden blood spattered her skin. She kicked up hard from the observatory dome and threw her wings open to catch the wind of her momentum. Then she twisted abruptly, angling her wings to steepen the dive.

Hai balanced on the observatory's parapet, legs braced wide, waiting for the angel to rise so he could take another shot.

As she swooped past, Lorelei tore the gun from the boy's hand. When she heard his cry, she wheeled around to catch him as he fell. She threw him down on the patio.

Hai's expression was a maze of fear, desire, and despair. "You don't love me," he accused.

"I never said I did, Tiger."

"I want to fucking kill him," Hai spat.

"It will take more than a gun to accomplish that." Armored once more, Azaziel dropped down from the dome and advanced on the boy. Uncertain why she did it, Lorelei lunged between them.

The angel looked from her to the boy and back. His eyes held the same distaste he'd shown her when they first met. "Do you have a contract with him?"

"I didn't need one."

The boy climbed painfully to his feet. Lorelei was glad to see she hadn't broken him in her fury. "What are you doing here, Hai?" she demanded.

"Yasmina told me where you were."

Of course she had. No matter the outcome, Yasmina benefited.

Lorelei gazed at Aza, filling her memory with him. This wasn't how she had wanted to say goodbye.

Hai's grumbling interrupted her thoughts. "You should've let me fall."

Aza drew his sword from the air. The keening hum of his blade made her shudder.

"No," Lorelei begged.

"I can end your life, if that's what you honestly want," Aza told the boy.

"He's no rival to you," Lorelei argued.

The angel gestured at the blood leaking out from under his breastplate. "I'm his rival. Jealousy is mortal."

"Please, Aza. He's as much my responsibility as I am yours. You couldn't consign me to the lake of fire..."

Azaziel regarded the boy: reading his soul, Lorelei suspected. Finally, the angel asked, "Are you going to save him? Will your sister or your prince allow it?"

"There's hope while life remains," Lorelei said.

The angel met her eyes and gave her a slip of a smile, to show he understood her remark. He lifted two fingers to his lips and offered her a benediction. Then he opened his wings and vaulted into the sky.

Lorelei grabbed hold of Hai's shoulder, sinking her talons deep enough that he wouldn't argue as she hauled him back toward the parking lot and his RAV-4.

Hai aimed the remote at the truck and unlocked the doors. Lorelei climbed in, thoroughly disgusted with herself. Azaziel's blood was drying across her skin like a talisman of failure. She tossed Hai's gun onto the dashboard and sank back into the passenger seat.

Hai scooped the gun up and aimed it at her. "Tell me why I shouldn't kill you, cunt."

Fear surged through Lorelei, sparking her nerves awake. Where were the words of compassion she needed to defuse this situation? In all her years, Lorelei had laughed her way past such threats, secure that no human could ever achieve her destruction. Now, with her soul quivering inside her, death seemed all too real. Damnation was only a heartbeat away.

"Say something, dammit." Hai's voice shook worse than his gun.

Lorelei gazed at him. Barely a man. Just a pawn that she'd used and discarded at will: if not unaware, then certainly uncaring about the continuity of the passions she'd inflamed in him.

"I've used you," she admitted.

That wasn't what he'd expected to hear. "Why?" he demanded.

"Because it served Floria's purposes."

Anguish clenched in him, making it difficult to cough the words out: "Why did you make me love you?"

"That was an accident."

Hai cracked the barrel of the gun against her temple. Lorelei shook off the ringing in her head and snatched hold of his wrist, twisting it hard. "Let go of the gun or I'll break your arm," she promised.

Hai twitched in a pathetic attempt to throw her off. Lorelei tightened her grip until his bones ground together. "Drop it or you lose the hand. I won't tell you again."

He struggled to regain enough control of his fingers to let the gun fall.

Lorelei unloaded the bullets into her purse, then slung the gun out the truck's window. "You don't love me, Tiger. What you feel is possessiveness and lust. If you loved me, you'd accept that I love someone else. You wouldn't hate me for it, like you do now. Maybe this is the closest thing you've ever felt to love. Maybe it's all that most people ever feel. But to call it love is a lie, when the only thing you want from me is unquestioned, immediate sexual service. I finally met someone who cares for me. I'm done working for people like you who don't give a shit about me. Stop thinking with your dick and your gun."

He sat up, flexing his fingers to get the feeling back. "Yeah, Lorelei? Well, fuck you."

"Fuck you, too, Hai."

The boy banged the glove box open, grabbed the pint of Cuervo inside, and sucked hard on it.

When she was sure he wasn't going to make another attempt to take her head off, Lorelei reached for the bottle and drank deeply herself.

Hai started the ignition and peeled out of his parking space. Lorelei tucked the bottle between her thighs and reached for her seatbelt.

Hai drifted across the centerline as they rounded a curve, only to swerve back to avoid an oncoming SUV. The vehicles missed each other by a hair's breadth. Hai fought to get the RAV back under control. Lorelei's fingers cramped from clutching the dash.

"Can we slow down?" she asked.

Hai checked his Apple watch. "We gotta be up in the hills by ten."

Something heavy and sharp seemed to lodge in Lorelei's throat. "We?" she managed.

"Yasmina says it's time I met your boss."

Lorelei felt her insides turn cold. "Hai, do you know what that means?"

"Yeah, she figured it was time I learned what your deal was." The boy turned a grin on her. "She said it's my reward for getting you away from your bad-news boyfriend."

Lucky boy. Lorelei ground her teeth together. If she wasn't careful, she'd be spending the rest of Hai's natural life paying for her definition of love.

CHAPTER 8: HELL TO PAY

Aza returned to his church. He didn't know where else to go. He didn't want to run into any of his siblings while they were hiding the children's souls. Santa Rosa's was the one place in LA that he was certain no one else would be. Even Joseph was secreted in a safe house, where Hell could no longer torment him.

Aza banked his wings, intending to land inside the upstairs bedroom. The pain from the gunshot wound made him misjudge his footing. He stumbled on the landing. Whatever he'd been hit with, the wound burned.

A single vigil candle flickered in front of the stained glass mural he had been assembling on the eastern wall. Aza knelt awkwardly before the candle to pray. He opened his heart, straining to hear his master's voice.

Instead he heard the beating of wings coming across the playground. Wearily, Aza climbed back to his feet to meet Muriel.

"Hello, Brother," she called cheerfully. Before he could respond, a shadow eclipsed her expression. "Are you injured?"

Aza put his hand to the blood soaking his shirt. "I've been shot," he admitted.

Muriel's halo went jagged with rage. For a change, it didn't seem directed at him. "How is that possible?" she demanded.

"I assume that Yasmina had a hand in procuring the ammunition." Aza stepped back into the room to allow Muriel to enter. "It stings. Would you be so kind as to help me remove it?"

"Of course," she agreed easily.

She stood only as high as Aza's jaw, flickering now between her mortal seeming—clad in snow-camouflage leggings and a pale gray zip-up hoodie—and the armor she had worn at Lost Angels. The echo of the Ever-Spun Hymn that circled continually at the back of her thoughts had gone silent. Something was deeply wrong, Aza realized, but he couldn't determine what.

He sank down onto the foot of the bed so Muriel could examine him. As she prodded his wound, Aza watched her face. He had seen Muriel angry many times. It was as much a part of her being as the Hymn itself. This time, her anger wasn't fanned by disappointment in him. It hadn't been spurred by some failing in the world. She had been in as good a mood as ever he'd seen her until she noticed his injury.

As he watched, a faint flush crept across Muriel's cheeks. "The projectile will have to come out," she said with false cheer.

"Please do it, Sister."

She nodded, all business. "Do you wish to prepare yourself?"

He looked toward the vigil candle. "I am ready."

With a slim silvered knife, Muriel pried the projectile from his abdomen. Unable to stop himself, Aza groaned deeply. But as soon as the cursed object was removed, he began to feel better.

"Thank you," he said, meaning it.

"Let me wash the wound as well," she said. She disappeared through the shattered doorway to the washroom on the landing outside. Only after she was gone did he realize she'd taken the projectile with her. No matter. It wasn't as if he wanted to keep it as a memento.

He hoped Lorelei was safe now, wherever she was.

Hai navigated cautiously up the steep drive. Several limos were already parked in front of Asmodeus's mansion. Among them stood half a dozen other cars, including Jequon's black town car and an SUV limo that probably belonged to Behemoth. Time to put on her game face. Lorelei checked the visor mirror, correcting the curve of her lipstick with the tip of her little finger.

Hai fidgeted. He'd dressed up, she noticed, wearing a black Tommy Hilfiger shirt that draped deliciously over his eighteen-year-old chest. His brand new Levis were the deepest black possible, over some newly polished Docs. He looked exactly like a thug going to his first job interview with the boss of the city. Lorelei chose not to say anything to make the boy any less nervous.

He dogged her up the flagstones to the front door, watched her stand there without pressing the bell. Belatedly realizing that he should be certain he had at least one friend inside, he leaned over to nuzzle her bare shoulder. "You look real nice," he offered. "New lipstick?"

She hadn't forgotten him hitting her in the truck. She showed him her teeth. "You look good enough to eat, Tiger."

The door was suddenly snatched open in front of them. There stood a badger-faced imp, his jeans so baggy that charm alone must hold them up. "You waitin' for a personal invitation, or what?"

Lorelei swung at him with the back of her hand, but he scampered off before she connected.

"Da roof," he called over his shoulder as he disappeared down the hall.

Lorelei stepped over the threshold with a sigh. She led Hai through the black marble foyer to the mirrored elevator.

"Do I bow or what?" the boy whispered.

"Just stand still and drop your gaze. And don't offer to do anything."

Lorelei led Hai out of the elevator onto the roof. Lazing in the morning heat, unfamiliar succubi ringed the pool. Some of Asmodeus's harem looked barely out of imphood. Lorelei realized that, if she were busted back to serving the boss personally, the competition wouldn't be much fun.

The girls perked up when they scented Hai. The boy himself fought to be stoic, but clearly he found himself in every rapper's paradise. Beyond the six potential supermodels sizing him up, beyond the mosaic-floored pool, beyond the obvious size of the mansion at his feet, the view spelled money. LA sprawled below them, cloaked in smog.

What appeared to be a young woman ambled over with the liquid grace of a panther. The gold lamé of her thong echoed the gold rings in her berry-black nipples. "Had breakfast, Honey?"

Speechless, Hai shook his head.

The succubus reached for his hand and drew him after her. Hai broke the dream long enough to turn back to Lorelei. "Okay?"

"Sure, Tiger." Lorelei noticed the other succubus flinch from the compassion in her tone, but it was lost on Hai. "Enjoy yourself."

As the girls descended on him, Lorelei stood alone awkwardly. In the past, her existence held meaning only in relationship to those around her, be they prey or infernal. Even at the Observatory, she'd been waiting for someone else to tell her what to do. Here, she was entirely at a loss. She didn't need to be part of the boss's seduction of Hai. In fact, she'd only get in the way. All the same, she didn't feel she could wander the mansion, without being summoned. Yasmina might be here, undoubtedly brooding over Azaziel's escape. Floria might even be around somewhere. As a matter of fact, there were getting to be more and more infernals in the service of her prince that Lorelei didn't care to meet in a lonely subterranean corridor.

She did what a mortal girl would do, when abandoned by her date: dug through her purse after a cigarette.

Before she'd taken a second drag off it, an unfamiliar archfiend reached around and plucked it from her fingers. Where Tibor had been big, this guy was massive, almost seven feet tall with fangs like steak knives. "He'll see you," the monster reported, crushing her cigarette beneath his boot.

Lorelei nodded for him to lead the way. She didn't look around for Hai. Even though they were young, the harem girls would treat him well. She was sure of that.

When Muriel reached Rafael, he sat in the pews in Our Lady of Angels. His white patent-leather shoe tapped jauntily as a high school junior choir belted out something about a "kiss from a rose on a grave."

Muriel would have liked to stride right up to the archangel with the news that Hell had attacked Azaziel. Instead, other angels clustered close to Rafael, absolutely basking in his good humor. Muriel wasn't sure she could get through the mob.

She stopped in a patch of light flowing through the alabaster windows and glared at the other angels. Didn't they have business to attend to? Somewhere in this cancerous cesspit there must be souls worth saving. If nothing else, someone—someone other than Barbelo—should be watching over Azaziel to make sure he wasn't sneaking off for any more liaisons with his harlot. Anyone could see that it was only a matter of time before the succubus tilted him too far. Her job was already half done.

The high school choir broke their song down into increasingly showy solos, singing as hard and loud as they could—as if this song, this moment of adulation from the crowd—could save them from the dangers and encroaching darkness of their brief, doomed lives.

One of the angels turned sharply, as if he'd overheard Muriel's thoughts. It was Zadkiel, master of her rank of angels. He leaned over to whisper to Rafael. Another angel turned, too: Michael, chief of the archangels. That three archangels had arrived in this sewer meant that something huge was going on, something more crucial than the transfer of the children's souls from behind the old Santa Rosa church. Muriel's heart soared, even as she sank to one knee in praise.

All the rest of the gathered angels turned to see who'd caught the archangels' attention. Muriel glanced over her shoulder, expecting to see Azaziel creeping up behind her, but she was alone. Feeling judged by her fellows' scrutiny, she twisted back to face them. The assembled angels turned away as one to applaud the finale of the children's song.

Muriel quivered with indignation. How dare they exclude her when she'd come to deliver so important a message?

Zadkiel stood over her suddenly. He reached down to take her hand. He raised Muriel to her feet and led her out of the cathedral as the high school choir flowed out to their school bus. "What is your message, Muriel?"

"In reward for her attentions to our misguided brother, Azaziel's harlot has been raised in Asmodeus's hierarchy. He gave her a fiend to serve as chauffeur and bodyguard, the better to expand his reach across the city. Last night, I killed the fiend and destroyed the succubus's conveyance, but one of Hell's minions retaliated by wounding Azaziel. I ask leave to put an end to this."

Zadkiel halted just inside the holy ground's open gates, letting the kids stream around him. The children remained unaware of the angels in their midst. As they passed, their hearts lightened for no reason they could name. Many students found themselves humming.

"What would you like to do?" Zadkiel asked.

Despite the mortals swirling around, Muriel hadn't lost the topic of conversation. "Please allow me to destroy the succubus before she nudges Azaziel any closer to Perdition."

"Who?" Zadkiel asked.

Muriel's mouth snapped closed abruptly. Did he know of the deal she struck with the blond succubus? Who else did he think deserved killing?

The archangel watched her, patiently awaiting her answer.

Michael was here in the "City of Angels." Rafael was here, and Zadkiel as well. Three archangels in a city that usually blundered along without so much supervision.

"Are we going to war?" Muriel whispered hopefully.

"Not yet." Michael had joined them, with Rafael by his side. The archangels surrounded Muriel in an equilateral triangle. She closed her eyes, drinking in the holy vibrations flowing from them. The audible major chord raised her spirits immensely.

She hadn't needed to report. Of course the Lord of All was already aware of developments in Hell's contingent. Of course judgment was already coming to pass.

"You can aid us in this," Zadkiel said.

"I would be most honored," Muriel answered.

"Give me your sword." Michael's voice was a bass rumble compared to Zadkiel's baritone.

Muriel manifested herself fully armed. She unbuckled her sword belt and laid the scabbard across the archangel's brown hands.

"Thank you," he said.

Muriel frowned and almost protested. She'd expected the archangels to bless her blade, to direct her as their weapon. Instead, Michael seemed to be confiscating her sword.

"You cannot take on Hell alone," Rafael warned.

Too stunned to respond, Muriel watched the school buses pull away from the curb, bearing the noisy children away.

"In Ypres," Michael said, "we warred with Moloch because his minions took souls outside their time. Hell circumvented the rule by inspiring the use of mustard gas. If you take Lorelei now, someone worse will take her place."

"The time is coming for combat," Zadkiel advised. "You must be certain you are ready when that time comes."

Then, as one, the archangels were gone, leaving Muriel alone, unarmed.

In his true form, Asmodeus sat at the head of a long teak conference table, a decanter in front of him. His skin glowed a rich dark brown, like the

Persians who had worshipped him as a god. Beneath black hair coiled as tightly as a newborn lamb's, he stroked his pointed black beard. Enormous glossy wings, as black as his hair, lay folded on his back.

He'd stretched one of his legs out from beneath the table. It was a mangled mess, shattered when he was thrown from Heaven's battlements. That he let Lorelei see it now was a warning about just punishments and battle scars.

He toyed with a pair of silver shears, then slid them down the table. "Lose the dress."

Lorelei shifted to her infernal shape. She set her purse on the table and picked up the scissors, slitting the Betsey Johnson dress from collar to hem. She stepped out of the shreds and left them lying on the floor behind her.

"Here." The demon pointed with his silver-headed cane to a spot near his chair.

Lorelei took her mark, hands clasped behind her back. Asmodeus slipped two fingers into his mouth, then wiped them across the blood crusting the upper curve of her breast. He licked the blood from his fingers, eyes closed to savor. A goat's smile curved his lips. "Your boyfriend's blood?"

"Yes, my lord."

"Who spilled it?"

"Hai Ng, my lord. Out of jealousy. He's upstairs with your harem now."

The demon nodded. He glanced past her to the archfiend still loitering in the doorway. "Tomur, why are you still here? Bring Jequon."

Asmodeus's goat-pupil eyes turned back to Lorelei. "Did you forget I gave you a phone? I told you to keep in close contact with me."

"I called Saturday night," Lorelei protested. "Didn't Floria give you my message about Barakiel?"

"Not as fallen as he'd like us to think?" the demon echoed.

"He's angry to have lost his only hope of salvation."

"Father Joseph, you mean?" Asmodeus uncorked the decanter and poured himself a snifter of extremely old brandy. He swirled the glass in his hand, but didn't drink.

Lorelei licked her suddenly parched lips. "I'm sorry, my lord. I used every enticement I could imagine…"

"Priests are tricky," Asmodeus comforted.

Lorelei was amazed to hear words of forgiveness from her boss. He smiled at her then, eager to be cruel, and added, "I trust you won't disappoint me again."

Lorelei dropped to her knees.

Her prince laughed. "Being too anxious to please is just as unacceptable as failure. Get up. Sit."

Lorelei pulled out the leather-upholstered chair at the demon's right hand and perched on its seat. Her prince poured a snifter of brandy and pushed it across the table to her. She didn't pick it up.

"What sort of ammunition did Hai Ng use to injure your boyfriend?"

Lorelei opened her purse. She thought the better of giving the demon both bullets, so she only pulled out one. She kept her gaze downcast as she snapped her purse decisively closed and held the lone bullet out on an open palm.

Asmodeus plucked it up and sniffed it loudly. "Interesting. Did Hai tell you where he got it?"

"Not exactly. He said Yasmina told him where we would be."

"Curiouser and curiouser. This, my girl, is of angelic manufacture. It was probably designed for you. Without my aegis, it would have most certainly ended your existence, for now and evermore."

Lorelei slumped into the leather conference chair.

"I was told, before you arrived, that your fiend Tibor was killed last night by the angel Muriel."

"I saw a fireball," Lorelei began.

Asmodeus nodded. "That was the death of your limo. This Muriel is becoming costly."

"I've already mentioned her to Mastema."

"Oh? Good. She certainly bears watching." The prince of the city had a sip of his brandy and turned the conversation back to Yasmina. "Clever of 'that bitch' to give the bullets to Hai, don't you think? Either the kid shot you and it ricocheted into your boyfriend, or he shot the angel directly... Yasmina couldn't have known that these bullets wouldn't pack a punch big enough to take her enemy down. Still, it's nice to see the old girl using some initiative to get back into my good graces."

Lorelei shivered at the thought. "Yasmina served you profitably for millennia..."

He cut off her apology. "I'll raise my tail when I want you to kiss my ass, Lorelei."

Still, she couldn't apologize for speaking the truth.

Asmodeus nudged the brandy snifter in her direction. Lorelei understood that it was important she accepted his hospitality, although she wasn't sure why. She picked up the glass, didn't bother with the niceties of sniffing and sipping, just tossed down a mouthful. It made her cough.

The demon's rich laughter warmed her like the breath of home. It included her, instead of mocking her. This was the boss she loved to serve, the one who made service such fun. "My dear," he said amiably, "ages pass between the falling of angels. Almost seems like there's a waiting period. We're due. Whether you tempt Azaziel into lust or his brethren shun him into despair, my ends are served. Any angel's degradation increases the glory of Hell." He draped an overheated hand across her thigh and leaned close. "Did your angel confess his lust to you?"

"He said he chose me." Lorelei knew her best bet was to be honest without giving too much away. "He said he loves me."

"Beyond all others?" Asmodeus prompted.

She frowned, trying to remember Azaziel's exact words. "He said he's watched me for years. It led him to fall in love."

"Getting there." Asmodeus rang his snifter of brandy against hers. "Keep at him."

"I exist to serve you," Lorelei whispered.

"Glad you remembered." Asmodeus refilled his glass and added a skosh to hers, so that she automatically joined him in a drink. The brandy coiled in her empty stomach.

"So Barakiel longs to be redeemed. Yasmina wants her place back. Azaziel wants true love." Asmodeus smiled. "And you, Lorelei, what do you want?"

It occurred to her to lie.

With his left hand, Asmodeus drew her glyph in the air, compelling her to speak truly.

Lorelei swallowed hard. "I want Azaziel," she admitted.

"For the honor of Hell?" the demon prompted.

"For my own."

"I remind you that you were created to serve Hell." He drew her glyph a second time. She didn't need to watch him do it: she felt the compulsion engulf her, constricting around her like a snake. "Succubi serve. They don't command service," Asmodeus reminded. "Perhaps you're angling to be elevated to temptress?"

Fuck, that would solve her problems. If she became a temptress and got Azaziel's signature, they could be together, perhaps even forever. She could certainly protect him, especially if Asmodeus continued to shield her with his aegis. She could face Yasmina as an equal and the bitch couldn't strike back.

"Well?" Asmodeus prodded.

Lorelei said cautiously, "I hope my service will be worthy of reward."

The demon took her chin in his hand, intentionally nicking her throat with his thumbnail. She smelled her blood on the air. He lifted her head to meet his gaze. "Have you anything more you wish to report to me?"

She had hoped not to be put on the spot. She'd thought she might have more time to weigh the betrayal, decide how to phrase it to protect herself and her angel. Now, with the compulsion upon her, she opened her mouth to speak. For the first time since she'd learned how, lies wouldn't come.

"At the old church—the one where he fucked me—Azaziel collected unsaved souls by the hundreds. He schools them there, in hopes of saving them after their deaths. He knows what he's doing is wrong, but claims it isn't forbidden."

Asmodeus watched her in silence, letting the weight of her treachery settle.

"I recaptured one of the souls," Lorelei remembered. She dug into her purse and pulled out the soul catcher. Erik's soul was still trapped in its pommel. Asmodeus took the knife from her, sucked the soul free, and sent it on its way. He returned the knife to her.

"Tell me what Azaziel will do about this project of his, now that you know of it." Asmodeus sipped his brandy, watching her. "Don't fear to guess," he directed. "Just be afraid to be wrong."

Lorelei swallowed hard. "They'll have to move the souls. I told Aza I wouldn't keep his secret."

The demon didn't praise her for behavior he'd already expected. Instead, he held her gaze, smirking, until her eyes watered. Once he released her, Lorelei protested, "I don't know if they have any way to move the souls en masse. Your spies would know that better than I."

"The angel told you nothing?"

She didn't dare admit she hadn't asked.

Asmodeus continued, "You are correct in guessing that, while you're under my aegis for the time being, I will remove it the instant I lose faith in you. At the moment, I want nothing so much as the destruction of those tarnished souls." The demon's voice thickened with some emotion she couldn't fathom. "I want my estranged brethren to understand they can't break Hell's treaties with impunity, not in my city. This is why I will continue to protect you, Lorelei: to revenge myself on angels who disobey Yahweh and go unpunished."

At the sound of the Holy Name, Lorelei convulsed, crushing the brandy snifter in her talons.

Asmodeus took her hand in his own and raised it to his face, inhaling the aroma of her blood. "So Azaziel loves you," the demon purred, changing the subject yet again. "Loves you with a specific, nearly human love. Lorelei, chosen from all Creation, as soulmate..."

The blood in her veins ran cold to hear the truth slip past the demon's black lips, bitten between his sharp teeth.

Asmodeus lowered her hand but didn't release it. He touched the sliver of glass embedded there, wiggling it to cut her more deeply, before he plucked it out. Blood welled up in her palm, liquid warmth around the pain.

"And you, my child—tarnished by a soul you earned through love. You love your angel with a scheming, possessive, but quite honest love in return."

He stared at her, daring her to deny it. Lorelei listened to the dripping of her blood, trying to find words that would save her. Finally, she could not bear Asmodeus's scrutiny any longer. "Yes, my lord. I love him. But it won't prevent me from doing my job. I am yours to command."

Asmodeus sat back with a sigh that expressed volumes.

Lorelei closed her fist around the pain and held it against her shoulder. Blood rolled down her breasts, mixing with the scabbed remnants of Aza's blood. The smell seemed like incense. She clung to the aroma, savoring it. It might be the last pleasure she was allowed.

Asmodeus sucked noisily on his fingers, lapping like a dog at her blood. When his hands were clean, her bleeding had stopped.

The demon pronounced her sentence. "Perhaps I will wish I had destroyed you, but for now I will allow you to continue to exist—solely, I remind you, because you betrayed your lover's hoard of souls. Do not forget for an instant that you survive on my good will. If I feel the slightest flicker of doubt that you ever put your angel's interests above my own, you will wish I had destroyed you now."

Asmodeus flicked his fingers. Lorelei snatched up her purse and ran from the room.

In the hallway outside, Jequon blew smoke into her face as he stepped past her into the conference room.

"Follow," the archfiend Tomur rumbled, setting off at a brisk pace. Lorelei jogged after him. When he finally stopped to open a door, Lorelei nearly stumbled into him. She caught herself just in time. Then Tomur gripped her elbow to thrust her into the darkened room.

A pair of fiends glanced up from the newscast on the television. A burning church filled the screen. The televised flames cast the only light in the room. Lorelei recognized it as Azaziel's church and her heart plummeted.

"What's that smell?" one of the fiends asked. Lorelei recognized him as another of Asmodeus's archfiends.

"Angel's blood." She set her purse down on the spare chair and crossed the room to stand before him. She raised her arms and twisted so he could get a good look at the blood dried across her breasts. "Go ahead and taste it, Tough Guy. I have. It's like sticking your tongue to the live end of a battery."

He looked up at her. Lorelei hadn't ever seen a bewildered fiend before. It made her laugh.

"How long since you been fucked, Lorelei?"

She looked back over her shoulder at Tomur. "Twelve hours, give or take."

"That's damn close to celibacy for a succubus," the other fiend growled.

Lorelei forced a smile, glad for anything that would keep her mind off her betrayal of Azaziel.

CHAPTER 9: LOOSE CANNONS

Floria wedged her Alfa Romeo into a parking space in West Hollywood. In the mood for some trashy lingerie, she planned to drop into Dream Dresser to see what was new.

As she climbed out of the car, the shop's window across the street gave her pause. In the display, an exaggeratedly male blond angel, dressed in black leather pants and a black latex shirt, stood against a background of thorny branches. The window glass in front of him had been painted with flames.

Floria spat on the sidewalk. Fucking angels were everywhere these days.

Still, she wanted what she wanted. Floria sauntered up to the corner of Santa Monica. As she waited for the light to change, a couple of devil girls stopped in front of the display across the street. One girl wrapped her arm around the other's shoulders, hugging her close to point out something about the angel. Then she grabbed her friend's hand and pulled her inside.

Floria didn't recognize the succubi, so they were probably newly raised from being imps. Just what they needed in this town: more dumb sluts who thought angels were playthings.

The streetlight changed. Floria was about to step off the curb when she heard an engine racing toward her. She froze in mid-stride as a Humvee sped toward her against the light.

The blond angel who had given Floria the ammunition glared from behind the wheel.

Before Floria could drop her mortal guise and fly, a town car made a screeching turn in front of her. An arm reached out its open back door and hauled Floria into the car's back seat.

The succubus didn't have time to register who her savior was before the town car bore her away, tearing at supernatural speed through the sludgy WeHo traffic.

After the fiends finally got their rocks off, Lorelei hurried into the shower. Standing under the scalding water, she tried to imagine what might happen now that Asmodeus knew about Azaziel's kids. Would Hell go to war?

Despite Lorelei's bluster when Aza first took her to his lair, succubi didn't fight angels. The dagger each girl possessed was used for opening veins to harvest "contract ink" and temporarily caching souls. Their horns, talons, and tail were mostly for show, things humans expected to see when they glimpsed a devil girl. Compared to fiends, succubi were so fragile that no one even bothered to train them for combat. She remembered Sasha, cloven in half by the angelic sword at Lost Angels, and shuddered.

Anyway, pitched battles against angels were extremely rare these days. Lorelei remembered hearing of only two in the last hundred years: at Mons, and then during the firestorm at Dresden. One loss, one gain. The last real throw-down she could recall had been the LA Riots, when Beelzebub attempted to burn the city down. A handful of angels repulsed Beelzebub's forces. Even though it cost him dominion over LA, it hardly rated as a skirmish in the War against Heaven.

A shadow loomed on the other side of the shower door. Lorelei shut the water off.

"Get out here," Tomur ordered.

She stepped out of the stall and followed the archfiend, dripping, into the bedroom. The fiends stood at attention, guarding the door. Jequon sprawled across the bed, watching how Lorelei moved. "Thank you for not bothering to dress."

Lorelei hadn't realized it was an option. The dress she'd been wearing was now a rag on the floor of Asmodeus's conference room. She wiped her wet hair back from her face and wished she'd grabbed a towel.

Jequon said to the fiends, "The prince waits to instruct you." They filed out wordlessly, leaving Lorelei alone with the fallen angel. None of the fiends even glanced over his shoulder at her. The last one out pulled the door closed.

Once they were alone, Lorelei was confused about what was expected of her in this situation. Had Jequon come to sample the freak or was this one of the propositions Asmodeus wanted her to report on?

Jequon regarded Lorelei with an expression the succubus could not decipher. "Let me put this in simple terms, Lorelei. With your shiny new soul, you have an attribute no other servant of Hell can offer. It's a shame to use that attribute to tempt only one of our enemies."

"You're suggesting...?"

"It seems to me that a creature who can lure angels to her bed shouldn't limit herself to just one. Think about your future, kitten. Nebiros demanded the honor of commanding Asmodeus's army here in LA. You might not know their saga, but on Heaven's precipice, Azaziel hit Nebiros so hard that the general became the twisted wretch you see today. Nebiros must remember every time he tries to sit down. So you can guess what that grudge augurs for your sweetheart. If I were you, I'd pick out the next object of my affection."

Lorelei swayed on her feet as if she'd been struck.

Jequon smiled like he'd swallowed a sinner whole.

"I have to go," Lorelei stammered, trying to shake herself out of Jequon's fascination. "I should…"

"Unnecessary," Jequon said. "I've brought your orders." He slipped a folded square of parchment from inside the sleeve of his burgundy silk robe.

Lorelei reached forward warily, but Jequon didn't tease her. Keeping one eye on the fallen angel, Lorelei unfolded the parchment. The penmanship was unfamiliar, but the words were pretty standard. Hai Ng pledged to serve Asmodeus, Prince of Los Angeles, in return for settlement of all his debts as long as he should live.

"That idiot!"

"He wasn't much of a negotiator with his dick in Fusao's mouth and Candy's tongue up his ass. Are you hurt that he didn't contract for you?"

"I—"

Jequon cut her off. "Actually, he did ask for you, but the girls persuaded him that they could satisfy him more completely than you ever have."

She was meant to be jealous, but Lorelei didn't feel anything but disappointment that Hai could be bought so cheaply.

"Don't pity him yet," Jequon cautioned. "As a token of his allegiance, he's offered to lead his friends into battle, when it comes."

Lorelei barely had time to assimilate the notion before Jequon delivered the postscript: "Of course, Floria will have to go along, to ensure credit for any of the boys Hai leads to their deaths. Asmodeus has become convinced you should accompany her."

"What?!" Lorelei shrieked, dropping the contract to the carpet.

Jequon called the parchment back to his hand. "After Nebiros kills your angel, you'll be at liberty to shop around for his replacement. If Asmodeus gets his will, every angel in LA should be there. Choose wisely, Lorelei. You fucked your way into this. You can just as surely fuck your way out."

From the doorway, the fallen angel delivered his parting shot. "Why don't you pick something sassy from Yasmina's closet? I'm sure she won't mind helping you get dressed."

Lorelei stood in the center of the room, trembling, as the water rolling down her back dripped onto the carpet. Into battle? Into battle with every angel in LA? Her mind refused to wrap around the concept.

On autopilot, she returned to the bathroom and toweled off. If these had been Yasmina's rooms, she wanted out of them as quickly as possible.

She wasn't sure if anything in the temptress's closet would fit her. Yasmina had a larger frame, though it was scraped of curves. Yasmina epitomized the "stick with tits" athletic build that was Lorelei's antithesis.

In addition, Lorelei preferred basic black clothing, while the elder temptress leaned toward patterns that hinted at the snake beneath her skin. Lorelei worried that anything she chose was going to look like a bad Halloween costume.

Still, while traipsing around naked had its attractions, she needed something closer to armor to make her feel like she could get through this day.

Lorelei opened the mirrored closet door and began to paw through the gowns within.

Yasmina settled into the back of the town car and grinned at the blond succubus she'd rescued. "That was close," she teased.

Sirens started up behind them. In response, Jezebel hunched over the steering wheel and poured on more speed.

Floria seethed with anger. "What is that bitch's problem?"

Yasmina smiled, revealing her fangs. She was well aware that most of Asmodeus's staff referred to her as "that bitch," so it entertained her to hear the epithet applied to the angel Muriel. In Yasmina's long-considered opinion, the angel deserved it much more.

"Somebody shot her brother," Yasmina explained. "Unfortunately, it didn't kill Azaziel."

Floria's normally golden complexion turned slightly green.

"You look like you need a drink," Yasmina observed.

Floria regarded the elder temptress through measuring eyes. "You're not one to do favors," she said, more politic than Yasmina might have expected. Floria wasn't known for holding her tongue.

"Your sister and her boyfriend are pissing me off," Yasmina said.

Floria's grin was sudden and sharp. "I will drink to that."

Yasmina pulled a bottle of Cristal out of the ice bucket.

As Lorelei was wriggling into one of Yasmina's Issey Miyake sheathes, Hai stumbled into the bedroom, knees barely able to support his weight. He staggered over to the bed and sank down on its corner.

Lorelei ignored him, bending over to straighten the seams on her stockings.

"You work here?" Hai finally managed.

"Yes," Lorelei hissed.

"You and Floria?"

Lorelei looked at him in the mirror. His unfocused eyes had gone black with pupil. His mouth hung slightly open, although he wasn't drooling. Not any longer.

Stupid little boy. He thought he'd finally hit the jackpot, finally discovered the secret stash of wealth and women that the world withheld from him. Before he met Floria, all Hai had known had been his mom struggling to work two, sometimes three, jobs, just to make rent and keep their fifteen-year-old Toyota running. Working for Tuan and Floria bought Hai new clothes, good booze, the shiny new RAV4. It gave him all the speed he could put up his nose, all the tequila he could drink, and made him feel all grown up. Even though he was only eighteen, Hai was damned for lust and damned for greed.

Still, Lorelei crushed out the pity that wriggled through her thoughts. Hai had just dragged Lorelei and Floria into the coming battle. Lorelei figured she'd better size up her bodyguards, decide who to hide behind, because she sure as shit wasn't fighting any angels alone. And if she could throw a big fuck-you to the angel who wouldn't run away with her before she could be sent into battle, so much the better.

"Why don't you call the boys?" Lorelei suggested. "A promotion like yours deserves a party." She handed him her cell phone.

"And tell them what?"

"Meet us up behind the Hollywood sign?"

Hai did as he was told. He called Sammy and directed him to bring the boys. All the while, he gave Lorelei a strange look. She suspected he wondered why she wanted the boys along. To be honest, it looked like Asmodeus's harem had about sucked him dry. Without a good dose of Viagra, which she didn't currently have on hand, Hai was not going to be much fun. Before long, he was going to want to curl up for a nap. Lorelei had no time for sleep.

She goaded the boy up onto his feet and into the hallway. Luckily, no one was visible in either direction.

Once they got back outside to Hai's truck, the teenager took a good last look around at the wealth on casual display. Then he unlocked his RAV4 and climbed back inside.

Jezebel ducked the town car into an underground garage an instant before the Humvee, followed by a phalanx of LAPD cars, screamed past. The ruined succubus coasted up in front of an elevator and put the car in park.

"Where are we?" Floria asked, slightly buzzed on the temptress's Cristal.

"Jequon's office," Yasmina said. "Go on up. He's expecting you."

Floria handed her glass back as Jezebel opened the car door. Yasmina's driver stood by, eyes downcast, long black velvet driving coat hanging open to reveal her scars.

Climbing out of the car, Floria studied the subservient girl. She didn't know the story of what Jezebel had done to rate her punishment, but it could be no worse than screwing an angel.

Floria's smile was mean as she considered that, perhaps, death was too good for Lorelei after all. It would be nice to have a driver, an eternal minion who could not disobey her slightest whim.

Aza stood in line at the street food park, content to watch his fellow Angelenos on this lovely afternoon. Now that the smoke from Lost Angels had finally cleared from the air, the sun streamed down from a reasonably clear blue sky.

The angel was feeling hopeful once more about trying to bring Lorelei a picnic. It was such a nice day, it would be delicious to find a shaded bower in Griffith Park and simply enjoy each other's company for an hour or two.

His wound seemed to have healed nicely, thanks to Muriel's ministrations. Aza wanted to make it clear to Lorelei that he bore Hai Ng no ill will. How could be begrudge another being who loved his succubus as much as Aza did? Hopefully, her intervention could turn that boy's life around, too.

Aza stepped up to the food truck's window and ordered a pork bahn-mi and two lemonades, trusting that would be enough to satisfy them both.

Eventually LAPD had Muriel boxed in enough that her only choice was to use the Hummer as a battering ram and try to get onto the freeway.

As she passed the spike strips and bashed through the barrier of police cruisers, she saw Michael and two of his warrior angels had parked their motorcycles across the top of the ramp. Rather than endure another scolding, Muriel threw the stolen vehicle into park and abandoned it before it could come crashing to a halt.

As Floria strode past the glass doors into Jequon's talent agency, the bottle blonde receptionist's gaze traced the plunge of Floria's neckline. The woman's puke-yellow suit didn't complement the orange tone of her tan. Her face seemed an artificial composite of the more famous features in the framed headshots on the wall behind her.

"Jequon is expecting me," Floria said.

"Mr. Jequon," the receptionist corrected icily, "is in a meeting. Please have a seat."

Floria ignored her, striding past the reception desk to push open the frosted glass doors to Jequon's inner sanctum. It was empty, save for a large glass desk.

"I told you—"

"Not a problem, Joyce," Jequon said smoothly as he materialized out of the shadows. "I expected Floria. Hold my calls, please."

As soon as the door closed in the face of the frowning mortal woman, Floria asked, "Who shot that fucking angel?"

"I'm surprised you don't know," the fallen angel said as he sank into his high-backed leather chair. "Doesn't Hai Ng run with your little Vietnamese gang?"

Floria felt her temperature rising. "What the fuck, Jequon? I asked for your help, not to take one of my boys and point him at the angel."

The lean black angel gazed at her over his steepled fingers. His black eyes had gone stormy. "Are you finished?"

Floria stared at him. Belatedly, she remembered she was here facing down a fallen angel without any borrowed fiends at her back. Unlike Lorelei, she had no aegis protecting her. "Sorry," she said—if not exactly contrite, at least less confrontational.

"Good." Jequon's gaze softened a touch. "I like you, Floria, but don't push me. There's a hierarchy and I'll see it respected."

"Sorry," she repeated. She knew there was a fucking hierarchy. He was a fallen angel, not a freaking demon, and he was subservient to Asmodeus, same as she was. Still, she put a little honey into her voice. "I was hoping you would find some way to get rid of my sister without the evidence leading directly back to me. I thought—I'd hoped—I made that clear when I called you."

"As a matter of fact, Yasmina herself got the ammunition into Hai's hands and has taken responsibility for the attack."

Floria hissed, but caught herself before she disparaged the fallen angel's favorite bitch.

Jequon's smile was subtle as a cat's. "If, despite our prince's aegis, the assassination of your sister had succeeded, then Azaziel might have fallen in despair. If the shot had ricocheted off the angel and hit Lorelei, it would have destroyed her and we could have counted it a lucky accident. As it is, we know that Azaziel can be wounded. That makes it a simple matter of bargaining for a weapon to finish the job. Once he's gone, our prince will have no further use for Lorelei. He will drop his aegis and you can proceed at will."

Floria dreaded to think what such a weapon might cost. It was almost too much to hope that Jequon could help her find one. Still, killing that damn angel would get her closer to having Lorelei under her heel.

Jequon changed the subject before Floria could daydream too long. "Do I understand correctly that you did not have a contract with Hai Ng?"

Floria's thoughts sharpened to a point. "I didn't need one. Hai is unquestionably damned."

"Then it won't disappoint you to know that he's no longer your account."

Floria screeched Lorelei's name.

Jequon tsked. "Lorelei merely rode along with him up to Holmby Hills, after the two of them had been summoned. Hai signed our master's contract of his own accord. Lorelei quite literally had nothing to do with it."

The stupid motherfucker, Floria thought. She'd have to get the other boys nailed into place quickly, before she lost them all. That meant the sooner she could get out of here, the sooner she could get back to work. "All right, Jequon, I owe you a favor. What can I do for you?"

Aza's plan had been to retrieve Lorelei's candle from La Rosa del Mundo, take it to Griffith Park, and see if that would suffice to summon her. Unfortunately, his cigar box had been stolen from its hiding place in the storefront church.

A sick feeling roiled Aza's stomach. When he arrived back at his home church, flames fully engulfed the structure. He flickered into his room, but it was empty, as were the old sanctuary and the vestry, kitchen, washrooms, basement. No one was in danger.

Aza returned to his room to bid it farewell. Shoulder-height flames shimmied and danced there, reflected in the half-assembled stained glass mural. Accelerant of some kind lit a path to his mattress, where a puddle burned. Lorelei's candle lay on its side, partially eaten away.

No one knew he had gone out to get lunch, so this was a crime of opportunity. The special attention paid to burning his bed put him in mind of Muriel's jealousy. Still, his self-righteous sister wouldn't have stooped to gasoline to make her fury known.

Mastema, if he could be believed, had warned that the fire would be set at Asmodeus's behest. Perhaps that meant that someone who had been at the nightclub had set the blaze. That limited the suspects to a couple dozen.

"Come away," Barbelo called gently from out on the sidewalk. Aza heard her sweet, melodic voice as clearly as if she stood at his shoulder.

He obeyed and found Barbelo standing across the street. She offered him the flask from inside her jacket pocket. Today it held Cathedral Cabernet from the gift shop at Our Lady of Angels. Aza savored a long swallow, trusting that the flask would refill itself for her to drink as well.

As they watched the flames, a fire truck braked hard in front of Santa Rosa's. The angels eavesdropped as the firefighters remembered the last time they'd saved this church. That arsonist had never been caught.

"Is Joseph safely hidden?" Azaziel asked his companion.

She had a silent conversation with someone else, then reported, "He's safe with Shebethiel now."

The fire crew unrolled their hoses as one of their number opened the hydrant. They hadn't yet begun to douse the flames when something tucked up under the roof exploded.

Aza and Barbelo injected themselves amongst the firefighters, shielding them as flaming debris crashed down on the street.

"Fall back," the captain shouted.

The fire crew hurried to obey before something else exploded.

"Hell is serious about leveling it this time," Barbelo noted.

"I was warned," Aza admitted. He wondered again over the conversation with Mastema. It still wasn't safe to be tempted by his offer about Lorelei.

Aza opened the plastic bag still looped, almost forgotten, over his elbow. He pulled out the bahn-mi sandwich, handed half to Barbelo, and unwrapped the white paper from his own half. Lorelei would have to fend for herself. He was needed here, protecting these firefighters.

CHAPTER 10: LORELEI'S RITUAL

Lorelei and Hai shared a joint, staring down the dry summer hillside at the megalopolis sprawled below. The young man no longer had the energy to shout at her or hit on her, so she tried to entertain herself with wondering what Aza was up to tonight. Would he forgive her for getting between him and the would-be assassin? Would the angel forgive her for reporting his swarm of souls? Would it have been better if Asmodeus had tortured her somehow that had left a mark? Would Aza like her better if she'd martyred herself for him?

It didn't fucking matter. She knew she had to get the boys on her side—most especially, Hai—before they marched into battle. She wished Jequon had given her some idea how much longer they had to live.

Finally, the Vietnamese gang came roaring up on Japanese crotch-rockets. Dressed in a riot of red leather—damn, but they were adorable. Lorelei felt a twinge of envy that her sister had all this candy within reach. Of course, Floria never availed herself of it. If a fuck didn't advance her career, Floria could hardly be bothered. Lorelei was done trying to school Floria that the fucks along the way were the only thing that made life worthwhile.

It took a little persuasion to keep the boys on their bikes, but Lorelei had a venue in mind. She climbed back into the RAV with Hai and slid close to him, letting her hand restore as much of his vitality as possible without opening his clothes. It was best not to leave him with much blood to think with.

She whispered directions into his ear, leading the boys farther into the hills.

Muriel waited across the street while Shebethiel talked with the knot of teenagers loitering outside the liquor store. Tonight Shebethiel wore pencil-thin black jeans, a motorcycle jacket with a constellation of sharp silver studs, and his immaculate purple fan of mohawk. He didn't fit in with the street children in their sagging jeans, but before long, he persuaded them to go shoot some baskets at the park up the street.

The childbed angel noticed Muriel standing under the awning of the shuttered vegetable stand. He raised a hand in greeting, but didn't seem inclined to cross the street to talk. Muriel took the initiative, stepping out into Monday evening traffic and trusting it to clear for her passage. "Hold, Brother!" she called cheerily.

"Hullo, Muriel." Shebethiel had always been shy, more comfortable singing lullabies to sleeping babes than making conversations with his own kind. Muriel felt affection for the gawky cherub. Especially since he had been posted so recently to LA that he had formed no attachments here.

"I come to beg a favor," Muriel said. "Rafael has commanded me to keep my distance from Azaziel's harlot. If you can believe that."

Shebethiel made no answer, not that Muriel had expected one.

She continued, "Could you watch her for me tonight? The succubus is keeping company with a troop of boys, some of whom could surely be ours, if they could be guided away from her influence."

Shebethiel met Muriel's eyes and offered her a shy smile. "Where might I find them?"

"The succubus was steering them up into the hills, who knows what trouble to cause. You will have to track her."

Shebethiel reached out for Muriel's hand. She blushed at his goodness. He was such an innocent creature, so unsullied by the darkness of this world.

"Thank you, Brother." She meant more than for simply taking her watch.

Night fell before Lorelei found the old coven house. It had been a long time since she'd been up there—and she'd always come by air before. Still, she knew when they were getting close. She sensed a familiar tinge in the air, the scent of very old blood and very black magic.

As Hai rounded the final hairpin turn, a blur rocketed from the brush at the side of the road. Lorelei saw the animal at the same instant that Hai slammed on the brakes. As the tires shrieked, the truck struck something with a thud.

Lorelei flung her arm out to prevent Hai's head from bouncing off the steering wheel.

They swerved wildly across the narrow road. Certain that they were headed into the canyon below, Lorelei resumed her true form and readied herself to jump through the windshield.

"Fuck, fuck, fuck, fuck," Hai chanted. He fought with the wheel, got the truck slowed, and finally parked on the margin at the side of the road.

One of the boys roared up on his motorcycle. Lorelei got her mortal guise back on as Hai slid his window down. Sammy demanded, too loud, "You okay?"

"What was it?" Hai panted.

"Coyote. It's not dead."

"I want to see." Lorelei unhooked her seatbelt and slid out the door.

They'd come a surprising distance from the impact. Lorelei walked back down the middle of the street. The boys had drawn their motorcycles up into a circle. Their headlights ringed the animal sprawled across the centerline, ribs heaving. Lorelei walked past the motorcycles to look down at it. The coyote glared back at her, half-heartedly showing teeth. Its blood puddled on the asphalt, reflecting white highlights.

"Give me a gun," Lorelei said.

Nobody moved.

She looked up from the suffering animal to find a ring of dark eyes watching her. "All right, tough guys," she snapped, "one of you do it."

Lam, recently out of jail, stepped up beside her, Glock in fist. His first shot sparked asphalt from the road. The second hit the coyote's shoulder. The third finally put it down.

"In the name of Satan," Lorelei breathed. She knelt beside the body and put her hands into the puddle of blood. The pavement beneath it was still warm from the sun.

Vin stooped beside her and started to tug the coyote off the road. Lorelei reached out quickly and traced the glyph that represented her name on his leathers with the middle finger of her left hand. Kim came to help, so she marked him, too.

Hai took her arm and pulled her out of their way. Lorelei smiled into his eyes as she wrote her glyph on his coat.

He looked down at the smear of blood. "Shit, Lorelei!" He grabbed her hand, crushing her fingers together. "What'd you do that for?"

"It's a protection spell, Tiger." She broke his grasp on her, then stepped close enough to straddle his thigh. She whispered into his ear, "I better do all the boys, just to be safe."

"Safe from what?"

"I don't want my ex to find us up here and fly into some kind of jealous rage."

Hai shivered. "Your angel, you mean?"

Lorelei touched a bloody finger to the boy's lips and nodded.

Horrified, Hai smeared the blood from his face with his T-shirt's hem. Even so, he ordered the others, "Come 'ere."

Despite their protests, Lorelei marked the jackets of the last two. The boys believed she and Floria were witches, so they accepted her explanation. Five of them and me, she thought. This should be a hoot.

While the boys examined Hai's RAV4 for damage, Lorelei slipped away. Nearby, not far from the road, had been a house where a coven worshipped her in the 1970s. People knew how to party in those days. Lorelei hadn't been back since the house burned down and killed them all.

As she dodged through the brush, she heard the boys cursing behind her. A motorcycle roared to life.

Lorelei quickened her pace through the semi-darkness. A little more wandering and she was there. The crescent moon lit the clearing between the live oaks. Some of the house remained standing. The crumbling walls threw shadows that were blacker than they should have been. Perfect. Evil still claimed this ground.

The succubus circled the ruin, trying to focus her will. She wanted to seduce all the boys, even virginal Kim, even Vin, who lacked the nerve to come out to his friends. She needed to be careful of Sammy, who would try to hurt her to prove his masculinity. "Relax," she teased herself. "They're just kids. This will be over before you know it."

The coyote's blood had dried on her hands. Lorelei felt it flaking away as she stripped off Yasmina's dress and spread it atop the dewy grass. The breeze was chilly on her bare skin. Dammit. The cold was another thing she'd never noticed before Aza inflicted Ashleigh's soul on her.

Lorelei raised her left hand to her lips and licked the dried blood from her fingers. "Hai, Lam, Sammy, Vin, and…" Dammit. What was the other kid's name? She'd been out of the game too long. It wasn't like her to forget the names of prey.

Scowling, Lorelei repeated the names she could remember, embarrassed that this was the sort of incantation to which she was reduced.

During the fifth repetition, Hai jogged out of the trees, Glock in one hand, cigarette in the other. His eyes were furious, even after he saw Lorelei dancing naked in the starlight.

"Not romantic enough for you?" she asked.

"I don't know why I don't just fuckin' kill you," he snarled, raising the gun.

Lorelei shrugged more casually than she felt. "Fuck me first, Tiger. You can always kill me later." She stared at the gun. Even if Hai missed the first few shots, like Lam had with the coyote, he would still kill her at this range.

Lorelei licked her fingers again and slid her hand between her thighs. Her black stockings framed her busy fingers.

Hai took a long drag on the cigarette, watching her. Lorelei gave him a good show.

Then he threw the cigarette butt down and stomped it out carefully. He slipped the gun into his coat pocket. Lorelei smiled as he unzipped his jeans. Hai didn't.

"Come on, Tiger," she crooned. "Lay down here and let me show you how good you can feel. I know those hos at the boss's made your head explode, but I can set your whole body on fire."

He wasn't thrilled about getting his leather in the grass, but when she crawled up the length of his body to take the condom from him, every fiber of his flesh yearned toward her.

Hai felt Lorelei's gaze locked on him as her whole appearance shimmered. It was if he stared at her through the haze of heat rising off the desert when he and Tuan ran out to the meth lab in Downey. Her eyes were red, like the cherry inside the RAV's cigarette lighter. Her skin had gone the color of her favorite cranberry and vodka drinks. Lorelei folded black wings behind her shoulders. A smile split her face, revealing teeth as sharp as a cat's. He remembered the dream he'd had about the exorcism and shuddered. The transition was much more terrifying in person.

The sight of her barbed tail lashing took his breath away. Her flesh gave off its own heat, steaming slightly in the chilly night air. She pressed something naked and warm against the only part of him that was bare. Then she pulled back to let him appreciate how cold the air seemed in comparison. He wanted her so badly it was difficult not to wrestle her onto her back and rape her.

A surprisingly cold voice inside his head told him no. He had to be smart now. He had to please her, seduce her. It was the only way to make her truly his.

He smelled her scent again, hash on the breeze at Griffith Park. Her burning fingers unrolled the condom on his straining cock.

It shamed him to beg her, but he whispered, "Please."

She trailed one talon under his balls. "Yes, Tiger?"

His cheeks burned with shame. "Please don't make it over too quickly."

Her appearance flickered between her human form and the devil girl she truly was. Hai had to close his eyes against the strobing. It didn't help. He could still see her.

"Are you suffering, Tiger?" She kissed him and he felt her smile against his lips. "You wanna set the pace?"

Summoned by Hai's moaning, Sammy and Kim ran out of the trees, guns drawn. When Sammy figured out what was going on, his laugh was vicious. "Look at the stupid whore go."

Kim ran a few more steps, before he clued in, too. Hanging awkwardly in the shadows, the younger boy turned his back. Sammy watched avidly.

Comfortably human-looking again, Lorelei wrung the last few drops of vitality out of Hai. Lying below her in the dry grass, he looked as if his limbs had been unstrung. Tears pooled in his eyes.

Lorelei wondered if he had the strength to get up and walk away. She swung her leg over him and knelt beside him on Yasmina's dress.

"I really want to party with all your boys," she said softly. "You don't seriously mind, do you?"

Hai rubbed the tears from his eyes. "Do what you want, Lorelei. Don't you always?"

"Not at all," she admitted.

He fumbled his fly closed. Lorelei helped him get back on his feet. He stumbled over to the other boys and told them what she wanted. Sammy stared at her speculatively over the red glow of his vape, before he ambled over.

This one could be trouble. Sammy was damned for murder; two that she'd witnessed and undoubtedly more she hadn't. He had a taste for killing.

"What's wrong with my boy Hai?" he demanded.

"What do you mean, Killer?"

"He ain't enough for you, slut? You're a joke, begging for it."

Lorelei tossed the hair over her shoulder, away from her bare breasts. Sammy watched her, furious at himself for wanting her. "Have I begged you?"

"What would you do if I said no?"

"Everyone would have me but you."

Sammy considered that. In the end, he decided this was a chance he didn't want to pass up. "On your knees, bitch."

Lorelei knelt on Yasmina's dress. Sammy tossed a Trojan at her. She ripped the packet open with her teeth and worked her mouth down over Sammy's dick, unrolling the condom as she went. She hoped he appreciated the skill that went into that trick.

"No teeth," he growled.

What kind of janky head was he used to getting? She made a sound deep in her throat that she knew he would feel.

Sammy grabbed her head, held her down, and thrust as hard as he could. Bored, Lorelei slipped a hand between her thighs and livened things up.

Before she could come, Sammy abruptly cuffed her backward. He came, despite his determination not to. "Stupid cunt," he growled, all the more humiliated because she watched him with a sly smile.

"Because you didn't want me to get you off? Or because I'm going to fuck all of you?"

He backhanded her. "I don't know what Hai sees in you, whore." As much as she wanted to, Lorelei didn't laugh. It would be truly stupid to get shot for dissing Sammy.

Before he could hit her again, Hai said, "That's enough, Sammy." He marched back to the others on wobbly knees.

Lam had joined Hai and Kim. He took a long slug from a bottle and grinned at her. Then he handed the bottle to Kim and shoved the boy in her direction.

The kid stopped halfway across the overgrown grass and sucked on the tequila. He wasn't old enough to drive, let alone drink. The older boys whooped at him.

Kim stumbled the rest of the way over to her. He didn't know where to look. "Thought you might wan' wash yer mouth," he slurred.

All the alcohol inside the boy hadn't given him courage. He looked like a horse about to bolt, too much white showing in his eyes. Generally, the older boys respected his innocence, using him as a lookout and keeping him away from the hands-on business. He hadn't yet gotten the chance to do anything damning. Lorelei wondered if one fuck would tip the balance.

She had a long swallow of the tequila. "Did they give you a rubber?"

With shaking hands, Kim pulled a red foil package from his jeans pocket.

"This your first time?"

"No," he lied.

Lorelei took his hand and pulled him down to the dress. When she kissed him, she kept it gentle. He tasted of tequila and vaping and sweet yearning. She worked on that.

Before long, the tension went out of him. Lorelei trailed her fingers down his arm until she located his hand. She raised it, tracing his fingertips across her nipple. "You can touch me," she whispered, "if you want to."

His fear transformed into enthusiasm. Lorelei was glad he wouldn't prove much of a challenge after all.

Yasmina accepted Jequon's chromed flask, holding it carefully so she wouldn't pierce it with her extra-long nails. She sipped the mixture of innocent blood and absinthe, gaze never leaving Lorelei and the boy-child she was riding in the middle of the clearing.

"She's slipped," Yasmina observed. "I've watched her work before. A little boy like that: Lorelei ought to have him singing 'Ave Satani'."

Jequon lifted the shadowy mass of hair and grazed Yasmina's shoulder with his teeth. "You think Azaziel has broken her?"

Yasmina's eyes flared copper, but she didn't rise to the bait. "Looks to me like she's sliding helplessly across the line to the other side."

"How unfortunate our prince has promised to devour her before that can happen."

Yasmina toasted to that.

Then Jequon changed the subject. "It's a shame she's using your beautiful dress as a ground cloth."

Yasmina rolled her eyes dramatically. "That old rag? If she was going to steal something from my closet, she's lucky she didn't take something I really liked."

Still, Jequon was correct. The bimbo would have Hell to pay before long.

When Kim finished, Lorelei thanked him with a kiss. The boy's eyes shone with dazed gratitude.

"Kim, sweetheart, do me a favor?"

He nodded, unwilling to trust his voice.

"Ask Vin to bring my purse when it's his turn? I left it in the truck."

Kim nodded. Lorelei stretched out on the dress. She'd done half of them, she realized. It was shaping up to be a good night after all.

Lam swaggered up as Kim wrestled his jeans back on. Lam was a small young man bulked out from lifting weights in the juvie. A gold grill flashed in his smile. "Now you got the kid broke in," Lam said, "want a real man?"

Lam's sins were covetousness and lust, which might be fun. "How do you want me, Big Guy?"

"Feet in the air and squealin'."

Lorelei stretched her arms up to him. Lam kicked off his tennis shoes and peeled out of his jeans.

Nearer to downtown, Aza stood amidst the ashes of his home. He had lived at Santa Rosa's for millennia, long before the first fire there cost Father Joseph his faith. Aza had done what he could to shore up the old building, hoping that someday the diocese would find a use for it again, restore it to its former glory, and make it a beacon of hope for the surrounding community.

Now all that was gone.

This neighborhood was still years away from being gentrified. This lot would remain vacant until some developer with a gleam in his eye built an overpriced luxury condo on it. Then the cascade would start. The survivors of his formerly Latinx neighborhood, filled with refugees from the drug wars in South and Central America, would be driven away from the heart of the city, out to the fringes where they could afford a roof over their heads. The community would shatter in the exodus.

Aza couldn't help but feel he had caused this. By taking up with Lorelei, he had drawn Hell's attention back to Santa Rosa's. Whether the fire was a belated slap for his pursuit of the succubus or a rebuke for his ghostly charges, it had the effect of punishing the community he had loved and served.

He wondered if there was anything he could do to make it up to them.

His eye caught on a flash of purple amongst the sludge of wet ashes. He bent to retrieve a facet of stained glass from his mural. Once the glass had glowed in the church's chancel window. Now it was only garbage. It panged him that the color of this shard reminded him of Lorelei's eyes. Aza wiped the glass clean with his fingers and put it in the pocket of his flight jacket as a memento.

The fire had burned hot enough that very little else survived. The angel shuffled through the ashes toward where the window overlooking the playground had been. What had appeared to be a shadow amidst the ashes turned out, once he drew nearer to it, to be a single crumpled black feather.

Had Barakiel left it behind as his signature on the fire? Or, as Joseph hoped, was the fallen angel asking for help as he struggled back toward the light? Aza pondered what he should do with the feather. Turn it over to Mastema and ask for Barakiel to be punished? Send it to Asmodeus with a note to acknowledge a job well done?

Instead, Aza picked the feather up, stroking its vanes back into place. He felt the essence of his fallen brother pulsing through the fragile object. If he set the feather ablaze now, no one need ever know that Barakiel, in fear and misery, craved forgiveness.

Tucking the feather inside his jacket, Aza swore to keep Barakiel's secret and find help for him, if he could.

Vin clutched Lorelei's purse in both hands when he crossed the lawn. Lorelei reached up for it and rummaged inside, giving the teenager time to collect himself. It didn't help.

"Lorelei, I...I can't do this."

"It's okay." She found the tube of Glide. Without looking up at him, she said, "I know your secret, Vin. I don't intend to let anyone else in on it. It'll be between us."

He relaxed so suddenly she thought he might faint.

Lorelei continued in the same soothing tone. "You can walk away, if you want to, but the others will wonder why."

His anxiety flooded back in a rush. "What'm I gonna do?"

"I'll do my best to get you off. Trust me. I know a few tricks I'm sure you'll like." Lorelei popped the cap on the lube. "Just close your eyes and pretend I'm Tuan."

"I've seen enough," Shebethiel said, turning his back. "Azaziel's harlot is willingly participating in the corruption of innocents."

Barbelo did not turn away. "In what sense has the succubus corrupted the boys? Seems to me that she's been remarkably gentle. As you know, loss of virginity in no way equals loss of grace in our Master's eyes."

Shebethiel gazed at Barbelo. The circumstances of her conception often colored her perceptions. It was inarguable that any amount of sex had not tainted the divinity of Barbelo's mother. All the same, Sophia was nothing like the angel she had been. Shebethiel still sometimes mourned the elder angel's transformation.

"Be that as it may," Shebethiel said, "I don't need to watch the succubus degrade these young men any further."

"Perhaps they are fated to undergo the succubus's tuition. Maybe she needs to put them through this to refine the goodness inside her."

Shebethiel sighed. "Either we intervene now before this orgy continues…"

"Are you that eager for a fight?" Barbelo nodded across the clearing. Shebethiel turned back, gazing through the faint moonlight. In the shadows beside the ruined house burned a fallen seraph. A serpentine temptress wound around him.

Shebethiel shuddered. "How many horrors must we gaze on in a day?"

Barbelo caught his jacket sleeve and pulled him away. "I agree with Azaziel. He's done good work with Lorelei. In fact, I think Aza has put the succubus's feet on the road to redemption. What's going on back there is a mystery unfolding."

Rather than debate, Shebethiel flung wide his wings and fled.

"Did you see that?" Kim gasped, unable to blink the vision from his eyes.

Sammy stared in more or less the same direction and burped. "You trippin'?"

"You didn't see it?" Kim repeated.

"Nothin' there, Kid."

Kim shook his head. He had seen something, he was certain. A flash brighter than a half-stick of dynamite had resolved into a figure with enormous wings. Lorelei's magic had called an angel.

Shebethiel landed behind Aza in the ruins of the church. Even before he turned, Aza could see the new angel was incandescent with fury. Aza wondered what had happened now and how he was responsible.

He didn't have to wait to find out.

"I tried to keep an open mind," the childbed angel said in a low, tight voice. "I can see how you find her pretty. But the succubus does not treat sex as the sacrament it's meant to be. Watching her with those young men… It reminded me of Sophia, swarmed by all the seraphs, one after another after another…"

Although he hadn't been there at the time, Aza remembered the stories about Sophia and her suitors. After the creation of the first woman, the

Almighty had inspired Lilith to adore Adam. Before long, Lilith's adoration had taken a physical turn. For that initial season of love, there was no separating the first humans.

Then, of course, Adam had to ruin it by demanding that his mate lie submissively beneath him. When Lilith left the garden and Adam to his uncomprehending grief, Eve was created. It didn't take long for Adam to initiate her into the pleasures of love.

The angels, most of whom watched from the Celestial City, were naturally curious to taste those pleasures themselves.

Aza and the others stationed around the garden were aware of the mass field trip to Earth, but since the ensuing orgy took place far from the garden, he and the other Watchers hadn't understood the ramifications of it.

Until Sophia's belly began to swell.

"Did you participate?" Aza asked Shebethiel. Aza was certain the answer would come to him, if he wanted, but it was always better to allow other angels to tell their own stories.

"What?" Shebethiel sputtered.

"With Sophia?" Aza clarified. "Were you there when Barbelo was conceived?"

The childbed angel glared at him. "I'm telling you that your hell-spawned girlfriend is conducting an orgy on cursed ground with a handful of young men…"

Aza considered the way that was phrased. "Conducting" made it sound as if Lorelei was in charge of the experience, that she wasn't in any danger from her suitors. He'd spied on her working before, watched her seduce and encourage her willing partners. Lorelei was not like her sisters, in that she rarely resorted to pushing her attentions on anyone unwilling. As far as Lorelei seemed concerned, there were simply too many fish in the sea to settle for bad sex.

Aza's thoughts turned back to Shebethiel. No childbed angels had been required on Earth originally. Before Satan tempted Eve with the apple, humans—like angels—felt no shame in their nudity. Once the Almighty discovered that his creations had tasted the fruit of the Tree of Knowledge, humans were ejected from the garden. From that point on, women were cursed to bear their offspring in pain.

As Sophia bore Barbelo in pain and blood.

"Are you one of Barbelo's fathers?" Aza asked.

Shebethiel shuddered. Without a word, he vanished. And Aza understood that the answer to his question was yes.

He wondered why the childbed angel had been assigned to Los Angeles. Shebethiel could do some real good here, with his genuine compassion and care for humans. That is, he could do good, if he didn't succumb to anger and hatred first.

After she'd pulled all the energy from the gang she could, Lorelei took Hai back to Chateau Marmont. He really didn't rate it and he certainly didn't deserve it, but she was tired and hadn't slept in a bed since she'd left the hotel on Saturday evening. After two very full days and all the trouble she'd seen, Lorelei wanted someplace familiar. She wanted the illusion of safety, even if there was no real security to be had.

Most mortifying of all, she didn't want to be alone.

In the morning, she roused Hai out of her bed and had him drop her off at the Galleria, so she could replenish her wardrobe. She'd decided that she sort of liked the Issey Miyake dress she'd left lying in the long grass at the old coven house.

CHAPTER 11: LEGERDEMAIN

As he stood in the vacant playground outside the ruins of his home, Aza removed Barakiel's feather from his coat pocket. He stroked it back into its simple, lovely shape. He formed a brief prayer in his thoughts: "Rafael, when you have a moment, could you send someone to check on Barakiel?"

Despite the scent of wet ashes on the breeze, Aza found himself smiling fondly at the name. Once Barakiel had been a Watcher, like Aza himself, assigned to Earth in the days before the Flood to guide humans as they roamed the Holy Lands.

In those far-off days, many angels struggled with their duties. The voice of their Creator, so distinct while they served in Heaven, was frustratingly distant—and occasionally distorted—while they went about their assignments on Earth. In Heaven, angels worked together in ranks: always we and never I. On Earth, they could be posted to small tribes of humans—or even smaller family groups—working alone amongst the creatures who had supplanted them in their Master's plans.

Many Watchers, in those days, found their jobs lonely. Some solved that by taking mortal wives, as Aza had. Others fathered half-monstrous children who became the Nephilim. Still others—Barakiel among them—taught humanity various sciences and arts, trying to recreate the Heaven they had left behind.

Barakiel taught humanity the science of probability, introducing them to games of chance. Aza could believe that Barakiel's instruction began innocently enough, but what started as entertainment turned eventually to addiction. And the demons, ever eager to swell their numbers, played upon Barakiel's guilt to tilt him into a crisis of faith that left him stranded on Earth, barred from Hell and longing for Heaven.

Father Joseph believed the fallen angel could be redeemed. Lorelei suspected it. Without a doubt, Asmodeus ordered the destruction of Santa Rosa's as a punishment for Barakiel's yearning toward the light.

Aza sent a second prayer upward to Heaven. "Father, if it serves Your will, please allow Barakiel to come home."

Lorelei sat in the bus stop outside the Galleria, mulling her next move. Shoplifting had gotten too easy to be satisfying anymore. Maybe it was time to start boosting Rodeo Drive again. Maybe it was time to find someone to "shop" for her. Maybe she was just craving Azaziel's company and nothing was going to satisfy her until she got it.

Still, her new Dolce & Gabbana pumps were awfully sweet. Lorelei curled her legs so that she could admire the shoes. They were a swoosh of chromed steel built like four-inch heels, but since the shoes were metal rather than leather, they required no heel to support them. They were polished enough that she could check her lipstick in them. And they were padded so generously inside that they were completely comfortable. She could stand around in these all day, with her legs stretched to best effect, and everyone would assume she was in excruciating agony for the sake of beauty.

She wished she had somewhere to show them off.

As if in answer, a gold-tone BMW M3 pulled up in the bus stop in front of her. Lorelei looked up from her shoes to find Tuan Nguyen leaning across the passenger seat. "Are you stranded?" he called out the open window.

"Considering my next move." Lorelei swept up the shopping bag stuffed with three new black dresses and leaned down to the window. The neckline of her dress opened up nicely, giving Tuan yet another reminder how she was built differently than her sister.

"I didn't really think you were waiting for the bus." Tuan bundled his satchel off the passenger seat onto the floor and pushed the door open for her. "Wanna get an early dinner?"

The invitation didn't have any warmth. Lorelei's eyes narrowed momentarily, faster than the boy could perceive. He wasn't asking her along because he had any desire for her company. He wasn't beaming especially friendly vibes at her. Was he here because Floria demanded it? And if that was the case, what did her sister want?

"What do you have in mind?" Lorelei asked skeptically.

"I'm off to a café on Melrose to do some business. They usually comp me for delivering to them at work."

That seemed harmless enough: free dinner from speed freaks. Lorelei didn't see how she could get into any trouble. And it wouldn't hurt to visit Daniel while she was up on Melrose.

"Sounds like fun." Lorelei tucked her shopping bag behind the seat and climbed in.

The "café" was funky swank. Lorelei stopped in front of the hostess stand, swaying in her tall shoes. The sweet slip of a boy stationed there studiously ignored her, to give her time to appreciate his position of power. Then he looked up. His gaze immediately slid past her to Tuan. Admiration glinted in his eyes. How could you not appreciate those pretty Vietnamese features?

"Is Marci working today?" Tuan asked.

"Would you like to sit in her section?" the maître d' asked haughtily.

"Please."

Without another word, the maître d' turned on one Cuban heel and strode off between the white-draped tables. His perfect gym-molded body swayed with restrained drama. Lorelei sauntered after him, marveling that none of WeHo's many incubi had snapped him up yet.

Tuan followed silently. Today he was dressed in black leather jeans and a soft, very black T-shirt, one whose maker Lorelei didn't immediately gauge. He looked very expensive. That was one thing Lorelei could appreciate about Floria's taste: her boys might be living the gangsta lifestyle, but when they were doing business, she didn't allow them to run around all flashy in bling and saggy pants. They looked respectable. They looked like model/actors or dancer/singers, but they didn't look like the street-trash drug dealers they were. It bought them access their wardrobe preferences would never breach, like this place. Heads turned as they passed. Lorelei was glad some of that attention was directed at her new shoes.

The young maître d' placed two menus on an empty table in the garden patio and left without another glance at Lorelei. His smile for Tuan went unanswered.

Lorelei took the chair facing the room before Tuan could get to it. They hadn't been seated long before a lovely African American girl in a long white apron bustled up. Her hazel eyes had an avid shimmer.

"Hi, Tuan! Want the regular?"

"That'd be great, Marci. Thanks." Changing the subject away from food, he asked, "You want the regular, too?"

"Yes, please."

In her anticipation, she barely remembered to look at Lorelei and do her job. "Can I get you something, too?"

The succubus hadn't had time to open the menu. "I'll have whatever Tuan's having."

The waitress nodded and rushed off.

"What are we having?" Lorelei asked.

"Pizza," Tuan said. "When was the last time you ate that?"

The succubus thought about it. "It's been a while."

As Lorelei touched up her lipstick, Tuan slipped Marci's envelope into the blue leatherette menu.

He'd barely finished when Marci scurried back with the wine list. She picked up the menus, checked inside the top one, and grinned.

"Have fun," Lorelei teased.

"I will," Marci said, already hurrying back to the kitchen.

"Service is fast here," Lorelei commented.

"You can see why," Tuan said unhappily. "They're good customers." He opened the wine list and surreptitiously counted the bills inside, before tucking them into his jeans pocket.

A Filipino girl, just as pretty as the first, brought a bottle of Chianti for the table. She gave Tuan a wink.

While they waited for their pizzas, Tuan seemed determined to work his way through the bottle of Chianti. Whether because he didn't want the comped wine to go to waste, because he didn't want to insult the staff's hospitality by not drinking it, or to assuage his guilt for amping up the entire waitstaff, Lorelei wasn't sure.

Finally he broke the silence. "Floria is really pissed about last night."

"What did you do last night?" Lorelei asked.

The young man's laugh was harsh. "I was in bed early. This time, it's you who set her off."

Lorelei had a sinking feeling. "What did I do now?"

"Hai was walking funny when he came by this morning. Didn't take her much to goad him into boasting about where he slept last night. Then she pushed him into spilling the rest of your gangbang."

Lorelei sipped her wine to give herself a chance to reconsider the really bitchy remark burning across her tongue. Turned out there wasn't enough wine to change her mind about venting it. "Floria's just jealous she didn't think of fucking all of them first."

"Prolly," Tuan conceded, too resigned to be provoked. "But you could have invited her along."

Lorelei realized it hadn't even occurred to her. The night had been about getting the cannon fodder thinking of her fondly. Floria's response hadn't even come into the equation. "Whoops."

"It doesn't matter now. Damage is done. But then Floria saw the blood all over Hai's truck…"

"He hit a coyote last night."

"That's what he said. But Floria went ballistic. Hai's gonna be detailing that RAV with a toothbrush, if he knows what's good for him. You know how Floria is about keeping a low profile."

Tuan fell silent as the pizza was delivered to the table. Lorelei raised her eyebrows at the chichi pie placed in front of her. It was covered in puréed spinach, mushrooms, and three kinds of cheese on a cornbread crust. She set to work on it with real hunger.

Muriel spun around, only to find herself trapped between the pillar-like arms of a ludicrous demon in a rainbow of mismatched clothing. He grinned at her with teeth like yellowed ivory as he backed her against the wall of the Beth el Rashael synagogue.

Muriel threw her body from one side to the other, trying to burst from the trap. The demon merely watched her with the same inane grin. He was as terrifying as a ventriloquist's dummy.

"Settle down, Little Sister."

"I'm not your sister," Muriel snarled. She wished she had her sword now. It was a full-body craving, a sickness like an addiction. "Let me go."

"You look like a moth trying to bash its way out of a killing jar," Mastema said. "I just want to talk."

"Talk to Azaziel," she spat at him.

"I have."

At that assurance, Muriel felt a modicum of calm settle over her. She drew a deeper breath. "Is it settled then? Azaziel is joining the infernal ranks?"

"As you know," the demon said, "our forces will soon join in glorious—" his tone mocked the word "—battle. Allegiances will alter as the battle rages," Mastema predicted.

Muriel shivered at something in his voice, something that sounded like fate. She didn't really comprehend why the Creator allowed such a creature to police the chasm between angelic and infernal, but she had seen Mastema before—from a distance—and knew he was charged with overseeing those too compromised to be true angels but not baleful enough to be admitted into Hell.

Now that she dwelt on it, that described Azaziel all too well. Perhaps...could Azaziel be a double agent? Did he actually work for Hell amidst Heaven's hosts?

The demon leaned back from her, still grinning. Now his expression held a hint of menace that chilled Muriel to her core. Like a three-card monte player in the back of a city bus, Mastema produced a business card.

"Call me, Muriel," the demon instructed. "When you see something, say something."

He vanished abruptly. The business card—shiny black, embossed with his glyph in crimson ink—drifted lazily downward like a feather.

Muriel contemplated letting it fall. At the last minute, before she needed to stoop after it, she snatched the card out of the air. She really didn't have anywhere to put it, other than the pocket of her warmup jacket, but she didn't really want it in there, for her hand to find whenever she had a quiet moment. As she stared at the card, trying to figure out what to do with it, it burst into a puff of acrid smoke, shriveling in on itself. When it disappeared, it left a blackened smudge on her palm.

Muriel frowned at the mark. She rubbed at it with her thumb, but the blotch wouldn't be erased. She pressed harder, without effect. Panicking, she chafed her hand against the leg of her pale gray track suit. The sooty stain would not be dislodged.

The breath caught in Muriel's throat like a sob. What was she going to do?

Then a thought came to her like the clarion peal of a bell. Maybe the demon's mark would evaporate when Azaziel finally completed his fall.

She drew a longer, soothing breath. She would have to watch for the time in the coming battle when she could unmask Azaziel at last.

On their way out of the cafe, Marci caught up with Tuan. "Thanks!" she chirped with intensity.

"You're welcome," Tuan muttered, less than gracious.

Lorelei couldn't help but smile. The girl was practically strobing. Floria had better start coming by to meet the staff here, or someone else was going to swoop in and collect their souls when they wilted like tulips. Floria would be left with their money, sure, but when did that really matter?

"Let me introduce you to Joshua," Marci continued. "He's new." She led them to the maître d' stand. "Josh? This is Tuan."

The boy's eyes were much brighter now. His smile was fast enough that it might have been a nervous tic. He shook Tuan's hand and nodded at Lorelei. "I'll remember you next time," he promised.

Lorelei grinned, certain that he would. The memory was probably branded into his brain.

Once the café's door had closed behind them, Lorelei asked, "Can we make a stop before you take off?"

She led Tuan down to the less fashionable end of Melrose, away from the designer boutiques and overpriced restaurants. When she stopped, the shop's windows were smeared with dust, less as a decorative motif than as a philosophical statement. A mangy taxidermy chimpanzee crouched on a threadbare purple silk cloth. Beneath one of its paws rested a human skull, spade marks still visible on the dirt-scuffed cranium. Secondhand paperback books on ritual magic and serial killers formed a circle around the monkey. Their covers were marked with masking tape that quoted very reasonable prices.

"What are we doing here?" Tuan asked.

"Picking up a gift for Floria." Lorelei swung the door open. The room smelled musty, with an undertone of unpleasant incense. Lorelei wound through the jumble of glass cases filled with charms. Tuan tore his eyes away from Lorelei's juicy ass, only to meet the gaze of the guy behind the counter. He looked like a wax figure with watery colorless eyes. Then he blinked.

"Hi, Daniel," Lorelei cooed. "I need to go through my stuff."

The old man shifted his gaze to her. He manipulated the ropy muscles of his face into a corpse's grin. "I've missed you."

"It's been too long, hasn't it?" She slipped into his arms, pressing herself against him, and pulled his head down to meet her kiss. When his tongue searched her mouth hungrily, Tuan turned away.

The old guy started to heave in Lorelei's arms. Tuan twisted back to stare at them in shock. Lorelei was smiling against Daniel's lips. With one painful lurch, he coughed up a key. Lorelei caught it between her teeth, then reached up to take it with her fingers. "Thank you, Daniel."

In an old man's emphysematic wheeze, he asked. "When will you come spend the night again?"

"Have you been missing me?"

He guided her free hand to the front of his trousers and let her find out for herself.

Tuan fought back a shudder, desperately looking for anything in the shop that wouldn't freak him out on some level.

"I'll work you into my schedule soon," Lorelei promised. "Maybe I can swing you a whole weekend."

"How long has that been?" He gave Tuan a death's-head grin and waggled his enormous gray eyebrows. Then he came around the counter and used a key from the ring in his pocket to unlock a closet tucked into the corner of the magic shop. Tuan noticed that the book Daniel had laid down on the counter when they came in—the one he'd been reading—was called Killing for Company.

Lorelei ducked into the walk-in closet. Tuan followed her, more comfortable in her company than alone with the skeezy shop owner.

Lorelei knelt in front of an old-style steamer trunk. Standing on its end, it was more than waist high. She fit the key Daniel had coughed up into the trunk's ornate lock plate and turned it three times. After the third twirl, the trunk unlocked with a thump. Lorelei pushed the two sides of the trunk apart. Each half was lined with heavy particleboard drawers.

As Lorelei opened the drawers and rummaged around in them, Tuan said quietly, "He doesn't look good."

"Who, Daniel? Always three steps ahead of death." She shrugged but didn't turn away from her chest of drawers. "He wanted to live forever. He didn't ask for eternal youth."

"One of yours?"

"One of the early ones."

Lorelei pulled out a couple of dresses, some prescription vials, and a roll of bills.

Curiosity got the better of Tuan. "Is this everything you own?"

"I've got a couple of other trunks stashed here and there. Floria does, too." She glanced over her shoulder for his reaction.

Tuan wasn't sure if he was meant to feel jealous that Floria kept her past and possessions from him. To be honest, he was relieved not to have been drawn into it. He changed the subject back. "You are powerful enough to keep someone alive forever?"

"It's a matter of separating the soul from the flesh," Lorelei said offhandedly. "In the state I found Daniel in, it wasn't as difficult as it sounds."

"Is his soul in Hell already?"

The succubus shook her head. "It's hidden."

"Does Daniel know where it is?"

She laughed. "He can't get it, give it up, or die, without my permission."

Tuan felt as shocked as he was fascinated. "What if he's in an accident or something?"

"He'd just better hope he's not in an accident."

"Why does he live in earthquake country, then?"

She looked at Tuan like he was stupid. " 'Cause somebody's got to watch my stuff, Tuan. Daniel watches my stuff and I keep an eye on his soul and he gets to live until he begs me to let him die. Not an elegant arrangement, but I was young when I set it up."

"How old were you?" Tuan asked.

Lorelei stepped out of the closet to ask, "How old are you, Daniel?"

He shrugged. "I was born the 19th of February in the year 1832."

"Had enough?" Lorelei teased.

"Not yet."

She grinned as she went back to searching through the trunk. "Eternal devotion," she marveled to Tuan. "Hard to believe he really meant it."

Tuan felt his stomach spasm in disgust. Every time he started to think that Lorelei was the better sister, the more compassionate one, he discovered something horrifying like this.

One of the drawers clattered, full of brightly colored laminated cards. "What's that?" Tuan asked, grateful for the distraction. He had to get it together.

Lorelei slid some of the cards out, turning them over in her fingers as she handed them to Tuan: The Rolling Stones, David Bowie, Pink Floyd, Led Zeppelin, The Doors...all the dinosaurs of rock. Most of the laminates said, "All Access." "Me and Floria worked the rock shows," Lorelei explained. "Back in the day."

She closed that drawer and opened the next. A stench oozed out like the damp, dense darkness of a swamp. Lorelei pushed that drawer firmly shut and opened the next without comment.

This drawer was filled with diamond rings. There were easily fifty or sixty of them, each representing a broken engagement. Lorelei dug through them as if they meant nothing to her. Tuan felt ill.

"There it is!" Lorelei pulled out a crumpled-up newspaper and handed it to Tuan. Afraid of what he might find, he gingerly unwrapped the package. Despite the closet's dim lighting, crimson gems flashed inside the nest of paper.

The succubus hooked the necklace with her forefinger and held it up to make it shimmer. Five square rubies burned like the deepest hearts of Hell among a constellation of diamond chips.

"Where's the newspaper from?"

Lorelei traced the name at the top of the paper with her left forefinger. "Pravda. The headline says, 'The Socialist Fatherland is in danger.'"

"What's that mean?"

"The Nazis had invaded Russia. 1941." She smiled. "That was a good year. People were lining up to get into Hell."

Tuan recoiled in horror. "A Nazi gave you this?"

"No, a communist did. Floria ought to love it. It is totally worth me gangbanging a handful of boys that she doesn't give a fuck about." Lorelei held the necklace out to Tuan. "Do you want to present it for me?"

"I'm gonna meet up with her tonight," Tuan said, staring, unseeing, at the gems. He had to play this very carefully. Floria had stressed repeatedly that Lorelei could not suspect a thing. "Wanna come along?"

"Might as well," the succubus decided. "Probably better if I apologize in person."

"Yeah," Tuan agreed. He thought his agreement sounded unconvincing. Lorelei didn't seem to notice.

CHAPTER 12: PANDEMONIUM

Tuan drove Lorelei over to Chinatown, circling around and around the little neon-spangled area to find street parking for his Beemer. Lorelei wondered why he didn't just avail himself of one of the many valets, but suspected—from the line of the boy's mouth—that he didn't want to spend the money. Even with the big drop-off on Melrose, cash was tight for the boy. Lorelei felt sorry for him, but what advice was she going to offer? There was no digging himself out of this hole. He'd gone in far too deep and he knew it.

A parking space, scarcely longer than the BMW itself, finally opened up on Yale. Tuan wedged his car between two SUVs without setting off anyone's car alarm. Lorelei wondered how many more payments he had on the Beemer, whether it was likely to still be sitting on the street when he returned. Maybe the insurance was worth more than trying to hold on to the car.

Tuan pulled a handful of leather straps from the glovebox and dropped them in Lorelei's lap. "Will you help me get these on?"

She sorted the silver-ringed cuffs from the spiked dog collar and helped him buckle each item on over his clothing. "This is making me hot," she confided.

Tuan laughed. "You don't ever stop, do you?"

"What fun is stopping?"

"You fucked all of Floria's boys last night. If you fuck me too, before we hook up with her tonight..."

"It'll be harder on you than on me," Lorelei understood. Floria's glyph was engraved on the dog tag swinging from his neck. "I'm not saying we should do anything. I'm just saying that suiting you up is getting me hot."

"Okay."

To her surprise, Tuan reached down to unzip his leather pants, lifting a rock-hard boner out of his Batman boxers. Lorelei scooted over on the leather seat, all but drooling, but Tuan halted her with a hand on her shoulder. "No touching," he said. "Floria will know. I'm not getting in any more trouble for you."

Her attention was drawn back to his busy hand. He wasn't interested in prolonging the sensation or making it good, he just wanted off and out of the car. Lorelei took his example and reached under her skirt. Still, she couldn't resist a pretty little moan as her fingers found the right trigger. They could still cum together, even if they were side by side.

They cleaned themselves up with a convenient box of tissues Tuan had stashed under the seat, then climbed out of the car. As they stood on the sidewalk and Tuan got his bearings, a cockroach ran past the open toe of Lorelei's shoe. The bug was practically big enough to skateboard on.

Lorelei hadn't been down to Chinatown in a while, at least not since Floria had hooked herself in with her gang of boys. The Vietnamese were a fairly marginal minority in LA, which made them a good place for a low-level player like Floria to begin. Not much in the way of infernal competition for them. The Chinese, however, had been in LA a long time, since the days of building the railroad and planting the orange groves. The devils that tended the Chinese went way back, too. They were powerful and touchy.

Tuan led Lorelei through Chinatown's Central Plaza, past all the gilt and red paint, the foo dogs and dragons, the show put on for tourists from the Midwest. Then he took an unexpected left turn down a back alley, filled mostly with a dumpster that reeked of rotting fish heads. He knocked on an unmarked door.

A little slot opened up, spilling a finger of light into the pungent alleyway. The fiend behind it looked them over, then slammed the window shut. After a long moment intended to inflict doubt on the unworthy, he yanked the door open.

Whoever had soundproofed the joint, they were good. Not a single beat trickled up the staircase behind the oversized fiend.

Lorelei handed over the company credit card before Tuan could pull his wallet from his jeans. Asmodeus's glyph burned in the holographic window.

Snatching his hand back before he touched the card, the fiend growled uncertainly, "Can't accept that."

"Since when is the boss's credit not good in his own city?" Lorelei demanded.

The fiend dodged the question. "Cash only."

"Fuck it, Tuan, let's go," Lorelei said, spinning on her toe. "You know Hai was up at Asmodeus's house yesterday morning. Ever wanted to see it for yourself?"

"Wait, wait, wait," the fiend begged. "Lemme check it."

Damn, Lorelei loved making him squirm. Clearly the fiend wanted to slam the door shut and have a little privacy to call the manager, but he was afraid that if he let her out of his sight, she was going straight to the Prince of LA to report the irregularity. The fiend thumbed open the microphone clipped to his collar and mumbled into it. His eyes never left Lorelei's cleavage.

In the end, he caved, just as Lorelei expected. "Come in. You're comped tonight," he grumbled, but the edge had gone out of his voice.

Lorelei wondered who could make fiends behave. This might be a fun little party. She let Tuan precede her down the extremely steep stairs. Since there wasn't any hand railing, she used the young man's shoulder to steady herself in the heel-less chrome pumps.

They passed through a series of doors like airlocks, each one guarded by a fiend in a matching red silk jacket with a golden dragon coiling up one arm and hanging its head over his left shoulder. The dragons' eyes were real emeralds, flaring and flashing in the progressively dimming lights.

When Lorelei and Tuan reached the third airlock, a bassline thumped beyond the door. The tiny anteroom throbbed queasily. Lorelei glanced over to see Tuan nervously licking his upper lip. He avoided her gaze. Lorelei was surprised he regretted their little circle jerk upstairs, since it had been his idea. She wondered if that was the sort of experience he shared with Hai or the other boys. The image made her grin. Too bad she hadn't gotten herself a show as a wrap-up to the gangbang last night.

The final door slid open to reveal the party beyond.

The club was the size of a two-car garage, jammed with more than a hundred people. They were, what, in the third sub-basement? For certain the fire marshal didn't know about this place. Lorelei thrummed with happiness. She trailed Tuan to the bar, admiring the exquisite corsetry modeled around her. It was like being in a candy shop, with beautiful people in varying stages of restraint hobbling around. Sexual energies swirled like currents in the ocean.

Unlike most sex parties, no one but Tuan seemed to be a tourist. They were all craving, all available, and all eager to be hurt. Lorelei's head swam. How had she not known this place existed?

To order their drinks, Tuan squeezed past an androgynous amazon who flaunted her mastectomy scars above a barbed-wire waist-cincher.

Lorelei turned slowly, studying the room to see if there was anyone she recognized. For all the desperate yearning going on in the room, there were surprisingly few devils around to enjoy it. Just how exclusive was this place?

Up on the little stage, a matched pair of incubi were playing with fire. The woman they were tormenting was tied between a pair of columns by hanks of her long black hair, rayed out from her head like beams from a black sun. She wanted to sag to the floor, but the locks of hair would have been ripped from her scalp. Vanity—and the threat of permanent baldness—kept her on her feet, despite the pain. The incubi were experimenting with the flammability of various potions, which they drizzled or sprayed against her skin, then burned away. Her skin glowed in patches of angry, sensitized red, but they weren't scarring her. She'd be back for more until they did. Lorelei's mouth watered. Gluttony. That was mortal.

Above pounding music which made conversation impossible and screams invisible, a voice insinuated itself into her ear. "Get out now, Lorelei."

Goose flesh shivered over her skin. She turned to find Barbas, the maître d' from Asmodeus's Isfahan, behind the polished steel bar. She pasted a smile on her face. "Are you talking to me?"

"Friendly word of warning."

Something icy slithered up her spine. Lorelei glanced back at the door she'd just come through, to see a pair of fiends, pitchforks in hand, staring at her. Daring her to make a move.

"I think I missed my chance," she said quietly.

"Probably," Barbas agreed. "Would you like a drink, then?"

"Is this your place?"

"I just work here on fetish nights." He curled a finger to summon her to look behind the bar. Lorelei hopped up, laying on her belly across the bar so that her ass strained her dress for everyone to enjoy.

The floor of the narrow area behind the bar was carpeted with naked people. Each of them wore a World War I-era gas mask, which erased the individuality of their faces. Something was clearly being filtered through their breathing apparatuses, though, judging from the nerveless sprawl of their limbs.

Barbas had manifested his true form below the waist. He was one of the old-fashioned goat-footed devils, with razor-sharp black hooves. Bruises and cuts marred the nudists' perfect skins where his hooves had danced over them during the evening.

"Wow," Lorelei said with honest appreciation.

"Home away from home," Barbas agreed, with a fanged smile. "Drink?"

"Absolut cranberry."

He whipped one together as she scanned the room for Floria. If she was here already, she must be on her knees under one of the tables.

Barbas held a shimmery red drink out. Lorelei pressed herself up onto her arms, arching her back for the best display of cleavage, and planted a kiss on his cheek.

Barbas's smile was appraising. Then his gaze drifted over her shoulder. "Looks like a table's opened up for you."

Lorelei accepted the drink and went to look for Floria.

The tables were actually semi-private high-backed steel booths lining the walls opposite the bar and stage. Lorelei wandered past some occupied booths, where various sharp objects were being inserted or twirled in all too willing flesh. Tuan was snorting lines off of one tabletop. Lorelei found the table Barbas had intended for her and slid over on the cold polished steel bench. Probably the metal would heat up nicely with a little provocation. It also undoubtedly made the place easy to hose down, come morning.

She sipped the shimmery drink Barbas had poured for her. She tasted Absolut and unsweetened cranberry juice, her usual preference, but it was jazzed up with Goldslager and just a hint of innocent blood. She admired the flakes of real gold slowly dancing in suspension.

"Want some company?" Hai shouted over the apocalyptic rumble of the sound system. Lorelei jumped. How long had he been standing at the edge of the booth?

"What are you doing here?" Even as the words left her lips, she realized he was wearing a dog collar like Tuan's, tagged with Floria's glyph.

Hai slid into the booth to hug Lorelei, hard. She turned her cheek to avoid a sloppy kiss that would have smeared her lipstick. To make it up to him, she dropped her hand into his lap and found exactly what she expected. She pressed the heel of her palm down hard enough to unstring his limbs. "You want me here?" she whispered into his ear, confident that her voice would carry to the core of him.

"I don't know," he said uncertainly. "Fucking you in front of the boys was one thing. This place..." He waved his hand over his shoulder. "Let's just say: performance anxiety."

Lorelei grinned. "I'll make an exhibitionist out of you yet, Tiger."

He shook his head and set his familiar Altoids box on the matte black tabletop. "You wanna get high?"

Not shy about doing that in public, Lorelei noticed. "What do you have?"

"Sensimilla."

"Lovely."

He slipped a single skinny joint out of the Altoids box and pulled a Zippo lighter from his pocket. Lorelei glimpsed the Playboy bunny on it and shook her head ever so slightly. Sometimes the brash innocence of mortals was terribly sweet.

Hai lit the hand-rolled cigarette with a series of quick puffs, not really inhaling, then held it out to Lorelei. She lipped it from his fingers and drew hard on the joint. The smoke hadn't hit the bottom of her lungs before she knew this wasn't sensimilla. She exhaled hard, trying to cough out as much of the smoke as she could. It was too late. Her vision seemed to detach from her head. She wasn't sure she actually asked, "Floria give you this?"

Hai shook his head in response. "Yasmina did. She said it was killer."

All the liquid evaporated from Lorelei's mouth, leaving her tongue as desiccated as an empty cocoon. She fumbled after her drink with her free hand. She couldn't believe she'd walked into Yasmina's trap so blithely.

Hai took the joint from her nerveless fingers and looked at it, contemplating a real hit. She could see that the small amount he'd inhaled had slowed his movements like he was underwater.

"Powerful stuff," Lorelei complained, unable to say more. Her heart fluttered like a hummingbird's.

"Yeah," Hai agreed. Although he'd probably never done it before, he stubbed the barely smoked joint out in the Altoids box before pushing the box back into his jeans pocket.

"Now that he's done his job, your boy-toy has to go," Yasmina ordered. She stood just beyond the edge of the table, where the overhead light didn't reach. Floria stood beside her. Jezebel hung a few steps back.

Lorelei's hand banged awkwardly into Hai's. He patted her arm reassuringly. "I want to stay," Hai protested. "I want to see you do magic."

"It might get messy," Floria cautioned, pushing Lorelei's purse into his arms. "Go wait with Tuan at the bar."

"You wanna see some magic?" Yasmina teased. "Tell the bartender you want to look behind the bar." Yasmina's cruel laughter sparkled around them like a broken mirror. Lorelei's eyes met Floria's and they shared a thought: Bitch.

Lorelei made herself smile at Hai. "Give me a kiss for luck, Tiger."

Hai pulled her into his arms. His tongue slipped between her lips and she met it with her own. He tasted of cigarettes and tequila, tinged by traces of whatever had been in the joint. Lorelei felt the connection with him spark inside her body, before Floria tugged him away.

Lorelei stared at the elder temptress.

She was rewarded with a vision of Jezebel, her fresh scars livid, cowering at the foot of Asmodeus's throne in Hell, with Yasmina swaying over her. She still couldn't remember what the former succubus had done to rate such a punishment.

Lorelei was sober enough to know she had nothing to bargain with. What could you offer a creature who'd lived for millennia that she hadn't already stolen, sucked the enjoyment from, and discarded?

"Bring her," Yasmina ordered.

Jezebel and Floria grabbed Lorelei's limbs and hauled her up into the air. She thrashed in terror, more out of reflex than in any real hope of escape. Yasmina led the way up on to the stage. Floria and Jezebel tossed Lorelei down on the floor there and quickly cuffed her limbs to the rusted iron columns, using a system of hand cranks to hoist her, spread-eagled, into the air.

How could they do anything to her with Asmodeus's aegis still protecting her? Unless he'd decided that Lorelei wasn't bringing Aza down fast enough and had withdrawn his protection?

"Why?" Lorelei asked.

Yasmina grinned at her, revealing her fangs. "Because I liked that dress you left in the grass at the coven house."

Floria drew her dagger from the sheath on her thigh and ran its blade up inside the front of Lorelei's new Issey Miyake dress, leaving it to hang from her body in a tattered shadow. Lorelei couldn't believe Floria sent Tuan to lure her to be sacrificed to the temptress they both loathed. So what if Lorelei had fucked all of Floria's boys? It wasn't as if Floria actually liked any of them. And Lorelei had been ready to make amends...

Yasmina opened a lizard-skin case and lifted out a small glass vial. Lorelei writhed, remembering her nightmare about the tattoos that bound her to mortal form, but Yasmina wouldn't have needed to undress her for that.

Needle in one hand, Yasmina knelt between Lorelei's legs and breathed deep. "What a pity you girls were bred to be sterile. Perhaps if you could offer me Azaziel's first-born..."

Lorelei couldn't help herself. Knowing how cold demonic piercing needles were, she moaned. When she'd lost her nerve in Siberia, Asmodeus had ground a needle through the bone spurs atop her wings, setting in rings that he used to lock her wings together for torturous months. Lorelei knew it wasn't her wings that interested Yasmina tonight.

Jezebel handed her mistress a length of coarse black thread. Yasmina threaded it through the needle dramatically. The audience crowded breathlessly around the edge of the stage, shoving each other to get the clearest view between Lorelei's legs.

The succubus closed her eyes. She vowed she would die before she offered the temptress her soul. It was a comforting realization. Fucking bitch couldn't take that.

"Give me more room to work," the temptress demanded. Lorelei's legs were roughly yanked farther open. Floria straddled Lorelei's shin, rubbing her bare sex against it. Floria was sopping wet, turned on almost past endurance.

Lorelei laughed at her, trying to wreck Floria's pleasure with her scorn. She heard the noise echo as the DJ picked it up from the mic dangling overhead. He set the sound to a dance beat.

Yasmina pressed a needle like a sliver of arctic ice against Lorelei's sensitive nether flesh. The chill radiated through Lorelei, tendrils of it creeping through her nerves, crushing the breath from her lungs. Then Yasmina applied some force behind the point. Lorelei felt every millimeter of the metal as the temptress forced it through her labia. The thread, trailing behind, stung. Tears rose in Lorelei's eyes. Yasmina jammed the needle through the flesh on the other side, wiggling it a little just to be cruel, and drew the stitch tight. Unable to control herself any longer, Lorelei screamed.

Somewhere in the room a fiend laughed, like a stone pounding a skull to dust.

Yasmina began the next stitch.

Floria worked herself up to a sweaty, laughing orgasm. She didn't curse Lorelei or even taunt her. Lorelei could have been unconscious or otherwise oblivious to what she'd done to rate this punishment, but Floria, Queen of the Long-Term Grudge, didn't care. At this point, it was all about Floria's pleasure. And she was gonna take it out on Lorelei's flesh.

The patrons of the club gaped at the show. Lorelei stared into their faces, memorizing them all, mortal and infernal alike. Most of them she didn't recognize, but she saw the tempter who'd pulled over Tuan's car the night Lorelei met the archangel Michael. He saw something in her eyes that made him flinch away. Lorelei's grin was short-lived, because Yasmina began another stitch.

Shivering with ecstasy, the two harpies clung to each other's shoulders, propping each other up as they gaped slack-jawed at what their mistress was doing. They still looked like under-age street trash. Damia's ratty plaid skirt and knee socks should have attracted the attention of a certain kind of pedophile, but the club's other denizens gave the girls a wide berth. Just couldn't cover that harpy stink, Lorelei thought.

She endured another stitch, then immediately went back to cataloguing her audience. There weren't any demons here. In fact, there were no devils who outranked Yasmina. Not even Jequon was here. Only the tempter Barbas was still polishing glasses, back behind the bar.

Yasmina reached over her head and angled the black mirror above her so that Lorelei could get a clear view of the needlework already finished. Worse, she could see how much was left to be done.

Lorelei didn't let herself be mesmerized by the image. She looked past it to find Hai. He sat at the bar beside Tuan, avidly watching the show in the mirrored bar-back. Tuan hunched miserably over a collection of emptied shot glasses. Lorelei wondered if he still had her ruby necklace in his pocket.

A dozen stitches later, Lorelei had screamed herself hoarse to absolutely no effect.

The power in the club suddenly went out. The abrupt blackness was less shocking than the subsequent silence that stuffed the room. With the sound system assassinated, the only noise remaining was Lorelei's ragged breathing.

Yasmina spat a curse that should have burned in the air. Instead, darkness swallowed it.

Before panic set in and people trampled each other in a rush for the narrow staircase, a thin thread of music began to play. The little music box melody grew steadily louder. If Lorelei had had any strength left, she would have laughed. Someone's ringtone played Mike Oldfield's "Tubular Bells"—the piece known more popularly as the theme to The Exorcist.

"Whose goddamn phone is that?" Yasmina roared.

The music continued, growing more self-assured. Finally, Hai spoke up. "It's Lorelei's. It's coming from Lorelei's purse."

"Bring it here," the elder temptress commanded, totally disregarding the fact that they stood in a pitch-black room stuffed with sharp-edged costumes.

Hai dug the phone out of Lorelei's purse. Its small white light barely penetrated the darkness. The soundtrack music grew more insistent. Whether the boy reacted from the programmed response of a human being faced with a ringing phone—or an even greater compulsion, he answered it. "Hello?"

Lorelei heard a sound that she suspected was the temptress gnashing her teeth, unused to being disobeyed.

"It's for you, Yasmina," Hai said. "It's Mr. Prince."

He used the glow from the phone's screen to light his way across the room. The crowd parted for him, shrinking from the tiny glow like feral creatures.

As she reached for the phone, Yasmina was visible as a towering snakelike monster, armed with hideously long talons. Still, she was gentle as she took the phone from Hai. Then she destroyed whatever cred she had among her sycophants when she bleated into the phone, "Yes, Master?"

Lorelei couldn't hear the other side of the conversation, but she could feel the heat of the shame radiating from Yasmina's skin. Moving silently around the stage, Jezebel uncuffed Lorelei's ankles. She gently lowered Lorelei's feet to the floor one at a time, then steadied her as she stood on her Dolce & Gabbana pumps. Lorelei drew her legs together gingerly. Every little movement tugged on the stitches and hurt.

When at last her hands were free, she reached down between her thighs and caught the silver needle. She pulled the thread taut, twisted it around her fingers, and broke it off. She flung the needle like a dart at Yasmina.

Whether Yasmina pulled her slave forward to take the sting or Jezebel threw herself in front of her mistress, the needle sank deep into flesh that could make no noise in response.

Lorelei met the ruined succubus's sweet brown eyes and mouthed, "Sorry."

Jezebel blinked in surprise.

Yasmina hung up the phone, shutting off the last light in the sub-sub-basement.

Then the club's music crashed in to fill the vacuum, full volume and pounding. The lights blazed back to life, all the more painful for the blackness they replaced. Even so, the party was clearly over. Everyone seemed deflated now, drained of energy, humiliated by their desires. A queue formed for the coat check as the crowd faced the long slow slog up all those stairs to the street, back to their everyday lives.

Humanoid once more, Yasmina snatched the purse from Hai, threw the phone into it, and shoved it at Lorelei.

Lorelei gave her a smile that promised every retribution she could bring to bear, from now until the sun burned itself out.

"Now, girls," Barbas chided. He took Lorelei's forearm and steered her offstage and down a little hallway toward the back office. She would have moved more slowly, without his hand pressing into the small of her back.

Beyond the office's open door, Lorelei saw a portal chalked on the wall. "Where does it go?" she asked, her voice hoarse.

"Someplace you'll feel safe." Barbas used his red silk pocket square to wipe the tear-smudged makeup from her face. "You still have your soul-catcher in your bag?"

Lorelei felt around inside the purse and found her little obsidian knife. She nodded.

"That ought to take those stitches right out," he encouraged. "You'll probably need a mirror, too, but you girls never travel without one, do you?"

Lorelei changed the subject. "Shall I tell the boss you helped me out of here?"

"Tell him whatever you like, Lorelei." The tempter shrugged. "He asked me to moonlight here on my days off from Isfahan."

"Is this his club or Yasmina's?" she demanded.

"What do you think?"

"Are you working here because you like her, or because you want to be standing there when she's brought down?"

He wagged his finger at her. "That's tough talk from someone who's just survived a little non-consensual embroidery. Asmodeus called her off, but he didn't come here to rescue you. Don't count on him backing you up when you get ready for payback. He's owned her for a long time..."

Lorelei interrupted him. "Since before the Flood, she said."

"Exactly. He's had a long time to play with her, to get attached to how she feels in his hands when he sets her to work. You're not going to get between them unless you bring Azaziel to heel." He smiled at her. "It's a pity you girls can't see eye to eye over that angel. Yasmina may be the Penultimate Bitch, but she's also good for laughs."

Lorelei snorted. "Speaking of which: why did he pick The Exorcist theme as his ringtone?"

"That movie has led more eager high school boys to the occult sections of their local secondhand bookshops than any other film Asmodeus caused to be made." He turned her around, swatted her on the butt, and laughed when she winced. "On your way. Go consider what your uses to the Prince of LA may yet be."

As Lorelei stepped into the opening in the office wall, she felt the portal's heat crawl over her skin like a thousand cockroaches, then stepped through the other side. There were a lot of places Lorelei expected the portal might transport her: poolside of Asmodeus's house, her room at Chateau Marmont, the back of the boss's limo. Instead, she found herself atop the dome of the Griffith Observatory.

So the question, of course, was why? Why would Barbas make a portal to this place? Why would he plant it on the back wall of Yasmina's office, unless to taunt the bitch with Lorelei's escape?

Lorelei spun to face the portal, determined to protect her back. She discovered that the portal's edges were already shriveling like paper gone to black ash, curling and flaking, blowing away on the wind coming from the desert beyond the San Gabriel Mountains. Barbas was closing the portal.

Why did he help her? The advice he'd given her sounded genuine. What was he going to want from her later?

Lorelei huddled atop the observatory dome, chin on knees. The city lights twinkled below, millions of stars, millions of lives. She had never felt so terribly alone. Even Floria had turned on her now, although that had always only ever been a matter of time, but she'd also been betrayed by Tuan and Hai. She'd made enemies fearsome and mundane, and for what? An angel who wouldn't run away with her.

She had been so foolish. She hadn't understood what an angel was, how different he was from human. As Asmodeus promised, an angel's fall could not be accomplished overnight, despite the myths of her childhood. Celestial time flowed differently than the progression of Earthly days and nights. Demons understood that—hell, the Fallen understood that—since they'd all lived under Celestial time before the First War. Lorelei realized she'd never had a clue.

Asmodeus certainly understood she'd never had a chance of success. Still he'd provoked her pride and set her to the task, then stood back to await the inevitable. Why not? She'd been created for one purpose: ensure the damnation of her prey. If she chose to prey on angels, she risked only herself. If, through some quirk of Azaziel's, he actually fell, Hell stood enriched. If—predictably—she failed, the only sacrifice was one foolish succubus. No doubt Asmodeus groomed her replacement even now. She'd probably been one of the girls lounging around his pool.

So where did that leave her, the compassionate devil? Sure, she'd fucked all of Floria's minions, but Lorelei had consciously left their souls alone. How could she continue to exist outside of nature?

The answer finally came clear to her: she wasn't outside of nature. Creation must have made a place for her.

She sat with that realization. The freedom she had tasted momentarily in Isfahan, when she snatched her own pleasure from Asmodeus's grasp, came back to her. She was a succubus with a soul. She was singular in Creation. Even Jequon had hinted at it: she was free to choose.

The thought chilled her all the way through.

Lorelei had believed that she was already damned for things done before she grew a soul, but that wasn't the way the universe worked. She was, in a manner of speaking, in a state of grace. She could ask to be saved.

Like that was likely. Maybe things would seem clearer, if her every thought wasn't tinged with pain. She opened her purse, pawed through it, and pulled out her lipstick case and the obsidian dagger.

The angle was going to be tricky. Getting her legs from closed to knees apart tugged the stitches and made the flesh swollen around them bleed. There wasn't much light on this moonless night, but Lorelei was determined and that always made her methodical. If only she'd been able to bring this much concentration to bear on bringing the angel down.

Fuck love, anyway.

At least the thought made her laugh.

Time for a little home surgery. She tucked the dagger's point inside the first stitch and gently, steadily, severed the thread.

Aza knelt on the roof of the tenement across the alley from Yasmina's club: Pandemonium, as if that was an original name for the place. He shook his head. You'd think, in all the long years of her life, Yasmina could have come up with something more creative.

People streamed out of the club's doorway. Some had knotted themselves into groups of twos or threes, but most were solo. Something had happened in the sex club that sucked the fun out of everyone's evening. It puzzled Aza. What had Yasmina done that jeopardized her hold on all these souls?

Lorelei was safely gone now. In his heart, Aza could feel the deep crimson pulse of her life-force back atop the observatory dome. She was in pain and angry, but no longer in danger.

Aza wasn't sure what he had meant to do here, anyway. He could have burst through the outer doors and fought his way through the fiends guarding each level, but whether he would have had the strength to fight his way back out, protecting the wounded succubus as he did so... Well, Shebniel was gone, Muriel was not likely to fight at his side again, and he could scarcely ask Barbelo to join him in this fight.

Aza was relieved that Lorelei had a friend inside the temptress's lair, whoever it was, to help her to safety.

Lorelei's sister Floria emerged from the club with Tuan Nguyen and Hai Ng. Even Floria, usually incandescent with rage, looked chastened. She'd molded herself close to the boys, trying to inspire them to some kind of protective lust. Whatever had happened in the club had frightened her. She wanted the boys as shields now.

Aza considered jumping down to demand some answers. He didn't relish being shot again by Hai Ng, but it might be fun to prove to the boy how little damage his infernal toys could do. In the end, Aza didn't see any point in antagonizing Floria. He had hoped that she might provide some protection for his Lorelei when she went among her own kind. Even if that looked no longer likely, Aza couldn't be the one who pushed Floria into becoming an active enemy. He let her pass in peace.

The humans had all gone by the time the ruined succubus Jezebel came upstairs to fetch Yasmina's town car. Yasmina herself waited until her driver had backed the sedan into the tight alley before she crept from the club's portal.

Aza jumped nimbly down in front of the car and impaled his sword through its engine block.

"Get him!" Yasmina screeched at her minion.

Even though Jezebel took no more than a half-hearted step in his direction, Aza didn't discount the harm she might do. "Don't interfere," he directed. He used the harmonics of the alley to amplify and echo his voice, but the words were merely words, not a divine injunction. Still, the succubus froze as if he had commanded her to.

"What do you want?" Yasmina demanded. She'd lost her semblance of humanity now. The oversized fangs that protruded from her upper jaw made her tricky to understand.

"This is your only warning," Aza told her. "If you ever harm Lorelei again, I will do what I should have done ages ago."

"What's that, Brother?" she bleated.

"Erase your miserable existence."

"But—"

Before she could remind him of his love for her sister oh so very long ago, Aza leapt for the sky. He gave it a moment, then called the sword to his hand, leaving the broken automobile blocking the alley beneath him.

CHAPTER 13: THE CONFLAGRATION BEGINS

While Lorelei watched from the observatory dome, fire broke out downtown. Flames leapt from the old Mission's roof, bright orange against the city lights, tinting a pillar of black smoke that swirled upward. Lorelei's heart sank. The attack had begun.

She wrapped her wings around herself and huddled into a shadow. She had no illusions that Asmodeus didn't know exactly where she was. If nothing else, his call to Yasmina's club proved that. The fact that he hadn't summoned Lorelei to go into battle yet meant little, other than he was too occupied to spare her a thought.

Lorelei wasn't sure how she felt about that. She should be getting credit for betraying the angel she loved, for giving Hell reason to fight. Instead, Hell had taken the opening she showed them and run with it. Her sense of indignation was followed by a wave of shame for having betrayed Aza, chased by a flush of anger, since she didn't understand what the angel had actually expected her to do about his little menagerie.

To be certain, Aza hadn't come to rescue her from Yasmina—and the temptress was much less formidable than Asmodeus. Clearly, that implied the angel would let Lorelei go to whatever punishment awaited her without stirring a feather.

For a moment, Lorelei missed Tibor. He was big and dumb, but he'd treated her well. She'd liked him. And he might have stood up for her against Yasmina and Floria.

More plumes of smoke rose over the city. Lorelei heard the faintest whine of sirens and sighed. She liked a good blaze as much as the next devil. It was so tempting to fly down and see what was going on, to join in the company of her own kind—except that her own kind had stitched up her currency, the heart of her existence, and made it a Grand Guignol lesson for mortals. Why would she even consider hanging out with her own kind?

Okay. Time to start looking ahead. Lorelei had done what she could to sway the cannon fodder into a self-sacrificing mood, but Tuan had served as the Judas Goat to deliver her to Floria's vengeance. Hai had gotten her too high to escape Yasmina—and he'd done it with intent and malice. Neither of them could be counted on to protect her when the shit poured down.

She'd best arm herself. Her little soul-collecting knife wasn't going to frighten anyone. She daydreamed about fearsome weapons. What if she had a bullwhip that would clear a radius around her? She imagined a deeply satisfying crack as the whip's end broke the sound barrier. Unfortunately, that would only be useful if the devils hunting her were armed with archaic weapons. She couldn't expect that to be the case.

Lorelei tore her gaze away from the conflagration building below. She reached into her purse and dug out the last remaining angelic bullet. It wouldn't kill an angel, which probably meant it wouldn't hurt a demon either. However, it might just take Yasmina out…if Lorelei could get a weapon to fire it. Maybe killing that bitch would get everyone else off her back.

Lorelei pulled the cell phone from her purse, turning it over in her hands. She couldn't call Azaziel even if she was inclined. He didn't own any conveniences of the modern age—no phone, no car, not even a gun—and he'd said that he wouldn't leave Los Angeles, so he didn't even offer her an escape.

Besides, her angel was undoubtedly busy squirreling away his surrogate children. He wouldn't have a moment to spare his would-be girlfriend. They hadn't parted on such great terms, anyway, arguing over whether she would allow him to send Hai's soul to its just destination. In light of current events, Lorelei wished she'd let Aza damn the stupid, greedy child before he could betray her. Twice.

Still, if she were honest with herself, she'd flounced into Yasmina's trap on her own two Dolce & Gabbana-shod feet. She'd known that Floria would be pissed about the little romp Lorelei had had with her boys, but in Lorelei's mind, the bribe she was offering had already been accepted. Lorelei had never doubted Tuan, even when the boy began to crack under the strain of playing Judas. She liked him. He liked her. Lorelei never looked beyond that.

She shivered. The outcome could have been so much worse and it would have been all Lorelei's own damn fault. She was very lucky to be alive.

She took a deep breath, trying to taste the ashes in the air. So. If you were the demon prince of LA and you planned to send a barely armed succubus who'd never had any combat training into a battle between the General of Hell's Armies and Michael, the warrior archangel, you were expecting to have that succubus quickly taken off your hands. Rather than done privately, in a club packed with damned souls, you wanted her sacrificed in front of the angel she had been lusting after. You wanted her executed at the best possible moment, to precipitate his fall through despair and remorse if concupiscence alone wouldn't tip the scale.

149

All she needed to do in the coming fight was to avoid all her enemies and stay away from Azaziel. No problem.

Lorelei switched the phone on. There was only one person who'd helped her in recent days. The question was how to get in touch with her.

Lorelei rubbed her thumbs over the phone's tiny screen. It couldn't be that simple, could it? She typed in the angel's name.

Of course, the boss would undoubtedly be made aware that Lorelei reached out to the angels. It couldn't be helped. With luck, he'd be too busy organizing his attack to concern himself with this particular conversation.

The phone had barely rung when it was answered. "Hello, Lorelei."

Lorelei heard a smile in the angel's voice. It sounded welcoming. "Hello, Barb. Have a minute to chat?"

"All the time in the world," Barbelo said sweetly, making Lorelei believe it. "Do you want to do it like this or should I come over?"

"This is better," the succubus said, "if it's okay with you. I'm more comfortable like this."

"I understand."

Lorelei stretched out on her stomach, hooked her ankles together, and kicked her feet up behind her. If only she'd had a phone cord she could twist around her free hand... "I have a rather large favor to ask."

"Yes?"

"Could you help me get a weapon?" There was a silence long enough that Lorelei diagnosed hesitance. She clarified, "I need a gun."

Barbelo's response came quickly. "Not anything powerful enough to take angels down?"

"Hell, no," Lorelei said, shocked. "I don't want to tangle with any more angels. One has been quite enough."

Barbelo chuckled sympathetically.

"And while we're on the subject," Lorelei said, "how is his gunshot wound healing up?"

"You know those don't slow us down," Barbelo said. "He's doing well, if that's what you want to know. Missing you. Wishing you hadn't parted with harsh words."

Lorelei closed her eyes against the fires burning down below. "For what it's worth, I wish we hadn't fought either. But he backed me into a corner and I fucking hate that. Did he really expect me to see all those souls and just turn a blind eye?"

"No one expected that, Lorelei."

The succubus was about to demand an explanation, when Barbelo added, "You know, I understand your sense of morality. Aza does, too. You see the collection of souls in black and white. It's why you turned Yasmina in to your prince over what she did to Ashleigh and Deion. To be honest, we all knew that eventually some devil would stumble across what Aza was doing with those kids. To be frank, we were stunned you didn't see them the first time he brought you to the church. Probably we have Ashleigh's mortal spirit to thank for blinding you to them. Even so, all of us knew it was only a matter of time until the jig was up."

"Does he forgive me for turning him in?" Lorelei asked.

"To believe it, you'd need that answer to come from him." Barbelo surprised her by changing the subject back. "How much firepower are you looking for?"

"I just want something that will keep devils off of me," Lorelei said. "Something that would make them turn tail and leave me the fuck alone."

"Something charmed?"

"If it was charmed against devils, wouldn't it be charmed against me?"

"The rules have bent for you," Barbelo said. "You know that's true."

Lorelei thought of her realization that Nature had made a place for her. It creeped her out that the angel had come to the same conclusion. "I worry that if I get something too powerful, the demons will start wondering where I got it, what kind of deal I cut for myself. So it's got to be something that will fly beneath the radar."

"You have a lot of conflicting criteria," Barbelo observed. "I think I can find something for you, but first: quid pro quo. Do you know the scope of Asmodeus's plan?"

Panic choked Lorelei. Every instinct told her to hang up the phone now, break the connection, and fly for her life. Her voice tight with fear, Lorelei wondered, "What are you asking me, Barb?"

"Do you know if there's more to their attack than a couple of fires? Do you know when the main putsch will come?"

Lorelei wrapped her arms around her shoulders, digging in her nails to feel the pain. "Betray my master, Barbelo?"

"You betrayed Aza's trust," the angel reminded. "Here's a chance to redeem yourself."

Lorelei felt tears prickle her eyes. She told Barbelo the same thing she'd told Aza: "I only want to be beneath Heaven's notice."

Barbelo chuckled sympathetically again. "It's much too late for that, Lorelei. But if you want my help, then help us out."

"I don't want it that badly," Lorelei said. "I can tell you this much: they'll kill me somewhere that Aza can watch. It will be spectacular and bloody. And if my death causes Aza to fall, then Hell stands enriched and I'll be accorded a martyr. Fuck you all, angel. See you in Hell."

Shaking, Lorelei severed the phone connection. She couldn't believe that she'd ever thought Barbelo might be her friend. The angel had been helping Lorelei all along only to shield and support Azaziel. Well, fuck them all, individually and in a big feathered pile. They could choose to protect their illegal store of kids or they could protect the succubus they'd dragged into the middle of their reindeer games. She was almost ready to cash out, anyway. The rules were getting so warped and bent around here that it was like staggering around in a funhouse. Lorelei longed for the old days, when enmities and friendships were clear-cut and the only person she was certain she could count on was herself. Time to forget about the Long Game and go back to looking out for Number One.

She wondered who else she might touch for a weapon. If Mastema helped her, what would it cost in exchange? Was there anyone who thought she was worth protecting, even if they wanted to use her for their own ends?

As if he'd been summoned by her desperation, Beelzebub stepped out of a portal to stand over her on the dome. The ends of his blood-red silk tie fluttered in the wind. He gave her a smile that revealed gold-capped fangs.

The former prince of LA wore a natty hat tilted above eyes as hard as granite. He was dressed immaculately in a bead-striped navy wool Italian suit: Zegna or something like that, more exclusive than your standard Armani. Lorelei read it as trying too hard.

She hadn't known the old has-been was still in town. All the same, he was a demon and expected deference. Lorelei kept her thoughts shielded and her gaze lowered.

Beelzebub picked up the conversation as if he'd been there all along. "You're looking for a weapon?"

Lorelei's heart skipped a beat. How much of the conversation with Barbelo had the demon overheard? Biting her lip flirtatiously, Lorelei hedged, "Sometimes a girl needs some protection."

"Too bad your prince isn't taking care of what's his." Beelzebub's voice was so low and deep, it made her shiver.

When Lorelei didn't answer, the demon pulled out a chromed pistol with an oversized bore from his waistband. "Show me the ammunition."

The pulse fluttering in her throat made her vision dim. She swallowed hard and handed over the last of Yasmina's bullets.

As Asmodeus had done, Beelzebub sniffed the bullet. Then he loaded the gun and handed it over to her, grip first.

"How can I repay you?" Lorelei asked. Her poor labia felt like hamburger, but if that was what he required, she'd oblige.

Instead, Beelzebub sat beside her and took her hand. He studied it in his, comparing her crimson skin with his ebony coloring, her sharp black talons to his blunt manicured nails. Lorelei felt a connection being made inside her body, one she didn't want to feel. The demon's granite eyes glittered in the starlight, a complete cipher to her.

She tried to remove her hand from his, but he held one of her knuckles in such a way that she would lose a finger before she got free.

"What do you want, my lord?"

"You." His smile was so oiled that Lorelei almost bought it.

"What do you want me for?"

He pulled her into his lap, breathing in the scent of her hair, tracing the side of her neck with his tongue. "A succubus with a soul," he marveled. "You're a delicacy I haven't had the pleasure of savoring."

Unlike everyone else in the back room at Lost Angels before the exorcism, she realized. What was going on between Beelzebub and her prince? And how would surrendering to this demon compromise her with her master later? Could things be any worse, Lorelei wondered, or was this one of those incriminating confessions Asmodeus warned would come her way?

Beelzebub leaned back enough to unbutton his waistband. Lorelei slithered off his lap to do as he expected. Whether or not he was aligned with her boss, he was a demon and she knew her place. He stroked the points of her horns.

"I was prince of this city once," he reminisced as she worked on him.

Lorelei was glad that her mouth was busy. Any comment she could think of would only ask for trouble.

"Your master orchestrated a coup." Beelzebub wound his fingers in her hair. "Your failure to bring down your angel seems no less spectacular than mine. Maybe they'll turn it into a musical."

He gave her time to dread that. Lorelei relaxed and let him do the work for a while. To her surprise, her surrender was enough to trip him into coming. Either her soul was more erotic than she suspected, or Beelzebub didn't get a chance at Asmodeus's girls very often. She thought she heard him moan.

After a final shudder, Beelzebub nudged her away. He handed Lorelei a silk handkerchief to wipe her mouth.

"I will be a prince again," Beelzebub promised.

Lorelei merely gazed downward, demure as could be.

The demon didn't go on to speak the treason she anticipated. The silence felt leaden. Clearly he expected her to say something. Lorelei couldn't think of anything that wouldn't be twisted against her somehow. Casting her hair to fall across Beelzebub's leopard skin loafers, she touched her forehead to the observatory dome. "Thank you for allowing me to serve you, my lord."

When she dared to look up, he was gone. The pistol still rested in her lap.

All Perdition seemed in a hurry. Instead of business as usual, devils darted here and there, starting fires, causing havoc, delaying the inevitable clash with hundreds of skirmishes designed to do nothing but test Heaven's patience.

Despite them, the watchers and guardians of LA forced themselves to concentrate on the task at hand, the immediate salvation of a few hundred souls in a city of millions.

Aza marveled at how readily the vacuum of guidance and protection around the living had been filled by the invisible hosts. It reminded him that, for every member of the manifested cadre to which he belonged, there were always two more invisibles ready to step forward. The knowledge reinforced a faith that had never faltered, filling him with confidence that the battle at hand would be won, as the others always had.

The only shadow on these thoughts was the question of whether he would be there at the final victory. Hell's entire battle plan relied on the falling of the physical angels, so that the unseen would be forced to take their place in the world. After that, Hell could begin a millennia-long battle of attrition, wearing and working at the new hosts. It was a long, slow process, but neither side was going anywhere.

Azaziel prepared for his own destruction, knowing that he could do no less after having put so many souls on the brink. Merely falling was unthinkable. He knew that Asmodeus's offer of employment back at Lost Angels had been sincere, since it superficially benefitted all concerned. However, after the sobering realization that his love had a soul, to be damned for love's sake was to become as separate a creature from her as he'd ever been. There had to be another way.

Aza dropped heavily onto a bus-stop bench, as full of weariness and weight as anything born of flesh.

Zadkiel grinned, clapping a warm hand on Aza's shoulder. "Come, there's business at hand. We have skirmishes to look forward to."

Aza looked at the archangel, reading a measure of anticipatory joy in his tiger-colored eyes. Aza realized that many of his brethren longed to continue the combat begun so long ago.

The thought invoked a chill of realized kinship. While fighting in the nightclub, Aza felt something indefinable within him change. He'd felt joy there: the joy of battle. That joy made him forget Lorelei long enough to leave her to the mercy of demons. Luckily, Barbelo had gotten to her first and had been able to squire his love to safety.

Zadkiel's touch carried Aza to the sidewalk in front of La Iglesia de Nuestra Señora la Reina de los Angeles, which stood on the site of the original Spanish mission church. Aza remembered when the Spanish came, two and a half centuries ago, and when they built their first little church.

This was the heart of faith in Los Angeles.

Only now, like a too-obvious metaphor, the church itself was on fire. Several companies of firefighters surrounded the building, laboring to save history.

Invisible to the human warriors, the full score of angels stationed in the city crouched around several blank squares of sidewalk. As Aza took his place in the circle, the others murmured greetings, accepting his presence. None balked, although Muriel sneered at him.

"Thank you all for coming," Michael said, standing alone at the center of the circle. He still wore his policeman's uniform and his polished black boots. "I'll keep this brief, since I don't want to delay you from your tasks." The archangel brought his boot down firmly on the concrete. The sidewalk shattered with a network of symmetrical fractures, turning the sundered pavement into a map of the city.

Waving one hand, Michael summoned hundreds of tiny flares. "Saint Mark's. All Saints. Church of the Blessed Mother. Beth el Rashael. Normandy Mosque," he recited, continuing until perhaps two-dozen flares glowed magnesium bright. "These we may count upon. The rest, however..."

The other lights guttered to sickly bluish-orange flames.

"Beyond the task at hand, you must be made aware of your true duty. We can only trust a fraction of the houses of worship in this city."

"Is faith so weak here?" Zadkiel asked.

Several angels rushed to take it upon themselves as personal failure.

Michael cut them off. "Faith itself is not a worry, but many of these temples will prove too easily breached and burnt."

Aza regarded the map sadly, then watched the other angels tally the number of weak flames, putting names, faces, and histories to each. Those flames represented centuries of work threatened, possibly destroyed.

"We've spent years establishing these safe houses, but we never envisioned a contingency like this: hundreds of souls to be saved at once and Hell eager to rise up against us." Rafael clapped his hands together. "This wonderful lesson teaches us not to grow complacent."

"But you've been moving the children for days!" Muriel protested. "Rather than leaving their souls in peril, we must retrieve them!"

Striding through the flames, Rafael shook his head, gesturing around at the assembled Host. "They're already collected. Here."

With the exception of those sent away from the playground, every angel present—seraph and cherub alike—placed a palm over its heart. The mortal souls were hidden inside angelic chests.

Those who remained realized they had been misled as much as any devil. Aza felt the coldness of Muriel's stare and the sorrowful acceptance of Barbelo.

"When we seemed to move the children, the foe watched and followed. They spread themselves thin, diffusing the power of their strike and giving us time to choose a stronghold. Now..." Rafael's voice swept through them, echoing another, greater source that left no doubt of its origin. "Like our dear warriors here, we must all be prepared to take up arms and protect these children, until they may safely be set free."

"Someplace safe," Aza guessed aloud. "Hallowed ground with many containers."

Michael nodded, pointing in the direction of Santa Rosa's parish cemetery. "Angelus Rose."

"But why there?" Muriel wondered aloud. "Especially when Forest Lawn has a veritable fortress atop its tallest hill!"

Barbelo gazed at her. "Why argue?"

"I only meant..."

Zadkiel touched Muriel's arm to forestall her tirade. "It has been decided. Let us fortify Angelus Rose and prepare for battle."

"Why are we waiting to attack?" Nebiros shouted in a voice like tortured steel. The beer foamed over as it heated in his hand. Throwing the bottle aside, he pushed away from Asmodeus's conference table and straightened as best he could. "Let's strike them now, at daybreak, when they least expect it. Why are you holding back?"

Asmodeus looked up from the silver head of his cane. "Finished?"

"I have to agree," Beelzebub said, contempt in his subterranean voice. "Caution right now smells like cowardice."

"Let me remind you, there are at least three archangels in my city," Asmodeus snarled.

"All the more reason to move decisively," Behemoth sniped, draining the pint of Guinness in his hand. "If the other side of the family doesn't take the city away from you, one of us may be tempted."

"Let anyone—above or below—try," Asmodeus dared, staring hard around the long teak table.

Jequon smiled behind a cloud of hookah smoke, but dropped his gaze. Tugging back one silk cuff, Beelzebub glared at his gold Rolex. Behemoth's armchair creaked as he slouched deeper. Mastema sipped his brandy and smacked his lips. Nebiros shifted at the end of the table, trying to find a comfortable position with his twisted spine.

"I want no all-out war with Heaven," Asmodeus said. "They could wipe this city off the map."

"Fact is, the demons of the other cities are not going to follow you," Beelzebub observed.

"They claim to have no pretext," Behemoth griped. "Because this is an LA cock-up."

Nebiros shouted, "What does it matter? Heaven's host is here. Their presence offends. Let's wipe them out."

"Your particular feud is well known," Beelzebub drawled. "And frankly, too personal for any of us to give a damn about." The Lord of Flies affected an inconvenienced tone. "If we're going to talk about aggrieved cases and personal affronts..."

"Stay with the subject," Asmodeus interrupted. "Will you support us?"

"Where was my support in '92?" Beelzebub answered. "All my expenditure, groundwork, and resources, but did the Valley burn? Did Beverly Hills? You let half the city cower behind barricades, while my fury was allowed to exhaust itself. I want to sympathize with you, Brother. I once sat where you do. When I called my council of war, what did you tell me? The time was not right. So I ask you now, what makes this occasion any more important?"

"There's no comparison..." Asmodeus began.

Beelzebub leaned forward. "You're right. Hundreds of unjudged souls were not on the verge of escape in '92. So tell us, how did you allow such a thing, Brother? I thought you had spies on every house of worship. How did this happen right under your nose? I was able to put my Crips and Bloods coast to coast at will, but you don't seem to know what's going on in your own backyard until you read about it in the trades. It looks to me, and I'm sure I don't speak alone, that your organization has been crumbling for a while."

"It's the only explanation—" Behemoth smirked "—why archangels feel safe enough to set up shop without so much as a by-your-leave."

Mastema sat quietly at his corner of the table, eating the whole argument up with a spoon. Asmodeus had his eye on that one. If Mastema could coax Azaziel into falling, he might defuse the whole situation. He might even take charge of LA, because the Cold Prince would surely reward him.

"Prince of the City!" Behemoth snorted loudly.

"Are you challenging me?" Asmodeus slapped his walking stick down atop the table with a thunderclap. "Are any of you challenging me?" he repeated, barely reigned.

Jequon set aside the hookah pipe and leaned forward, apparently ready to join in if it came to a throwdown.

Beelzebub pushed himself to his feet, lips rolling back from gold-capped fangs. Then he paused to let a façade of composure cloak him. His voice took on the patronizing calm he had often used on recalcitrant city council members. "All this is unnecessary. In another week, no one will need to challenge you. One of us," he nodded graciously to the other demons present, "will merely have to sort through the rubble and reorganize what's left of your people under a new, more profitable banner."

He strode unchallenged out of the room. Behemoth heaved himself up and waddled out too. In the end, Mastema stayed behind.

Once the door had slammed behind them, Asmodeus chuckled. He drew a cigar out of the humidor on the table, then used his cane to push the humidor toward Nebiros, Mastema, and Jequon. "Thank you, gentlemen. Your support will be rewarded."

Sucking fire into the cigar, Asmodeus told Nebiros, "All the soldiers I command will be at your disposal."

"How soon can I have them?" Hell's General asked.

"They're gathering now in storm drains near the graveyard. The only thing they lack is your leadership."

Nebiros's chair scraped back from the table as he stood.

"Don't be in too much of a hurry," Asmodeus chided. "Before I place an army under your command, let's be clear about their objectives."

Growling, Nebiros settled back into his chair.

"I want those souls destroyed, if they can't be damned."

"I'm sure the other side of the family will see that your army works up an appetite."

"I want the graveyard razed."

"A pleasure."

"I want those archangels chased from my territory."

"Rely on it. And the angel to blame for all this?"

"Formless or fallen—" Asmodeus shrugged "—it's all the same to me."

Nebiros wheezed out an ugly chuckle. "He won't get off that easily." The General leaned into a crabbed bow, never taking his eyes off Asmodeus. "If that is all, my prince?"

"For the glory of Hell," Asmodeus said, blowing out a long plume of cigar smoke, "do your worst."

CHAPTER 14: SETTING THE BOARD

Aza walked into the old cemetery, trying to see past the dusty monuments and drought-crisped grass to the defensive possibilities of the space. A high red-brick wall surrounded Angelus Rose, which could be reinforced to slow down the attack. Through the soles of his boots, he could feel that the ground itself had been sanctified, which would dissuade the lower-level minions in Hell's army, at least in the beginning. The cemetery had several buildings—the caretaker's house, the chapel, the columbarium, the public mausoleum—that would be targeted by arsonists once the wall was inevitably breached.

As he tried to decide where he could best take his stand, Rafael appeared to hand Aza the dented chrome martini shaker from Asmodeus's Lost Angels. Once, the martini shaker had been the repository for Ashleigh's soul. Only an echo of the girl's goodness remained in the container now that she'd been released to Heaven.

Rafael said, "I'd like you to take 'young Ashleigh' and place her with the others."

Aza started to query the archangel when Rafael nodded toward a couple of damned maintenance men pretending to fix a sprinkler nearby. Once the men exited through the front gate, they were a phone call away from reporting to Asmodeus.

Muriel manifested, smiling tightly. "It would be so easy to just drop them in the ocean somewhere." Her tone brightened. "But we can't do that, can we? Wonder what they'd say if they knew we only allowed them to live so they can say they'd seen the soul of Ashleigh, still unreleased."

It would be an unquestioned point for Hell to destroy the girl's soul, Aza realized. Praise Heaven she was already safe.

Rafael continued, "Place the receptacle in the chapel. Hell will strike there first and we'll be able to gauge the strength of their attack."

Cradling the martini shaker against his chest, Aza sighed heavily. He hated that this was all a show to misdirect Hell—and there would be one more holy site destroyed because of him.

Just as he was about to do as asked, a welcoming shout came from across the graveyard. Michael, holiest of archangels, had arrived, bringing through the gate a dozen mortals. Although they were still some distance away, Rafael threw his arms wide in greeting, echoing Michael's shout.

With a single step forward, Michael left the group of mortals and entered Rafael's arms, his blazing white wings a fading blur. The mortals he left behind halted, murmuring amongst themselves at the undeniable proof of the company they'd joined.

Aza recognized most of the group: Father Joseph. His friend Noc. Ernesto, who'd sold him the pupusas he'd fed Lorelei before the possession. Dolores Gutierriez and her sister Rae. The pretty Latina girl Aza had smiled at outside the Golden Door. The gum-cracking waitress from Canter's. As Aza watched, a shadow eclipsed the small knot of people. He knew—with the kind of certainty by which he knew too many things— that they would never leave this holy ground alive.

Shebethiel, standing sentry at the fence, pulled the gate closed behind them.

The only man that Aza didn't recognize carried a couple of gun cases in one hand, a bowling bag full of ammunition in the other.

"Max Phillips," Muriel said. "He drove the car in which you and your whore escaped to the Chateau Marmont."

Before Aza could attempt to defend his actions, Rafael interrupted smoothly, "A month from now, Max's heart would've given out in rush-hour traffic to LAX."

"Working with us, he could save three hundred souls," Michael pointed out. "You can guess which death he chose when I laid it out for him."

"Thank goodness some people have their priorities straight," Muriel chirped, always eager to be on the winning side of the argument.

Other angels moved to greet the mortals. Aza realized this was every mortal with whom he'd connected in the past week. Everyone whose life Aza had touched was being erased. He wondered what arrangements had been struck with these people. Had Rae and Dolores been promised they'd see their parents again? Had Noc been told he'd rejoin his wife? How, Aza wondered, had his friends been enticed to come to their deaths?

Personal contracts entered into for some brief gain… Suddenly, it seemed a much thinner margin between how angels and demons achieved their ends. How, he wondered, did that make angels any better than the creatures they fought?

The very ground seemed to yaw beneath him. It became all he could do to hold onto his faith. Surprisingly, Muriel came to his rescue. The instant Aza felt himself slipping, Muriel cast a sharp, appraising glance his way. Had she picked up on something? She gave no cry of alarm or support, made no attempt to notify the other angels. Aza steeled himself and gazed Heavenward. He clutched the martini shaker to his chest as if it still contained the girl's soul, not to mention his faith in God's plan, and his love for Lorelei.

Without a backward glance, he strode past the maintenance men into the chapel to play his part in the ruse.

A monstrous black SUV twisted up the observatory road. Asmodeus's glyph burned on its roof, bright crimson in the smoggy air. Lorelei watched the vehicle come for her, wondering who the boss had sent. Floria would have arrived in Tuan's car or a cab. Anyway, Asmodeus must know Lorelei wasn't ever going to be alone with Floria again, if she had any choice.

When the SUV jumped the curb onto the patio in front of the observatory, scattering tourists, Lorelei guessed who had come. That bitch.

The SUV pulled to a stop at the base of the steps to the observatory's second level. Lorelei stretched out her wings and resettled them on her back. She wasn't sure how far Yasmina could reach with that tail, but wanted all the advantage that wings would give her if it came to a fight.

Instead of the elder temptress, a fiend climbed out from behind the SUV's wheel. It was Tomur, the archfiend from Asmodeus's mansion.

"Get your ass down here," he ordered.

"Why?" Lorelei countered. The edge of the observatory dome was directly behind her. She could fling herself off and fly like a bat out of hell. Like the fiends they commanded, archfiends couldn't fly, but they could jump a hell of a long way and throw those damn pitchforks even farther. She grimaced, not liking her odds.

The gun in her handbag tugged at her thoughts. If she used her only bullet to erase the archfiend, that would buy her a little time. Unfortunately, she still had nowhere to go. Worse than that, she had no one to protect her, beyond that washed-up has-been Beelzebub.

"If I have to come up and get you, you're gonna be fucking sorry."

"Okay, Big Daddy. Take it easy. I'm coming down."

Lorelei stood, switching her hips to swing her hemline back into place. The fiend watched the movement and licked his lips. Lorelei smiled, but didn't push him. She opened her wings and used them to slow her fall as she hopped down. "Where we going, Daddy?"

"Knock that shit off. We're on a schedule now. Just get in the car."

Lorelei winked. Her labia still ached, but she'd had sex under worse conditions. "In the back?"

"In the front, where I can keep an eye on you."

Muriel followed Michael as he moved from one knot of angels to another, not so much giving orders as strengthening courage and bolstering will. He could inspire the other angels with a simple word or a hand on the shoulder. Once again, Muriel burned with a desire to be Michael.

Finally, after Michael made the rounds of the graveyard—with Muriel creeping ever closer behind him—he turned to acknowledge her. "How can I help you, Little Sister?"

Muriel bristled at something in the nickname, a timbre she hadn't heard before. In the past, it seemed to include her in the family. Now it felt belittling, dismissive. Like she would never outgrow it.

She shook that feeling off. "No one has given me any direction," she said. She meant it to sound like a wry observation, but her true feelings leaked out and she sounded like a wounded child.

Michael gazed at her, unreadable. Had he forgotten her? Did she not fit into his plans?

"I—I haven't got any weapon with which to fight," Muriel clarified.

"I remember," Michael assured.

"How can I join the battle without a weapon? Must I sit this fight out, too?"

He ignored her questions to point out, "You descended to this plane to teach our mortal brethren to praise the Creator, but you have faltered in the praise that formerly illuminated your own existence."

Muriel stumbled over a fallen headstone and barely kept her feet. For the first time, she heard the silence in her thoughts where the Ever-Spun Hymn used to ring. Worse than that, she couldn't be certain how long it had been missing. "What happened?" she moaned.

Michael reached out to her, clasping her shoulder. Even though she had just watched him use this gesture over and over on his rounds, she still felt its power flow through her. The Hymn stuttered like an old-style movie that jumped a sprocket and caught again, grinding back up to speed.

"Don't forget that we are ministers of love," Michael commanded.

"I won't," Muriel promised.

"Then I will return your blade." It manifested, still sheathed, in his left hand. He held it out to her.

"Hell will use humans, just as we do," Michael explained. "You may disregard them. Concentrate instead on the foot soldiers of Hell's army and thin their ranks before they can approach our collection of souls. I rely on you for this, Muriel."

"I am yours to command," Muriel swore. She donned her armor and buckled her sword back on. When she looked up from that task, the archangel had moved off to inspire someone else.

Muriel smiled at the thought of the humans on their battlefield. Perhaps, if one of them survived, he would be the poet who would record Muriel's deeds and bring her the renown she craved. She would have to ensure that they all knew her name, just in case.

The archfiend halted the Mercedes SUV outside Tuan's apartment building in the Valley. "Go up and get your sister."

Lorelei blurted, "You're joking."

"Think so?" Tomur asked. His knuckles cracked as he made a fist.

Lorelei put her hand on the door handle but didn't move any farther. "You know what she did to me last night?"

"Everybody knows." The archfiend's lascivious grin made Lorelei's blood turn to ice. "And as much as I'd like to get me a taste of that, we got places to be. So go get your fucking sister and let's get a move on."

Floria screeched, "They want what?"

Watching Floria glancing around for something to smash, Lorelei sank down onto the sofa in Tuan's living room. It had been a mistake to come up to Floria's alone.

"Succubi don't go to war!" Floria insisted.

"Not all succubi," Lorelei repeated. "Just us." She wished she knew what it felt like to be numb with fear. At the moment, she felt fear with knives in her stomach.

"I understand why he's sending you, since you fucked up so badly." Floria paced across the room. "I can't believe he's sending me because of you. Shit. Haven't I suffered enough for knowing you?"

"Your boy Hai volunteered your gang, Sister," Lorelei snapped. "You wanna keep credit for their souls, you better go watch them die."

"That's another thing," Floria said. "It took me two years to pull these kids together. I don't wanna waste any more time tempting such boring prey. I was hoping to use those fucks to step up to something better. That's all wasted if they bite it tonight."

"You wouldn't have had them for much longer, anyway," Lorelei pointed out. "They would've driven down the wrong street or had a run-in with the cops."

"Yeah, but that would've happened when I set it up," Floria snarled. "I would've gotten something for it. What the fuck do I get out of this?"

"You get to prove you're a good little slave, just like me," Lorelei answered. "Surprise, Sister. You're just as expendable as I am."

Floria's eyes flared red as the change shimmered over her. She swiped her talons toward Lorelei's face. Lorelei flung up her forearm to block the blow, shivering into her own infernal form as she launched herself off the sofa. Floria hadn't expected a counterattack and lost her balance. Lorelei rode her to the floor. They struggled to reach the knife sheathed on Floria's thigh.

Something hauled them apart. It happened so quickly that each reacted instinctively, forgetting her opponent and reaching back to claw at the fist wrapped in her hair. Tomur gave them each a good shake, then held them at arm's length. "The first one of you who snags a thread on this suit is gonna wish she'd never been hatched."

Floria's claws scrabbled against the carpet, trying to get a purchase. The archfiend shook her again, hard enough to rattle her teeth together. "Save it for the angels, bitch."

Floria wrapped her hands around his wrist, trying to lessen the weight on her hair. "Don't either of you think I'm going to forget this."

"What's a succubus going to do to me?" Tomur swung her against the wall. Lorelei winced as her sister's head bounced off the door molding. "The boss wants us to move out. Call those little pricks of yours and have them meet us at the Beef Bowl on Olympic and Western." He dropped Floria and gave Lorelei one final shake. "And you, shut the fuck up. You're down to Friend Zero as it is."

The Vietnamese boys were lounging against their bikes when Tomur pulled the Mercedes SUV into the parking lot behind the Beef Bowl. A twelve-foot cinderblock wall enclosed what was essentially a blind cul-de-sac. They would be safe here from prying eyes.

Lorelei stayed in the front seat of Tomur's Mercedes, arms crossed sulkily. Floria followed the archfiend around to the hatch in the back.

"New toys!" Floria gushed as Tomur handed out semiautomatics.

Lorelei had seen Hai shoot Aza, without effect. Oh, the bullet had drawn blood, but it sure as shit hadn't made the angel any less dangerous. She wondered if Floria knew the weapons were just set-dressing, or if she even cared. Certainly didn't sound like it.

"My, look at all the big guns," Floria cooed theatrically as the boys inspected their brand-new firearms.

"Handle 'em with care, children." Tomur passed out boxes of ammunition from a Louis Vuitton duffel. "These loads are blazin'. We're talkin' the meanest stuff that Hell could send up."

Hai rolled a handful of rounds, glossy and dark, in his palm. "This stuff is scary warm," he observed.

"I'm not sure about this, Floria," Tuan groused. "Maybe we should head down to the river and shoot some first."

"No time for that," Floria answered. "Just believe me when I say they are some badass shit."

"Gonna make your pieces kick like a motherfucker, too," the archfiend added. "Keep that in mind and don't pull any sideways Tarantino shit, or you'll blow the head off the guy standing next to you."

Sammy tried to toss his new gun, a darkly gleaming 50-caliber Desert Eagle, back into the bag. "Fuck this wrist-breaker," he growled, full of macho indifference. "I want my Tec-9 back."

"No exchanges." Tomur deftly shoved the gun into the boy's waistband. "You'll do the job you're told with the tools you're given. That goes for all of you," he added menacingly in Floria's direction before climbing back into his car.

"So what's up with these?" Lam wondered aloud. "We takin' down an armored car?"

"You wish." Floria smiled slyly. "Tonight you boys get to show me what you're really made of, by fucking up some angels for your favorite girl."

Tomur distracted Lorelei from the boys' responses by asking, "What the fuck are you waiting for?"

"He's not sending me into battle unarmed, is he?" She hated the quaver in her voice.

"Hell, no. You've got your soul collector, right?"

Lorelei nodded slowly.

"You know those guns aren't shit, so you know you're not shooting any angels with them. You wanna kill yourself, that dagger will do you just fine. Now get the fuck out of my truck, before they leave you behind. I got shit to do."

Arranged around the funeral chapel stood dozens of containers, all of them empty. They'd been brought in to encourage the assumption of Hell's watchers that the children's souls were being collected here. Rather than set the martini shaker among them, Aza continued to cradle it.

A knock at the doorway brought his thoughts back to the present. It was Max, the maimed soldier with the heavy conscience. "Hope I'm not bothering you. I was wondering...could I talk to you?"

Walking carefully between the bottles and jars lining the center aisle of the chapel, Max approached Aza. He set down the bowling bag, his expression a combination of bewilderment and resolve. He offered his thumb-less hand, then paused, uncertain if he should even touch an angel.

Aza couldn't grant absolution. Before he could admit that, the young man began. "Michael asked me to come here today 'cause he kind of knew what I'd been through some years back."

"Afghanistan, where you were sent to be a peacekeeper." Fully aware of the events Max was ready to relate—down to details of dust, heat, stench, and fear—Aza wondered if Max knew how unnecessary it was for him to confess. Aza decided not to tell the man. Speaking it aloud might be release enough.

The young man projected an air of apprehension that the angel would judge him harshly. "I was supposed to be a peacekeeper...but everything was wrong there," Max said. "That place was like Hell on Earth: crooked people, mistrusting innocents, death, starvation, anarchy..." The memory had melded into a shadowy, half-waking nightmare, which still filled the young soldier with shame.

He sat down on a pew, then jumped up again, unable to settle. "The last couple of times we went out to try and do good, everything fell apart. We wound up fighting the people we wanted to save. This one day..." Max choked up.

"The day the two of your helicopters were brought down, you and your friends tried to rescue the pilots," Aza continued for him. "You volunteered to go out, even though you had that terrible fear you shouldn't have to. You wondered where my kind were, where the Almighty was. You worried that the whisper of fear that told you we didn't care was true."

Max looked up. His eyes were accusatory, as if he'd been observed in his time of need, without help being offered.

"To get everybody out—or what was left of them—we wound up in a running fight with hundreds of heavily armed outlaw militia, all mixed in with thousands of civilians. They tore up the bodies of our dead and paraded them on TV."

Aza eyed the young man carefully. "If I told you there were no good wars, just good causes, you'd want to hit me. I know it was bad there. It became your problem, even though it wasn't your fault."

"I had to kill kids to get at the bastards shooting at me." The young man's voice dropped to a rushed, emotionless drone, as if he wanted nothing more than to get the story out of the way. "One of the guys figured out that our ammo, real high velocity stuff, was going right through the militia guys... Seven or eight shots. Nothing. Someone said—I swear to God someone said this—to shoot through their human shields, so the bullets would slow down enough to kill the gunmen."

Aza felt the still-sharp terror, the sick remorse flooding through Max like putrid adrenaline. He wondered if it had been an infernal or divine voice that whispered the fatal advice.

"We got out, but I'll never know how many I killed. Civilians, I mean." Max paused. "Can you tell me?"

The exact number came to Aza. Though it was far lower than the young man feared, it wouldn't change the fact that even a single life taken unjustly would distress him. "Is it important now? All that matters to Heaven is that a young man like you is willing to give your life in the protection of these helpless souls."

"Part of me will never get away from that place. If everything ends tonight, that's fine. Problem is, I don't think I deserve Heaven and I'm afraid of Hell." Max scrubbed his fingers over his eyes, careful not to touch the scar tissue of his hands to his face.

"Dangerous talk there, friend. Suicide isn't the reason to be here." Aza smiled with carefully engineered joviality, doing his best to emulate Rafael's style. "Ask me something else."

Clearly a man who had backup questions, Max shot back, "We're supposed to be in God's image. Which is it: white, black, brown? Male, female? Why are we all so different?"

Aza nodded. "An old question, but a good one. None of those attributes apply, because you're not quite cast in the Almighty's image."

Max's expression fell at the words. He sank onto a pew, trying to absorb them.

Despite his best efforts, Aza didn't possess Rafael's gift for answering questions with a cheerful aplomb that made everything fine. He hurried his explanation, trying to find something reassuring. "Put simply, your question is an old misconception: mutable words spread by mortal lips, put down by imperfect hands, and shaped by all-too-mortal longing. Not to sound self-important, but we angels were made in the image of the Creator. In turn, you mortals have been cast in ours. You come in many colors, shapes, and aspects, because we do."

Max shook his head. "That can't be right."

Aza smiled, even though it was clear this simple truth wasn't accepted. "Why do you think so many of our kind were upset when told to honor weaker, wingless, essentially vulnerable versions of ourselves?" Aza slipped past Max to sit on the pew next to him. "Mind you, this was well before the fall of Adam, when mortals were still more concept than reality." He smiled sadly. "The truth is, angels by and large, fallen or otherwise, still consider themselves above man."

Max looked taken aback. "So you don't always help us because you choose not to?"

This was spinning farther out of his control. Aza tried another tack. "Max, have you ever considered how many more of you there are than there are of us? We act first and foremost for the Almighty's purpose."

The soldier considered what the Almighty's purpose might have been in Afghanistan.

Emulating Michael, Aza clapped what was meant to be a reassuring hand on the man's shoulder. The contact only made Max flinch. Letting his hand drop, Aza said, "I promise you, you are all very much part of that purpose. I don't know why humans continue to hate each other so much. If it'll make you feel any better, there are times my kind doesn't get along any better than yours. While held to a higher standard, angels are far from perfect."

"Some less than others, which is why some of us keep our ears open at all times." From the doorway Muriel glared pointedly at Aza, not bothering to hide her true aspect as she entered the chapel.

Max's jaw was still hanging from trying to process what he'd been told. He'd asked for a revelation and gotten an admission to boot. The sight of this second angel opened Max's eyes. Suddenly he was aware of Aza's wings as well. This proved to be the young man's limit. Mumbling thanks to both angels, he sidled past Muriel.

She smiled radiantly at him, only making matters worse.

Wearily, Aza turned to face his constant judge, wondering if she realized how well she'd underscored his point. "Aren't you needed out there?"

"And in here, it seems."

Aza felt a rush of impatience, fought it back. He thought how badly his bout of truth with the young ranger had turned out, how he'd come within a hairsbreadth of being no better than the mythic serpent in the garden, making poison of knowledge. He wanted to go after Max and set things right.

Muriel must know his sorrow, but she ignored it. "We need to talk about your...girlfriend, before this fight starts."

Any thought that Aza had of Muriel coming to him—at some higher behest—vanished. He pushed past her out into the graveyard.

His shadow tagged along. "I've felt you wavering, trying to keep your love for her from being an obstacle. While you really haven't managed to do well with that most of the time, I believe you should be commended for trying...and encouraged to continue."

He realized that, from Muriel, this might be an effort at smoothing things over. "Are we making up to present a unified front? Is that Rafael's directive?" Aza felt terrible for saying it. Worse, that it felt like the truth.

Muriel compounded his discomfort by changing the subject. "Do you believe, even for a minute, that she's thinking of you? New-grown soul or not, your girl is thick within Asmodeus's coterie."

She placed a firm hand on Aza's arm, shaking him as if to rouse him. "I swear to you, she has spared not a thought for you in this past hour. Before I saw you terrifying the ranger, I thought perhaps you might have a few words with the mortals levied here today, to explain to them that you are the reason they've been put into the path of imminent death."

"Azaziel doesn't need to explain anything." A new voice joined them, strong, clear, and filled with purpose.

Both angels turned. Muriel's face shone in delight as Michael manifested on the mausoleum ahead of them.

"These people face Hell willingly, selflessly. That is reason to rejoice." Michael's eyes glowed with holy joy. With a surprisingly tender hand, he reached down to Aza and drew him upward to join him atop the tomb.

Muriel stared up at them, too rapt at the sight of the archangel to mind that she had not been similarly raised.

"There is no precedent for what's about to occur here. That said, it was bound to happen, simply because of the infinite breadth of the Almighty's purpose."

Aza repeated what constituted angelkind's oldest watchword and joke: "The only plan being that we can never know the plan."

Michael nodded. "I've come to warn you that you've a visitor waiting out front. An infernal."

"Now, who from the other side would be asking for you?" Muriel inquired. "No doubt hoping that you'll make a choice today."

Aza strained to see if they were talking about Lorelei. What if she had come to seek asylum after all? For all the stock-in-trade hope that defined his kind, Aza fought the impulse to entertain the possibility that he could rescue her. Push come to shove, he could hide her soul with the others— but he didn't want to think about that, because that would mean she was as dead as Ashleigh.

Michael drew a gleaming long sword from the sheath on his back. The blade danced with tongues of iridescent flame. Aza recognized it as Raphael's. "I heard you made good use with this at the nightclub the other night," Michael said, handing it over. "Go take care of your unfinished business."

Sheathing the sword across his own back, Aza hopped down from the mausoleum and made for the front gate by the most direct route possible through the tombstones.

The grounds around him hummed quietly with angelic song and the growl of traffic on the street outside. The air was so sluggish and hot, Aza felt the grass dying beneath his feet. With a mordant smile, he could imagine Samael trying to blame him for that as well: "Death goes with you, Azazi-El, and peace eludes your every step. Cursed should you be in Heaven and placed among the low hosts of despair and denial."

Lorelei had been too much to hope for. Outside the closed gates paced Mastema, unsuccessfully striking match after match. An unlit cigarette drooped from one corner of his mouth. The demon brightened at Aza's approach.

"Damned if I can make fire here," Mastema remarked. "Let's try a trick, shall we? Put your finger through the bars and see if you can light me."

"Tell me what you want," Aza said. "Keep it short."

"It's not what I want." Mastema shrugged, breathing an orange glow into the tip of his Benson & Hedges. "This is more a joint request on behalf of Paradise and Perdition."

"I don't believe you for a moment." Aza matched the demon's steps along the length of the closed gate.

"Put simply, you're about to be the agent of great misery here in this fair town." Mastema proffered a handshake through the bars. "Congratulations."

Aza stared at the hairy hand with its sharpened thumb and pinky nails.

Snapping his fingers twice, Mastema produced a second cigarette, already lit. "Smoke with me, Brother. Show you can at least be friendly."

Accepting the cigarette, Aza flicked it to the dirt and ground it to powder beneath his boot. "Stop wasting my time or I'm walking."

"Part these gates, walk away with me, and Hell won't attack tonight." The demon gestured toward the mortals inside the gate. "These good people can die in bed, or a crosswalk, or wherever."

"I wouldn't believe that if I were mortal," Aza snapped. "You and I both know Asmodeus wouldn't miss this chance to strike at us. It's the closest thing he's had to cause since Rafael ruined his wedding night."

"Ah, ha!" Mastema exhaled jets of smoke through a too-wide grin. "You admit Hell has cause for complaint. That's progress." With a sidelong glance, the demon put his face close to the bars. "Between the three of us—that is to say, you, I, and the Almighty—" Mastema paused expectantly, then smirked for having gotten away with giving God third billing. "It would please all concerned if we could deny the lame prince his shot at restitution. You agree to descend right now and I'm prepared to give the Creator's guarantee that no action will be taken against your stash of children, corporeal or otherwise."

Aza stopped in his tracks, sensing truth in every word the demon spoke. "Choose to fall?"

"The universe demands a sacrifice to redress the upset you've caused," Mastema said reasonably. "Make this your final show of faith. While chances are you still won't get the girl, you'll save your mortal friends."

Eyes flashing, Aza demanded, "So faith has nothing to do with this offer, only expedience?"

"No more part than pride in your refusal."

"Not pride, but love," the angel insisted, buoyed by the truth of the words.

"Have you ever stopped to consider that what you keep insisting is love is really unacknowledged sin?" Mastema grinned smugly, like a pulp story detective wrapping up every loose end. "Wise up, Brother. You do the Almighty great disservice when you ignore the intellect you were given, thinking instead with your loins. Tacky." Mastema flicked his cigarette through the fence toward the dry grass. "Tacky and self-delusional. Quit hurting everyone here. Just give up and be true to what everyone else already knows you to be."

"I've loved two women with my flesh, and numberless thousands with my deeds."

"Now you're sounding like some stupid mortal. You know this is different," Mastema whined derisively, "we're in LLLOOOVVVE."

Aza cut the demon off. "What would you know about it? You weren't there."

Mastema shook his head pityingly. "News for you, Aza, my boy: I was there. I always am, waiting on the nearest sideline, never far enough away that I can't take you by the hand if need be and lead you to your destiny. That is my power."

"I didn't know demons had power; only strength."

"Really?" Mastema arched a bristling eyebrow. "Before you go bandying about the D-word, consider this. Which of us has been to Heaven recently?"

"Yet you manage not to stay," Aza shot back.

"Whatever happened to the Azazi-El of old? When the Almighty told you to scourge Heliodorus in the temple, you didn't hesitate." Mastema recollected proudly, "Striped him up and bore him away without a second thought. One succubus makes a pass at you and suddenly your life could be mistaken for the plotline of a Meatloaf song."

Aza walked away.

The demon called after him. "I didn't want to bring this up, since it's supposed to be a surprise, but your sweetheart is going into battle tonight. She'll be up in the front lines. I'm just letting you know so you can look out for her—'cause you know nobody else is going to."

Aza shouted over his shoulder, "Succubi don't fight!"

"Not very well," the demon agreed.

Aza forced himself to continue walking. There was no reason to continue this pointless discussion. It was taking him away from more important work.

"See you later!" Mastema called after him.

"Not if I see you first," Aza muttered.

CHAPTER 15: HELL BREAKS LOOSE

Yasmina smoothed her Alice + Olivia dress over her hips, rearranged her décolletage in the deep V-neck, and nerved herself to push open the door to the conference room. She found Asmodeus alone, puffing meditatively on a cigar.

"Why are you here?" he growled.

"My lord, I…I don't know where else to go." She slunk into the room, but halted before reaching him.

"I'm willing to forgive you for marking up Lorelei in defiance of my aegis, since you didn't do any permanent damage," he said, drawing on the cigar again, "but don't push me."

"Please," Yasmina said. "All I want is to use Lorelei against the angel. If she'd submitted to us, there would've been no more potent weapon against Azaziel."

"Your threats against Lorelei before the exorcism caused her to save the mortal girl's soul. That helped her decide to spare the priest. You cost me two mortals that would have counted against Azaziel. This I find difficult to forgive. I wonder what my girl will decide to do, now that you've made it clear you've turned Floria against her," Asmodeus said.

Yasmina crept closer. "My lord, you know no one in Creation desires to see the destruction of Azaziel more than I. To that end, I made bad decisions. I regret them. I accept my punishment for them. But if he is to fall, Master, please, please, let me be part of it."

He sucked on the cigar again, breathing out a long plume of smoke. "The problem, as I see it," Asmodeus said, "is that you don't understand Azaziel at all. You've spent too much time studying Jequon, when in fact he was half a devil all along. Jequon pimped for the other angels long before he fell because of it. For him, it was less a matter of falling than of finally wising up. Azaziel is not like that, nor was I. Creatures like he and I need to be cast out from our false principals to discover our true selves."

She lifted the bottle of brandy and poured some into his glass. Asmodeus watched her, then leaned forward to slap the bottle out of her hand. He grasped her wrist and pulled her closer.

"This is no game," he said severely. "Nebiros leads my army to protest the inequity of God's favor. Opposing him is a score of angels led by the archangel Michael. All I have to hope for out of this fiasco is the

172

castration—and banishment—of an angel who thought momentarily with his penis. If Lucifer himself could not stand against Michael, Nebiros certainly goes to his doom."

"Then let me follow him to mine," Yasmina begged. "Master...if Azaziel falls, or is cast down, or by some twist of fate is destroyed...Please, Master, let me be there to witness it."

"You hate him that much?" He smiled at her, baring goatish teeth. "Are you armed?"

"You have only to say the word and I will be so."

He tapped his cigar over the ashtray as he considered her fate. "Beneath the altar in my chapel," he said at last, "you will find the weapon I carried in Lucifer's army."

On the steps of the cemetery's columbarium, an unfamiliar man held out his hand to Dolores Gutierrez. "My name is Noc." He pronounced it "Now" with a "k" on the end. Dolores, who spent her days typing in names as people rented cars at the Burbank airport, wondered how it was really spelled.

"Mrs. Gutierrez," she said, shaking his hand. "This is my sister—"

"Rae," she said, holding her hand out. Rae had always been the more outgoing sister, the one who joined the church choir and knew everyone's names by the end of the first rehearsal. "My sister's name is Dolores," she told Noc as they shook hands. "There isn't any Mr. Gutierrez. She just calls herself that so people will think she's widowed."

Dolores flushed and turned away from them.

Noc changed the subject. "Do you know my friend Aza?"

"I don't think so," Rae said.

The man pointed out an angel standing on the gable above the chapel door. It was clear from the shadow thrown on the lawn in front of him that he was an angel.

Dolores's hazel eyes widened. "Yes, I recognize him," she said. "He brought the news of my son's death."

The smile collapsed from Noc's face. "What a terrible loss," he said. "I am so very sorry."

A smile flickered across Dolores's face before it evaporated. She stared at the angel, remembering now all the times he had crossed her path, all the little kindnesses he had done for her.

"Did you know he was an angel?" Rae asked.

"We call them bodhisattva," Noc said, his warm humor returning. "No, I didn't know. But now that all is revealed, I am not surprised."

Without looking away from the angel, Dolores asked, "Are you a Christian?"

"I am not," Noc said. "But Rafael, when he asked me to come, said that it was not important I be."

"How did you meet him then?" Rae asked, nodding toward the angel atop the chapel.

So Noc told them the story of his desperate escape from home, the leaky boat, the threat of starvation—and Aza, waiting on the shore, ready to make everything right by giving Noc a chance at a new life. He told them about feeding the homeless and caring for the needy and the concept of karma and his need to work off his debt. And Rae told him about singing to the dying and the warm coat drive. And Dolores talked about her struggles with her wild husband and her wilder son, how she loved them but couldn't fix them, and how she felt she owed the world for the things they had done.

As the hours passed, the three of them came to be good friends.

The mansion seemed all but abandoned as Yasmina strode through its halls. Everyone had either been sent to prepare for battle or they were in hiding, hoping they'd be forgotten by the prince of LA until the dust could settle.

If she'd been smart, Yasmina knew she should've been among those hiding. However, this was the night when everything would change— Azaziel couldn't duck out of this. Tonight he would fall or be made formless. Yasmina couldn't imagine anything he might do to slip back into Heaven's good graces, so falling seemed a solid bet.

If he was rendered formless—and Nebiros didn't immediately devour him—Yasmina wanted to be ready to pounce. She'd given everything she had left to Jequon to acquire an amphora that had formerly imprisoned a djinn. Jequon promised the enspelled jug would be strong enough to hold an angel cast out of Heaven and banned from Hell.

To capture Azaziel, she just needed a weapon to destroy his body, and then to get close enough to open the amphora.

She arrived outside Asmodeus's chapel in the depths of the mansion. No guard stood there today. No doubt all the fiends had been eager to do some damage at their master's command. They were probably already massing at the graveyard.

Yasmina pulled the chapel's double doors open. The darkened room was redolent of spilled blood and rich red wine.

She plucked a lighter from her clutch and lit one of the torches near the door. Once the flame caught, she lifted the torch from its sconce and approached the altar.

Asmodeus's weapon wasn't apparent. Yasmina had expected to find it atop the altar, being consecrated by the atmosphere of the room.

As she circled the altar stone, a flagstone shifted beneath her feet. She knelt, tracing the edges of the loose black stone with her nails. She had no idea how to lever the stone up, but she was certain this was what she had been looking for.

Aza perched halfway up a palm tree overlooking the far eastern corner of the cemetery. The low brick restrooms concerned him. They could provide cover—and there weren't enough angels to guard every approach. Faith would have to be their bastion, more than the high red-brick wall that ringed Angelus Rose.

As he scanned the perimeter, three fiends drew themselves to the top of the wall. They inspected the terrain below before the first leapt off. A gout of smoke and steam rose when his weight smashed into the sod below. With a whistling hiss, the fiend hopped up onto a headstone. His steel-toed Thom McCanns had burned away, revealing clawed feet swollen from his foray onto consecrated soil.

One of his companions tossed him a pitchfork before leaping down onto the protection of his own patch of granite. He waved others forward before leapfrogging to another marker a few feet ahead.

Aza drew Rafael's sword, raising his other hand in warning. The three fiends burst into raucous laughter. "Come on down, Soul Daddy! Give us the chance to take you out," one of them taunted.

Aza sprang to the ground. The fiends drew up short, teetering on their respective gravestones. Their oversized shoulders bunched as they tried to maintain their balances. The center fiend's marker lurched forward under his weight. Seeing this, he commenced waggling the loosened stone back and forth. His companions stared at the angel, jaws widening into defiant, hungry smiles.

The center fiend allowed his weight to carry the precariously lurching stone over to smash down atop a child's lamb-shaped monument. Digging his pitchfork into the sod, the fiend vaulted forward to a much larger stone.

Aza stared him down, knowing full well what the fiend and his companions were up to. The longer he delayed with them, the more of their kind would attempt to slip past elsewhere.

Leaping forward, he met the first fiend head-on. Its pitchfork caught Rafael's sword, knocking Aza's blow wide. The fiend laughed and swung one muscular arm. His claws connected with the small of the angel's back.

A beat of his wings carried Aza forward. He toppled the rearmost fiend neatly from his stone. There was nothing nearby enough for the fiend to use as a steppingstone. He flopped around on the holy ground, flesh sizzling as his dark clothing erupted in flames. Aza pinned him neatly with the archangel's sword, leaving it in place while divesting the screaming devil of its weapon.

Unmindful of the way the pitchfork smoked and sparked in his grip, the angel sent it flying toward the lead fiend. It went wide. As the fiend stretched to snatch it out of the air, Aza yanked Rafael's sword from the dead fiend at his feet and pitched the weapon with considerably more accuracy.

Skewered through the shoulder, the fiend lost his footing and rolled off his monument into the grass, squealing like a teakettle.

The third fiend had made his way a considerable distance into the graveyard. He pitched an incendiary at the caretaker's house. Flames exploded across its porch.

Aza started forward in frustration, then realized that the fire had to be left to others to handle. He heard the chink of steel-toed boots on the wall as more fiends chinned themselves up.

The storm drain outside the cemetery wall was dry and cold. Lorelei found a shadow cast by the flickering torches and hid herself in it, like soaking into a shallow and changeable pool of water. Waiting was excruciating. Her hand felt clammy on the haft of her knife. It would be no protection against angels. She wondered if perhaps her best bet, when Azaziel's brethren cornered her as they surely must, would be to throw herself on their mercy, begging them to obliterate her miserable soul. Or maybe she ought to just slit her own throat here and now. In her human form, she wouldn't even have to put much strength behind the blade—and if she was extra, super lucky, it might even capture her soul as she died.

Hai stumbled into her by accident. Panic washed across his face until he recognized her. Then he huddled close, clutching her free hand.

Lorelei let her eyes flare. She didn't much pity him. He'd done this to himself in accepting Hell's bargain—against her express direction. In return for whatever he'd been offered, he'd committed the boys to this attack. They weren't the only mortals present, but devils outnumbered them a hundredfold. Lorelei wondered if any of the kids other than Tuan guessed what that boded.

At least Hai had seen Hell's contingent before, from his foray into Asmodeus's mansion. Lam, little Kim, and the others were as terrified of the allies around them as they were of the battle in which they were about to take part. Children, Lorelei thought, feeling true compassion for them. If they knew the words in which to pray, they'd be saving their own souls right about now. And their "allies" in the drain would tear them apart for it.

The still air of the tunnel was a labyrinth of smells that made Lorelei homesick: her sister's musk, the sour tang of the fiends, the bitter aromas of the tempters, the complex odors of the higher devils. The unwashed stench of Nebiros, the only demon to take part in the attack, burned her nostrils, even at a distance.

If the stories were true, in the First War with Heaven, Azaziel had vanquished Nebiros with one mighty punch. The blow broke the general's jaw, shattered half his teeth, deformed his beautiful face, and twisted his spine into the hunched wretch he was now.

Rumor said that Nebiros was a warlord who never tired of the taste of blood. She'd heard that his representatives whispered in the ears of defeated generals the world over to keep the human race in turmoil. Standing atop a gilded chair dragged down for the purpose, Nebiros looked like he'd just as soon tear a succubus apart to get warmed up for the fight. More than anything, Lorelei wanted to remain below his notice.

A trio of imps scampered toward him down a side branch of the tunnels. The army parted to allow them to pass. Nebiros turned toward them, one haughty eyebrow arched.

"The first company of fiends is over the wall," the lead imp panted.

Nebiros raised both hands and drew a sigil in the air. "Serve well. Annihilate the dead. Ruin all you touch," he screamed. The exhortation hung, sparking and spitting, above the army. Lorelei closed her eyes, wishing she could draw the protection down around her shoulders. Then the mob surged forward and she was hustled along.

Despite the pain it caused her tender nether flesh, Lorelei took her turn climbing the ladder out of the tunnel. She found herself inside a small octagonal crypt turned into a tool shed. Cobwebs draped its corners. A pair of dusty lawn mowers had been shoved aside to allow the army to pass. Whoever the original inhabitants had been, they hadn't gone saved into their tomb. The ground she stood on, at least, had been de-sanctified by the dead mortals' presence.

The reek of Nebiros filled the small room. Before Lorelei could locate him, he grasped her arm with one crabbed hand and hauled her over against his armored chest. "Bring me your angel," he ordered. "I'll allow you to have what's left of him when I finish."

Lorelei's eyes widened involuntarily. "But..."

With a lopsided grin that revealed strings of meat hanging from his broken teeth, Nebiros warned, "Here and now, you are under my command."

His normal hand rested on the hilt of his scimitar. Lorelei wished there was someone, anyone, she could trust to watch her back. Instead, Floria shepherded the boys past the demon and out into the graveyard.

Lorelei let her hair curtain her face. "I understand, my lord."

Coiled around his shoulders, the snake he carried as rank of office peered out from under the general's straight blond hair. It hissed as it gathered to strike.

"Go," Nebiros suggested, flicking his fingers at her. "Now."

Lorelei dodged out of the tomb into the honeyed golden light of late afternoon. Blinking, she hurried between gravestones after the boys.

The army had scattered ahead of her. She saw fiends perching atop grave markers, jumping from one to the next to avoid touching the blessed ground. Such tempters as had wings vaulted into the sky. Clear shouts rang out as angelic sentries spotted the attack pouring out of the crypt.

Lorelei spun around, trying to locate the enemies. Widely spaced around the large cemetery, most of them stood guard near the red-brick outer walls. There weren't as many angels as she'd feared, but even a dozen was treble the amount she'd fled from before. Now that the call had gone out, how many angels in Creation would swarm to this fight? More than enough to wipe out the army who violated their repository.

Any of those few angels already here would probably be proud to show bloodstained palms to their Creator and say, "This was the slut Lorelei, the one who dared to love one of us." She thought about changing into her true form, but decided that any camouflage she could manage might better her chance of survival.

A loop of tail across her path caught Lorelei's foot. She toppled like a tree, her head dropping toward a marble marker. Even as she curled up in a vain attempt to miss the headstone, the tail hauled her backward. She landed safely in the grass.

Lorelei flung herself over onto her back to find Yasmina swaying above her.

"Should've made a deal with me, Little Sister. You could be somewhere else, safe in bed, and Azaziel could have been servicing you even now."

"Spare me," Lorelei snapped. "If anything you could do would've made him fall, he would've been in Hell long before I hatched."

Yasmina's eyes flashed copper, but she smirked. "Are we speaking plainly, then?"

"Might as well. The boss made it clear at the exorcism that you're no longer Queen Bitch."

"What's to keep me from destroying you for your insolence?" the elder devil hissed.

"Gonna talk me to death?" Lorelei taunted. "I'm under the boss's aegis, at least where you're concerned, or you would've struck first."

Yasmina's grin gave nothing away.

Lorelei glared at her. If Yasmina expected her to start something so she could strike Lorelei and claim self-defense, she was dumber than she looked.

"Actually," Yasmina said, her voice taking on a singsong confidence that set Lorelei's teeth on edge, "I'm here to remind you of one thing."

"Want me to guess?"

"No, I'll tell you, since you asked so nicely. No fleshly spirit has been allowed into Hell since the days of Orpheus—and you know that entrance has long been sealed. You, my dear, with your flawed new soul, are exiled for as long as your flesh may live." Yasmina checked the slim gold watch on her wrist. "Watch your back."

"Be careful no one drops a house on you," Lorelei countered.

Yasmina's tongue flickered out. It was clear from the distaste in her eyes that she respected the aegis. Then her gaze dropped to Lorelei's hands and she smiled. "What pretty little wrists you have, child. I can't wait to see how they'll look in cuffs."

She slithered away and Jezebel trotted unhappily after her. Across the ruined succubus's back hung a quiver of wicked-looking arrows. She clutched a bow in her hand. At least she didn't have breasts to get in the bowstring's way, Lorelei thought. Poor thing.

Fuck. Exiled. Lorelei should've thought of that. So much for being posted back home in safety. Now she really was going to have to watch out for angels and be careful around Floria and not get shot by a panicked human being. That fucking sucked.

A strange noise, like wind through silk curtains, drew her attention upward. An angel swept overhead. Lorelei couldn't guess the angel's gender beneath its lavender and gold chain mail. All that mattered was that it was certainly not Aza. She dove for cover. The angel sailed past, uncaring.

Looking around, she saw that only the infernals flinched at the sight of the enemy. Even the bulkiest fiends stooped their shoulders a little. Tuan and the boys merely stared upward in wonderment. They weren't so much brave as stupid, completely unaware what angels could do.

Though most of the boys hadn't been brought up Christian, they'd lived long enough in the United States to be exposed to saccharine Christmas tree angels and harmless Valentine's cherubs. If they'd considered it at all, they believed that angels stood on your shoulder, whispering ineffectual platitudes, like in cartoons. If Hai'd had any clue what he was doing, he never would have shot Aza on the observatory. Lorelei shrugged. They were all about to become a lot wiser in the ways of Creation. If it'd been up to her, they would've been home watching pay-for-view porn. Hell would still get its cut.

Sammy took his stance as he brought up the squat, vicious-looking Desert Eagle and fired off a short burst at the angel. Half the shots went wild. Even so, they shattered the top of a nearby obelisk into powder.

The boy swore and tried to get on target. Stupid fucker, Lorelei thought.

The low sun sparkled off its armor as the angel wheeled around. It ignored the gunfire whizzing past. With a slight flex of its wings, the angel dove straight through Sammy, shattering him like so much bloody crockery. As the angel beat its wings to regain altitude, Lorelei could see what the boys couldn't. The angel held a writhing blue-black mist that was Sammy's rotten soul. Lorelei wondered if the angel would carry it back to where the other souls were corralled.

The angel looped around and tossed the soul down toward a pack of fiends. They reacted like starving dogs falling onto a piece of meat, rending the soul apart with fangs and claws. Lorelei blocked her ears. Poor Sammy kept screaming as one of them gathered his fragmented soul into a silvered belt buckle.

The angel drew a gleaming long sword from a sheath on its back. It slashed at the distracted fiends, hacking off limbs while their backs were turned. Hell might have fired the first shot, for all the good it did them, but Heaven spilled first blood.

The angel sprang back into the air, shaking ichor from its sword as it gained height. The encounter was over before Lorelei could shift from the shadow in which she huddled.

One thing was for certain: the boys would never think of angels as harmless again. They'd be even more afraid of death if they understood how much misery could continue afterward.

Kim collapsed onto the ground. The others stared down at the scattered hunks of Sammy's flesh, unable to believe what they'd just seen. Sammy was the oldest of them, the toughest. If he could be killed like that, what were they doing here?

"What? You didn't believe me?" Floria threw her hands up in exasperation. "I told you these angels were a menace and I always play straight with you."

"This whole deal is bullshit!" Lam yelled, no longer trying to cover his fear.

"Bullshit?" Floria echoed incredulously. "Which part of the deal are you referring to? The part where I took your ass out of Westminster, living in your grandma's garage? Or when I set you up with a crib in the middle of Korean turf, and made it so none of the fuckers dared even look at you? Enlighten me, any of you... Was it the respect, the cash, the chicks, and steady jobs you got under Prince Asmodeus? Where did any part of that deal go wrong?"

None of the boys looked at her, least of all Tuan. Floria grabbed the nearest two and shook them hard.

"Guess what, kids? You took the thirty silver, and shit on everyone else doin' it, so you're in now. All the way in." As she finished her diatribe, Floria transformed fully into her infernal shape for the first time in front of them. The effect on the boys was dramatic, if not the way she'd hoped.

At the sight of her horns, wings, and tail, Lam pressed the barrel of his gun under his chin and fired.

Floria rolled her eyes in amused disgust. "Believe me," she told the survivors, "he just made things worse for himself."

She pulled the compact out of her little Gucci backpack and teased his soul out of his cooling flesh.

What a crock of shit, Lorelei thought. Floria was going to lose them all if she didn't get control pretty damn fast. If they underwent battlefield conversions... Lorelei didn't want to think of all the eminently damnable marks that she'd known who'd come back from war irretrievably saved.

Still clinging to her own mortal form, Lorelei dodged through the boys to snatch Sammy's gun out of the carnage. "Look," she told them, "the only way you're getting out of here alive is to stick together, watch each others' backs, and do what we tell you. If I've learned anything in the last week, it's don't set off any angels." She said it in a perfectly reasonable tone of voice.

She checked the action of Sammy's gun, then wiped her bloody hands on the nearest unhallowed gravestone. "Get your shit together and draw your weapons."

On the roof of the chapel, Rafael and Michael continued to debate with the recording angel Yehudiah about the removal of the hoarded souls now, before the siege escalated out of control.

"I cannot risk taking the sullied with the pure," Yehudiah said, fingers untying the elaborate knots on his ledger scrolls.

"No risk of that." As Shebethiel alighted on the corner of the roof, the last minuscule beads of Sammy's blood evaporated from his armor. "Most of the mortals in their thrall are irredeemable." He opened his hand to reveal a dozen spent slugs. His own blood oozed slowly from the rents in his armor.

Michael nodded. "Direct our own mortal warriors to be careful. Tell them there are children about with dangerous playthings."

As Rafael went to obey, Yehudiah consulted the scroll in his hand. "What was the young man's name?"

"Sammo Ha," Shebethiel said.

Yehudiah added it to Hell's balance.

Commotion arose in the western corner of the cemetery. The stone angels atop monuments glowed with warning iridescence. "They mean to keep us busy," Michael observed. "If need be, we can summon more help, but I'd prefer not to. We dare not leave the rest of the territory unguarded."

Aza flung his wings open to fly in that direction.

"Stay," Michael commanded.

Aza froze, as still as one of the monument angels.

"You've already taken enough part in this," Muriel said as Shebethiel leapt to take Aza's place in the fray.

The archangel soothed Aza with a hand on his shoulder. "There's a reason for you to remain here," Michael assured. "I've seen your Lorelei and know her judgment. If she is killed tonight, I want you to save her soul with the rest."

"How can she be saved?" Muriel protested. "She's a succubus!"

Michael smiled. "Though the spirit Lorelei has seen centuries, her soul is but a week old. In that week, it returned a priest to us for the sake of Heaven and saved a young girl for the sake of love. You've done well, Brother. Bide here and lure Hell's attack, but save Lorelei if death finds her."

Floria felt a hand clutch her forearm, manicured nails biting deep enough to hint how much damage they could do if their owner chose.

Like the sound of an unfolding lockblade, Yasmina's voice hissed in her ear. "You'll be watched tonight, Special Girl. Time to cash in all your boys." The temptress's breath rolled over her in a mix of smoke and soiled fangs, impossible to ignore.

"I wanted to ask you..." Floria swallowed hard. "How did you bring Jezebel to heel? If I could get Lorelei under my thumb—"

Yasmina swung around to face her, mouth twisted into a sneer. "Fuck your sister, Little Girl. Sometime tonight, undoubtedly very soon, Asmodeus will lift his aegis from her. Watch her carefully. As soon as it's gone, make sure Lorelei gets shot before her angel's eyes."

"But—"

The temptress's copper eyes glowed brighter. "It's crucial that, whatever the outcome of all this, the angel suffers tonight. Once Lorelei is dead, you will be allowed to leave the graveyard. The sooner you do what you're told, the sooner you'll be safe. So go say goodbye to your boys and make sure we get full value out of them before that happens."

Tuan found a cast-off pitchfork smoking in the grass atop a grave. He circled it, trying to figure out if it promised to be enchanted enough to protect him. Then he stumbled over the handle of a sledgehammer abandoned amidst the rubble of what had been a marble statue. Whatever had been wielding the hammer had been reduced to a puddle of oily goo. Tuan wiped the hammer's handle with his bandana, which he threw away. He swung the hammer experimentally. It seemed like a much more certain weapon than Floria's damn guns.

The longer he wandered around in the open, the more likely he'd be to come across someone else, devil or angel or terrified human with a high-powered weapon. The only cover he could see were the family tombs dotted here and there through the grounds. The stone was probably fire-resistant, too. Tuan expected that would be a good thing before long.

He needed a place to hole up until he could get out of the graveyard. Then he'd go to the nearest church, make a full confession, and try to find a way out of his damned contract. Tuan didn't care if the priest sent him to jail, or worse, a madhouse; he just couldn't deal with Floria any longer. Their relationship was worse than a bad marriage and probably more expensive to get out of.

Tuan felt awful about abandoning the boys, especially since it was clear they'd been brought here to die. He wasn't sure about the states of their souls—other than Sammy's—but he knew where his own was headed once it was separated from his body. He wasn't ready for that trip yet.

The battle had fragmented out of control around him. Even fiends couldn't seem to stand against the angels, so Hell's default plan appeared to be merely to fuck up the graveyard as much as possible. Tuan had too much respect for the dead to join in.

And the boys' objectives—kill any humans they came across, leave the angels alone—what a fucking joke. Other than Sammy, his boys weren't killers. They were just kids, trying to make a living in an expensive world where the best they could hope for was room and board courtesy of LA County.

Floria couldn't couch what she wanted them to do in any sort of terms that made sense. She was no leader, that was for damn sure. The way she drove Lam to suicide—then calmly collected his soul—had been the last straw. Tuan loved his friends too much to watch them all die.

He circled one little tomb built like a miniature church, complete with spire and frilly stonework dripping off its roof. The easiest way in might be to break its stained glass window, but Tuan hadn't the heart for that. He lifted the sledgehammer from his shoulder and took a practice swing at its ornate iron gate.

A fiend leapt onto a tombstone nearby. Its too-big teeth flashed beneath burning eyes. "Good work, kid," the monster growled, before springing away.

Shivering, Tuan raised the hammer again and attacked the door with more determination.

CHAPTER 16: DROPPING LIKE FLIES

Aza was looking for Lorelei when a trebuchet outside the cemetery wall flung a flaming Christmas tree onto the chapel's roof. The tree exploded on impact, raining burning needles everywhere. Although he had done his best to clear the leaves from the chapel's decorative ironwork, debris in its downspouts caught fire.

Aza sought aid, but his siblings were scattered across the graveyard, each engaged in a separate battle.

Another trebuchet strike spattered burning pitch across the chapel's roof.

Aza spotted a crimson flash across the central drive of the graveyard. The hourglass contours of her form were unmistakable. His Lorelei had joined the battle, just as Mastema predicted.

Then Aza's attention was called back to the situation at hand. A pack of fiends vaulted onto the chapel. Aza swung Rafael's sword in a broad arc, scything the tines from their pitchforks all at once.

Even as he dispatched the fiends, Aza realized that Lorelei wore only another iteration of her black party dress, instead of any sort of battle gear. A thought, in a voice almost like Lorelei's own, echoed through his mind: at least she could've worn a leather dress, rather than the scrap of shadow that provided no protection at all. He felt his heart contract. How could he possibly help her escape?

Taking advantage of the angel's distraction, a tempter dropped from above, flattening Aza to the chapel's burning roof. Before Aza could regain his breath, the tempter's weight was swept away.

Aza tossed himself over onto his back, only to find Michael standing there, a huge grin on his face as the second wave of fiends tripped over each other, howling as they fled across the consecrated ground. The tempter himself had vanished.

The archangel held a hand down. Aza clasped it and allowed himself to be raised to his feet. "Thank you, Brother."

"My pleasure, Azazi-El."

Michael surveyed the conflagration surrounding them. "The chapel is a loss," he decided. "Fall back to the columbarium and await further orders there."

Unquestioning, Aza leapt for the sky.

As he rose, he scanned the cemetery for another glimpse of Lorelei. When he found her, he confirmed his earlier observation: the sigil that had burned above her—Asmodeus's aegis—had been extinguished. The demon had withdrawn his protection. She'd been sent here to die.

Aza swung toward her, ready to swoop down and rescue her. Then he noticed that Michael was still observing him, watching to see if Aza would leave the children's souls at risk for even an extra moment. It was a terrible, heart-rending choice to make, but in the end, Aza turned away from the succubus to do as he was bidden.

Lorelei would have to find her own safety, if she could. Too many other souls were reliant on Aza's protection now.

Even as he touched down on the columbarium roof, preparatory grief stabbed through Aza's chest. He hated himself. He could not believe that Lorelei's betrayal of spirits she never met was as great as his own when he abandoned a creature he loved above all others. Everything she accused him of was true.

Not far from the burning chapel, Max crouched in wait atop one of the family mausoleums. His forearm was wound tightly through the sling of the deer rifle he'd brought. Someone, he didn't know who, called his name and warned to be ready. Max almost had to laugh. Here he was: in the middle of a graveyard, a sniper for God, and he had no idea what he was supposed to be ready for.

Until he looked through the scope. Max had never seen anything like the man-shaped bulldozer that sprinted away the chapel, puffs of smoke marking every footfall.

It still shocked him that he somehow managed to sight and squeeze the trigger, placing a shot squarely into the creature's face. Less surprising was the way the monster kept coming, now headed directly for him.

Out of nowhere, an angel dropped down to cleave the fiend in half.

"Thanks!" Max called. "I…"

The angel turned. Several blackened holes gaped in her armor, trickling golden blood. "Do me a favor," she said. "Don't waste your shots on them. However, if you see anyone with a gun, kill 'em. They can hurt us, Max."

"I'm on it."

"Good man." Muriel took wing and left him alone.

After Vin got separated from the others, he found himself with his back against a low headstone, cowering beneath the spreading branches of an old pine. In the treetop, an angel kept watch on something at the far side of the graveyard. Vin learned from Sammy's example not to confront angels directly. He slipped the Zippo from his pocket and touched a tongue of fire to the dry needles around the tree's base. The flames raced up the trunk as if following a trail of gasoline. After the long dry summer, the bark was like tinder.

With a sound like shredding bubble wrap, the tree exploded into a torch. The acrid, sweet scent of pine resin filled the air. Filament-like embers swirled around him as burning needles fell.

Vin smelled a stench that could only be singed feathers. Got him!

Vin dodged back from the heat. He looked around, hoping one of the others would see what he'd managed.

Unfortunately, no angel fell from the tree. Scorched and blackened pigeons tumbled down out of the fiery branches. Vin gasped in pity but feared to allow himself to be distracted for long. He had to see where that angel was. He backed up for a better look and bumped against a cool and very solid body. Before the boy could turn, the angel pierced him with its spear.

Lorelei halted. She'd been going back for Vin, but the angel ended that plan damn quick. The succubus dodged behind a granite obelisk to spy on the creature, aware that Floria's boys were running on without her. Lorelei didn't want to call out and draw the angel's attention, so she let them go. They weren't really much protection anyway.

She sized up the situation from behind the obelisk. Asmodeus's army, which had looked so large jammed into the sewer, had spread across the graveyard and been absorbed. She was alone in this moment of quiet. She wondered what would happen if she simply left the battlefield and went out for a drink someplace. Surely, everyone would be too busy to drag her back here. Better to beg for forgiveness than to ask for permission…

Before she could formulate a plan, a polished black limo, so mundane as to be completely out of place amongst the spreading fires, rolled up the road to the columbarium. An ember-colored sigil sparkled in the air, drifting forward in pace with the car. As it parked, Lorelei speculated on who could be inside the limo.

Black windows completely blank, the car waited with doors closed until one of the angels stepped to the edge of the columbarium. Lorelei recognized the archangel who'd rescued her from Yasmina's henchmen on the highway: Michael, Heaven's champion. A shudder ran through her.

Michael burned with white light inside his golden armor. He traced the limo's sigil in the air before him.

Floria arrived at Lorelei's shoulder. "What're they doing?"

"Some kind of parlay?" Lorelei guessed.

"It's a little late to be stating terms," Floria bitched. Several of the pines were aflame now, casting up black columns of smoke. "Can you read the sign?"

Lorelei shook her head. "Maybe it's Enochian or something."

"What's that?"

"Angelic script."

"Something your boyfriend taught you?"

Lorelei fired a glare at her. "Not yet."

Tomur climbed out of the limo, boot soles smoking on the asphalt as he removed a Persian carpet from inside the car. He kicked the carpet open, unrolling it on the parking lot to give the occupants of the car somewhere to stand. More fiends piled out, taking positions around the edges of the carpet, clearly unhappy and—as clearly—unarmed.

Jequon stepped out of the limo and waited to be recognized by the angels above.

"Maybe he's going back," Lorelei said.

"Oh?" Floria raised an eyebrow. "That'd knock you out of the headlines." She lit a cigarette. "Unless you'd care to join him?"

"Why do you have to be such a cunt?" Lorelei asked rhetorically. "I'm here following Nebiros's commands—just like you, Sister. Maybe we ought not to let the boys get too far ahead of us." She dodged off toward the sound of gunfire.

As Lorelei ran off, Floria raised her hands to mime a gun. She squeezed off a handful of imaginary shots at her sister's back. Now that the aegis had been lifted, there would be no repercussions for killing Lorelei. Maybe the boss would even be in a mood to hand out rewards.

Yasmina had said it needed to be done for maximum dramatic value, preferably somewhere that Lorelei's soul daddy could see her brought down. Floria scanned the graveyard, clocking various angels, but didn't recognize Azaziel. She wondered if he'd snuck off with his next honey already.

Floria turned back toward Lorelei. As clearly as she could see the aegis was missing, she could also read Lorelei's soul. It certainly wasn't damned, despite her orgy with the boys. Then again, she wasn't entirely saved either. Lorelei was too selfish for that.

Looked like she'd make a good midnight snack for someone. And if anyone was going to eat Lorelei's soul, Floria figured she deserved it most. Then, once the bitch was devoured, Floria's advancement could get back on track.

Until she located Azaziel, Floria had to figure out how to keep herself alive. Nebiros was one obsessed motherfucker, if the gossip about his behavior at Lost Angels could be believed. He wasn't likely to have the sense to fall back until the angels' cache of souls was razed. While Floria was all for pissing on the angel's corpse, she didn't plan to go to her destruction reclaiming a lot of flavorless gray souls.

First things first. Floria ran off after Lorelei, imagining, then rejecting ways to kill her former best friend as impactfully as possible.

From his place on the Persian carpet, Jequon looked up at his former brethren. "Are you going to come down here so we can converse like civilized beings or are you going to shout our business so that all and sundry can hear it?"

"Spread your wings and come up," Michael invited. "That is, if you're not ashamed to."

Jequon unwound his crimson wrap sweater and shrugged out of it. He handed it to the nearest fiend, who folded it over his arm. Then the fallen angel stretched out his oily black wings and bounded up onto the columbarium.

Once there, he checked that the sigil for truce continued to shimmer at the corner of the roof.

"Have you come back to us?" Rafael wondered.

Jequon grinned, glancing down at the fiends standing on the carpet in the parking lot below. The fallen angel said smoothly, "I'm merely here as Hell's envoy."

Zadkiel said, "Give us your master's message."

"Hell is incensed by this sundering of the natural order. Mortals die and are sent to their judgment or are consumed and forgotten. There has been no other way for them since time began. But this…" Jequon gestured at the graveyard. "You must agree that the unblessed souls unlawfully gathered here are forfeit."

"No," Aza protested.

"I do not speak to you, Brother," Jequon said haughtily. "This enterprise, after all, is your conception. You kept your secret long and well, but as you know, every crime has a way of being found out. Since you revealed yours to one of Hell's choicest minions…"

Michael cut him off. "You haven't been sent to bear witness against our brother, Jequon. What incentive can you offer to keep us from destroying all the servants of Hell ranged across this holy ground?"

"These are expendable." Jequon offered a bitter smile as he glanced again at the sigil burning overhead. Even so, he understood that the expendable might include himself. "However, Asmodeus pledges that in return for the destruction of the fifteen-score souls you've kept illegally, he's prepared to stop the holocaust of your temples and dwelling places across the metropolitan area. For every proscribed soul you retain, you jeopardize a hundred times that number of living."

Rafael shrugged. "Temples are but structures. The Creator's true place is in the heart. Faith tested by fire is usually strengthened. Asmodeus should know well enough not to create martyrs."

Jequon's wings ruffled in the smoky breeze, but he resettled them. "It appears Asmodeus is doing you a very large favor. How could Hell have blundered into this shrewd arrangement on your part? It's a pity he'll have to destroy the city in order for you to save it. I'm sure he'll think his assistance worthy of reward."

The fallen angel turned his back on the angels to survey the graveyard. Now that the trees were ablaze, the brown summer grass was catching as well. Shouts and infernal curses screamed through the air. Wailing sirens converged outside the walls. Gunfire crackled sporadically. Night had come, made blacker by the smoke. "Your new city looks remarkably like the Plain of Fire."

The truce sigil burned itself out.

Jequon knelt abruptly on the columbarium's roof, resting his palms on the tiles. An electric tremor ran through the building, as if all the souls hidden within quailed at his proximity.

He looked up expectantly. "They're all here, aren't they? It became obvious when you didn't make more than a token effort to save that tacky little chapel. Come on, comrades: throw open the doors of your treasury and allow Asmodeus's army inside. Put an end to this conflagration before it spreads beyond the cemetery walls. All that Hell requires is the destruction of these unsavory souls—and the status quo returns."

"Impossible," Aza said, drawing Rafael's sword.

"Of course you continue to change the rules to suit your whims. Some things are eternal." Jequon offered a knowing smile. "All that follows rests on you, my brother." He looked to Yehudiah. "Record that in your ledger. Hell will of course prosecute its grievance to the full extent of the law—for which my brother Azazi-El accepts full responsibility."

Floria looked back in time to see Jequon hurled from the columbarium onto the hood of his own limousine. That ended the theory of his defection. Too bad. She hated that motherfucker.

She vaulted up onto the nearest tombstone, then sprang into the air. Bursting through a wall of heat thrown off by a row of burning palm trees, she found herself suddenly in the midst of an aerial battle between a pair of arch-tempters and an angel. Floria folded her wings and plummeted, targeting a safe landing on some scorched earth.

When she rolled to her feet, the silhouette of another angel sent a bolt of lightning through her. Floria whipped her knife out of the sheath on her thigh and dropped into a crouch. Doubt crossed her mind that the angel on the granite column might be a statue. Then it leaned forward into a swan dive. The updraft from the fire swept it into the sky to help its sibling.

Floria sank against a tombstone, laughing weakly.

"I wouldn't laugh yet, harlot," a female voice said. "We have unfinished business."

Floria spun, flipping the knife into her other hand.

The angel swooped down at her. Rather than face the sword with golden flames licking its edges, Floria dodged around behind the tombstone. Momentum carried the angel past her.

Floria zigzagged between markers. One misstep brought her foot down onto a holy grave. The resultant shock made her pounce backward like a surprised cat.

Ahead of her, two unfamiliar African American boys huddled behind a tomb, backs to one another, guns swiveling this way and that like characters in a Jon Woo film. One snapped off a pair of shots toward Floria before she remembered to put her human disguise back on.

"Help me!" Floria pleaded.

The pitch of her voice motivated the kids. The cry of a beautiful girl touched the childish, elemental core of their manhood. Floria glanced around for the angel, smiling to herself as she ran toward the boys. They bolted in her direction, guns drawn, not yet thinking about what it was they meant to do.

The angel dropped to the ground behind her, demanding that she halt. Floria pushed past the boys, thrusting them in the angel's direction as she leapt into the air. She didn't turn to watch them die, hoping the angel would content herself with foes that didn't run away at the first breath of confrontation.

So what if she was a coward? Floria congratulated herself on keeping alive.

Lorelei located a remnant of Floria's boys crouched behind a mausoleum near the front of the graveyard. Kim curled up against the granite wall, his head on his knees. Hai was pacing, trying to inspire him with visions of what they could expect in payment for their service to Hell.

Tuan had either gotten separated from the boys or, more likely, chosen to absent himself. Lorelei suspected Tuan was questioning the circumstances under which he'd signed his contract. Still, Lorelei knew she had to leave Tuan for Floria to worry about.

Stepping out of a shadow so the boys could see her, Lorelei asked, "What are you guys doing here?"

Little Kim was too shell-shocked to respond. Hai fumbled out his gun and demanded, "How do we know you're really Lorelei?"

She offered him a smile that went straight to his groin. "Any questions?"

"Yeah," Hai answered, "is your fucking angel boyfriend here?"

"You fucked an angel?" Kim wondered.

"He wasn't the only person I fucked this week," Lorelei reminded. Kim flushed crimson and dropped his gaze.

Hai pushed it. "Is he?"

"I haven't seen him, Hai. Why? You want another shot at him?"

Rather than look at her, he checked the action on his gun. "For all the good it fucking did me."

"He's not the one who got you into this," Lorelei pointed out. "You volunteered. So what's your plan for getting out of here?"

Kim muttered, "Some monster came by here to say there was a truce on 'til the guy in the limo leaves. He said there'd be Hell to pay if the limo's paint got scratched by some stray shot."

Hai led Lorelei over to peer around the tomb toward the front gate. "See those guys?"

A loose row of ordinary people stood with their backs to a dump truck parked across the entrance. They looked utterly doomed.

"The monster said they were doin' Hell the favor of blockin' the gate. As soon as they move the truck and the limo passes, we're supposed to take out as many of them as we can and run like Hell."

Lorelei nodded. "Just don't shoot the angel."

"I'm not stupid," Hai snapped.

"That dude with the purple mohawk? He's an angel. He'll reveal himself as soon as you start gunnin' down his people."

Kim peered over their shoulders. "Seriously?"

"No shit," Lorelei agreed. "My advice would be to pick your targets, spread out, cap 'em, and duck."

"Are you gonna take out the angel?" Hai asked.

Lorelei pulled the knife out of her purse. "With this? Fuck, no."

The battered limo rolled down toward the gate. A Nicaraguan man hoisted himself up into the dump truck to shift it out of the way.

"Get over here," Hai ordered. To Lorelei's surprise, Kim obeyed. Hai relayed Lorelei's directions and Kim trotted off.

When he was gone, Hai turned on her. "You can't even cover our retreat, can you? You're scared of him." He nodded toward the angel.

"I'm scared of all of them," Lorelei admitted.

"Except the one you're fucking."

Before she could add, "Him, too," somebody opened fire. Hai turned to aim at his own target. As he took his first shot, Lorelei transformed and stretched her wings. She let Hai squeeze off three shots, then hauled him up and away.

The boy struggled in her grip, so she dug her talons in. It would be too easy to lose him as she swooped and swerved between the pillars of smoke.

Hai swore in Vietnamese and emptied the Glock's clip at something behind them. Lorelei didn't dare turn to see.

There was nowhere to set him down safely. Small clusters of tempters threw themselves at angels, unholy weapons howling. Fiends kicked over tombstones and tore open graves. Gangs of imps defaced stone angels with spray cans and baseball bats. The eucalyptus trees literally erupted in flames. Fire was spreading everywhere. Though she could stand it, Hai could not. Throughout the chaos, angels marched forward, slaying everything without remorse.

With a wrench, Hai was torn from her fingers. Lorelei somersaulted out of control, before crashing into a flaming palm tree. Then she was falling, sliding down the trunk and flailing to catch herself.

An angel, darker than the punk rocker at the gate, held Hai loosely in her arms. This one was a pretty girl, all curly brown hair and soft brown eyes. Panic coursed through Hai, even as the angel leaned down to bestow a kiss on his brow.

Pushing her off, Hai stuttered, "W-what do you want?"

In Vietnamese, the angel said, "You're to be damned, Hai Ng, for the sins of covetousness and lust. Because you willingly signed your soul over to Asmodeus, Prince of Lechers, I'll ask this but once: do you repent?"

"You must be fuckin' kidding."

Disappointed, the angel released the boy from her arms.

Hai grabbed after her, but the angel didn't spare another glance as she beat her huge blue wings and flew away.

"Lorelei!" Hai screamed.

Somehow, as his limbs pinwheeled, he managed to turn himself over. Then he was falling face downward. He didn't spare a glance up from the ground to see Lorelei launch herself off of the palm tree, straining to reach him but coming too late.

Lorelei bent over Hai's broken body and collected his soul in the polished knob on the hilt of her knife. She felt dead inside herself.

A hiss of scales on dry grass warned Lorelei and she flung herself into the smoking ruins of the cemetery chapel. The smell inside its broken walls made her think of the angel's lair: the aromas of grief and frankincense intertwined. Yasmina reared back outside, casting a snake's shadow on the chapel's delicate mosaic floor.

Yasmina shrugged. "You have to come out of there eventually."

Lorelei flipped a finger in Yasmina's direction.

Yasmina laughed. "You wish, Little Girl."

Jezebel ran up to Yasmina and pointed urgently back toward the heart of the cemetery. Yasmina snarled, but her displeasure melted away when she recognized whatever her minion pointed at. Lorelei's heart sank. She could guess who had snared their attention.

"Well?" Nebiros snapped as he bent down to talk to Jequon inside the battered limo.

"The holy ground grows blighted, as you foresaw," Jequon reported. "Your soldiers should be able to cross it safely soon."

Nebiros's spine crackled as he nodded.

Jequon fiddled with his crimson sweater. His skin still crawled at the feeling of the archangel's hands upon him. "The chapel was a decoy. The souls are concentrated inside the columbarium."

Nebiros gestured sharply. Two archfiends loped away to carry the message into the graveyard.

Jequon continued, "You'll be thrilled to know that Azaziel stands guard atop the columbarium."

Nebiros's serpent reared back, hissing, as its master's tortured face worked into a grin.

"He's still carrying Rafael's accursed sword," Jequon warned.

"It won't matter," Nebiros promised. "Azaziel was lucky to escape me Friday night. Tonight I won't be dragged away until I've made a chalice of his skull."

On the balcony of Asmodeus's mansion overlooking LA, an archangel materialized in the middle of the party. The succubi surrounding Asmodeus slouched away. The few fiends on duty drew their weapons and moved toward their master.

Asmodeus halted the fiends with an upraised hand. "I don't recall inviting you," he told the angel.

"Everyone else is fighting tonight," Rafael answered. "Why should we?" He held up an earthenware jug as a peace offering. "It's Galilean. I wager you haven't tasted its like in a millennium or two."

Asmodeus waved the fiends away. They stepped backward into the shadows, slipping on their sunglasses against the angel's radiance. "There are a lot of things I haven't tasted, thanks to you," the demon said.

"You're not still mad about that princess, are you? That was a long time ago."

"True," Asmodeus conceded. "But that's no reason why I have to tolerate a double standard these days."

"You're a prince of Hell. You can rise above…"

"So you actually approve of this pairing?"

"The one that started all this trouble?" Rafael finished for him. "I'll tell you how I feel about it: I'm told to watch and wait."

Asmodeus turned toward the fiends and gestured for goblets from the bar cart. Only one of the hulking monsters had the balls to step forward. Asmodeus accepted the drinking cups, then held them out for Rafael to fill.

They savored the wine silently. Asmodeus's eyelids flickered with ancient memories.

"Simpler days," Rafael remarked.

"Better wine. The fools in Napa have no idea how much they've forgotten." Asmodeus raised his glass, looking through it at the flames below. "If you've brought something to drink, I assume you've come to bargain. I'll split those hoarded souls with you fifty-fifty."

"The souls aren't mine to give away." Rafael sipped his wine. "Neither is Azaziel."

"So why did you come?"

"You wouldn't be drinking my wine if there wasn't some trace of love for Sarah still in your heart."

"That was before I learned to grow my own girls." The prince drained his glass. "Which is why I can still claim Lorelei as mine, to do with as I like."

"Except for that soul of hers." Rafael refilled his own glass and waved the jug toward the demon. Asmodeus held his goblet out. While their hands were busy, Rafael said, "It's that issue of free will again. I'm sorry about that: Sarah should have been allowed to choose you."

After a long pause, Asmodeus drawled, "I believe I just heard an apology from an archangel."

"You did. I meddled in something that was none of my business. I know you made her happy, which is more than we can say about Tobin."

"I'm still pondering that unsolicited apology." Asmodeus sipped his wine. "I don't know what to say."

"Say this: whatever punishment you inflict, you won't kill Lorelei."

Asmodeus snorted. "For what it's worth, I can promise that I won't kill her. But you're assuming I have more control over my people than I do. Hell is the realm of the disobedient, after all."

The archangel didn't answer, gazing out instead at the columns of smoke rising from the city's churches. Asmodeus followed his gaze, drinking the old wine with a smile.

CHAPTER 17: THE WORLD'S AFLAME

The gun was too big for Kim's small hands to hold steady. Blinded by tears, he let his forehead rest against the cold stone base of an angel statue. He tried to imagine himself pulling the trigger, but all he could think was that maybe those people guarding the gate had been dragged here by angels the way his friends had been dragged here by monsters.

This whole night was horrible and wrong. Kim had never been this scared, except maybe in nightmares. This nightmare seemed like it would never end unless he turned the gun on himself. Maybe suicide was the only way out, despite what Floria said after Lam's death.

Kim heard gunshots and lifted his head to see a winged sex monster flying away with a screaming young man in her talons. Kim bolted in the opposite direction, hurdling over gravestones, unsure where he was headed, but fleeing all the same. He was across the cemetery's central drive before he realized that he'd abandoned his gun at the stone angel's feet.

His foot skidded across a polished marble slab and he landed hard on his ass. Even though nothing pounced on him, Kim started sobbing.

When he could hear over the wheeze of his own breathing again, he knew he was in Hell. The night echoed with the roar of flames, sirens, and curses he didn't want to understand. He was lost in a maze of fire and monsters, unarmed and helpless.

He forced himself to his knees. The stone that had tripped him was a glossy black granite slab. The dates were clear enough: 1981—1999. 18 years old. Etched in the marble, the dead boy's portrait had sharp eyes beneath bushy brows. He looked a lot tougher in death than Kim felt alive. His name had been Carlos.

To either side of Carlos's grave lay his brothers: hermanos, one Spanish word Kim had learned in school. To the left lay Emilio, 1983-1998, two years older at death than Kim himself. The other boy was Roberto, 1980-1999, buried two months after Carlos's death. Reprisals, Kim realized. Brothers killed trying to avenge brothers.

Kim thought of his older brothers, both in prison, one for car theft, the other for strong-arm robbery. Without them, Kim had felt unprotected and small. Tuan had seemed to be the brother he needed, the one who'd look out for him in the world.

But where was Tuan now? Where were any of them? Hai had ordered

Kim to shoot a stranger—kill him—and Kim couldn't do it. Now he was alone.

One of the palm trees dropped a burning frond with a rustle that scared Kim back to his feet. The heat boiled around him as the dried grass took fire.

An angel appeared in front of Kim without having seemed to land.

Too frightened to move, Kim stared at the angel, noticing the bare toes that peeped out from her Birkenstocks. Thin bands of gold held her loose brown curls back from her beautiful face. Wordlessly, she held one hand out.

In what felt like the bravest moment of his short life, Kim stretched out his arm and laid his fingers in the angel's cool palm.

Not far from the columbarium where Azaziel stood guard with a glowing sword, Joseph raced from faucet to faucet, blessing the taps as he turned on the water. His original plan had been to use the sprinklers, until he'd discovered that every single one had been sabotaged. He wondered how many taps he could get going without losing water pressure.

A pair of fiends loped toward him, flinging globs of flaming tar into the dry fronds of the gigantic palms that lined the cemetery's main avenue. Joseph didn't have anything beyond a prayer to fight them. Although Max had offered him a rifle before the fighting began, Joseph had been unable to accept it. Even now, he didn't regret that choice.

A slap of cool wind splayed the hair at the back of his neck, making him turn. A winged shape loomed overhead. The shadows of the fire dancing all around them made its feathers ripple. Joseph's first thought was that it was a brown granite statue, illuminated by the blazing trees, until the angel gestured to him, part benediction, part motion to stay down.

"Joseph, it's not wise to remain here. Your soul may be safe, but your body isn't."

Joseph pointed mutely behind him toward the fiends' methodical progress down the lane of trees. The archangel unsheathed his sword with a sound like golden bells, nodding grimly as something flashed overhead. Another angel swept back and forth across the lane, severing the heads from the burning palms. They hurtled down like short-range comets. One struck the pitch wagon the fiends had been hauling along. It erupted in a volcanic splash of flame.

Vaulting over Joseph, Zadkiel waded into the burning morass, slashing at the blocky silhouettes of the fire-throwers.

Another breeze plucked at Joseph, though he was unable to take his eyes off the skirmish in the inferno. The archangel continued to battle the lumbering shapes on all sides of him, dropping them with brief economical attacks, like a movie samurai.

A steamy hiss was followed by a string of curses in a feminine voice. Joseph whirled around in surprise and nearly lost his footing on the muddy grass. Floria sat atop a thick gravestone, rubbing her taloned feet.

"Who the fuck put holy water there, Joe?" The devil girl tossed her blonde locks. Her glittering eyes flicked toward the brawl in the flames. "Bet you're the cause of that, too. Right?"

As if in answer to her question, one of the fiends leapt free of the flames to escape the angelic blade—only to explode into steaming chunks when he hit the sodden grass at the roadside.

Joseph grinned. He wondered if he could splash some of the puddled holy water up at this terrible beauty, or maybe anoint himself.

"Yep, it's all you, clever boy," Floria scolded. "Messing with my crew, helping those good-for-nothing feathered fucks."

Leaning down at an impossible angle, the succubus sniffed at the priest.

"Ooh, and check out his soul."

"It's out of your hands."

"So they said. Bet they told you you're already dead too, like all the mortals they trick into doin' their chump work."

Joseph put as much force into the words as he could: "Get thee behind me…"

The succubus cut him off with a bored sigh. "Okay, that's it. If you're gonna babble the classics, I don't want to hear it. I'm gonna cut to the chase and give you one shot at this, so I can get back to work."

Leveling a razor-tipped index finger at Joseph, Floria's eyes locked on him, angry and yellow in the dark. "All you have to say is, 'Floria, get me out of this and my soul is yours.'"

He almost laughed at her, but caught himself just in time.

"Make it worth your while, Joe," she offered, keeping one eye on the archangel. More shapes had entered the flames, trying to drive him off and get the pitch wagon back on course.

Joseph shouted for the angel's attention. "Help!"

In a single lightning movement, Floria's spaded tail lashed out to encircle the priest's throat and drag him back toward her.

Clutching a faucet, Joseph tried to resist the pull, praying the angel would catch sight of his peril. The prayer was answered, but not the way he'd hoped. The archangel shook his head sadly, calling, "I tried to warn you," before turning back to his fight.

"A lot of good he did you," Floria teased, dragging the priest toward her. His feet slipped out from under him in the puddled grass. His head struck the base of her monument hard. Everything went black.

Floria watched the water bubble up around the priest's face. When he didn't get back up, she hopped down atop the prostrate man's back, jabbing a single talon into the back of his head to see if she could rouse him before he drowned in the sanctified mud. No response. Tearing into Joseph's back, she probed for his soul, only to find it gone, safely seeped into the holy ground beneath them.

"Why am I not surprised?" she muttered sourly before leaping back into the safety of the smoky darkness. She wanted to be elsewhere before the archangel fought clear of the fiends swarming over him.

A familiar scent caught Floria, stopping her in mid-flight. Her mouth watered at the aroma of Marlboro smoke, stale CK, and fresh sweat: her boy Tuan.

She circled back to find him sitting inside a holy little tomb with his back against the altar. Over his head, a stained glass window was fitfully lit by the flames outside. It showed that pallid messiah, fey hands clasped atop a rock, doe eyes upturned toward the sun.

Tuan wasn't praying. He wasn't even really thinking. He just sat there in the dark, working through his cigarettes. Weird.

"You jacking off in there or what?" Floria wondered.

Tuan flicked the butt of his cigarette out the door at her, but didn't answer.

"Come on, boy. There's work to do."

"There's work for you, Floria. I'm done."

"How do you figure that?"

"Our contract says that you serve me. I don't serve Hell 'til I'm dead. I don't kill people, not with intent. Not with a gun. And I'm done selling death a gram at a time. I don't give a fuck about angels, so I'm just gonna sit this one out."

Floria's tail lashed. The light flickering through that stained glass was giving her a screaming migraine. She glanced down at her feet, found a suitable chunk of marble, and pitched it. The glass shattered with a musical crash.

Tuan sighed. "You didn't have to do that."

"What does it matter?" Floria answered. "Come morning, this whole place is gonna look like Vietnam after the war." Floria arched an eyebrow. "That's before your time, Baby, but your folks must've told you what it was like. Grandad was never afraid of getting into the shit, back in the day." She whistled appreciatively through her fangs. "He threw a lot of lead for Uncle Ho. What would he think to see you now, cowering in a shrine to the running dogs' god?"

Tuan took a step forward, as if he might close the door in her face.

Just a little closer, Floria thought, searching for a better goad, wishing she'd listened to the young man more closely over the months.

"Yep, Ông nôi really knew how to play the game. Fucked the Yankee back home, then emigrated here to make money at the Man's expense. Your slackin' now would probably kill him, if he weren't gone already."

Since Tuan had hardly known his grandfather, he merely shrugged the taunt off.

Floria prowled past the doorway, tail switching. She had to get the boy out of there and back to business before anyone important saw him inactive. If word got back to the boss that the lynchpin of her organization balked at her orders, on tonight of all nights...

More humiliating, the closer she got to Tuan, the more clearly she could smell the change in him. Not only was he ignoring orders now, he didn't plan to follow orders again. His soul had lapsed from being wonderfully, deliciously damned to teetering on the brink. If she didn't get him out of that tomb soon, he was going to slip from her clutches despite their contract.

"What's the matter, Baby?" Floria purred. "Didn't you get everything you ever wanted?"

"Except a woman who really loves me. I been thinkin' a lot about Lorelei, 'bout how she really loves her angel. Loves him enough to wear a broken handcuff as a token. Loves him enough to stand up to you, and that bitch, and a prince of Hell. Loves him enough to allow herself to become a spectacle at Pandemonium. I wonder what that's like, having a love like that."

Floria swallowed the bile that rose in her throat. As sweetly as she could manage, she asked, "Didn't we have good times?"

"It was fun," he said, "but it was just sex."

Floria's tail slashed through the air. "Great sex," she corrected, working the connection between them for all it was worth.

She heard the intake of his breath and knew she'd gotten through. Tuan shifted in the darkness, his jeans uncomfortably constrictive. He laughed at himself. "Prolly the best sex I'll ever have," he admitted. "If it had stayed fucking, I might not have a problem now. But this...all this bullshit..."

She gave him time to think about it. Really, she was curious what he was going to say. It would be instructive, she suspected. It might help her keep prey in line in the future.

"The sex was worth my soul," he said finally. "This bullshit is not. Watching my friends die for you is not. Killing people because you say to is not. I didn't sign up for this. And the sex would've been better if you'd loved me, or at least knew enough to pretend that you did. Once I figured out it wasn't about me at all, that I was just part of your plan... Sex isn't enough anymore."

Floria paced past the door of the tomb. "You're telling me you want out?"

"Yeah," Tuan said.

"Everything's in your name: the BMW, the penthouse, TV, PlayStation. Nothing's paid for. You stop selling drugs, you kiss all that goodbye."

"I know. I'll go down for it. It's worth some jail time to have tasted it. But I want all the way out. I want the contract broken, too."

"Okay," Floria said.

That caught him off-guard. "What's the catch?"

"You do one last thing for me and I'll have the contract annulled. You can tear it up."

"Give it to me now," he shot back.

Floria reached out, calling the contract to her hand. "This is just parchment. Tearing it up doesn't end our deal. We'll need a witness to break it."

Tuan walked to the threshold of the tomb. Floria wondered if he knew the tomb had been consecrated and she couldn't get at him, or if it was just dumb luck. His luck wouldn't hold much longer, if she had any say in the matter.

"All right," he said. "What do I have to do?"

"I've got one goal for this whole night. Just one. And you're the man to help me accomplish it. Still got your gun?"

"Shooting angels doesn't do shit," he protested.

"It's not for the angel. It's for Lorelei."

Floria watched Tuan absorb that, surprised by the cold dread that washed over him. He wrestled with his affection for her sister.

"I said I didn't want to kill anyone else."

"She's not anyone," Floria corrected. "She's one of us."

"What's to keep me from shooting you?" Tuan answered.

"Wouldn't do anything but piss me off." Floria bared her teeth. "Now that Lorelei's sprouted a soul, she's in the same boat as you. Her soul gets separated from her flesh—say, someone shoots her between those pretty purple eyes—and she's on the express elevator to Hell. Her soul for yours, Tuan. That's my deal."

He lit another cigarette, sucking on it hard as he thought it over.

"I'll get you safely over toward the columbarium," Floria promised, waving over her shoulder in that direction. "Lorelei's boyfriend is stationed on its roof. Sooner or later, she's gonna try to link up with him. I have to stop her. You stop her for me, and you're free to go."

The combat grew steadily nearer to the columbarium since Michael had been called away. Aza paced the rooftop. "Rejoice, I have entrusted thee with a great and holy task, thy love a mightier shield than the charge of any foe." Micha-El's voice swelled within Aza's mind, recalling the words of the Almighty during the Rebellion in Heaven.

Barbelo settled next to Aza. Her halo was radiant in the gloom. She gave Aza a companionable smile.

"I wish I could join you in the fight," he said.

Chestnut locks swinging around her shoulders, Barbelo's eyes were afire with purpose. She hadn't fought in the War. Vicious as it had been, Heaven hadn't needed more than a third of its loyal host to put the rebels to flight. Still, she'd been in some noble fights over her mother. Once permitted, angels loved few things as much as a good brawl in a righteous cause.

"They're safe with you here, Azazi-El," Barbelo assured, before taking wing again. Her lance lit the air around her with a golden-blue glow.

Aza strained to see what Barbelo leapt so hurriedly to attack. Something in his chest burned down to a stony pain as he saw Yasmina coiled up along one of the obelisks nearby.

A cohort of fiends hacked down several of the pines between the obelisk and the columbarium. At Yasmina's direction, without a doubt. Using their claws, they set to work stripping the massive branches to use as breastworks to mount the walls in the event that the angels could stop them from using the trunks as battering rams.

Harpies dodged to and fro among the remaining trees, staying out of the fight whenever they could. It would be their task to swoop amongst the scattered souls once Hell managed to breach their refuge. The harpies would collect up the children and bear them back to their master, so that Asmodeus could dispose of them as the law directed.

Shrieking, Yasmina worked as far up the obelisk as possible, using the trees at her back to keep Barbelo from getting height on her. With her serpentine body wrapped tightly, she was free to twist, turn, and meet any attack.

In one hand, the arch-temptress whirled a hooked blade of red bronze, which trailed a shimmering vortex at every spin. In the other, she held a fan of gleaming darts, each fletched with the mottled quills of fallen angels and dipped in the polluted blood of cardinal sinners yet alive.

Swooping in, Barbelo thrust her lance at the snakelike creature. She would be only too happy to rid Creation of this monster. Yasmina had endured virtually the entire age of mortalkind, eternally refreshed the dark springs of jealousy and spite.

Yasmina called for her bitch Jezebel. The cowed servant scrambled from behind a family tomb. Nocking a black arrow, Jezebel drew back the bowstring, fingertips tightly clutching the shaft. Its bristled fletching scraped along her mutilated cheek.

With neither breath to still nor heartbeat to time from, Jezebel sighted on the angel. Her screeching mistress castigated Jezebel for the lazy disobedient slut that she was, demanding that she fire for the sake of Hell.

I am a creature of Hell, Jezebel reminded herself. It is my home and rightful place, the realm of the disobedient. Without a dreg of remorse, she turned the bow on her mistress and released the string. What harm can this do?

The arrow sang for an instant of its too-short flight, burying itself completely in Yasmina's trunk at the junction of flesh and scales. A spasm bent the line of Jezebel's mouth, the closest thing to a smile she could manage.

The curse Yasmina screamed made the blood roar in the fallen succubus's ears. Unable to conceive that the arrow strike had been deliberate, Yasmina ordered Jezebel to fire again, to aim with greater care.

Practically a blank check, Jezebel thought, eyes alight with malign joy.

Even as she drew and fired again, the angel fell upon her mistress, pinions a pearly bluish blur, lance darkening with devil blood. Although Jezebel hadn't intended it to, the second arrow found its mark, ripping through the muscles that webbed the arch of Barbelo's wing. The shaft split into cruel slivers as it glanced off the angel's pretty little head.

Jezebel ground useless teeth behind the fused scar tissue that had been her lips. The angel's cries of pain and glory made her wish that Yasmina had taken her ears along with everything else, so long ago.

All the same, something stirred in Jezebel, like the thrill a mortal would feel when it broke something irreplaceable.

No longer caring which creature she hit, Jezebel sent shaft after barbed shaft screeching up at the pair locked in sinuous combat. She wished she had an arrow for every thwarted ambition she'd known. For every sweet clutch of orgasm she'd been denied. For every time her eyes had lowered in unending submission.

Then her knuckles scraped the inside of her empty quiver. Thirteen shafts gone as swiftly as a mortal heart could beat so many times. Jezebel dropped to her knees, shaking through the last of her rush. The larger battle around her had faded into a muffled cloud of noise. She had no idea that her ears were clogged with blood, ruptured by the screams of both creatures she'd been trying to kill.

Jezebel quickly tallied the arrows sticking out of the antagonists, writhing now with decidedly less energy. Six each, not counting the one she'd bounced off the angel's hard head. Not bad shooting. Downright wicked.

She wasn't the only one keeping count. Yasmina cast aside the wounded angel. The arrow shaft that had pinned them together twisted and snapped, messily dragging its barbs across the temptress's scaly belly as it came free.

Smearing one palm across a gout of inky blood, Yasmina healed the wound with a squelch of steaming flesh, then turned her gaze on Jezebel. Vengeance and fury lit her eyes copper as she gestured a spell to hold the mutinous succubus fast.

Not waiting for her to finish, Jezebel snapped the now-useless bow over her knee and vaulted the nearest tombstone. She dodged amongst the headstones, not caring if her feet sizzled on holy soil. All that mattered was putting as much granite between the mistress and herself.

With any luck, the bitch would go back to the wounded angel and leave her alone for a change. If Jezebel was especially lucky, Yasmina would be destroyed and she could be free.

And if any questioned the arrows sticking out of her?

That realization wasn't enough to make Jezebel break stride. After all, she had been nailing the angel, but Yasmina, enraged beyond reason, wouldn't clear back. How could poor silenced Jezebel warn...no, plead...for the Mistress to stand clear? Why, she couldn't! And she didn't dare spare the angel. It was a great excuse. Hell valued audacity more than honesty any minute of the day.

Heaven, however, had no use for Jezebel—as the angel dropping down before her, all glittering armor and golden wings, surely would attest.

Jezebel looked up into his eyes, marveling at the stern sorrow in them. Being merely elevated, Jezebel had no clue regarding the angel: not his name or what his deal was, nothing.

He was as brown and beautiful as anything she had ever longed for. A mass of raven dreadlocks framed tiger-striped eyes. Taking her in his arms, the angel bore her upward, above the smoke and din of the fight.

No time for regrets, Jezebel realized. Just one last act to define who she was.

Reaching down abruptly, the succubus pulled the dagger just inside the waist of her driving coat. With a single swift plunge, she brought the blade up, trailing blood from a raw slice in her crotch. Even as the angel reacted, Jezebel trailed the knife's edge against her lips, freeing her mouth for the first time in centuries.

"Do us a favor?" she rasped, her teeth dingy with blood. Jezebel locked her legs around the angel's hips.

He regarded her with a mix of pity and rage. It almost seemed he was angriest about having to destroy her. Jezebel went for broke, pressing the ruined slash of her mouth to his lips.

Smeared on the angel, her tainted blood became purple-red flames that raced between them like Saint Elmo's fire. The very blood in her open wounds caught, fire burning her from inside out.

Not a bad kiss to go out on, she thought.

Zadkiel dove back toward the conflict, letting the rushing wind fan the succubus's immolation, holding her as tenderly as she could have desired. Ashes and cinders blew from his grasp into a thinning trail behind him.

Shaking her head as the ashes settled in her hair, Lorelei backed away, trying not to compare the angelic embrace she'd just witnessed to the one she longed for.

Once she focused on the battle again, Lorelei saw Tuan stumble. He crashed to the ground hard enough that his breath huffed out. Then he didn't move.

Was he dead? Was he still damned? Lorelei couldn't stand not knowing. She crept between the headstones to reach him.

Tuan saw her coming and lifted a gun in his shaking hand.

"Are you okay?" Lorelei asked gently.

"I been shot."

Lorelei crawled forward, disregarding Tuan's gun. She perceived his soul trying to melt free of its flesh. Her mouth watered.

Tuan let his gun fall. He rested his cheek in the grass and sobbed.

Lorelei lay beside him and wrapped herself around him: arms, legs, and tail. She turned him over as gently as she could. Blood welled out of the wound in his back. It was hot against Lorelei's skin.

"I don't want to die," Tuan moaned.

The sound of his anguish stabbed her heart. Tears pooled in her eyes. "I'm sorry," she whispered.

"I don't want to go to Hell. Lorelei, I didn't understand... I thought I'd live longer. I thought I'd get out of it. She was supposed to serve me..."

Lorelei hushed him with a kiss. Tuan pushed her feebly away.

"I hated you in the beginning," he confessed. "I hated how Floria would do stuff to impress you..."

"Doing her job," Lorelei corrected.

His blood slicked her from shoulders to thighs. The warmth, which she'd always found sensual, nauseated her now. Tuan shivered against her, growing cold in her arms.

"I'm sorry," Tuan whispered. "I'm so sorry for everything..."

A low thrum disturbed the air. Lorelei recognized it as the sound of a naked angelic weapon. She cringed, wondering if she could hide behind the death vibrations flowing out from Tuan.

"He's mine," Floria snarled.

Lorelei felt the boy twitch at the sound of his mistress's voice.

"Sounds to me as if he's ready to repent," the angel answered.

Lorelei didn't dare look up at them. Instead, she watched Tuan, stroking his face with the back of her taloned fingers, wondering how she could ease his pain.

Parchment crackled as Floria shook open the scroll. "I have a contract, duly signed and witnessed, that Tuan Nguyen, this young man, does upon his death award his soul to me." She smiled down at Tuan. "Isn't that right, Baby?"

"Only parchment," the angel said. "There's still time." He knelt and stretched out a hand toward the boy.

Floria slithered off the gravestone on which she'd been sitting. Her talons smelled of priest's blood.

Lorelei knew she had to do something soon. If a minion of the Enemy stole a soul out of a corpse she held in her arms, nothing would save her from Hell's wrath. But this new feeling she had—this damned compassion—made her understand all too well Tuan's terror.

The end was very close. He was gasping, trying to gulp enough air to ward off the oxygen starvation caused by massive blood loss.

There was only one way she might rescue him. Lorelei began to tell him a story. "Remember the night we met?" she whispered. "You and Hai on the highway so late, your truck dead, and Floria and I stopped to pick you up in the convertible. Remember how we looked? You felt like you'd stepped into a music video. You felt blessed. You wanted to live forever in that moment. You were so young and innocent…"

She felt the change in him and knew the others did too. They leaned closer, but she moved over him first, sealing his mouth with a kiss. His eyes met hers and she saw permission—just a flash of it—before life bled away. Lorelei drew his soul out and swallowed it whole, consuming it entirely.

Floria let out an unearthly howl. Shebethiel clapped his wings together and rose into the air. Lorelei was watching him leave when Floria caught hold of Lorelei's hair and yanked her head back.

"Tuan was mine," Floria said between teeth clenched so tight the cords stood out in her throat.

A high-powered shot whistled by, slamming Floria off the monument she'd been perched on. It knocked her into a puddle of holy water. Floria screamed, thrashing, unable to right herself.

Lorelei told herself it was the horrible noise that made her grab her sister and toss her clear of the water to safety.

Then she soared upward, winging toward the ranger like the fury of Hell. She landed with a crash atop the Egyptian Revival mausoleum on which he lay. He fired at her twice, missing, before she wrenched the rifle from his deformed hands. His thumbs had been removed in some horrible, scarring accident.

She smashed the rifle down against the roof and threw it back at him. "You shot him in the back," she snarled. "Tuan was a child."

"Oh, God," the man whimpered. "Not again."

"He might have redeemed himself in time," Lorelei continued. "He might have gone to Heaven. But you took it upon yourself to judge him and take his life. What gave you the fucking right?"

The man was shaking. Huge fat tears rolled from his eyes. Remorse clogged the air around him.

Lorelei didn't relent. "The only thing I could do for him was devour his soul and save it from damnation. That's the only blessing I dared give him. It's not my business to save innocents, you stupid fuck, because you get some a sick rush from murdering children."

Lorelei could see the man hadn't heard a word she'd said. Max Phillips shoved himself heavily onto his knees, then smashed his head down hard against the granite roof. His face left a bloody splotch as he pushed himself up to bang his skull down again. He repeated the motion over and over, chanting and whispering, already in a Hell deeper than Lorelei would be likely to drive him into herself.

Completely puzzled, she stood over him, wondering if it was possible for humans to kill themselves in such a way. She'd never seen a person behave like this before. Then his skull gave way with a sickening crack. He collapsed in spasms at her feet. Her mouth watered at the thought of another soul to devour.

As she knelt to turn him over, Lorelei smelled the complex aroma of his soul. The angels had chosen him as a test of his faith, but once here, the glory of the angelic presence hadn't lifted his guilt at being a killer. The Commandments prohibited taking lives, yet the angels required it. Max could not reconcile the two. All the outside forgiveness in the world couldn't wash away his sense of disgust. Everything they revealed only confirmed to him that God was a bastard, working out sick experiments on a defenseless world.

Damned, at the hands of angels. Lorelei shook her head as she drew her knife and collected his soul in its pommel.

If God was a bastard... Lorelei struggled with the concept of predestination. Had He known Asmodeus would send her here? Had the Enemy protected her when so many others of her kind had died? She hadn't had as much as a conversation with any of the angels swirling around the graveyard. Did something more than a demonic aegis protect her?

Lorelei looked up to see Aza standing atop the columbarium, gazing at her across the rank of fiends preparing to batter down its door. When their eyes met, the battle was erased from Lorelei's awareness. She was here because of Aza. There could be no other reason.

Then her angel smiled sadly and returned to protecting his children.

Shebethiel returned to face Floria. "You should have let me have the boy," he said.

Floria gritted her teeth against her pain. "Tuan worked hard for me. You would have had to store him with your other gray souls—and oops, we're about to take those away from you."

"You won't be among those who do. Get thee hence," Shebethiel growled, his soft voice becoming more forceful as he conjured a banishment. He traced fiery lines in the air, which lingered like a jagged corona above Floria's head. The angel raised his hand as if to strike the succubus, then spun her forcefully around.

Floria felt her wings manifest of their own accord. A hundred unseen points jabbed at her. "But Lorelei..." she protested, already moving away from the angel, trying without success to veer back toward the battle.

"Get thee hence," Shebethiel repeated. Clearly not a suggestion.

Unwillingly, Floria jumped into the sky. Perhaps the banishment only reached as far as the cemetery wall. As relieved as she was to be paroled from the fight, she wanted to witness its resolution.

Barakiel watched Floria disappear in the smoke wreathing the graveyard. The battle had moved past him now, as Hell's forces converged on the columbarium.

The fallen angel stepped out of the sandstone pyramid where he had hidden. He knelt in the sodden soil beside the priest's corpse, hands hovering in the air above his friend's body.

"I've missed you," Barakiel said softly to Joseph's corpse. "I wanted to apologize for misleading you for so many years. For finally burning your church to the ground. For so many things. Your friendship meant the world to me. I'm so glad you regained your faith and that you've gotten your heart's desire now."

He was startled from his litany by a hand on his shoulder. Shebethiel stood behind him. "May I pass your regrets on to Rafael?"

The fallen angel stared, unseeing, at the fire raging around them. They were alone here, in this oasis, thanks to the water Joseph had blessed. Even so, Barakiel said bitterly, "Hell will never let me go."

"Perhaps we can arrange a prisoner exchange," Shebethiel suggested. "Give me permission to help you, if I can."

"Why?" Barakiel asked.

"I only met Joseph toward the end of his life. He spoke well of you and hoped you could come back to the light, as he had. I'd be honored to assist you, if I can."

Barakiel nodded, then clasped his hand over the other angel's. Then Shebethiel leapt upward to return to the battle and left Barakiel alone to grieve.

CHAPTER 18: DIES IRAE

Barbelo raised herself painfully, leaning hard on the shaft of her lance. She tried unsuccessfully to steady her legs.

The slick of Yasmina's gore staining her armor smoked and shriveled as it mixed with the angel's own blood. Around her, the battle crashed and churned. Within its tumult, she heard the screams and curses of wounded infernals and the moans and prayers of mortals who lay dying.

Yasmina's attention shifted suddenly from her fleeing slave back to the wounded angel. With a sharp flick, she swung the bulk of her serpentine body around, flattening tombstones in a bid to lash the angel's legs out from under her.

Barbelo leapt awkwardly skyward. Unfortunately, her damaged wing dragged low. She pitched back to the ground. The wing curled painfully beneath her until it snapped where the arrows had pierced it. She cried out, breath trumpeting from her throat out of proportion to her size.

At the sound of her cry, the battle lulled. Every other angel realized they were losing one of their own.

Atop his perch on the columbarium roof, Aza strained against the impulse to leap to Barbelo's aid. He'd known her all her life. He remembered her exceptional birth and the ecstatic song Sophia sang as she held her daughter for the first time. He recalled Barbelo as a child, laughing and playing in the streets of the Celestial City. He treasured Barbelo's delight when she was posted to the world of humans. All the moments of their friendship passed through his memories. His existence would be massively devalued if Barbelo were removed from it.

Aza oscillated between ingrained obedience and the very essential need to rescue his wounded friend. He searched the flame-lit skies for other angels, seeing only their shapes darting amidst the smoke. The entire row of palm trees lining the central avenue of the cemetery was aflame. The path, limned in fire, pointed straight to the columbarium. The fiends and tempters creeping nearer on all sides made it clear that he couldn't leave. He could only watch and pray his friend received the aid she required.

If she did not, the hole in his life was yet one more thing he would simply endure, as the Name willed.

Nebiros turned his attention from the siege to the wounded angel. Here was a creature who had aided and even—according to his spies—befriended his sworn foe. A hungry grin slashed the demon's disfigured face.

Tracing a pattern on the ground beneath him with one taloned toe, the demon opened a passage to the tunnels converging to undermine the columbarium. Snapping out a string of instructions to the damned still lying beneath the soil, he turned them to attack the area beneath Barbelo's feet.

In response, the bruised turf around the angel heaved and tore. Hands groped blindly upward, claws of bone followed by limbs swaddled in rotting cloth.

Barbelo thrust her weapon at her corrupt attackers time and again, until they were reduced to twitching fragments. In the end, the lance head broke free of its shaft.

Seeing this, Yasmina surged forward, eyes hard with terrible confidence. She dipped close, intent on dispatching the angel.

Intense agony jerked the temptress to a stop, just out of talon's grasp. Twisting around, Yasmina saw that a bright angelic sword transfixed her to the ground. A portion of an archangel's blade gleamed above her scaly flesh, blinding her with its terrible radiance.

Frantic, Yasmina looked around for her assailant.

Azaziel stood at the nearest corner of the columbarium, arm still extended from throwing the sword which pinned her to the ground. When it was clear the temptress couldn't reach Barbelo to continue her attack, he turned away.

Yasmina screeched with inarticulate hatred. Her intended prey was torturously close, yet out of reach.

Barbelo plucked her lance tip from the torn-up earth. With a grimace, she crawled painfully toward Yasmina, bringing the fight back to her.

Crazy bitch needed dispatching now. Straining forward, Yasmina threw her will into her talons, extending them threefold. Even as they poised to sink into the angel's forearms, the ground between them exploded, spraying sod and shattered bones upward.

Nebiros rose from the ground. His arms enveloped Barbelo's head. The angel's clear hazel eyes went wide in surprise. The demon pulled her back sharply with one spurred knee at the small of her spine. Her holy armor shrieked against his damned skin. Then there was a muted crunch and Barbelo went limp.

Nebiros grasped her torso, ripping the armor from it. With a fat-bladed knife, he stabbed her twice in the chest. The force of the blows drove Barbelo to the ground.

Roaring with a joyous fury unlike any he'd known since the Fall, Nebiros laughed. His warped body felt unimaginably powerful from compounded millennia of hatred and preparation.

Swiveling his head toward Azaziel, Nebiros wrenched Barbelo into a kneeling position. The demon's voice cut through the tumult. "Make no mistake, Brother. I'll feast on her, but only to whet my appetite for your heart."

Thrusting her hands skyward, Barbelo cried out again. Her very essence leapt free of her flesh just before Nebiros shattered the angel's husk in his arms as if it had been spun from glass.

Throughout the graveyard, every angel paused as if drawing an unending breath. A swift, rushing quiet descended over the riot and fury converging on the columbarium.

Formless now, Barbelo flashed heavenward through the growing silence. Below her, Nebiros clawed through her remains, rending the chunks of flesh and scattered feathers at his feet.

Unwilling to accept that he could be cheated of his feast, he leapt to the air after her, but was too bound by his deformities to stay aloft.

Desperate to appease the General's frustration, Yasmina spat a command for Damia to follow and find the formless angel.

Beating her wings furiously, the harpy gave chase.

Barbelo sped upward.

The hush conjured by her brethren betrayed every beat of the harpy's wings, every hissing gasp of exertion Damia made in the pursuit.

Far below, devils cheered the harpy, never realizing that their shouts of encouragement were masked so long as the angels kept up their silent cry.

Lorelei craned her head backward. Damia was already invisible in the swirling smoke.

Abruptly, the angels ceased their call of silence.

An undulating shriek sounded overhead, to be cut off mid-cry. A chunk of meat, with dirty feathers still attached, whirled downward. Damia's mauled carcass crashed to earth mere paces from Nebiros. A single angelic sword gleamed amid her ruined flesh.

The force of Damia's impact echoed within the cemetery walls, swelling to include the previously muted clash of weapons, the crackle of flames, the obscenities, taunts, and screams. The returning sound exploded outward in a physical blow, knocking most infernals from their feet.

The angels struck fiercely in unison, with terrifying effect. Hell's forces wavered and broke as their entire front rank was erased. All the ground gained near the columbarium was lost again in less time than it took to realize it.

Nebiros and Yasmina found themselves cut off from help. The temptress writhed in agony and frustration. She raked herself with hands encumbered by overlong talons that she was too terrified to withdraw.

"Terrible One, I beseech you, unpin me so I may better serve you," she implored.

Nebiros ignored her, pausing at the edge of his portal to watch as the angels drove his forces back.

"Great One," Yasmina tried again, attempting to prostrate herself in the filth before him. She scrambled upright when the blood-soaked ground caught flame around her. The angel's spilled blood corroded her skin.

"Remain here to draw the foe away from me," Nebiros sneered dismissively.

Climbing atop a broken column, he leapt for the columbarium's roof, scimitar in hand.

Summoned by a sense of terrible wrongness, Aza dropped through a hole punctured through the columbarium's roof. Animate powder fogged the heavy air. The room clattered as the metallic urns danced in their niches. Some urns had already smashed through their glass partitions, adding sharp fragments to the swirling filth.

A pair of bodies lay crumpled near a stained glass window. Sweat pasted a coating of ash to their skin. More ash obscured the colors of their clothing. These mortal warders were dead, lungs clogged with bone grit and ash. Noc, the Cambodian cook, lay where he fell, his shirt wrapped around his face in an impromptu mask.

The woman had been Dolores Gutierrez. She lay curled around a book-shaped urn that held the soul of Willy Goldenstern. Aza could feel the boy defying the evil which tried to pry him out and carry him away on a wind of damnation.

Other souls also barely held out. Despite their makeshift containers, each was battered by the growing whirlwind of fouled remains.

Aza wondered how the other angels could have overlooked this possibility. Even if the niches in the columbarium around him weren't hallowed ground in and of themselves, they were surrounded by it, ideally presenting a safe haven for the loose souls. But no one seemed to have considered removing the urns spaced throughout the structure that had contained the unredeemed dead. Perhaps there simply hadn't been time.

As the General of Hell drew closer, his influence called to the dust of once-damned flesh. The mausoleum hallway hissed with the sound of whispering voices as the damned entreated the children to join them.

A shape swept up to meet Aza, coalescing into a twisted starfish of soiled gray. Nebulous and solid by turns, the ash wraith struck, attempting to suffocate the angel as it had the mortals.

In the cemetery outside, Aza could have dispelled the wraith with a few powerful strokes of his wings. In the narrow confines of the columbarium's hall, he had no room for that. Instead, Aza approached the creature, speaking a banishment to drive it back.

The wraith fled around the corner of the columbarium's corridor, before melting into the wall of niches. It rattled among the urns, trying vainly to open them before its destruction.

Aza didn't give the creature any respite. Drawing a mighty breath, he forced the wraith's physical components back into the corridor where he drove it out through a shattered window.

The ceiling overhead whispered and scratched with the sound of heavy wingtips and talons. A powerful stench rolled down through the gap in the roof, announcing the presence of Aza's oldest adversary.

The yowling song of Nebiros's unholy scimitar acutely reminded Aza that he'd cast away Rafael's sword to thwart Yasmina and his own sword to dispatch Damia.

The next archangel to appear at Asmodeus's mansion had the manners to ring the doorbell. He waited calmly on the step until a fiend ushered him up to the roof to meet the boss.

"I expected you would come next," Asmodeus said. "I appreciate you leaving the armor behind."

"I couldn't imagine that I'd need it." Zadkiel stepped over to the balcony's edge, to survey the city below. "Nice place."

"I've been happy here," Asmodeus answered.

"Happy?" Zadkiel echoed.

Asmodeus wasn't inclined to debate. "Can I offer you some refreshment?"

"I'll have some of that cognac. It smells divine."

"Hardly." Asmodeus poured a pair of snifters while the angel gazed out at the massive fire burning at Angelus Rose.

"Have you come to give me what I want?" Asmodeus asked.

Zadkiel smiled. "The souls aren't mine to give away. Neither is my brother Azaziel."

"Then why have you come? You know there can never be peace between us."

"Sure, if that's your choice." Zadkiel sipped his cognac appreciatively.

Asmodeus shrugged. "You know I don't have any choice."

"I've been hearing that a lot lately," Zadkiel answered. "Lorelei has no choice but to love Azaziel. He had no choice but to rescue those children's souls. You have no choice but to make war on us for things you honestly couldn't care less about."

"It passes the time."

"You sound old," Zadkiel teased.

"Merely bored. This fixation between Azaziel and my Lorelei is the first interesting thing to happen in a long time."

Zadkiel held out his glass in a toast.

"What are we drinking to?"

"The unexpected?"

The demon chimed his glass against the archangel's. They turned as one to watch the conflagration.

"It's almost over," Zadkiel said at length. "Will you come sign the accord yourself or have you arranged for a proxy?"

"It's not over yet," Asmodeus corrected, "but I'm honored to accept your invitation. Since you adhere to the most ethical and rigorous business practices, I'm sure no one will mind if I look over the bookkeeping."

The temptress watched the demon who had just abandoned her scrabble to a halt atop the columbarium's roof. Even if she saw no angels around, she smelled them everywhere. It was only a matter of time before one of them dropped down to finish her off.

Crawling backward, Yasmina put her weight against the holy sword that pinned her, hoping to topple it so she could escape. Instead, the weapon sliced into her tail, widening the original puncture into an excruciating gash. Eyes brimming with black-blooded tears, Yasmina gave up on pushing the blade and tried instead to pull herself forward, worsening the wound, bisecting her lower body.

Finally her hands reached the hot churn of rotten soil that marked the edge of Nebiros's portal. She'd only crawled a few cubits to get there, but it felt like leagues. She snatched up her fallen weapons, intending to lay them at Asmodeus's feet as she abased herself.

With a vow of gratitude to the dark father who dwelt below and eternal hatred to all who'd led her to this state, Yasmina disappeared below the surface, dragging her torn and bloodied tail behind her.

From her vantage point atop the mausoleum beside the dead soldier, Lorelei watched Yasmina's bifurcated tail disappear into the ground. The succubus laughed with pure childlike joy, the way Ashleigh might once have.

"Where are you tonight, my friend?" Lorelei whispered. "Are you watching our enemy finally vanquished? Are you cheering along with me?"

She gazed upward, trying to see the stars beyond the smoke. She hoped the girl who had once possessed her was enjoying this evening as much as she was. "Will you greet Barbelo when she reaches Heaven and ask her to intercede for us?"

Craving the girl's company, Lorelei swung her feet over the mausoleum's Egyptian façade and waited for an answer.

Aza paced through the columbarium, looking for a weapon that might serve him when Nebiros came down from the roof.

The souls around him, the youngsters he'd rescued so carefully, quailed with terror at the proximity of such powerful evil. Aza did his utmost to emanate reassurance and strength. "Be thou not afraid," he whispered. The echoes repeated it in every language.

The only thing he found with potential to become a weapon was the baseball bat leaning in the corner near Noc's body. Taking it up, Aza smiled at the words "Anaheim Angels" burned into the wood. Even in martyrdom, Noc had a sense of poetry.

A familiar hiss brought Aza's guard up. Nebiros's serpent swung down from a stained glass chandelier. Its saw-toothed mouth brimmed with the same molten venom Aza had been lucky to survive after Lost Angels.

Swinging the bat, Aza connected with the creature in mid-strike. As the serpent's fangs sank into the wood, it burst into flames. Without hesitating, the angel shoved the bat—snake and all—through the nearest window, stirring it around in the jagged stained glass until the snake's lacerated body hung crookedly from the wood. Flames consumed its head.

The victory was minor with such a deadly enemy poised above. Nebiros's scimitar carved the edge of the hole wider so he could enter. Breathing hard, Aza approached the opening, terribly aware how close to destruction he and these souls were.

Leaping for the flat of the blade, he attempted to bash it to one side with the bat, hoping to knock the weapon from the demon's hand. Nebiros laughed at him.

"Brethren," Aza whispered, "come to this place so that if I'm destroyed, those within will not be."

Even as he prayed, the ceiling around the hole gave way. Nebiros tumbled inward.

Hands closing on the sphere of granite that had caused the hole in the ceiling, Aza tried to yank the polished globe upright, in order to smash it down onto the General's head. Unfortunately, even Muriel's healing had limits. The remnant of the tainted gunshot wound undermined his effort, causing Aza to stumble to one knee with the heavy stone barely held aloft.

With a savage smile, Hell's General rose up from the floor. He slapped the stone easily from Aza's grasp. "Rage is strength, my brother, but you'll have to take my word for it. Unendurable misery is all you'll know in your final moments."

"But first things first," the demon slurred. With his free hand, Nebiros gestured toward the columbarium's doors, tearing them from their hinges and flinging them into the graveyard beyond.

The very walls of the place shuddered with the lamentation of souls.

The sound of the columbarium doors crashing open roused Lorelei. She stared hard into the building, seeking her angel. Her heart actually seemed to freeze at the sight of Nebiros facing off against Aza.

She pulled out Sammy's Desert Eagle, sighted on Hell's general, and held the trigger down. Tomur wasn't kidding when he said it would kick like a motherfucker. Aza and Nebiros each scrambled away from each other, seeking cover.

That was the best she could do from here. She knew the gun's ammunition, however hellish, wouldn't kill Nebiros.

The succubus launched herself off of the Egyptian mausoleum. She didn't know what she would do to that ugly fucker when she reached him, but she knew she had better be sure to kill Nebiros with her first blow. She was learning, from Aza's example, not to leave enemies alive.

The pistol in her purse, with its stolen ammunition, would not be powerful enough. What she needed was a truly deadly weapon. Perhaps Yasmina had dropped one of hers before dragging her sorry ass back to Hell.

Lorelei swooped low over the battlefield. Damned corpses, dismembered by Barbelo's spear, lay in singed fragments across the shattered earth. The rich, rank aroma of home flowed out of Nebiros's unclosed portal. Lorelei sailed past it, not even daring to be tempted.

The sword that had pinned Yasmina still protruded from the earth. Its sanctity flared magnesium bright in the darkness. Sure, it would kill anything Lorelei came across. However, a voice cautioned her not to touch it. For once, Lorelei felt inclined to obey.

Her gaze caught on the heap of cooked flesh and burnt feathers that remained of Damia. Amongst the harpy's carcass lay unclaimed the weapon which had killed her. Lorelei recognized it as Azaziel's sword.

Lorelei set her feet down and folded her wings. The sword was embedded through Damia's breast into the ground beneath. If it had killed a harpy, it was good enough for Lorelei. She hoped she could hold it without Ashleigh's ghost to make her safe. Tentatively, she stretched out her hand. Her tail lashed nervously behind her.

A screech split the air over Lorelei's head. The succubus leapt toward the sword and rolled to her feet with its hilt clenched in both hands.

Keisha dove out of the roiling smoke. Lorelei met her with a two-handed swing that batted the harpy aside like a piñata. Too bad the flat of the sword didn't split her open with Lorelei's first swing.

Keisha crashed into a gravestone and shook her head, dazed. "What are you picking on me for?"

"Not so tough now, with your mistress crawled off to Hell," Lorelei taunted.

"This is all your fault, you stupid cunt." Keisha beat her ratty wings, zigzagging wildly through the air at Lorelei.

Instinctively, Lorelei jabbed the sword forward. She barely caught the harpy's shoulder with its point. Keisha screamed like she was being boiled alive. The wound spread open as if being torn from within. Every beat of Keisha's wings pulled the edges farther apart. She couldn't fly fast enough to escape the pain. Silver light burned inside the wound, consuming the harpy from the inside out.

"Fuck you," Lorelei said as the harpy dropped, burning, from the murky air. She turned away, gripping the sword, and went after Azaziel.

Snatching up the granite ball, Nebiros advanced on Aza. There was nowhere to run and no hiding now. Nebiros pitched the heavy ball at him. Aza dodged unsuccessfully. He thought he heard a rib break.

Shouting "Lex Talionis!" Nebiros swept Aza's feet from under him and knocked him to the floor. Grinning with far too many teeth, the demon planted his foot on the angel's chest. His talons pierced the holy armor with a tortured shriek.

Aza looked up, trying to recall the way Nebiros had been before the Fall. Clearing his eyes to transpose that memory over the ruined visage above him, Aza tried to project this vision to reassure the panicked souls.

The demon's smile became as beatific as his twisted features would permit. "You're lying to them, although I'm touched that you haven't forgotten what I once was. And what I am no longer: servant of Yahweh."

Setting the rock aside, Nebiros lowered himself, keeping one knee pitched firmly on Aza's chest. Casting his eyes to Heaven, the demonic General jerked a clawed thumb behind him, toward the accumulated urns. "For what we are about to receive, we shall be truly grateful," he intoned, full of mock humility.

The scent of Barbelo's blood radiated from the twisted appendage that held Aza down. Her blood spattered Nebiros's armor. At the thought of his destroyed sister, Aza quivered in sudden resolve. Throwing back his head, the angel opened his throat in a single pure chord of wordless song. He strove, in that single cry, to express every remembered moment of Heaven, the glory and sorrow of his existence on earth, his idyll with Anah, the banishment and solitude.

He sang of love, not only for the lost Barbelo, but for his harbored souls and for Lorelei as well. His heart was suddenly full of thanks to the Almighty for having been granted even an hour of love for the succubus. Finally, he sang with faith that all could still be salvaged.

Nebiros screwed up his face in disgust. "Leave that noise to the saved," he bellowed in an effort to shout Aza down.

At the sound of Aza's voice, Lorelei's legs gave way. She dropped helplessly to her knees. She didn't understand the ancient words any more than when he'd spoken them at the church, to bind Ashleigh to her flesh— except now she recognized her name. Somehow, she grasped that Azaziel was confessing to the Enemy how much he loved her.

Tears of joy flooded Lorelei's eyes.

Out in the graveyard, the other angels joined Azaziel's song of praise.

The rout of Hell began.

The lesser devils could not withstand the heavenly music. Lorelei watched a gang of imps simply pop, exploding to oily black threads. Their cast-off clothing dropped, burning, to the ground. All around her, fiends writhed, groaning, as they burrowed into unsanctified dirt. Harpies squawked overhead, flapping crazily away as fast as they could. Hell's General seemed mesmerized, his own voice raised in a wavering roar that failed to compete with the swelling hymn.

Angels strode forward throughout Angelus Rose, bathed in a light of relentless glory. As they converged inexorably on the columbarium, they killed everything—infernal or damned—within their sight, allowing no one to escape.

Kneeling beside the dead harpy, Lorelei's tears spilled unheeded as she drank in the song. Somehow she was able to separate Aza's voice from the others. The sound of it filled her heart with a rapture that clarified everything. They were meant to be together. They would be together. No creature in Heaven or Hell could prevent that fate now.

A discordant note in the midst of the harmony caught Lorelei's attention. "Run, harlot!" an angel ordered. Lorelei spun, raising the stolen sword just in time. Even so, she barely deflected the flaming sword in the hand of her blond nemesis. "Why doesn't our song drive you away like all the rest of your kind?"

Lorelei didn't answer. She hadn't fled because she wasn't leaving without Aza—and that was definitely not going to please this honey-blond bitch. Lorelei jabbed half-heartedly toward the angel. She was certain she didn't have the strength to penetrate that holy armor.

Using the flat of her sword, Muriel batted the blade of Lorelei's weapon to one side and continued to advance. "When did Azaziel give you his sword?"

"I found it in the carcass of my enemy," Lorelei said. "Sheath your sword and I'll give it back."

"No deals, whore. I'll scrape your hands from it after I've cut them from your wrists."

Lorelei skipped backward. Her feet touched briefly on holy soil, but it gave her an electric tingle, a pale echo of the taste of Aza's blood, nothing more.

Though momentary, the distraction was enough. Muriel swept forward, wings outstretched. Lorelei stumbled back against an obelisk, thumping her skull against the marble. The stars she saw were nothing compared to the flare of the angelic blade as it flashed to rest beneath her jaw. Oh, my love, Lorelei thought, I am so sorry to leave you...

"Muriel! Hold!" A towering figure with black-quilled wings dropped out of the smoky darkness. With one skeletal hand, he pulled Lorelei from beneath Muriel's sword.

Lorelei stared wild-eyed, awed at the beauty of this terrible angel. He was so different from the rest. His bones shone like polished marble, robed in thunderhead-dark raiment. Stars glittered in the dark sockets of his skull as he regarded her.

Holding her like a rag doll in his enormous fist, Samael traced a bony finger down her chest. Lorelei felt her heart stop.

"You are the creature for whom Azaziel risked his grace." It wasn't a question.

Lorelei's heart pounded back to life. She nodded.

The angel of death released her and turned away to collect his sister, pulling Muriel after him as he melted into the shadows of the graveyard.

"Why did you stop me?" Muriel shrieked.

"Her survival has been ordained," Samael reported in a low voice.

"By whom?" Muriel demanded.

The angel of death halted abruptly, black eyes aglitter. "Quiet yourself, Sister. Not another word."

Lorelei wanted to feel some kind of triumph—or at least a sense of relief. Her angel loved her in the face of Heaven and Death had taken her side.

Unfortunately, Samael was too close to the columbarium and her angel. Mustering every ounce of willpower, Lorelei continued on her way.

"No," Muriel said, stepping out from behind the base of a marble angel who had somehow escaped demolition. "Come no further."

"Out of my way," Lorelei ordered, buoyed by her new sense of divine protection. "You can't kill me."

"Perhaps not." The angel's smile was worthy of any of Hell's elite. "But after you've been beaten within an inch of your life, you will beg me to end your misery."

Muriel tossed her flaming sword off into the darkness and rushed at Lorelei with her hands outstretched. One of her palms had a black smudge as if she'd been burned.

To Lorelei's credit, she stood her ground and slashed Azaziel's sword hard across Muriel's face, laying her skin open to reveal the grinning skull beneath.

Then Muriel was inside Lorelei's reach. She grabbed hold of the sword's hilt and turned, wrenching the weapon out of Lorelei's grasp. Muriel spun so fast that Lorelei was nearly gored. Instead, the succubus flung herself down on her back. The sword blade whistled over her...straight into the armored glove of the archangel Michael.

He disarmed Muriel as neatly as she'd disarmed Lorelei. "What part of 'hold' did you fail to understand?"

Muriel looked from the archangel to the succubus and struggled to find words for her disgust. "How can she be spared when so many, more worthy, were not? What possible purpose can her existence serve? There's clearly been a mistake. A miscommunication. We can sort it out..."

"After she's dead?" Michael asked.

Muriel's hand wandered to her slashed cheek, touching bone and teeth. She stared at her bloodied fingers uncomprehendingly.

"Bear it as the mark of your folly," Michael said, "and come away."

"And her?" Muriel spat.

"Lorelei's destiny is up to her."

"But mine is not?"

"You have two choices," Michael said gently. "One of them is wrong."

Muriel rubbed her fingertips together, marveling at her own blood.

Even though Lorelei expected it, Muriel turned on her quicker than she could react. The angel was almost atop her when Mastema stepped out of a nearby tongue of flame. He snapped a heavy chain like a whip. Its end coiled around Muriel's throat. He wrenched it backward and tugged her from her feet.

Michael bent over Muriel and quickly bound her hands.

"I can't believe you're in on this!" Muriel shrieked.

"I obey my Master's will," Michael answered. "My counterparts and I were sent here to watch you. Not to protect this city. Not to guard these souls. We are here because one of the Host stood upon the lip of mutiny and set her will to oppose the directives of the one voice she should heed above all others. You've elevated hatred above obedience. Therefore,

Muriel, once of the Choir, be thou accursed of Heaven, cast from its ranks, and sentenced into servitude at the whims of the Adversary."

"Wait!" Muriel shouted at Michael's back.

Mastema bared his teeth as he loomed over the bound angel. "For someone who's inflicted more than her share of injury, who's so often cast herself as a vengeful judge, you've escaped miraculously unscathed." The demon in charge of the Fallen on Earth seized her chin, digging his hooked nails into her wound. When Muriel opened her mouth to protest, Mastema snatched hold of her tongue with a wicked pair of tongs. And yanked hard.

Lorelei retrieved Aza'z sword as she fled the newly fallen angel's screams.

As Nebiros raised his weapon for the killing blow, Lorelei plunged forward to tangle Azaziel's sword in the scimitar's curve. She couldn't jerk the weapon from the demon's hands, but she distracted him long enough that Aza could roll out from beneath him.

Nebiros wrenched the scimitar back. Lorelei barely managed to keep hold of the sword. She trembled, aware that she was fighting one of Hell's ablest warriors with an unfamiliar weapon on a slippery marble floor.

Aza felt the song falter on his lips. He scrambled to his feet, wishing desperately for a weapon of his own so he could join the battle. He dreaded to think that he was fated to stand by helplessly as his true love died.

Nebiros swiped at the unarmed angel. Lorelei swung the sword hard at Hell's general, hoping to break his weapon with her holy blade.

"Where are your feathers, Little Angel?" the demon taunted.

"Stand aside," Samael commanded. Lorelei jumped. Silhouetted against the burning graveyard, Samael mounted the steps to the columbarium behind her.

Nebiros swung at her. She scarcely blocked the scimitar in time.

Aza met the Angel of Death's eyes and saw no trace of pity in them, only implacable will. Defeated, Aza stepped away. Samael's scythe sliced the air with an unearthly scream. The blade caught both Lorelei's sword and Nebiros's scimitar and carried them down to embed in the marble floor of the columbarium.

"I have been forbidden to take Azaziel tonight," Samael rumbled. "You, Nebiros, were not expressly mentioned."

Lorelei realized that both she and Aza had been given a pass. Someone truly was looking out for them. She quivered at the implications of the knowledge.

"I'm not leaving without something to show Hell. Let me put Azaziel's face in my pocket." Nebiros tugged on his weapon, tearing it free of the floor. "Give me his arm."

"You've already taken our dear Barbelo," Rafael said from his position above the fissure Nebiros had carved in the ceiling.

"She's only gone, not destroyed," the demon argued. "That's not good enough."

Michael appeared from the back of the mausoleum, interposed between Nebiros and the last avenue of escape. His massive sword flamed in his hand. "Greed on top of arrogance on top of pride. I think you must be odious even by Hell's standards, so we'll spare them your return."

"Fuck you all!" Nebiros turned toward Aza. "Come on, Brother. We're going now." As he charged, the scimitar formed an unholy blur over his head.

Samael reversed his scythe and slashed the demon neatly from shin to shoulder. The scimitar clattered to the marble at Aza's feet. The General's flesh shivered into coils of ash. On the floor of the mausoleum, his ashes extruded tentacles that reached for Aza.

As Aza retreated from them in horror, the winds from the firestorm outside the columbarium caught the ashen tentacles and tore them apart.

Aza stood looking down at the black stain on the floor in front of him. Without a doubt, he knew Nebiros's death as a mercy for which the demon wouldn't have dared to beg. Still, Creation felt diminished by the loss of another of the eternal Hosts.

Michael said, "Blood drinks blood," and extinguished his sword.

Zadkiel, who had only just arrived, began to sing a lament for Nebiros.

Lorelei stood in the columbarium's foyer, more alone than she'd felt on the catafalque at Lost Angels. Three archangels and an angel of death surrounded her. She was the last of Hell's soldiers uninjured in the graveyard, but for how much longer? While she had been spared death, what worse torments might these creatures devise? Now that she knew Aza was safe, Lorelei wanted nothing so much as to flee.

Samael turned back into the graveyard to assist in the mopping up. Once he was gone from the doorway, Lorelei saw a chain of limousines snaking up the curving cemetery drive.

"He's coming." Rafael stepped through the puncture in the ceiling and floated down to the floor. "Zadkiel and I have played our parts, Michael. There remains only for you to do yours."

The exits were clear. Lorelei realized that she could walk out of the columbarium and resume her place in Hell's hierarchy. She could remain where she stood and perhaps serve some purpose under Heaven. But what she yearned for with all her soul was for Aza to put his arms around her, kiss her in front of the assembled hosts, and pledge himself as hers. She looked expectantly at her angel, but he stared down at the blotch on the marble floor and did not meet her gaze.

The archangels moved to greet the limousines. Unwilling to face the prince of LA, Lorelei leapt up and pulled herself out of the hole in the ceiling.

CHAPTER 19: THE FINAL TEMPTATION

Asmodeus climbed from the limo with the aid of his walking stick. He limped worse than usual, as if his old wound pained him more in the presence of so many archangels.

He hobbled silently to Nebiros's portal. His boots crunched over the bone fragments of the damned as he observed the trail Yasmina's wounded body had dragged through the mud. Using his cane, he turned over a single shining blue feather. Stoic, he twisted back to face the victors.

Beelzebub strode from the second limo. Behemoth waddled out of the third. Jequon climbed out of the last one. They formed a reluctant honor guard behind the Prince of LA as he climbed the columbarium steps.

"Greetings, cousins," Michael said.

"Welcome to Los Angeles," Asmodeus returned. "I hope our hospitality has entertained you."

"Uncommonly diverting, even if the outcome was never in doubt. You've been a congenial host," Michael said, without a touch of irony. "Would you care to hear the casualties?"

"If you'd be so kind."

Yehudiah, the recording angel, stepped forward with his scrolls. "On this sad evening, our sister Muriel, formerly of the Choir, has fallen from our ranks. No one shall receive credit or blame for this, since no one provoked her fall more than she herself. Also this evening, our sister Barbelo was rendered formless at the hands of Nebiros. She has returned to the Realm of Glory."

Asmodeus inclined his head, clearly pleased.

"The demon Nebiros chose destruction rather than retreat. He will not be returned to you."

"Just as well," Asmodeus said. "A broken toy has limited utility."

"The temptress Yasmina crept back to Hell, sorely wounded."

Jequon received that news with the slightest twitch of his sensual lips.

Yehudiah rolled the scroll open a little farther. "Of the human combatants here gathered, only one survived. Kim Tran has been returned to his mother with his soul secure. Eleven of the others died as martyrs and have ascended."

"Does that include the priest?" Asmodeus asked.

The scribe consulted his scroll. "It does."

"Pity."

Yehudiah shook the dark curls back from his face and asked icily, "May I continue?"

"Please do."

"In Hell's contingent, eighteen mortals were damned and one contracted soul, Tuan Nguyen, consumed by Lorelei. Of the devils assembled here, only the succubus Floria and those fiends accompanying Jequon earlier continue in your service."

Asmodeus asked, "And Lorelei herself?"

Managing to exclude Aza, the archangels exchanged a glance. "Lorelei persists in confounding expectations," Michael said at last.

The demon prince bared his fangs in a smile. "That leaves us only to divide up the souls cached here around us," he said. "Surely, some were tempted or frightened into coming my way."

Aza turned his back then and descended the columbarium's rear steps. He had to get away from this discussion or he knew he would do something he'd regret later.

As he walked through the graveyard, a breath of cooler air parted the tendrils of smoke. Amidst the flickering lights atop a fire engine outside the cemetery wall stood a silhouette he could not mistake. The light and distance made it challenging to see Lorelei clearly, but he was certain that she smiled at the sight of him. Then she took wing into the night.

Aza launched himself after her. Despite the singing throb of his wounds, he felt a connection to the succubus that drew him: not as a lure now, but as a beacon.

The lights had gone out across most of LA. The blackout kept the police busy and most people in their homes, out of harm's way. Aza was relieved that the archangels had thought of that. He'd been too focused on surviving the night to worry about the city beyond the graveyard walls.

The Equitable Life building rose before Aza, a monolith veiled in drifting haze. Cresting the skyscraper with painful exertion, the angel clung to the railing surrounding the building's helipad. His balance was uncertain, as if the natural weight of his wings might pull him backward toward the street far below. He struggled to catch his breath against the pain suffusing him.

Mastema stepped over to the rail. With a surprisingly gentle grip, his strong hands took Aza's arm to haul him over the railing and onto the deck. Shrugging him off, Aza stood as best he was able. He found himself looking at Muriel, bound with chains. Worse, her tongue had been drawn past her lips, stretched grotesquely long and wound tightly around her throat. Beneath her shame, Muriel's clear blue eyes burned with powerful hatred, focused on Aza.

"Be nice!" Mastema smacked Muriel hard on the back of her head. The blow caused her to bite down painfully on her transformed tongue.

Aza prevented himself from intervening. Now fallen, Muriel could no longer be his concern.

"Smart fellow." The demon chuckled. "Once she manages her transition, you'd best watch your back. She can hate you legally now." With a snap of his fingers, Mastema sent her stumbling back a few paces.

"Then you're not after me any longer?"

"I won't promise you that," the demon answered. "However, I did get what I came for this time." He waggled his fingers. "It's all about misdirection."

Changing the subject abruptly, Mastema continued, "I remember the day they sent you here. This place made the perfect prison for you: empty, so distant from the tribes of mortals that all you could do was convince yourself that—at least—it was full of the Almighty's grace and beauty." Mastema winked. "You did surprisingly well with your solitary confinement, until a certain succubus shook her sassy little tail at you."

Ignoring the sarcasm, Aza stared off at the blurry tapestry of fire below, seeing the land-as-it-had-been overlaid on the present. His exile here seemed like a long dream.

Mastema cleared his throat and spat over the side of the building. "Speaking of honeys," the demon continued, "we watched Lorelei go past not long ago. It occurred to me to hold her for you, since I suspected you might follow."

Aza pushed aside a pulse of disappointment. "Why didn't you stop her?"

"In part," Mastema replied evenly, "because you're acting from free will, same as she is. That's always amusing to watch. Mostly, though, I let her go by because it would have agitated the new acquisition over there."

"What happens to her now?" Aza refrained from glancing at Muriel.

"Why, the Almighty's will. And that of the exiled Morning Star, of course. Once our Muriel gets herself accustomed to the notion of which side of the family she's landed on, she'll be another weapon against those of you yet unfallen."

The rotor wash of an approaching helicopter ruffled the demon's bushy red hair. Aza and Mastema gazed at the craft until they were content that the pilot could land safely. As soon as the 'copter blades slowed, the doors flung open. The occupants rushed to the far side of the building. They stared down from a safer vantage than being airborne afforded them tonight.

Aza shook his head. "Imagine what they've seen."

Turning his back on the mortals, Mastema shrugged. "What they didn't see, the humans almost certainly felt. The skies have been crowded with warriors from both camps tonight, signs and portents there to be divined."

Aza sighed. "I'd hoped this would all turn out to be a minor skirmish. I'd hoped that the trouble at the exorcism would be the worst of it."

"The final fallout remains to be seen. This affair of yours has so far left a general of Hell's armies destroyed, a high temptress thwarted, Muriel in my hands, and Barbelo and Shebniel lost to this plane..." Mastema's gaze focused intently, watching something far below or in the future. "Not to mention the still-unresolved matter of your succubus."

Aza's hand found the demon's shoulder, clutched it tightly. He was startled to hear Mastema of all people refer to Lorelei as his. "Is there any truth in what you're saying? Do I dare continue after her?"

"Sounds to me like it's approval more than truth you're seeking," Mastema observed. "Don't ask me. I suppose you've worked hard and served Heaven and mortalkind as best you could." The demon gave him a grudging smile. "You've done well these last decades, even with recent events. Nonetheless, it's time to admit to yourself that love of one above all others has changed you more than all the loneliness of the last few thousand years. In my opinion, you've never recovered from what you shared with Anah."

Mastema smiled. "My gut says you're not coming back to your own. Not out of punishment, but from your own choice. Your heart no longer looks to Heaven for happiness. Now it falls to you to find out whence it lies. I don't pretend to know if Lorelei is your punishment or your reward. Whatever she turns out to be, you're entirely deserving."

Mastema gestured Aza in the direction Lorelei had gone. "Good luck, my friend."

Once more the wind over Aza's wings was a mixed blessing. His injuries—recently inflicted, healed, and reopened in his battle with Nebiros—all quivered. However, something sustained him in flight, propelling him beyond the mix of Heavenly means and physical mechanics that kept angels aloft. Shouts of encouragement rang in his ears, from voices unknown. Neither angels nor devils—more likely his own delusion, Aza decided.

Perhaps Mastema had been trying to tell Aza something he was too distracted to realize. What if all of this was a dream while falling? What if this lonely flight was all eternity held for him from now on, ceaselessly winging toward mountains he'd never reach, in hopes of a lover who wouldn't be waiting?

Shaking his gaze away from the eerily distant hills, Aza watched the landscape sliding beneath him. The power had come back on now. Fires had reduced a number of houses of worship to voids between the city lights. Constellations of dying embers flowered in the gaps. Aza felt worry and despair emanating from some of them as he passed. Others were filled with courage and determination. He could only pray that Rafael's projection of greater good would prove to be true.

Swooping low, Aza was astonished to see no fire trucks crowding the boulevard in front of Sunset Saint Mary's. Cracked and stained by smoke, the rose-colored adobe of the old church still expelled dark rushes of heat. Amid the stench of ash and ruin, Aza smelled tears and burned flesh. Misery ascended in waves so strong that it made him ache when he chose to disregard the impulse—the need—to drop down and help. There would be other angels for that, now that the cemetery fight was won.

Aza feared that, if he stopped, he might not have the strength to take wing again. While he acknowledged that might be for the best, he swept on, past Sunset Boulevard.

Lorelei was not holed up in her room at Chateau Marmont. Where would she have gone now that Asmodeus's army had been vanquished? Aza opened his senses, trying to detect her perfume on the wind.

As he continued on, he noticed that the untouched parts of the city had fallen unnaturally still. The regular bustle of LA, even at this hour of night, had vanished. Patrol cars and city service vehicles blocked intersections, many lit with prayer.

Then the angel soared over Bronson Canyon. Its hillsides were etched with a lazy twining of streetlights where an occasional car made its way home like the inhabitant of an exposed but nearly empty anthill.

Something pulled Aza's attention to the shadowy base of the canyon.

Circling tightly back, Aza swept toward the Bronson's sole landmark, a shallow cave. A familiar mix of infernal flesh and perfume rose from the darkness there, drawing him. It seemed like Lorelei, but was not.

A fusillade of sling stones whirred up at him from the shadows. Whoever it was, they were willing to risk his being armed.

He contemplated calling out to them, to Lorelei, in case that was her scent among the devils there. As he came around for a final pass, another volley rattled off his wings and chest. One projectile sliced his cheek.

Aza snatched another stone out of the air as it sailed past. It throbbed with deep-soaked grief and compounded hate, leaving no doubt as to its Hellish origin.

"Lorelei!" he barked, his tone as sharp as the Hell-mined obsidian.

A chorus of yelps and jeers chased the echo of his cry.

Why was he allowing these minions to waste his time? "Lorelei!" he sang, this time with force and fury. He made her name his sword. No sound answered, save for the wet slop of imp pitch.

Higher up the hillside, Lorelei called, "I'm here!" Her voice was melodious with joy and hope.

Smashing the air with his wings, Aza pulled skyward, catching another bewildering breath of his lover's scent. Reaching out by instinct, he swept a hand through the branches of an oak tree. His fingers caught up a shred of Lorelei's black dress. Aza realized he'd wanted so badly to find her that he'd tried too hard.

Still, the intensity of her scent on the fabric told him she was near. Taking strength from that, he turned toward the observatory's lights. He prayed as he flew that, in finding her, he wasn't making a mistake worse than being deceived by imps.

Drawing up at the observatory's parking lot, he settled atop the sculpture of James Dean. Above Aza on the dome stood Lorelei's unmistakable figure, darkly incandescent: wings swept back, arms outstretched toward him. He couldn't move. Strength remained in his wings, but his legs seemed ready to crumple.

Without a word, Lorelei came down to meet him. Her leathery wings weren't made for hovering, but she did her best. Aza's eyes searched hers when he realized that words were useless.

"We should kiss," she offered helpfully.

Aza gathered her into his arms and held her close. She'd told him in her hotel room that she loved him, but now, with ashes in her hair and soot smudged across her forehead, he believed her. She had stepped up against one of Hell's most ferocious warriors to save Aza's life. Michael himself had been surprised by her bravery.

Her lips on his were warm, eager, and Aza could no longer pretend that he didn't love her as passionately in return. Still, he broke the kiss to say, "This is too exposed."

Lorelei laughed, twisting his words.

Aza shook his head. "If one of my brethren saw us, they'd think I was in trouble."

"Aren't you?" she mocked.

"Oh, yes."

He could see that his honesty surprised her. Unwilling to say more yet, Aza hopped down from the statue. Luckily, Lorelei was there to steady him when his knees buckled.

"Should we head to holy ground?" she wondered.

"I have a better idea." Wrapping his hand around hers, Aza led her down the hill and into the shadows between the trees.

She was content for a while, then curiosity got the better of her. "Why did you follow me here?" she asked.

"Isn't it obvious?" He squeezed her hand. He hoped the gesture felt more possessive than restraining.

"The last thing I heard you say was how happy you were to die for your Sky Daddy and how much you loved me. Lover, you've outed yourself. But now—" She gestured toward the dark lace of branches overhead. "You've got me and we're keeping a low profile."

Aza turned toward her. Her eyes shone as red as blood in the darkness. Her proximity gave him courage. "Stay with me, Lorelei. I don't want damnation, but I will forgo Heaven for you."

Lorelei pressed herself into her angel's arms, wrapping every limb and even her tail around him, making a kiss that they'd be fools to break.

An unholy screech split the night, setting all the coyotes yipping in the hills. Lorelei's attention wrenched upward. Floria perched on a gnarled branch of the oak stretching over the path. She'd glamored herself so that Lorelei couldn't see how badly she'd been burned by the Holy Water.

"What is wrong with you?" Floria snarled. "How are you too stupid to grasp that he is the enemy?"

"How do you not grasp that I don't fucking care?" From her purse, Lorelei drew the pistol Beelzebub had given her.

Floria laughed until Lorelei broke the chamber open and pulled out the oversized bullet. Floria's cackle choked off in mid-breath.

"Yeah," Lorelei said, "I thought you'd recognize it, bitch."

"Where'd you get it?" Floria demanded.

"Them," Lorelei corrected. "I got them from Hai when he didn't shoot me like you intended—and Aza didn't allow the kid to take a second shot at him."

Aza took the bullet and rolled it around in his free hand. "Muriel gave you this, didn't she, Floria?"

Lorelei stared at her sister, surprised.

Floria only said, "Someone else who hates you as much as I do, Angel."

Lorelei snatched the bullet back and reloaded the gun. "So, Sister, why don't you fuck off right now, before I blow a hole in your pretty little dress?"

"You don't have the balls," Floria dared.

"Wanna test me? Even if it doesn't kill you outright, it's gonna be a drag slogging through eternity with a gaping hole where your tits used to be." Lorelei raised the gun.

Aza helpfully nudged her arms up a little, adjusting her aim. "A head shot ought to do it." His voice was low and serious enough to give her a pleasant shiver.

Floria flung herself off her branch, zigzagging erratically as she fled for her life.

Lorelei let out her breath and eased her finger from the trigger.

"Want me to do it?" Aza offered.

"Not yet." Lorelei grinned at him. "I only have the one bullet."

"You lied to her?"

"Wasn't the first time." Adrenaline left her shaky, another unwanted souvenir from her days trapped in mortal form. Lorelei tucked the gun back into her purse. "I don't want to waste the bullet. We may still need it."

"Fair enough. I'm not sure I'll be allowed to wield an archangel's sword ever again."

"I really hope you won't need to."

They came out of the trees at the edge of the park, hand in hand, unseen. Los Feliz Boulevard ran past them, a conduit of flowing steel.

"What now, Lover? Cross the road?"

Azaziel nodded, grinding his teeth against the pain where Nebiros's talons had pierced his chest. "The fountain," he whispered.

Had Lorelei been human, the angel's voice would've been impossible to pick out from the rush of traffic. The wounds he bore glowed faintly from Nebiros's venom. "I know you're worn out, but you gotta have one more hop in you?" she asked.

Aza slumped against her, shaking his head. Lorelei took that moment to unfurl her wings and leapt forward with enough force to carry them both across the street. To her delight, the angel proved virtually weightless when taken unaware.

"What now?" she asked, easing him onto a bench at the far side of the fountain. The angel stretched out on his stomach, pressing his wounds to the cool concrete bench. Fresh blood slicked the bench. Lorelei wanted to trace her talons through the streaks, to scrawl sigils of claim in it for all that could comprehend them.

Instead, she sat beside him and lifted his head so he could use her thigh as a pillow. What a blessing it was just to touch him, to smooth her fingertips across his brow. "I wish it didn't hurt," she whispered. Aza didn't reply, so she sat there, waiting, breathing the chlorine-tinged air and listening to the helicopters rushing overhead.

"I need to bless the water and wash myself, cleanse the hellspite from my wounds," he said.

"Do you need my help to get into the water?"

He suggested, "You could join me."

Lorelei felt the slightest shiver from being tempted by someone else for a change. Some part of her still wanted to believe that everything had been an elaborate setup to get her into a holy water bath, a sanctified trap. Perhaps she'd be changed back to mortal form the instant she dipped a talon in the pool. Aza would spring upon her, fucking her as the waters washed over her head, his lips against hers to take her soul as her flesh drowned.

She'd be part of him then, possessing his flesh as surely as Ashleigh had hers. Then she'd show him a time 'til he couldn't stand it. 'Til he dumped her into mortal bitch after mortal bitch, sweet lust the only thing unchanging. He'd just go on loving and keeping her hidden from Heaven and Hell alike, until the Trump of Doom when they'd fly away, plunge into a distant sun, and end like some deliciously bad opera...

Or she could just let him bathe and get out while the getting was good.

Too late for that now, she decided. Feeling a rush of possessiveness, Lorelei inclined her head over his, her hair curtaining him in a veil of darkness, making a tiny universe where the only sight to meet his gaze would be her own eyes, glowing red.

He was suddenly gone. She didn't know if he'd meant to tear himself away, or if he'd simply shifted on the narrow bench and fell from her grasp. It had to have been the latter, judging from the way he was trying weakly to regain his feet. Helping him up, Lorelei led him to the edge of the fountain's reflecting pool. Testing the water, she was surprised at how warm it was this long after sunset.

Moving back a step, she allowed him to commence the blessing. Iridescent circles spread from his fingertips, crossing the water as he drew holy signs and murmured sacred verse.

She searched the skies, more for her own protection than his.

Aza straightened, running moistened hands down his neck. He smiled that damned peaceful angelic smile. Lorelei felt cold hatred for the water he'd just blessed, for his god. Why couldn't she make him smile like that?

He leaned to kiss her, but she turned her head to avoid it. The angel looked as if she'd torn something vital within him. Lorelei hoped she had. Wanting his divinity and sin all nice and swirled together like that... Screw that shit.

"Get in your water," she instructed. Flicking a talon toward the upper basin of the fountain, she said, "I'll wait up there." With a vulture-like hop, she sprang up to the upper fount, watching sullenly.

The angel climbed awkwardly over the edge of the basin. He walked around the circumference of the pool, west to east, leaning down periodically to draw handfuls of water over his shoulders. The blood from his wounds ran down his body in a thin sheen, trailing phosphorescently in the water as he moved. By the time he'd completed three tours of the fountain, he was walking more normally.

Lorelei slipped between the rushing jets of unblessed water in the upper basin. They sprayed a protective curtain around her, although the colored lights in the basin must have silhouetted her true form for all who cared to see.

The water around her shifted from violet to emerald. The fountain's powerful splashing blocked all sound as she stood there, curtained but unhidden, wondering if her lover would still be there when she looked out.

At length, the waters ceased to sound like rushing wings or devilish whispers and became monotonous noise. The lights changed again and again around her. Patience was not her virtue. Surely Aza knew that. Lorelei felt compelled to look.

The angel—without a doubt her angel—was climbing up the fountain to her. He was bathed in a golded glow that sparked highlights from his wings. The light presently shifted to lava orange, then wonderful hell red, as if he were climbing out of his little pond of divinity into the inevitability of sweet damnation.

Lorelei reached for Aza, pulling him into the center of the fountain. The waters sighed for her as the colors changed around them. The spray diluted the last traces of holy water on his skin. When the world flared all ruby-orange again, she kicked back, catching the insulated cable that fed power to the lights.

In the sudden darkness, Aza asked, "Do you trust me?"

Lorelei nodded, despite the corner of her mind railing at her for making another blind agreement with this angel.

"Do you accept me, Lorelei of Hell, for what I am?"

Lorelei fiercely pressed her lips to his, letting the kiss wander so she could take his earlobe between her teeth. "Yes," she hissed.

Taking her hands in his, he slipped the plain circle of heavy gold from his finger. Aza transferred it to her ring finger, bringing her hand to his lips as he did.

The ring's weight galvanized her even more than the words. He was serious.

Mind racing, she returned the band to his finger, even as she made his words her own. "Azazi-El, seraph of LA's host, do you accept me for all that I am, all that I have done and will yet do?"

He can't, she reassured herself, waiting for the angel to take wing, fly into the night, destroy himself with heartbreak somewhere out of her knowing, so she'd be free.

Even as she hoped it, Lorelei turned her face from his to hide the tears brimming behind her tight-closed lids.

In her ear, he whispered, "Yes, I accept you, Lorelei. I love you."

His eyes snared her gaze. Understanding passed between them: what they'd done was serious and binding. Lorelei felt her tears spill, but Aza hugged her hard against him. Lorelei clutched him, fingers pressed against his soft gray feathers. Their lips met. Lorelei breathed in his sweetness, his tarnished light, and loved him with all her being. Was this how it felt when a devil fell? Had there ever been such a thing?

With a gurgle, the fountain shut off. The jets of water surged one last time, became leaden in midair, and dropped back into the basin.

Suddenly exposed but no longer caring, Azaziel swept his lover into a joyful embrace.

When Aza jumped down from the fountain with Lorelei in his arms, a fiend's whistle cut across the sweet silence. The hair rose on the back of Lorelei's neck. She asked softly, "Are you armed?"

"Only with my love for you."

"No worries, then," Lorelei play-snarled at him. She opened her purse again, ready to snatch the gun out.

A limousine pulled to a stop at the edge of the walk. Tomur stepped out of the driver's side and faced them unarmed. "The car's for you, Lorelei."

"Why?"

"One angel fallen, one angel formless. The boss is pleased. You've got yourself a promotion."

"Temptress?" Lorelei asked skeptically.

"Yeah. With 'that bitch' out of the picture, there's an open slot in the hierarchy."

It was too sudden for Lorelei to absorb. She was being given credit for the two angels lost tonight, a feat unmatched in these modern days. The Prince of LA was grateful to her. She had finally become a temptress...

"Is this what you want?" Aza wondered.

She looked at her angel, still surrounded by his halo, still holy despite all else. "If I take the promotion," she said uncertainly, "I could protect us."

"As long as such protection suited Hell."

"If I don't take it, I insult him and we have nothing."

Aza left the choice up to her.

To die by his side would be Heaven: wasn't there a song like that? Lorelei tried to hum the melody as she pulled the dagger from her purse. She handed the knife, hilt first, to Tomur. "There are a couple of souls in there. Deliver them for me and I'll decide if I want to get in touch."

"That's your answer?" the archfiend ground out.

"If Asmodeus feels he owes me a favor, he can leave me the fuck alone." Lorelei took Aza's hand again. "Wish us luck."

"I wish you sanity," Tomur said as he got back into the limousine.

Aza kissed her. "Why did you make that choice?" he wondered.

"Because I have a soul now," Lorelei said. "They can tempt me—and I can say no. That's how the world works."

He laughed, a beautiful melodic sound that made her heart soar. Lorelei pressed against him for another kiss. Her angel might still not be fallen, exactly, but he was most definitely hers.

Then, arms around each other's waists, Lorelei and Aza walked down the steps to the river. His feathers were softer than anything she could imagine. The feel of them against her skin made her wet with desire.

"We'll figure something out," he promised, offering his hands. "Give me time, Lorelei. I have faith this can be made to work."

Lorelei launched herself into the angel's arms, wrapping every limb and even her tail around him. Not fallen, of course, but definitely hers.

If you enjoyed this book, please consider leaving a review. Even something as simple as awarding stars on Amazon or Goodreads will help other people find it. Not only do reviews help sell books, they give authors a reason to continue writing.

ABOUT THE AUTHORS

Loren Rhoads is the author of *The Dangerous Type*, *Kill By Numbers*, and *No More Heroes*, which comprise the *In the Wake of the Templars* space opera trilogy. Her Lorelei stories have appeared in the books *Sins of the Sirens* and *Demon Lovers*. Other short stories have appeared in Occult Detective Quarterly, Space & Time, Weirdbook, and *Best New Horror 27*. Keep an eye on her at https://www.lorenrhoads.com or join her mailing list at https://mailchi.mp/aa9545b2ccf4/lorenrhoads

Brian Thomas's writing has followed the modern course of fanzines, newspaper work, promotional copy, screenwriting and script doctoring, to annuals including *Morbid Curiosity* magazine. He was a researcher for 20th Century Fox for ten years on over a hundred films and TV shows, including The X Files, Simpsons, Firefly, and fittingly, Brimstone.

He previously collaborated with Loren Rhoads on 2016's *Lost Angels*. Brian resides in Flint Michigan, in a full-time artists & writers collective, where he hopes to return to writing, seeing as he's just had an unhappy love affair and doesn't see why anyone else should have a good time.

HOW THE STORY BEGAN...

Lost Angels — *As Above, So Below: Book 1*
by Loren Rhoads and Brian Thomas

In the days before the Flood, Azaziel was a Watcher, sent down to guide God's creatures on Earth. He fell in love with one of Cain's granddaughters and they passed her mortal life in bliss.

The succubus Lorelei doesn't know any of that when she sees Azaziel in her master's nightclub. All she knows is that the angel's fall will bring glory to Hell and acclaim to any succubus who accomplishes it.

Of course, Lorelei has no way to predict that Azaziel will try to tame her by possessing her with a mortal girl's soul. Can the succubus find an exorcist before the fury of Hell is unleashed?

ALSO AVAILABLE FROM AUTOMATISM PRESS

Black Light
by Martha J. Allard

Los Angeles, 1983. Trace Dellon knows exactly what he wants: the white heat of the spotlight. When his band Black Light is offered a record deal, Trace grabs for it. He will do anything to make it.

Bass player Asia Heyes knows what he wants, too. It's not fame or the adoration of groupies. It's Trace. It's always been Trace. Though it's been unspoken between them, Trace's other lovers—his audience—push Asia aside.

With the record contract, Albrecht Christian comes into their lives. He has everything but what he needs to live: the energy that runs just under Trace's skin.

Rock and roll, like magic, requires both love and sacrifice.